I0761822

FEYLAND
BOOK SIX
MARNY
USA TODAY BESTSELLING AUTHOR
ANTHEA SHARP

MARNY

FEYLAND BOOK 6

ANTHEA SHARP

Cover art by Mulan Jiang

Subjects: Young Adult Fiction/Fantasy/Contemporary, Fiction/LitRPG

Quality Control: If you encounter typos or formatting problems, please contact antheasharp@hotmail.com so they may be corrected.

This updated version of *Marny* includes the novella, *How to Babysit a Changeling.*

This one's for my brother, Colin: third-degree black belt, awesome cook, and kickass orc.

PROLOGUE

MARCH

The first time the enchanted forest appeared in his bedroom, Nyx Spenser wasn't exactly sure how it had happened. Or even *what* had happened.

He'd finished questing in the new game called Feyland, pulled off his gear and powered down the equip, then got out of his sim chair to find half of his room engulfed in a magical forest. He'd blinked hard, bent down and put his hands on his knees, took some deep breaths, rubbed his eyes...

When he stood up again, the trees were still there. Sunshine slanted through the silver-leafed branches, and a mysterious wind ruffled his hair. Beneath the trees lay a mossy forest floor. Red and violet flowers bloomed on clumps of bushes, and butterflies flitted in and out of the shafts of sunlight, turning orange when the light hit them, then blue in the shadows.

Legs unsteady, he'd walked over to the nearest tree and put his hand on the pale bark. It felt real—slightly rough and cool under his palm.

But it couldn't be.

He swallowed back fear and wonder and curses. What the hell was going on? Carefully, as if the remaining half of his room might disappear at any moment, he sat on his bed. *Breathe. Think.*

Birds chirped overhead, and the smell of damp soil mixed with the reek of Nyx's sweaty workout clothes piled in the corner. As he watched, a small, gold-furred creature the size of a mouse crept out of the underbrush. It lifted its pointed nose and sniffed, then dashed over to the discarded pizza box that hadn't made it into the trash yet.

Unbelieving, Nyx watched while it hopped inside, then emerged a moment later, carrying a pizza crust in its nimble, definitely un-mouselike hands. The thing looked up at him, then winked—*winked!*—and scurried back into the forest.

"No." Nyx covered his eyes with his hands. "This is not happening."

His heart pounded frantically while his mind scrabbled for an answer.

Somebody had slipped him drugs, or piped hallucinogenics into his room. Except that he'd been home from school for hours, and nobody in his family would do something like that. For one thing, they had no imagination, and for another, their life out in the suburbs of Newpoint was almost stereotypically squeaky-clean.

Maybe the meatloaf his mom had made for dinner had

gone bad. He burped experimentally, but only ketchup and broccoli aftertaste filled his mouth.

He dropped his hands from his face and looked again. The forest was still there. It started partway across his room, the tan wall-to-wall carpet rumpling up and becoming tree roots and soil and emerald green moss. The far wall was just gone—only trees stretching away, and a path that seemed to beckon to him.

Okay. Okay. He could deal with this. He'd dealt with crazy stuff before—though never as completely tweaked as this. His martial arts training kicked in, though, and he made himself center, breathe.

First thing was to figure out if it was him, or if the forest was actually there—impossible as it seemed.

He stood and backed to his bedroom door, keeping a wary eye on the trees. He fumbled at the handle, turned it, and slipped through into the absolutely normal hallway of their split-level home.

Resisting the temptation to open the door again, he quietly hurried down the hall to his sister's room. Emmie was supposed to be asleep, but he knew she'd be up, reading her tablet under the covers.

For that matter, he was supposed to be asleep, too. The parents were big on getting to bed early, but Nyx couldn't even deal with turning his light off at ten o'clock. That was just ridiculous. After a serious shouting match a few months ago—where he'd reminded his parents he'd be eighteen soon—they'd finally caved.

"Stay up as long as you like, then," his mom had said. "But don't whine at me when you're exhausted the next day."

"Natural consequences." Dad shook his head. "You'd better get a loud alarm, son."

So far, though, Nyx hadn't missed any of his classes. Been late a couple times, sure—but he was practically done with high school anyway. And he wasn't headed for college, so he only had to keep his grades up to a minimum standard. It wasn't like he had a brilliant academic future ahead. He was "clever," his mom liked to say. Which meant not necessarily academically gifted.

But since he'd already made over a hundred thousand credits from his entrepreneurial ventures, his parents didn't give him too much grief about not going to college, beyond the occasional suggestion he should look into business classes. Nyx figured he could hire accountants and managers, though. He was good with people, and already had his friend Durham crunching numbers for him.

He gave his sister's door a quiet tap, then slipped inside. The glow emanating from under her blankets went out.

"Hey, Emmie, it's me," he whispered.

She turned her tablet back on, then stuck her head out from under the covers. The blue light illuminated her pale skin and her bleached hair, all frizzed out.

"What," she said.

"I need you to come look at something," he said.

She rolled her eyes. "If it's another live-stream idea, it can wait until tomorrow. I just got to a really good place in my book."

"Why can't you be a normal teen and stay up late gaming instead of reading?"

"Normal teens read, too. Not that you'd know anything about that, mister illiterate."

He had plenty of comebacks for her endless store of cracks about his supposed stupidity. Most of them had to do with money and usually shut her up. But whatever was happening in his room was severe. Way more important than arguing with his younger sister.

"Just come," he said. He needed to know if he was going insane in the brain.

Emmie let out a gusty, impatient sigh, but set her tablet aside. "This better be good."

He didn't say anything, just held the door open and waited for her to get up. With another long-suffering look, she grabbed a fuzzy blanket off her bed and wrapped it around herself, cloak style.

Again, Nyx bit his tongue. Usually he'd make a comment about the fact that winter was over. His sister was a complete wuss about the cold. She was wearing flannel PJs, too, and paused to slip her feet into her fuzzy pink slippers before following him down the hall.

He hesitated a moment in front of his door. Maybe the trees had disappeared.

The thought left him half relieved and half disappointed. It wasn't every day weird magical stuff happened, like enchanted forests taking over bedrooms. Probably he'd dreamed the whole thing.

Only one way to find out.

He pushed the door open, his breath catching when he saw that the pale-barked trees still extended past his bed and into the sun-dappled shadows. The thing was, did Emmie see them too?

"Holy crap," she breathed, stepping into his bedroom. "How did you do it? Projection holos? MR console? This is amazing."

Thank God—he wasn't having crazy hallucinations.

"Not exactly," he said, carefully closing the bedroom door behind them. The last thing he needed was his parents seeing this and completely freaking out.

"It looks so real." Emmie went up to the nearest tree and swung her hand, clearly thinking her fingers would pass right through the illusion.

Instead, her palm slapped against the bark.

"Ow!" She stared at her hand. "You set up some columns and are projecting the images over them? That's dumb." She glanced up at him. "But kind of interesting."

"I wish it were me." He swallowed, hard. "Em, believe me. This stuff is real. I was gaming, and then the forest was just... here."

"Right." She smirked at him. "Nice try, bro. Still, it's pretty believable. Though you'll need a bigger place than your bedroom if you want the final installation to work."

"It's not a trick," he said, frustration starting to burn through him.

She watched the butterflies flit through the sunbeams. "That's a nice touch."

He wanted to take her by the shoulders and march her into the woods—except he didn't trust those deeper shadows. Strange creatures lurked in enchanted forests; at least he knew that much.

"I'm touched you think so highly of my skills," he said. "But this isn't me, I swear it."

"Does anything else happen?" she asked, completely ignoring him and staring into the forest. "Or is it just static?"

He dragged the pizza box over with his foot, then bent and grabbed the last piece of old crust.

"That's disgusting." Emmie wrinkled her nose. "I don't want your moldy pizza. Get some personal hygiene."

"Shut up."

He crouched at the border where his rug turned into mossy forest floor, and waved the crust around.

"Wait, is that your magic wand?" his sister asked. "You're doing a transformation spell? Turn me into a pepperoni. No, no—an olive."

She cracked up, but Nyx ignored her, his gaze fixed on the bushes where the little golden mouse-thing had first emerged.

"Come on," he coaxed. "Come out—yummy yummy."

Nothing happened. The shrubbery didn't rustle, and no creature appeared to snatch the crust from his fingers.

Emmie folded her arms. After a minute, she yawned.

"So, that part's broken," she said. "Whatever. It's still a super illusion, but I'm going back to bed. You can show me more tomorrow, after you get it all fixed."

Nyx set the crust on the moss and stood up. Clearly his sister wasn't going to believe him—at least not yet. He was just glad he wasn't crazy. Though it would help if Emmie would actually wake up enough to see that there was no way he could have engineered such a complex setup.

In the light of day, maybe the otherworldly aspects would be more obvious. If the forest was still there tomorrow.

"Fine," he said. "Good night."

Though how he would get to sleep with a creepy magical forest in his bedroom, he had no idea.

"Night," she said, opening his door and shuffling out like an old woman, blanket still wrapped around her.

She didn't close the door behind her. Typical.

Nyx shut it, then turned at the rustle of leaves behind him. The little golden-furred creature was sitting by the pizza crust, sharp nose twitching.

He almost yelled down the hall for his sister to come back —but she was probably under the covers already, lost in her book. And he didn't want to wake up his parents.

"*Now* you show up," Nyx said to the little creature. "Nice."

It grabbed the crust and, with a flick of its long, fuzzy tail, dived into the underbrush.

"And stay there." Nyx folded his arms. Stupid mouse.

He was thirsty, the back of his throat dry with the aftermath of fear. All the water bottles on his floor were empty, though, except for one that seemed to be growing algae.

"Don't do anything," he said, eyeing the forest. "I'll be right back."

There was no answer. Just the brush of a breeze riffling the silvery leaves, and the distant trill of a bird. It would be peaceful, if it wasn't so freaky. Nyx gave the woods a narrow-eyed look and slipped back out of his bedroom.

It would be all right to go down to the kitchen, since the trees hadn't followed him when he'd gone to get Emmie. At least, he hoped everything would remain stable.

He listened hard as he headed for the stairs, the carpet soft under his bare feet. His dad's snores filtered from the master bedroom, but that was it. No weird sounds coming from his own room.

He padded down to the lower level of their house. When he hit the kitchen, the cold tiles made his toes curl.

Halfway to the sink, something happened. A sub-audible *pop,* a feeling like his ears had just cleared. Nyx shook his head, then hastily gulped a glass of water.

Still moving as smoothly and quietly as his karate training had taught, he hurried back to his bedroom. He took a deep breath and opened the door.

The forest was gone.

Dammit. He folded his right hand into a fist and tapped it against his leg.

Except for the fact that Emmie had seen it too, he'd think he'd just had a super-intense, vivid dream. But no.

The enchanted trees had been real. The creature that had eaten the pizza crusts. The flowers and butterflies—those had all been there. A magical forest had manifested in his bedroom.

Somehow, he'd figure out how it had happened. And find a way to bring it back.

Deep under the hill, through misty halls and jeweled forests, a king sat in the center of a shining glade. His hair was golden, nearly as bright as the crown rising above his severe, unearthly face, and his armor gleamed like the sun.

High above, a brilliant ruby cast warm light over the gold throne and emerald grasses of the Bright Court. Harp music filtered through the air, lilting a jig that a half-dozen gnomes cavorted to. Pixies darted, bright sparks, through the jade leaves of the nearby trees and over the heads of the fey folk.

Some of the court were beautiful as the dawn; nixies with eyes a mortal could drown in, faerie maids with wings like glimmering rainbows in the clear air. Others, like the hobs and brownies, were squat and hairy, better fitted to concealment among the stumps and shadows. Twig-limbed spriggan guards surrounded the clearing, holding spears made of sharpened blackthorn.

The Bright King raised his jeweled goblet, his gaze distant and thoughtful. Something stirred in the air of the Realm of Faerie, something mortal—and innocent. The king's lips curved in a faint smile. The lines of fate and foreshadowing shimmered about him. It seemed that, once again, a human would stumble into his court—and no doubt prove to be a very useful tool.

CHAPTER 1

JUNE 21

Marny Fanalua crossed her arms, earbuds fixed firmly in her ears, and tried to ignore the smell of the long-distance bus, a mix of grease, old sweat, and recycled air. The man across the aisle from her was snoring sloppily, and the kid in the seat ahead lit up the space with the blue glow of his screenie game.

At dawn, she'd be in Newpoint—the biggest city she'd ever visited, over eight hundred miles from her home in Crestview.

Anxious homesickness rose in her chest, and she thrust it back down. She'd be fine.

It was just for a couple months, after all. Landing a summer internship with Intertech was a big deal. Even if she didn't know how to navigate a large city, she'd figure out how to get around Newpoint. Growing up on the edge of complete poverty gave a person skills.

Besides, somebody from Intertech was supposed to meet her at the station. Sure, the bus ride was a grind, but she'd be there in... she flicked on her tablet and checked the time. One hour and forty-three minutes.

She must have dozed. The sound of the driver announcing their arrival in ten minutes made her blink awake, her mind hazy from strange dreams of fey folk and fantastical magic. A few wispy images remained: a silver-leafed forest, a young man with gray eyes, an enormous white deer.

Impatiently, she shook her head. No more faerie stuff.

Crestview, Feyland, and the creepy Realm of Faerie were behind her now. This summer she was all about expanding her world and figuring out more about herself as part of Intertech's student team.

"Wait, what?" her best friend Tam had said, when she told him she was going away for an internship. "How come you didn't tell me about this?"

"Hey." She patted his arm, gratified by the hurt look in his eyes. "You've been busy, you know."

Busy in all kinds of ways. His girlfriend Jennet came first and foremost, not to mention his part-time work with Virtu-Max, which, while cool, he wasn't supposed to talk about due to "trade secrets." Add in a terminally broken family, and the fact that he was living with said family in Marny's uncle's apartment over the garage, and—well. Tam had a lot going on.

Still, she was glad he cared enough to be bothered that he didn't know all the details of her life.

"Yeah," she'd said. "Uncle Zeg found out about this program, and we applied. I'll be interning for Intertech—you know, the big communications company—in Newpoint. They want to expand their multigenerational platform." Whatever that meant.

"Good for you. But... Newpoint?" Tam had swiped his hair out of his eyes and stared at her. "That's a million miles from here."

"I know."

It was appalling and exhilarating all at once. But next year was her last year of high school, and how was she supposed to figure out what direction to take in life when she'd never even been out of the Podunk town where she was born?

"This is because of No Compromise, isn't it?" Tam asked.

"Mostly."

Nobody had expected Marny's app to go viral the way it had. She'd hoped that a few gamers would use the avatar-modification plugin, but millions of people all over the world adopted NoComp to change their virtual selves. Within a couple weeks of the app's release, chatrooms and forums all over the 'net were full of avatars modified using her program.

And the gamers had gone wild, taking Marny's program to crazy and fun extremes she'd barely envisioned. Even though she'd offered it as freeware, Jennet had made her set up a donation button.

"What you've created has value," Jennet had said. "If some people want to pay you for it, let them."

Marny hadn't expected much, but in the several months the app had been live she'd made almost enough credits to help her family move someplace fancy, or buy them a grav-car. Not that they wanted either of those things.

"Save it," her mom had said. "College is coming up. And

you earned that money, fair and square. We know how much time you spent on that program."

True enough. While her friends were diving deep in the prototype game of Feyland—and saving the world along the way—Marny had devoted hundreds of hours to her app.

For years she'd had a fierce desire to be able to make an in-game character that reflected who she was. A big, dark-skinned girl who could take on whatever the world threw at her. Not a skinny, overly busty cartoon caricature with big eyes and pouty lips, or a fearsome warrior princess with tusks and tribal tattoos. So, she'd written the app—and it had exploded.

"Huge congrats on the internship," Tam had said, giving her a hug. "We'll sure miss you."

"Same. Maybe I can come visit, if I get a few days off."

Doubtful, though. From what she knew about Intertech, their internships were coveted. Once accepted, they worked you hard. No extra days off to run home.

"You know," Tam had said, a wheedling edge in his voice. "You could always start sim gaming and come meet me and the crew in Feyland."

"Keep dreaming." She'd scowled at him, to show she was serious.

No way was she enclosing herself in a sim system. The thought of sitting in the formfitting chair and pulling the sensory helmet over her head made her breath tighten.

"You can get therapy and meds for claustrophobia," Tam had said.

"Sure. How about you pay for it."

He'd held up his hands. "You're a prime gamer, Marny. I

just wish you wouldn't limit yourself to screenie systems when there's a whole immersive world to discover."

She'd shrugged. They'd had this argument for years, ever since Tam started simming when they were in elementary school. Her first try with the sim equip had convinced Marny she was not made for sim gaming, and subsequent experiences had only proven the point.

"I'll message you," she'd said. "Keep me posted on... things."

She'd meant fey things, magical things.

Tam, her very own Uncle Zeg, Jennet, and the arrogant-but-getting-better Roy Lassiter were all part of the Feyguard; a group of humans deputized to watch over the boundary between the mortal world and the Realm of Faerie. Mostly via the sim game of Feyland, which, in a strange way, had managed to straddle both those worlds.

Marny wasn't a Feyguard, but she'd seen plenty of tweaked things, including her time babysitting a changeling, and looking for traces of feral redcap goblin in the Exe. She knew that freaky magic could seep over into everyday life and create all kinds of havoc.

But she was leaving that behind. Crestview might be a nexus for the Realm of Faerie, with the gaming company VirtuMax setting up headquarters there and the frequent crossovers between it and the magical Realm.

Newpoint, though, was perfectly normal.

Big, yes. Industrial and crowded and noisy, for sure. She was ready for it, though. Ready to face the world on her own terms. Without magic, thank you very much.

"Check around your seat and collect all your belongings,"

the driver said in a flat, bored voice. "Next stop, Newpoint main terminal, end of the line. Luggage compartments under the bus will be accessible from both sides after disembarking."

Marny watched out the window, eyes gritty from lack of sleep. The late bus was the cheapest way to travel from Crestview to Newpoint, and, frankly, she didn't have *that* much left over for food and fun money. She'd taken her mom's advice and put her app donations into a fund for college—all but a few extra creds to get her through the summer.

Intertech was housing and feeding the interns, but she'd need more than just a bed and some corporate cafeteria food for the next two months.

Pale light seeped into the sky, illuminating a few dozen skyscrapers. One of the downtown buildings was Intertech's HQ, and she squinted, trying to make out the company logos on the top of the buildings. Maybe the tallest one, but it was hard to tell through the smeary bus windows.

The bus exited the highway just past the tall buildings and went through a warehouse district. As the light strengthened, Marny's first impression of the city was gray. Cement and glass and shadows, but a blue sky waking up overhead. The top of the silver skyscraper suddenly caught fire, windows reflecting the flame of the rising sun.

With a lurch and squeal of brakes, the bus pulled into a dingy-looking station. The guy across the aisle woke and scrubbed his tired-looking face with his hands. The kid in front of Marny closed his tablet, grabbed his backpack, and was the first one off the bus.

Marny waited. No point in squeezing herself up the aisle when a little patience would make it simple to walk freely off the vehicle. Under her feet, she felt the clunk of the luggage compartments being opened.

The last passenger other than Marny, a frail old lady, got up from her seat. She struggled to reach her flower-decorated case in the overhead rack.

"Let me help you," Marny said.

One-handed, she snagged the case. It was heavier than it looked, but she was strong.

"Oh, thank you." The woman blinked watery blue eyes at her.

"I'll just carry this out for you, okay?"

The thing was wretched heavy for an old lady to handle, and Marny didn't want to be stuck behind the woman as she lugged her case up the aisle.

The tedium of the long bus ride was done. Now that she was finally in Newpoint, she was eager to take the next step of her adventure. She'd been patient, but the fresh dawn air called to her.

The woman still moved excruciatingly slowly, gripping the back of every seat as she traversed the length of the bus, but at last she hobbled down the stairs. Marny practically leaped off the bus and set the flowered case beside the old lady.

"Here you go."

"You are a dear child." The woman patted Marny's hand, then turned away as a middle-aged man greeted her.

The crowd was thinning, most of the passengers grabbing their luggage or already gone. A single duffel bag stood on the stained concrete beside the bus, but it wasn't hers. Marny ducked, peering into the luggage compartments for her bag. Completely empty.

Irritation tightening her chest, she strode around to the other side of the bus. Those compartments had also been cleared out.

The bus driver lingered by the front of the bus, sucking on a vapor stick.

"Hey," Marny said. "My bag's missing."

"That's not it?" He gestured to the black duffel bag.

"No. I mean, I have a duffel, but it's green, and a little bigger than that."

The driver frowned. "Looks like somebody took yours off accidentally. Maybe when we stopped in Nelco—lots of traffic there."

"So, what am I supposed to do?" Everything she needed was in her duffel: the new clothes Jennet had helped her buy, all her toiletries, her pillow from home.

The driver took one last puff, then tucked his stick in his pocket. "Go to the office over there, give 'em your contact info. Your bag'll show up."

She hoped so. All she had in her backpack was her tablet and charger, her messager, her new jacket, and the small loaf of coconut bread her mom had thrust at her as she left.

Marny went over to the office window the driver had indicated, glancing around for her Intertech liaison. The station had emptied out, and she didn't see anyone who seemed obviously there to pick her up. Maybe they were running late—city traffic or something.

After leaving her messager number and Intertech details with the bored-looking woman in the office, Marny settled on a nearby bench. The metal was cold against her jean-clad legs, but she didn't care. She glanced around once more, but the only person even looking her way was a scruffy old guy wrapped in blankets in a nearby doorway. With a silent sigh, she pulled out her messager.

Intertech had given her a few contacts, and she scrolled through until she found the number for Brenna Dalton, the intern liaison.

:Hello,: she typed. *:This is Marny Fanalua. I'm at the Newpoint downtown bus station. What's the best way to get to Intertech from here?:*

There was no immediate answer. Marny glanced at the time readout glowing on the plain gray wall. Six thirty-three, Sunday morning.

She yawned, then grimaced at the taste of exhaust fumes and stale vapor. Surely she could find a better place to wait than the cold and empty bus station. She stuck her messager in her jeans pocket so she could answer as soon as it rang, then pulled her jacket out of her pack. Jennet had made her buy it, insisting that the bright scarlet looked great on Marny. Maybe so, but what Marny liked best was the soft fleecy lining. She buttoned it up, then slung her backpack over one shoulder and stepped out onto the street.

"Got any spare coin?" the blanket-wrapped man asked from his doorway. His voice was scratchy, and he smelled like he was in dire need of a bath.

"Sorry," Marny said.

"Eh, right." He scowled at her.

"No, honestly." She went to stand in front of him. "I just got here, and I don't have anything, not even my luggage. I'd help you out if I could."

The man's glare faded, but he was still frowning.

"Really," she continued. "Are you here every day? I could come back and—"

"Go away." He flapped a grimy hand at her. "You'll do just fine in this city. Now leave me alone."

Dissed by a homeless guy. It would make Tam laugh when she told him the story. In fact, it was pretty funny in the moment, too. Smiling a little, Marny turned away.

Then caught her breath at the scale of the buildings. She stood at the bottom of a canyon made of skyscrapers, so tall they felt like they were leaning in on her. A scrap of pale blue sky shone way overhead, but chilly night shadows still clung to the streets.

Even at this hour there was traffic; mostly yellow grav-taxis zipping around, and a long city bus that roared off down the street. A woman on a bicycle sailed past, her blue scarf fluttering in the breeze.

Newpoint. The city.

Despite the scratchy sleeplessness under her skin and her dismay at not having her luggage, a bubble of joy percolated up inside Marny. She was here, in the middle of a real adventure that she could smell and taste and feel.

Chin up, she strode down the street. The block ahead seemed full of stores and restaurants, from the look of the colorful animated signs and advertising flags set out. Although she didn't have any spare cash in her pockets, the card in her wallet certainly had enough credits for a hot drink, at the very least.

Of the two coffee shops, one had a line out the door. Marny joined it, then pulled her messager out and checked, just in case. Nothing incoming.

Guess she had time to drink a nice big cup of tea, maybe have a scone or pastry, before she tackled whatever came next.

As the line shuffled forward, Marny people-watched. She was used to some diversity in Crestview, so the range of skin tones and features didn't throw her, but she sure wasn't used to such a well-dressed array. They almost made her feel self-conscious in her canvas high-tops and worn jeans, but her new jacket carried her through. Not that she cared *that* much what random city dwellers thought of her.

Still, it was interesting. Jennet was the only person she knew who made a production over looking good before she left the house, but it seemed like that was normal in the city. At least judging by the tall man with a fancy necktie, the lady with carefully applied makeup, the girl with a costume made of lace and leather, and the overall polished look of everyone else in the line.

Marny surreptitiously watched as she got closer to the counter. About a third of the customers were paying by waving their wrist-chip over the scanner, instead of by card or cash. It didn't seem to be a big deal either way. Not like Crestview, where the elite rich folks wore their chips like badges of honor and stayed together in tight cliques.

Or maybe that was just high school.

And to be honest, Jennet had a wrist-chip and was friends with Marny. Not to mention that Tam was of even lower social status, having grown up in the Exe. Maybe things changed as people got more mature. Or maybe Crestview was just that provincial.

When she got to the counter, Marny ordered a large black tea and one of the apricot scones displayed in the pastry case.

She blinked a little at the cost, and scanned her card. Good thing she'd made some extra creds, or she'd go broke in a week. Things in Newpoint were seriously expensive. She could buy an entire meal back home on the amount she'd just dropped for tea and a small bakery item.

The shop was jammed with people, and Marny didn't feel like wedging herself against the stand-up counter. She poured a liberal amount of soy milk in her tea, glad to see they had that option (unlike most of the cafes in Crestview), and tucked her wrapped-up scone in her coat pocket.

Maybe there was a park nearby where she could settle and enjoy her breakfast.

Two more blocks into the heart of downtown she found a cement sculpture garden, complete with a splashing fountain. Plasmetal benches ringed the fountain. She settled on one, then nearly got drenched from sitting too close to where the random jets of water sprayed up. Quickly, she scooted to a drier spot.

The expensive scone was delicious, and the tea tasted nice and strong. Feeling warm, she sat for a moment and watched the sunlight slide slowly down the face of the building in front of her. The bottom was still in shadow, though, and would be all day, judging from the angle of the light coming between the skyscrapers. It was weird to think that some parts of the city never got direct sun.

A guy jogging with a rotund bulldog paused at the edge of the fountain.

"Go get 'em, Pancho," he said, unsnapping the leash.

With a joyful bark, the dog barreled into the middle of the fountain, dashing from one spurt of water to the next. Whenever a new squirt came up, Pancho would leap on it, snapping at the spray—but somehow the water always got away. Marny watched for a while, amused, until her messager pinged.

She pulled it out of her pocket to see that Intertech's liaison, Brenna Dalton, was finally responding.

:Hey, so sorry. Thought you were in at pm. Take a cab to Intertech building and will reimburse.:

:Okay,: Marny sent back.

:Ping me when you get downstairs.:

Marny found a trash receptacle—or more accurately, a composting station—to dispose of her cup and scone wrapper. Another thing Crestview didn't have, though word was the city was trying to go greener. At least people there recycled, unlike some places she'd heard of.

The street beside the sculpture park seemed busy enough to hail a cab. She hoped. Standing at the curb, she raised her arm and tried to make eye contact with the drivers. It didn't take long for one of the little yellow grav-cars to pull over beside her and the door to slide open.

"Where to?" the driver asked, his English heavily accented.

"The Intertech building," Marny said.

"Okay. Scan." The driver pointed to the scanner mounted between the seats.

Marny climbed in and scanned her card, and a holographic display popped up, showing "5.25."

"What's that?" she asked.

"Passenger charge. Standard fee."

It cost over five credits just to get into a cab? She was glad Intertech was picking up the bill.

"All in?" the driver asked.

Marny set her pack on the seat beside her and belted up. "Yep."

Barely looking at the traffic behind him, he pulled out into the street. Horns blared, and Marny braced herself for the crunch of plasmetal.

The driver grinned at her in the mirror. "No worry. I never get hit."

There's always a first time. But she didn't say it aloud.

As they went down the block, the fare readout continued to climb. When the cab stopped at a light, Marny leaned forward.

"How far is it to Intertech?"

"One more street," he said with a big smile.

"Are you kidding me? I could have walked."

"Maybe your leg hurt." He shrugged. "I don't ask why people take cab, I just drive."

The light changed, and he zipped forward, cutting across two lanes of cars. Marny took a deep breath. Even Roy Lassiter didn't drive so carelessly.

"We here," the driver said, coming to a sharp halt before an enormously tall silver building.

Marny grabbed her pack to keep it from sliding off the seat and glanced at the readout. The total fare was a little over eight credits. Robbery. Next time she'd do a little more research—like looking at a map—before jumping into a grav-taxi because somebody told her to.

Add tip? the readout blinked.

Fine. Marny keyed in an extra half-cred.

"I need a hardcopy receipt," she said.

The driver let out a gusty sigh, but hit a button and the

scanner spat out a slip of paper. She took it and her pack, then got out of the car.

"Thanks," she said as the door slid closed behind her.

"Have a good day!" He grinned, then swerved suddenly back into traffic, accompanied by another blare of horns.

Marny slung her pack over her shoulder. She'd survived her first taxi ride, and was a little wiser for it.

She turned to face the gleaming expanse of the building. It towered over its neighbors, an edifice of angles and hard surfaces. The company logo, a blue circle with a stylized feather through it, was suspended over the main entryway.

Intertech—at last.

CHAPTER 2

The Intertech building took up the entire block, with a restaurant on the bottom floor at one end and some upscale retail stores at the other. The big front doors were shaded by a blue awning where a uniformed doorman stood guard, like at a fancy hotel or something. Marny didn't suppose she could simply walk into the building.

"Hi," she said to the guard. "Could you ping Brenna Dalton? She's supposed to meet me in the lobby."

"Your name?" the guard said, his voice disinterested.

"Marny Fanalua."

He put a hand up to his earpiece. "Miss Fanalua," he said to whoever was on the other end.

After a moment he nodded and stepped forward, flashing a key card at the door sensors. They whooshed open.

"You may wait inside," he said. "Miss Dalton will arrive shortly."

"Thanks."

She wasn't sure if she was supposed to tip him, or how to even do that without any spare change, so instead she just walked into the building. Warm air rushed over her, and she relaxed a little as she surveyed the lobby.

It was at least two stories tall and all done up in gold and cream and brown. To her right were acres of couches and chairs grouped together in small seating arrangements. Beyond that was a bar with a long polished wood counter and dozens of glass bottles of varying shapes and colors. Beside it was an espresso bar, the sound of the coffee grinder a low grumble in the air. A line of people waited for coffee, which surprised her until she remembered that many of the Intertech employees lived in the building. She and the other interns were going to be housed there, too.

On Marny's left was a tall counter staffed by two women wearing blue blazers with the Intertech logo embroidered over the heart. Another uniformed guard stood beyond the counter, his hands clasped behind his back.

"Miss Fanalua?" one of the women said.

"That's me." Marny stepped up to the counter.

"Why don't you have a seat." She gestured to a nearby cluster of couches. "Miss Dalton will be down soon."

"All right."

Marny headed past the hefty marble table in the center of the lobby. Bigger than a bed, it bore a huge golden vase of flowers. She thought they were fake until she walked by and smelled the lilies and some spicy scent that made her nose wrinkle. Eucalyptus, maybe?

Behind the couch arrangements stood shiny banks of elevators—a half-dozen doors all pinched shut in the middle, like lips closed tight on secrets they would never tell.

She settled on one of the couches, surprised at how comfortable it was, and pulled her messager out of her backpack.

:I'm downstairs by the elevators,: she sent to Brenna.

:Yep. brt: was the reply.

After a moment, Marny keyed in a message to her family, copying the text to her Uncle Zeg, and Tam.

:Arrived safely. The city is big, but not too scary. Will vidchat later, once I'm settled.:

True, she hadn't yet met her Intertech contact or seen her room, but Marny felt like she'd been working on an epic questline called "Arrival in Newpoint" since she'd gotten on the bus yesterday. Now it was nearly complete.

On cue, the elevator doors dinged open. A woman in her thirties with dark, curly hair stepped out. She wore jeans and a gray T-shirt, *Checkswing Comics & Games* emblazoned across the front above stylized representations of superhero logos. Her left ear was studded with piercings, and the edge of a flower tattoo showed above the neckline of her shirt. A silver streak ran through her hair, beside her face, and Marny wondered if it was natural, and if her own hair would ever do anything that cool. The woman scanned the lobby, then made eye contact with Marny.

"Are you Marny Fanalua?" she asked.

"Yep." Marny stood and grabbed her backpack. "Brenna Dalton?"

"Yes." Brenna strode forward and offered her hand. "I'm sorry I wasn't at the station this morning. I'm a complete night owl, and it never even *occurred* to me you'd be arriving this early. For me, there's only one six in a day, and that's p.m." She gave Marny a rueful smile.

"It's okay—I got to see some of the city," Marny said. And got to prove to herself that she could handle unexpected mishaps, even in the big streets of Newpoint.

"Still, I owe you. Do you like sushi? There's a great spot around the corner. I'll treat you to lunch later today." Brenna glanced around at the couches. "Where's your bags?"

"Lost, apparently."

"That's tweaked. How do you lose luggage on a bus?"

Marny lifted her shoulder in a shrug. "They said they'd contact me as soon as they found it."

"We can swing by one of the department stores after lunch," Brenna said, "grab you anything essential in case your bag doesn't show up 'till tomorrow. But first, let's get you settled."

"Sounds good." Weariness tugged at Marny, hanging off her like a whiny little kid who wanted attention. A nap was definitely in order.

"Since you don't have any bags to lug, we'll make a quick stop to get your ID." Brenna flashed her key card at the elevator. "Hold still. The scan only takes a second."

A laser flicked on above the door and thin blue light traveled over Marny. She didn't feel a thing, but it was weird to be inspected so thoroughly.

"Miss Brenna Dalton and visitor," a metallic voice said. "You may enter."

The metal doors slid open. Marny glanced up at the

cameras overhead, tracking their movements. Intertech took their security seriously.

"Since I'm a mid-level employee, I can bring extra people in without clearing them at the desk," Brenna said. "Your visitors will need to get checked out—they won't be able to just come up the elevators, so don't imagine bringing boyfriends home after hours."

"Wasn't in my plans."

"Good." Brenna gave her a grim smile. "You won't have much time to socialize, anyway. The pace here is grueling."

At least it was only for nine weeks. No matter how bad things got—and Marny was certainly expecting some horrors—she could take it for that long.

"How many interns are there?" Marny asked as she followed Brenna into the brightly lit elevator. Her shoes squeaked faintly on the polished floor.

"This year there's three of you. A big crop. Usually we get one or two. Once, nobody, if you can believe it."

An Intertech internship was a golden ticket. Half the people who interned were offered full-ride scholarships to the colleges of their choice, and the rest went straight into high-paying jobs with the company as soon as they graduated from high school. At her Uncle Zeg's urging, Marny had applied, but she really hadn't thought she'd land one of the coveted spots. When the acceptance notice came, she'd been sure it was an elaborate prank.

"Of course they want you," her uncle had said. "You're a smart coder and a creative thinker who clearly has a clue about what people want. That's exactly what Intertech is looking for."

Once the truth had sunk in, she'd been elated, in her own quiet way.

Then—unusual for her—she'd started second-guessing. She'd only gotten in because she was a minority. A poor one. And a girl. Good PR for the company to show how inclusive they were.

Still, she couldn't have been the only applicant that fit the politically correct criteria. And Newpoint seemed to contain a huge variety of peoples and cultures. Maybe she really *had* gotten the internship on her own merits.

The elevator whooshed smoothly up, numbers flashing by on the readout over the door.

"The business offices are on floor fifteen through thirty-eight. Dining's on thirty-nine," Brenna said. "The top floor—level seventy-six—is the CEO's domain. You'll never go there. Under that is middle-management apartments—that's me—and forty through fifty are the apartments for the cubicle workers. And you interns. All told, around seven hundred people live in the Intertech building."

It felt a little claustrophobic, like Intertech was its own hive. Which would make Marny a worker drone, she supposed. She took a deep breath to dispel the feeling.

"Are the other interns here yet?"

Brenna nodded. "You're the last to arrive. You'll be sharing a triple. Nice thing about living in the building is that it's easy to get to work."

"So about my new roommates—"

The elevator stopped and the doors dinged open.

"Soon as we're done here, I'll take you up to meet them," Brenna said, setting a brisk pace down the hallway.

Marny followed her into a large office that, despite the fact it was Sunday morning, was full of busy people.

Her surprise must have been clear on her face, because Brenna gave her another quick smile.

"Intertech has branches all over the world," she said. "There's always somebody here, day and night. This is the office command central—the international heartbeat of the company."

"You make it sound like a living organism," Marny said.

"It kind of is." Brenna snagged a tablet off the pile on the receptionist's desk. "Hey, Shawn," she said. "Checking in a new intern."

"Good, good," the redheaded man said. "I'll get the fingerprint scanner primed."

Marny blinked. "Do you want a DNA sample, too?" She couldn't quite keep the sarcasm from her voice. Intertech was really over the top.

"Nah—you won't be here long enough for that," Brenna said, in all seriousness. She handed the tablet to Marny. "Fill everything out, we'll get your prints and picture, and you'll be in the system."

"Great." Meaning the opposite, of course.

Marny had spent her entire life living on the edge—of poverty, of social acceptance, of being a large, strong girl in a culture that didn't really honor that model. So she'd embraced everything that made her different. She was comfortable with edges. This *being assimilated* thing made her feel itchy under her skin.

But it was part of the package. She could hardly work here if she couldn't even get the elevators to open, now could she?

It was like playing any other game. Follow the rules, learn the patterns and expectations. Then, later, break them as necessary.

For a bureaucracy, it took surprisingly little time for Marny to finish getting registered. Processed. Whatever they called it.

The machine spat out her new badge, and Brenna glanced at it before handing it over.

"Not bad," she said. "Most people look scared out of their wits or like severe criminals."

"Good thing I'm not either," Marny said.

The liaison gave her an approving nod. "I like you, Fanalua. Okay, time to see your new home."

Before clipping on her badge, Marny glanced at the photo. Her unsmiling face looked back at her. Not frightened. Not a felon. Just a broad-faced Samoan girl with kinked brown hair, serious eyes, and a determined expression.

Yep, that was pretty much her.

Brenna waved goodbye to the receptionist, then led Marny back down the hall.

"What should I know about being here?" Marny asked.

"Oh, God." Brenna let out a humorless laugh. "Everything. At least you three interns can learn the ropes together. It's good to have a support system."

Marny wasn't going to count on that until she met the others. Could be they'd bond into one happy group. Or conversely, become one another's worst enemies.

"Tell me about them," she said.

"Anjah Lee is a brilliant mathematician, and Wil Cutter's an engineering genius."

"Okay." A spurt of anxiety jumped up in her stomach, and Marny pushed it back down.

She wasn't a genius anything. Sure, her app had gone viral, but what if had all been luck?

She made herself take a deep breath. No need to get all tweaked. Intertech had picked her for a reason. She'd just have to believe they'd made the right choice.

Brenna paused before the elevators, and the blue light scanned them both. This time the system identified Marny by name. It was a little freaky, but no stranger than the networked house AIs that her rich friends had.

"Floor forty," Brenna said.

The elevator hurtled upward, and pressure built in Marny's ears. She opened her mouth, trying to ease the sensation.

"Yeah," Brenna said, noticing her discomfort. "Try yawning."

Marny did, and with a soft pop, her hearing returned. The display above the door showed they'd gone up thirty floors in less than a minute—but the elevator was slowing. Thirty-six. Thirty-nine.

With a ding, the doors opened, and Brenna tipped her head. "After you."

Marny adjusted the straps of her backpack and stepped into a brightly lit hallway. The tan carpet underfoot had a subtle pattern that probably hid dirt well, and the walls were painted a warm shade of yellow. Pictures of fields of flowers lined the far wall, which was ironic, considering they were in a skyscraper thousands of feet above the ground.

Beside the elevator hung a photograph of a stern, silver-haired man. The ornate gilt frame surrounding it made his face seem even more austere in contrast.

"Our esteemed founder and president," Brenna said, a hint of sarcasm in her voice. "Dettwiler von Coburg."

"Okay." He didn't look particularly friendly. "Is there a picture of him on every floor?"

"Of course. Wouldn't want the proletariat to forget who's in charge, now would we?" The edge in Brenna's voice was more pronounced.

Marny didn't voice her opinion that the man clearly had a huge ego. She glanced at the white ceiling. Though she couldn't see any cameras, she assumed the entire building was wired for surveillance. The company certainly seemed paranoid enough.

As her uncle always said—assume the worst until proven otherwise. Especially where corporations were concerned.

"So, this is the dorm?" Marny asked, as Brenna led her down the hallway.

It seemed more like a fancy hotel, with art on the walls and even a few tables with actual potted plants. She'd imagined a big white room with metal beds and shared dressers.

"Yep. Not what you thought it would be, is it?" Brenna shot her a knowing smile. "We just call it the dorm—it's really more apartments. You're down here at the end of the hall. Number 4027."

They reached the door and Brenna waved her ID card at it. The plasmetal slid open to reveal a tiled entry area leading into a large living room, with plush beige carpet in a nicer pattern than the utilitarian one in the hall. A bank of windows looked out at the tops of nearby buildings, and Marny caught a hazy glimpse of mountains on the far horizon. Mostly, though, the view was all city. She bet it looked prime at night.

A big open room with a large screen took up one side of the living area. A sim system was installed there, and a couple of console devices. Next to the living room was a kitchen larger than Marny's bedroom at home. A hallway led off to the left, presumably going to the bedrooms and bath. She made herself say nothing, although part of her wanted to ask if this was the right place. The apartment seemed way too nice to house lowly student interns.

A pair of large black athletic shoes lay in the entryway, laces tangled. The open coat closet showed a colorful array of jackets and matching purses. She'd be living with a slightly slobby guy and a girl who took her fashion way seriously. This would be interesting.

"I'm sure your roommates will be out to greet you in a moment," Brenna said. "I pinged them while you were filling out forms."

Right on cue, a tall, lanky guy sauntered into the living room. His blond hair was messy and overlong, but at least it didn't flop over his eyes and remind her of Tam.

"Hey there," he said, coming over to shake Marny's hand. "I'm Wil. Welcome to our humble abode. Whoa, you're tall."

Clearly he wasn't used to meeting girls over six feet in height. Not that the world was necessarily full of them.

"Thanks," she said, taking it as a compliment.

He grinned at her, and she thought maybe sharing a space with Wil wouldn't be too bad.

"Anjah?" Brenna called. "You here?"

"Yeah, she is." Wil waved his hand toward the hallway. "Had to put on her makeup or something."

"Coming!" a high voice called, and a moment later a beautiful, petite girl with exotically tilted eyes and perfect lips emerged from the hall.

Marny swallowed back her stab of jealousy. When people talked about gorgeous Asian women, they meant girls who looked exactly like Anjah. Not robust Samoan gals with full mouths, wide cheekbones, and even wider shoulders.

Damn. Marny thought she'd gotten over that particular issue. She'd worked through hanging around cute white girls like Jennet, but clearly had some issues with mixed-race beauties. She let out a quiet breath.

"Hi," she said. "I'm Marny."

"Anjah." Her roomie strutted forward on what had to be three-inch heels and extended a perfectly manicured hand. "Pleased to meet you."

Even wearing heels, the top of her head didn't reach Marny's chin.

"Right, then," Brenna said. "Marny, I'll come get you at one for lunch and a little shopping. Then tomorrow morning, crack of seven thirty, I'll be here to take you all down to the thirtieth floor, where you'll receive your assignments. Meanwhile, I'll leave you three to get settled."

"Thanks," Marny said, trying not to feel a little forlorn as the metal door whooshed closed behind Brenna.

"Shopping?" Anjah raised a graceful eyebrow. "Aren't we special."

"It's not that." Marny calmly held the other girl's gaze. Anjah's eyelids glimmered with blue eye shadow. "My luggage got lost in transit. I have nothing except what's in my backpack."

"Aw, bummer," Wil said. "Though it's not like there's any more room for stuff in the bathroom. Anjah's girly potions have completely taken over."

"They have not," Anjah said. "I left one of the drawers empty."

"A drawer will be fine," Marny said.

She was used to sharing a bathroom with her two older sisters, younger brother, and Grandma Harmony, who lived with them half the year. Having only three people sharing would be a luxury—even if one of them was evidently quite fond of her makeup.

"Your room is this way, at the end," Anjah said, turning to lead her down the hall. "Bathroom's on the right."

Marny peeked in as they went past. Despite Wil's warning, she was a little amazed at the amount of cosmetics and lotions and perfumes spread out on the pale marble counter. A basket held an array of hair curling/smoothing/straightening/rumpling appliances, their cords escaping like tentacles, and the walk-in shower was lined with colorful plastic bottles.

The first bedroom door was ajar, showing a spill of jeans and T-shirts and an unmade bed. Wil's room.

The second door also stood open. In addition to the standard furniture, Anjah had a hot pink upholstered chair, a white and gold vanity table, a screenie system, and a fluffy cream-colored rug laid over the carpet.

"When did you arrive?" Marny asked. It looked like both Anjah and Wil were pretty settled in.

"I've been here two days. My mother and I drove down

from Vane, and she helped me move in." Anjah waved her rose-tinted nails. The sparkle of a gem set into her wrist-chip caught the light. No shock there. Marny was fully prepared to be surrounded by 'leet rich people at Intertech.

Although she had covertly checked out Brenna's wrist, and the liaison didn't have an embedded chip. She thought back to her observations from earlier that morning, that maybe having a chip or not wasn't such a big deal in the city. It would be nice not to deal with the gaping social divide between the haves and the have-nots.

"Here you are," Anjah said, gesturing to the last room. "Home sweet home."

Marny stepped into her bedroom. It was comfortably furnished with a desk, dresser, and bookshelf, a nondescript picture of a tree on the wall, and best of all, a window that looked out over the city.

"Nice," she said.

"If you like tiny rooms, I suppose." Anjah gave a dismissive sniff.

"Right. So, did Wil get here two days ago, too?"

"He arrived yesterday—flew in from the West Coast," Anjah said. "Where are you from?"

"Crestview." Marny shrugged off her backpack and let it land on the bed's tan and white coverlet.

"Never heard of it," Anjah said.

"Yeah, it's not that big a place."

"Isn't that where VirtuMax relocated?" Wil asked from the doorway. He grinned when Marny whirled to face him. "Didn't mean to surprise you, but I heard you girls say my name, and was hoping for something juicy."

Anjah narrowed her eyes at him, as if no one in their right mind would find him attractive. Marny didn't think he was that bad looking, though he didn't particularly spark anything for her.

"That's right," she said. "VirtuMax is headquartered in Crestview now. Are you a simmer?"

"Yeah," he said. "That's my rig in the living room. Had to ship it out special." He leaned against the doorframe. "Got any insider info about what the company's working on next?"

"Nope." She didn't mention that her best friend worked for VirtuMax. Already there was a too-interested gleam in Wil's eye. "Also, I don't sim."

"What?" he straightened. "Everybody sims."

"I don't," Anjah said, pursing her perfect lips.

"Okay, *almost* everybody." Wil cocked his head at Marny. "You look like a gamer."

"I am. Just not a simmer."

Anjah gave an exaggerated sigh. "You two can squabble over this later. We should show Marny the rest of the apartment."

"I saw there's a kitchen," Marny said. "Are we supposed to do our own cooking?"

"Of course not!" Anjah looked horrified at the thought. "That's what the dining room is for. I keep a few things in the fridge, but you won't see me *cooking*."

"Speak for yourself," Wil said. "Personally, I'd rather sleep late and grab a protein shake than get up and go to breakfast."

"But you guys won't mind if I cook sometimes?" Marny asked, although she wasn't planning on it.

For starters, she didn't have a lot of extra money to buy

food, and the dining room was included as part of her internship. But it was nice to have the option to make her own meals, especially since she had no idea about the quality of the Intertech food. It might be decent, judging by the apartment. Still, she never knew when she'd need to cook up some comfort food. Spicy chicken curry, coconut bread—two dishes she'd bet were not offered on the dining room menu.

"Sure, cook away." Wil shrugged. "But if whatever you make is good, I want some."

"It'll be delicious," she said. "Maybe too spicy for you, though."

"Hey, I'm adventurous."

"Stop flirting with the girl," Anjah said. "I have to get ready to go to brunch."

"That's not for another two hours," Wil said. "Jeez."

"I need to choose something to wear, and redo my make-up," Anjah said, in a tone of voice that implied Wil was an idiot.

"You just want to get there super early so you can sit at a table with that cute tech guy," Wil said.

"Lies." Anjah blushed though, just a little.

"I saw you chatting him up last night," Wil said.

Clearly, two days were long enough for Anjah to start on a love life. Privately, Marny thought it was foolish to go down that path. Work and romance didn't mix, and besides, interns were only around for two months. Any relationship would have to come to an unhappy end at that point.

But she wasn't going to say as much to Anjah. The girl clearly had a sharp side, and Marny didn't relish the idea of getting cut up over something small. She'd save herself for the big fights, which she had no doubt lay in their future. In direct contrast to Wil, Anjah didn't seem like the easygoing type. At all.

"I guess I'll get settled in, then," Marny said. Not that it would take her long to empty her backpack.

"Welcome to your new temporary home," Wil said.

"Yes. I'm sure we'll become good friends." Anjah sent her a gleaming smile.

Her teeth were unnaturally white. She looked like a perfect doll, but Marny knew better than to judge by appearances. If Anjah had scored an internship, she had formidable brains and talent behind that glamorous façade.

When her new roomies left, Marny closed the door and took a breath. Well. Here she was.

Ignoring the zing of homesickness in her belly, she strode over to the window and looked down. The streets were laid out in orderly patterns, with bars of shadow thrown across the city from the taller buildings. The faint vibration of traffic drifted up, and people scurried around on the sidewalks. It was a strange perspective, like she was floating above the world. What did the air even smell like up here?

Not that she could crank open any of the windows and find out. Everything this far up was sealed shut, which made sense. Didn't want some overworked employee taking a swan dive from the Intertech building—the PR would be terrible.

Still, half of her believed that if she opened a window and stepped out into that high, clear air, she could fly.

CHAPTER 3

APRIL

"My liege." The woody form of the spriggan guard bowed before the Bright King's throne. "It is as you said. A mortal boy has stepped into the Realm."

"Good." The king brought his fingertips together. "Bring him to me."

"I fear... there is a difficulty, your highness."

The spriggan trembled, like a tree whipped by the wind. Behind him, his brethren took a step back. It was never wise to upset the monarch.

The clearing of the Bright Court quieted, the harp falling silent as the king's gaze filled with wrath.

"Pray tell me why you cannot lead the human here. Has he dealt with the Realm of Faerie and its creatures before, and thus is wary and wise?"

"I know not." The guard's voice scraped like branches

rubbing together. "The mortal appears, remains for a short time, and somehow carries a piece of the Realm with him when he departs."

"Then follow him!" The king's voice was sharp.

"We have tried." The spriggan gestured to his comrades, and they nodded in confirmation. "He goes, and the way is closed to us. We can see a part of the Realm, but it exists as in a bubble, floating separate and unreachable beyond our grasp."

The Bright King's eyes narrowed, and the light falling over the court deepened toward sunset. "Be quicker. Next time he must not be allowed to escape."

"Yes, my liege."

"Go—and return successful, or not at all."

The king dipped one long-nailed finger into his goblet, then flung a droplet at the spriggan. It landed on the guard's arm, the spot smoking and hissing, but the creature knew better than to flinch. He made a low bow and, in the red glow of the king's anger, backed away and rejoined his comrades.

They patted his knobby shoulders, awkward in the knowledge that he would never again set foot in the Bright Court.

May

Nyx stood at the doorway of the empty warehouse, satisfaction swooping through him like a hawk spotting its prey.

"This could do," he said to Babs, the real-estate agent helping him find the perfect building to rent. "Let's go inside."

She gave a dusty little sigh. For the last five weeks—in between studying for finals, graduating from high school, and figuring out his crazy new ability—Nyx had been searching for the ideal space.

As far as he'd been able to determine from hours of searching the 'net, he was the first and only person able to create magical forests from playing a sim game. That was an ability that deserved to be showcased. And he knew just how he wanted to do it.

At first, the real-estate agent had been energetic and positive, showing him office complexes and storefronts. But none of them had been right for what his imagination, and new business venture, required.

"Could do," Babs said, clearly tired of presenting him place after place with no luck.

But this...

Nyx flipped the lights on and strode forward, his boots thudding over the concrete floor. The space was tall—over three stories high. In addition to the huge main warehouse, smaller offices lined the west wall and there were a couple outbuildings butted up against the outside.

Big windows let in light, but he could paint over the lower ones so nobody could see in. Even better, the building took up a whole city block, just south of downtown Newpoint. The surrounding area contained more warehouses, some abandoned, and a beverage-bottling plant that shut down from ten p.m. to six in the morning. No neighbors to pry and ask nosy questions, or lodge complaints about his hours of operation.

"Yeah," he said, the word echoing through the quiet space. "I think this is the place."

"You do?" Babs hurried over, her expression perking up. She could smell the commission.

"Let's look at the whole thing," he said. "If there are no surprises, I'd like to discuss terms with the landlords today."

"Excellent! I believe the bathrooms are this way." She turned to the right, a sudden bounce in her step.

Nyx glanced at the metal-girded ceiling high overhead, and smiled. The space was big enough to host his magical forest. He'd have to do some work with the positioning, of course, to make it seem like it was an illusion cast inside the warehouse, but it was way doable.

In addition, there was plenty of room to put an espresso and juice bar in one corner, figure out the dance floor situation, and install some comfy seating and gaming equip. Plus fix up an area he could live in. Extra bonus: the warehouse was even bigger than the dojo where he went to work out, and would make a great space to practice his martial arts.

It was going to be perfect.

Club Mysteria—where enchanted worlds become real...

Of course, everyone would think it was all high-end mixed reality generation and special effects. Look at the amount of convincing it had taken to get his sister to believe the magic was actually real.

The very first thing he'd had to do, back in March, was figure out how and why the enchanted forest had appeared in his bedroom. It had something to do with playing Feyland, he was sure, so he needed to spend as much time in-game as possible until he found some answers. He'd pretended to be too sick to go to school, making loud retching noises in the bathroom where his parents could hear, and refusing food.

As soon as everyone left the house, though, he'd scarf down peanut butter and banana sandwiches, pound a couple energy drinks, and start simming. After that first night the forest had appeared, it had taken him four days of practically nonstop gaming to find the answer.

Day One: Nothing except a ton of in-game questing and killing monsters. No glimmering trees growing in his bedroom that night.

Day Two: More of the same. Still no forest.

Day Three: Time to play smarter. He started retracing his steps, trying to recreate the adventures and remember the quests he'd done on the day of the magical manifestation.

Day Four: Halfway through tromping around in-game, he finally recalled he'd done a small quest to gather fallen leaves from the Sylven Glades. For some reason, he'd ended up with an extra leaf in his character inventory. At the time, he'd thought it just a glitch.

Was that it? He couldn't imagine how an extra in-game item could conjure up a magical forest in his room, but it was the only unusual thing that had happened. With a shrug, he turned his Archer character toward the Sylven Glades.

Leaping through the meadows of bright flowers, feeling the sun and breeze on his face, Nyx had to admit that the immersion tech of Feyland was prime. The company had done an amazing job with the game. Seriously, he felt like he was really there.

Ahead, the silvery trees of the glade rose into the purple-tinged sky. He slowed down and pulled an arrow from his quiver. There was a big, wicked boar that guarded the glade. On his last visit, it had taken him by surprise, and only Nyx's extra

Archer agility had kept him from failure. He'd used a Death-Defy leap and managed to land an arrow in the creature's eye.

This time he crept forward, arrow nocked to the string. The mossy ground cushioned his footsteps as he moved into the glade. Pale trunks rose around him and a faint wind shivered the leaves, their undersides flashing like moonlight. Breathing quietly, he moved toward the center clearing where the huge copper-leafed tree stood.

A stray sunbeam illuminated the tree, making the leaves glow like little suns. Nyx paused. He'd turned in the leaf quest already. Would he even be able to pick up one of those gleaming leaves scattered on the ground?

He took one step into the clearing, then whirled at the sound of grunting and rustling behind him. Fast and fierce, the wild boar charged. Its tusks were long and pointed, its eyes full of rage.

Heartbeat racing, Nyx shot an arrow at the creature. The shaft bounced off its armored hide, and the boar kept coming.

Forcing his hands steady, he grabbed another shaft and sent it flying. This one landed in the boar's chest, and it gave an angry squeal. But it didn't slow down. *Ah, crap.*

Nyx glanced at the dagger strapped at his waist. Nope, he didn't think his chances of hand-to-hand—or tusk-to-blade—were very good. Whirling, he dashed to the tree dominating the center of the glade.

He circled the huge trunk, half his attention on the animal closing in on him, half on the coppery branches. Come on! There had to be a limb low enough for him to climb.

One time around the tree. Breath rasping in his throat, Nyx risked a glance behind him. The trunk was so enormous he couldn't see the boar, but he could hear it grunting. Getting closer. He kept going.

Twice around. Should he make a stand, hope for a lucky shot? He pulled another arrow from his quiver, but something made his feet keep moving. He imagined he could feel the boar's hot breath at his heels. Good thing the animal was too dumb to switch directions.

Adrenaline pumped through Nyx. Running around the copper tree yet again was ridiculous. This was it. He'd have to turn and face the boar.

He slowed, then blinked at the big branch just above eye level. Why hadn't he seen it earlier?

He leaped, caught a decent handhold, and swung himself up. Without stopping to think, he balanced on the rough, coppery bark, nocked his bow, and shot at the boar racing below him.

The arrow plunged into the top of its skull. It kept running a few more steps, then suddenly fell over. No blood, no cries of pain. A moment later, the body disappeared in a shimmer of blue light.

Nyx let out a long breath.

"Thanks," he said to the tree, reaching over to give the trunk a pat. For sure that branch hadn't been there before.

The leaves rang together, with a sound like jingling coins. One perfect, shiny leaf drifted down, right past his face. Nyx swiped at it, missed, and lost his balance. The tree shook, as if it were laughing at him.

Luckily, his enhanced agility stat kept him from crashing too badly. He rose from a crouch, dusted off his leggings, and bowed to the tree. The copper leaf shone against the greenish-brown mosses and gnarled roots.

"Okay, then." Nyx picked it up.

The leaf was smooth and cool against his fingers. He slipped it in his pocket, and his character inventory lit up, showing that he'd added one copper leaf.

Distantly, he heard the ping of an alarm. Crap. Emmie would be home from school in ten minutes. If she found him simming, she'd tattle to the parents out of jealousy. After all, who *wouldn't* want to stay home from high school and game all day? It didn't matter that he was keeping up in his classes. Mom and Dad would come down hard on him for lying.

Nyx keyed his character back to the village inn that was his in-game home and hastily logged out. He pulled off the gaming helm and sim-gloves, then hopped up out of the chair.

Something poked his thigh, like there was a pin in the pocket of his sweatpants. Wouldn't that be just like Emmie, to sabotage his clothes? He could tell she thought he was totally faking being sick. Curses on perceptive little sisters.

He perched on the side of his bed and reached into his pocket. Something cool and slick met his fingers and he caught his breath in disbelief. It couldn't be.

Carefully, he drew the item out of his pocket and stared at it. A perfectly formed copper leaf. From Feyland. The back of his neck prickled with disbelief.

Nyx looked from the sim system to the leaf cradled in his palm, then back again, his mind insisting it couldn't be true. Things couldn't appear in real life from out of a video game.

He swallowed, feeling dizzy. Was he going crazy?

He set the leaf on his bedside table. It looked strange and magical beside his tablet and half-empty can of energy drink.

Downstairs, the front door slammed. Emmie was home. He wanted to call her in to look at the leaf, but she'd only laugh at it, saying he was trying to hoax her again. He rubbed his eyes, sudden exhaustion crashing over him. Maybe he really *was* getting sick after all.

With a last glance at the magical leaf, he curled up on his side and pulled his covers over him. It would be gone when he woke up—the whole thing just a fever dream.

"NYX! OHMIGOD, WAKE UP."

Emmie's voice, her hand on his shoulder shaking him insistently.

"Go 'way," he mumbled, trying to roll away from her annoying presence.

"Open your eyes. Please!"

The panicky note in his sister's voice penetrated his foggy brain. Nyx forced his eyes open.

His sleepiness shocked away like he'd been doused with a bucket of cold water. Slowly, he sat up and stared at his room.

His bedroom. His forest. Oh yeah.

The pale-trunked trees started by his bedside table and faded away into the misty distance. Bright flowers bloomed in clumps at their roots, and orange-winged butterflies danced in and out of shafts of sunlight.

"I told you," he said to Emmie.

Wide-eyed, she sank down to sit beside him on the bed.

"It can't be real," she whispered. "I thought you'd just... you know. Made a really prime MR simulation."

"What changed your mind?"

"Just look at it." She glanced around. "I came in to ask you a question about my data homework, and thought you'd left your projectors on. But then I felt one of the trees. Really felt it. And a drop of water splashed on my face, from a leaf."

She brought her fingers to her cheek.

"If it helps, I didn't believe it at first, either," he said, glancing at the copper leaf gleaming on his bedside table. "This is the second time it's appeared."

Emmie took a deep breath. "It even smells like a forest."

She was right. The air smelled like wet soil after a rain, with a faint underlay of crushed herbs.

A nearby clump of green-leaved bushes shook, and she grabbed his arm.

"Relax," he told her.

He couldn't reassure her that the forest wouldn't hurt them, but he had a pretty good idea of what was hiding in the shrubbery. Luckily, he had a half-eaten protein bar around somewhere, probably under a pile of clothes. He peeled Emmie's fingers off his arms and slid to the edge of the bed.

"Wait," she said. "You can't just get up and go in there."

Nyx ignored her. He knelt on the floor and started rummaging through his clothes. The flash of a foil wrapper caught his eye. Tossing his armful of laundry aside, he grabbed the bar and stripped off the wrapper, then moved to the perimeter of the lush green moss.

"Come out," he called, waving the bar. "Tasty treats."

"Seriously?" Emmie didn't sound scared anymore, or awed

—which meant the usual sarcasm couldn't be far behind. "You're trying to coax some creature out of the forest that *shouldn't even exist in your bedroom* with a stale bar?"

"Shut up," he suggested.

She narrowed her eyes at him, but at least she stopped talking.

After a moment, a pointy-nosed golden head popped out of one of the bushes. Nyx smiled, but kept his hand steady. Cautiously, the mouselike creature crept out of hiding. It paused and tilted its head, and Emmie made a little cooing noise.

"Here." Nyx broke a piece off the bar and reached out, setting it partway between him and the creature.

In a flash of gold fur, it darted forward, grabbed the hunk of protein bar, and disappeared back into the bushes.

"That was sooo cute," Emmie said. "I hope it's not like the attack bunny in that old movie Mom and Dad like so much."

"I saw this creature before." Nyx settled cross-legged on the floor, keeping one eye on the place the golden mouse had disappeared. "I don't think it's dangerous."

"Um." His sister picked at a loose thread on his coverlet. "So, I guess you were trying to tell me about this before. I should have listened better."

It was as close to an apology as he would get.

"Hey, it's pretty hard to wrap your brain around." He glanced into the misty depths of the forest. "It's like those books where kids walk into an enchanted closet and emerge into a magic land or something."

"But why us?"

"Us? Excuse me, this is *my* room."

Emmie rolled her eyes, but her usual snarky expression faded as she looked back at the woods. "Did you, like, pick up a magic coin or meet a sorcerer on your way home from school?"

"Not that I know of."

He wasn't about to try and explain, not when he himself had only a shaky grasp of what was going on.

The clank of the garage door opening vibrated through the house.

"Oh, crap." He got to his feet. "Dad's home early. What time is it?"

"Time for me to run interference." Emmie hopped off his bed. "I'll go talk at him while you do something about this. You know he's going to want to check on you, you big faker."

"I had reasons." Nyx raised his brows and swept a hand out at the forest.

"Well, undo them or whatever." She hurried to the door and opened it, then looked back over her shoulder. "Nyx?"

"You better get down there."

"If that mouse thing comes back, can I have it as a pet?"

"No. Now move it."

"Emerald? Onyx?" Their dad's voice drifted up the stairs.

Emmie slipped out, closing the door behind her, and Nyx glanced around. The forest was way too big to conceal. No way he could even drape the closest trees with blankets—the idea was ludicrous.

"Here." He chucked the rest of the bar into the mouse's bush, and was rewarded with a squeak of gratitude.

Muffled by his door, he could hear Emmie talking to Dad. Their voices were getting closer. Dammit. He really better be right about this.

Heart racing, Nyx picked up the copper leaf. It was cool and polished under his fingers. He grasped it in both hands, closed his eyes, and snapped it in half.

The sound of it breaking was a tiny click, but it seemed to shake all the way through him. He gasped, like he'd been punched in the stomach, and opened his eyes.

"There you are, buddy," his dad said, pushing open his door. "Wow, you really don't look good. Can I bring you an upchuck bowl?"

"No, thanks." Nyx clenched his hands around the remains of the leaf and staggered over to his bed. "I'll just rest."

"Hang in there. I think your mom is bringing some fizzy soda home. That might help."

Nyx nodded and lay down, giving his plain old walls a grateful glance.

At least he'd been right in his suspicions that the leaf was connecting Feyland to the real world. Somehow.

"Is he okay?" Emmie peeked her head in, but she didn't even bother glancing at him. She scanned his room, managing to look both relieved and disappointed at the same time.

"We'll let him rest," their dad said. "Out you go, squeak."

"Don't call me that." Emmie withdrew, Dad right behind her.

Nyx exhaled shakily, then uncurled his fingers. Instead of shattered bits of copper, his palms were coated with dust. Even as he watched, it seemed to float away, mingling with the dust motes in his room.

Head pounding, he sat on his bed and tried to make sense of the whole afternoon.

Somehow, he'd brought a leaf from inside a video game

into the real world. Where it had conjured a magical forest to life in his bedroom. Then the leaf had disappeared into a handful of ashes when he'd broken it, causing the enchanted trees to fade.

Yep, that pretty much summed it up. He rubbed his forehead. Too bad he had no idea what this all meant, or what to do about it.

But over the weeks, as he figured out how to bring various items out of Feyland and conjure up different environments—the silvery forest, a swamp, rolling meadows filled with flowers—a plan had formed.

This was magic, and he wanted to share it with the world in a way that people could enjoy.

"You'll be lying to them," Emmie had said.

"Nobody will believe the truth. And if they did, they'd just want to monetize it."

"The way you're planning to do." His sister's voice was dry.

"Yeah, but I'm not exploiting it—just delivering it in a way that will cover my costs."

Emmie had folded her arms and given him a sour look. "What if it turns out to be dangerous? How are you going to explain *that*?"

"I've had that forest in and out of my room for nearly two months now, and nothing has happened." He'd even gotten comfortable sleeping in its presence.

"What about that pile of sticks you told me about?"

Nyx had woken up one morning to find a small heap of twigs and branches in the middle of his bedroom floor. When he'd gone to pick them up, they'd disappeared. Not into silvery dust, either, just a shimmer in the air, and—poof!—gone.

"They were harmless, and it never happened again. I shouldn't even have told you about it."

"But I'm your partner." She had the stubborn look on her face that meant trouble.

"You're my *employee*. Big difference."

Actually, she was somewhere in between. She'd been a surprisingly good sounding board to bounce ideas off, and when the juice/espresso bar idea came up, she'd convinced him to let her manage it.

"You'll be too busy running the place," she'd said. "You don't want to be trapped behind a counter, making lattes. Besides, I'll have fun, and you'll pay me well."

"I hate it when you make sense."

She'd stuck her tongue out at him, and they had a deal. When he got his plan up and running, she'd be a part of it.

And finally, nearly three months from when the enchanted forest had first appeared in his bedroom, he'd found the place that would become Club Mysteria. A huge warehouse with a set of rooms he could fix up to live in, plus a couple more for offices. An entire city block, waiting for the magic to begin.

"This is perfect. Let's go sign the lease," Nyx told the stunned-looking real-estate agent. "Did I mention I'm paying cash?"

CHAPTER 4

JUNE 22

Marny's alarm, a cheerful blend of birdsong and gurgling water, rang way too early. She hit the snooze button, her brain struggling up from smoky dreams filled with vague disquiet. Probably trying to adjust to the fact that she'd never been this far from home, and anxiety about the internship.

Normally, she was not a worried kind of girl. Whatever came up, she dealt with it, and stressing beforehand wasn't useful. But as she sat up and pushed her hair out of her eyes, she had to admit she felt a touch afraid.

What if she couldn't meet Intertech's expectations?

Oh, stop it, the smarter part of her said. *You wouldn't be here if they didn't think you were worth it. Now get up.*

She sounded like her own mom. Half smiling, Marny pushed the soft covers aside and stood. The large bed was very comfortable. It was nice to have enough space to stretch out without bumping into the wall or stubbing her toe.

She'd outgrown her single years ago, but the bedroom she shared with Grandma Harmony didn't have room for a double bed. It could barely handle the two singles squeezed in on either side of the little room. Sometimes, when it was clear there'd be a few months between her grandma's stays, Marny pushed the beds together and stuffed a blanket in the crack between the mattresses. It was better, but nothing like a real double.

Everyone in her family was big. That was just part of her Samoan heritage. But so was helping out family. So whenever Grandma Harmony came back, Marny pulled the beds apart without a complaint.

She heard stirring in the room next door, and quickly pulled on her T-shirt and jeans and hurried into the hall. If Anjah got to the bathroom first, Marny had the feeling she'd monopolize it until they had to leave.

Marny brushed her teeth, swiped a comb through her hair, and was leaving the bathroom as Anjah came out of her room. She wore a set of silky pajamas that wouldn't look out of place at a fancy dinner party.

"Are you planning to shower?" Anjah asked, her eyes still half closed.

"Not this morning."

"Okay. Good." Anjah yawned and bumped into the bathroom door. "I'll be out in a half-hour. Maybe longer."

"I'm done in there," Marny said.

Anjah blinked. "Really? What about your makeup?"

"I rely on my natural beauty," Marny said dryly. It wasn't

entirely true, but a swipe of lip gloss and a dab of eyeliner certainly wouldn't count as makeup in Anjah's world.

"You could be attractive, with a little enhancement. We'll talk about that, later." Anjah yawned again. "God, I hope Wil makes some coffee."

"I don't think he's up yet." Marny let the "could be attractive" comment pass. Whatever.

"Maybe you'll make the coffee?" Anjah peered at her hopefully.

"I'm more of a tea drinker," Marny said. "Enjoy your shower."

She had no interest in becoming Anjah's personal chef. Or in submitting to a makeover, no doubt complete with catty comments about all her physical shortcomings. Tallcomings, heh.

Back in her room, Marny donned the new clothes she'd bought yesterday from the store Brenna had taken her to. The dark pants and tailored burgundy top were adequate corporate work clothes, but she hoped her duffel would show up soon. The clothes Jennet had helped her pick out had a little more character, and besides, they'd remind her of home. Make her feel that she hadn't been completely assimilated as an Intertech worker-drone.

She went to the mirrored closet door and tried to see herself as a stranger might. The clothes made her look adult. And was she almost attractive? She leaned forward, trying to determine what about her wide cheeks, dark eyes, and broad nose was particularly appealing.

Years ago, she'd given up on being beautiful—at least the kind of beautiful found on the vids and netscreens. As far as she knew, there hadn't yet been a Samoan supermodel. And that was actually fine. She was proud of her strength, and her family. Proud of the particular collection of features that made her Marny Fanalua.

Whatever Anjah was talking about, Marny didn't see it. Then again, the girl was a bit obsessed about appearance, not to mention half-asleep. It was obvious Anjah wasn't a morning person.

Neither was Wil, judging from the snores emanating from his room as Marny walked past. She paused, wondering if she should knock on his door, when a shockingly loud alarm jangled from inside. He mumbled and she heard him smack something. The noise abruptly cut off.

Right, then. If she ever overslept, his alarm would definitely rouse her. Good to know.

She shook her head and continued to the kitchen. Far better, in her opinion, to wake to the soothing waterfall-and-birdsong melody programmed into her tablet.

She flicked on the electric kettle, then rummaged in the cupboards until she found the mugs. They were all too small, and standard boring white. She mentally added a big, colorful tea mug to the list of things she needed.

On her way past the dining hall the night before, she'd grabbed a few tea bags and sealed containers of creamer. Soon, she'd get to the store—she really did prefer soy milk—but for now, Intertech could keep her in tea. The Celtic Breakfast in its bright green packaging looked promising.

The kettle dinged, and she poured boiling water over her tea bag. Stainless steel and black, the appliance matched the rest of the stylish kitchen. Dark granite countertops, a stove that looked brand new, and cupboards made of some reddish wood, stocked with dishes. And regrettably small mugs.

When her tea had brewed nice and strong, she took her cup over to the window and watched the morning traffic zip around the streets below. Almost half the cars were the bright yellow grav-taxis—something she didn't see much of in Crestview. Either people drove themselves (or had chauffeurs, in the case of the rich kids), or took the bus.

"Yo." Wil shuffled into the kitchen, wearing sweat pants and a T-shirt with holes in it. His hair stuck up on one side like a fan.

"Morning," she said, turning to greet him.

Lucky Anjah; it looked like he was, indeed, making coffee.

Most of Marny's family loved the beverage. Her uncle even owned a simcafé, but Marny had never developed a taste for coffee. Too bitter.

Though she did enjoy the smell as Wil ground the coffee. It reminded her of home.

He rubbed his eyes and leaned back against the counter beside the gurgling coffee machine.

"I hear they set out a tray of bagels and pastries in the dining hall," he said. "For people who just want to grab something and go during their breaks. In case you were wondering about breakfast."

"Sounds good."

She usually wasn't too hungry in the mornings, but it wouldn't hurt to have a little bite. Although this morning, her stomach was so tight with nerves she was particularly uninterested in eating.

Calm down. Sheesh. You'll be fine.

Whatever the day held, she'd handle it. If she could battle crazed smoke-drifters and wicked goblins, babysit a changeling, and fight off faerie glamour, she could face her first morning at Intertech.

Before the coffee was done, Wil grabbed a mug and poured himself a cup, letting the still-brewing coffee splash down and scorch on the burner. Marny wrinkled her nose at the acrid smell, but she didn't say anything as Wil dashed back to his room. She could hear Anjah singing in the bathroom.

For a second she missed her sisters and parents with a deep stab of homesickness.

But at home there was no view of a waking city outside her windows. No way to prove herself against a larger world. Crestview was where she'd grown up, but it was constricting, like an old sweater that had shrunk in the dryer until she could barely get her head and arms through, let alone wear it comfortably.

She wasn't sure what kind of future would fit her, but that was part of why she'd applied for the internship. Why she was here in Newpoint.

"Coffee?" Anjah called plaintively, cracking the bathroom door open an inch.

Wil didn't respond, so after a moment Marny did. "I'll bring you a cup. Black?"

"Oh, thank you! Black, two sugars."

Marny supposed it didn't hurt to preserve harmony with her roommates. She'd need a favor in return at some point, and it didn't take long to fix Anjah's cup.

"Here you go." Marny rapped on the bathroom door.

Anjah cracked it again, and stuck out her hand. Her nails were now peacock blue.

"A million thanks," she said from behind the door as she grabbed the mug.

"Welcome," Marny said to the rapidly closing door.

Oh, well. Some people really weren't human until after their morning coffee. Though she had the suspicion Anjah had a selfish streak as wide as the Pacific.

Marny went back to the window, and her tea. The last couple sips were cold, but she finished it anyway as sunlight illuminated the side of a nearby skyscraper. Gray windows turned to silver, flat metal sparkling as it caught the light, and colors burst from wan to brilliant.

She liked being high enough to see the sky. Mentally calculating that the window faced southwest, she figured the apartment would get some nice afternoon sun.

Though whether she'd ever have free time in the afternoon remained to be seen.

She glanced at the screen mounted on the wall, currently displaying the time and weather. Brenna would be there in five minutes to take them downstairs for their first day of work.

Marny rinsed her cup in the kitchen, then went back to her room. She grabbed her tablet and slipped on the new pair of shoes, dressy but still relatively comfortable. Wil was moving around in his bedroom, and Anjah was still in the bathroom.

"You guys coming?" she called as she strode down the hall toward the front door.

"Right here," Wil said, stepping out of his room.

Marny pursed her lips and nodded. "You clean up nice."

His wild hair was tamed back with gel, showing off his strong features. Wearing slacks and a button-down shirt, he didn't look quite so gawky and uncoordinated. Not that she was any more attracted to him, but it was an interesting transformation.

"Glad you approve." He winked at her. "You look pretty sharp yourself."

Anjah threw open the bathroom door and sailed out on a cloud of steam and flowery perfume. Of course she was dressed perfectly, in a blue-green ensemble that was like a sunlit sea.

"Let me get my shoes," she said. "And my bag."

She led the way to the entry, where she deftly donned a pair of aquamarine high heels and plucked a matching purse from the closet.

Somebody knocked on the door.

"Come in," Wil said through the speaker interface, and buzzed the door open.

It slid back to reveal Brenna standing in the hallway.

"Good," the liaison said, giving them each a once-over. "After today, you guys need to get yourselves down to the offices, but this morning there's an introductory meeting to attend."

"Aye-aye," Wil said, snapping a salute.

Brenna gave him a look. "This isn't boot camp. You all ready?"

"Yep," Marny said. "Let's go."

"Wait a second." Anjah set her hand on Marny's arm, pulled her to the hall mirror, and handed her a tube of lip gloss. "Put this on."

"I'm fine—"

"Humor me. Besides, you have beautiful lips."

"Hurry up," Brenna said, folding her arms.

It was quicker for Marny to slick some gloss over her mouth than keep arguing with Anjah. Besides, she could always wipe it off when Anjah wasn't looking.

"Nice." Anjah nodded. "Keep it—it's not really my color."

Marny had to admit the subtle sheen did look good on her, and not too obviously like she was wearing makeup. Maybe she wouldn't wipe it off, after all.

"Guys," Wil called from the hall.

Moving alarmingly fast in her high heels, Anjah hurried out the door. Marny was right behind her.

"Finally." Brenna gave Marny a stern look. "Do your primping a little earlier next time, okay?"

Marny just nodded. No use arguing.

They were silent as they rode the elevator down ten floors. When the doors dinged open, Brenna led them down yet another hallway and past several offices and official-looking meeting rooms.

"This morning you'll meet your supervisors and get your assignments," Brenna said. "If you have any questions or concerns, make sure to speak up. And here we are."

Marny looked through the glass window into the conference room Brenna had indicated. It seemed full of people, and her stomach tightened again.

"Sure looks busy in there," Wil said, voicing her own worry. "Do they really need nine people to run herd on us?"

"Ten," Anjah said. "You missed the guy in the dark blue suit at the far end of the table."

"Don't argue, just come in." Brenna swiped her ID card at

the door. It slid open and she strode inside, heading for the four empty chairs at the close end of the table.

"Fine, ten people," Wil said to Anjah. "After you, your majesty."

Anjah sniffed as she swept past him, walking gracefully into the room as if she really were royalty.

Which, for all Marny knew, she was.

"Ladies first." Wil lifted his brows at her.

Marny couldn't quite manage the princess walk, but she did her best to appear calm and unruffled as she followed Anjah into the room. Brenna beckoned them to the chairs beside her. Anjah promptly took the middle one. Marny pulled out the chair on her right, glad to find it was nice and roomy, and Wil settled on Anjah's left.

The man in the blue suit stood, and Marny saw with some surprise that it was the CEO, Dettwiler von Coburg. As soon as he rose, everyone else stopped conversing and set their tablets down. For a long moment, Mr. von Coburg studied the people seated around the table. His eyes were steel gray in his stern face. Marny wondered if his silver hair was fake, it looked so thick and shiny.

At last he sat down again, his gaze fixed on the interns.

"Welcome," he said, a faint trace of an accent in his voice. "I am sure I needn't tell you what an honor it is for the three of you to be sitting here, in the heart of one of the greatest corporations in the world."

The other people in the room applauded, and Marny couldn't tell if it was in greeting or because they were supposed to respond like that to everything Mr. von Coburg said.

"It's an honor, sir," Anjah said, hitting just the right note of respect.

"Miss Anjah Lee." The CEO didn't bother glancing at the tablet in front of him. "Your mathematics scores are impressive. We're placing you with the data and statistics team. I'm sure you'll be able to assist with their various projects."

He waved to three people seated across from Anjah, who each nodded at her in turn.

"I'd be delighted," Anjah said, with a demure smile.

"Mr. Wil Cutter." Mr. von Coburg leaned forward. "Mechanical genius at a young age—very nice. You will be working with the structural engineering team."

"Prime," Wil said, grinning.

Three guys who had the rumpled look of engineers nodded to him, and he lifted his hand in return.

"Miss Marny Fanalua." Mr. von Coburg's gaze pinned her to her chair. "You created an app that has swept the globe, providing a modification scheme no one had envisioned the need for—until you invented it. We're assigning you to the social interfaces design team."

He nodded at the two women and one man seated to his left.

"Thank you," Marny said, though she had very little idea what she'd just gotten herself into.

Social interfaces design team? It sounded like calling the cleaning guy an "environmental alignment specialist." Except at Intertech, the job was probably way more involved than mopping floors, and required top-level clearance.

"Now." Mr. von Coburg held up his hands. "I trust you three to give Intertech your best work, cooperate with your team members, and, of course, abide by the nondisclosure agreement you all signed before arriving."

Yeah—that contract had serious teeth. If Marny breathed a word about Intertech to anyone outside the company, she'd be booted out so fast she probably wouldn't even have time to gather her belongings.

Provided her duffel bag ever showed up.

"It's been a pleasure welcoming you to the company." The CEO gave the interns the barest hint of a smile. "I look forward to weekly updates on your progress. Now, teams, gather up your hatchlings and get to work."

He rose, and the rest of the people around the table quickly stood, as if it wouldn't do to idle there when the boss was on his feet. Marny, Wil, and Anjah got up, too. Nobody said anything as Dettwiler von Coburg paced out of the conference room without a backward glance.

"We do okay?" Wil asked Brenna in a low voice, once the CEO was gone.

"You guys are fine," the liaison said, waving her hand. "The boss practically smiled at you—a real coup."

Marny raised her brows, while Anjah preened a little.

"You heard the man," Brenna continued. "Get over to your assigned people. I'll see you at lunch."

"Good luck, everyone," Anjah said, tossing her hair back.

She sauntered over to her team, and after a quick conversation, they left the room. Wil did the same, trading backslaps with the engineers in some kind of dude-recognition ritual.

Marny's turn. The three people who represented the social interface design team surrounded her, but not in a scary way.

"Hey," Marny said.

"Welcome," the blonde woman said, with a decidedly French accent. "I am Madame Fontaine. These are my colleagues, Ms. Hanley and Ser Jellicoe."

Marny nodded and shook hands all around. She guessed Ms. Hanley was American, but Ser Jellicoe stumped her. He looked Native Australian, maybe, with tribal tattoos snaking down his arms, and a smile that gleamed whitely in his dark face.

"Come on down to the twenty-ninth," he said. "Meet all the gang. We'll get you settled."

"Okay." She followed Ser Jellicoe into the hallway.

"Nice work on that app," Ms. Hanley said. "Really creative stuff."

"Thanks, Ms. Han—"

"Please, don't take Madame's formality to heart." The brown-haired woman smiled at her. "Call me Angie. And he's Jelly." She nodded at Ser Jellicoe.

Marny could handle using the name Angie, but she didn't think she'd be comfortable calling anyone Jelly, let alone a supervisor. Madame clearly would always be Madame—and nobody suggested otherwise.

"How did you come up with the idea of No Compromise?" Madame Fontaine asked as they stepped into the elevator. She keyed in the floor number with one flawlessly manicured finger.

"I was tired of the same old types of avatar choices," Marny said. "Especially the skinny ones with idealized proportions. I mean, it was either play them, or go for the really gross monster avas. I'd been trying to mod my gaming characters for a couple years, and finally found a way to make it stick."

"I'd say." Angie laughed. "Got anything else you're working on?"

"I'm pretty open right now. Maybe an idea or two, nothing solid. I'd love to see what you guys are working on."

"Our team specializes in primary customer interfaces," Ser Jellicoe said. "That includes things like avatar creation as well as social media outreach."

"One of our projects involves designing new voice modules," Madame Fontaine said.

"Really?" Marny couldn't curb her enthusiasm. "I've been starting to think about different dialogue options. What people say and *how* they say it is nearly as important as how they look. I'm not sure the regular settings give enough nuance, you know?"

"Excellent." Madame gave her an approving nod. "Miss Fanalua, sit down with Ms. Hanley and familiarize yourself with our current projects. I'll be interested in your feedback. That will be your first assignment."

"Great." Marny grinned at Angie, who winked back at her.

Maybe this internship wasn't going to be so fearsome after all.

CHAPTER 5

MID-JUNE

A light breeze swirled through the Bright Court, setting the gemmed flowers on the jade-leafed trees clinking. The floating motes of pixies spun and glowed, their chiming laughter drifting over the court. A jig lilted through the air and the feasting tables were crowded with cheerful denizens of the Bright Realm. Yet despite this levity, the Bright King's expression was pensive as he sat upon his throne.

His spriggan guard had not returned, and the king had come to the reluctant conclusion that the creatures of the Realm of Faerie would not be able to use these so-called bubble worlds to enter the human realm.

There were other ways, however, of crossing the boundary between the worlds.

The king gestured to one of his courtiers, a slender youth

garbed in pale green with wings of the same color tightly furled against his back.

"Verdan," the king said as the faerie made him a low bow, "I desire to speak with Puck. Go search him out and ask him to present himself as soon as he might."

"Yes, my liege." The courtier leapt lightly into the air, his wings opening to bear him away.

The Bright King watched until Verdan disappeared beyond the shining trees. While he wished he could summon the sprite to appear immediately, Puck was a tricksy faerie and not the king's to command. If Puck felt too put-upon, he would remove himself in rebuke to the Dark Court for a time, well beyond the king's reach. It behooved the king to tread carefully—though being forced to issue such a polite summons grated upon him.

Still, Puck was a useful fellow, and a good ally when he chose to be. And for the errand the king had in mind, there was no better emissary than the mischievous sprite.

Nyx stood in the center of the warehouse, hands on his hips. The buzz of drills and the steady thwack of an air-compressor nail-gun filled the air, along with lots of dust particles and the smell of new paint.

It was all his, and it was prime.

The process of leasing the building and starting the remodel had been mostly seamless, although jumping through permit hoops at the city hall had been a pain. But now it was just about finished and he was ready to move in.

First priority had been fixing up the living space. The

construction crew had done a good job with it, and now the bedroom, spare room, bathroom, and little kitchen/living area were complete, plus extra bathrooms for the club side.

The next step was putting in some furniture and making the place his own.

"We'll miss you, hon," his mom had said at dinner the night before. "Are you absolutely sure you want to move out?"

"I'm eighteen now," he'd replied. "Isn't that what I'm supposed to do?"

She'd given him a sad-eyed look that was only partially in jest. "You know we love having you around."

"Speak for yourself." Emmie made a face at him over the salad bowl. "He's loud and annoying and leaves messes all over."

"It's not my fault you have an issue with my socks," Nyx said, mostly to rile her up.

"They're disgusting! You leave them right there on the couch, and—"

"Stop." Their dad held up a hand. "Carolyn, maybe it's not a bad thing for Onyx to get his own place."

"No kidding." Emmie narrowed her eyes at him.

"You'll have to do my portion of the chores now, don't forget." He gave her an evil smile.

"*So* worth it."

"At least plan to have dinner with us a couple nights a week," his mom said, ignoring Emmie's drama.

"I will." He'd patted his mom's arm. "It's not as if I'm going far."

"Unlike me in three years, when I'm actually going off to college like the smart people do," Emmie said.

"You'd be lucky to make a fraction of your brother's income in three years," Dad said mildly. "I believe he's on track to be a millionaire by the age of twenty-five."

"And you'll have a pile of debts, instead." Nyx took a bite of mashed potatoes, then grinned at her, letting some of the potato slip through his teeth.

"Ew. You are so immature. I don't understand at *all* how you manage to make so many credits—or have so many fans. People are idiots."

Nyx shrugged. The truth was, he'd been surprised at how many people had subscribed to his Flail channel to watch him and his best friend play old-school games.

"Durham has all the fans," Nyx said, though he knew they both had plenty of followers.

"At least he's good-looking. You, I just don't get." Emmie shook her head.

"Some people appreciate the subtle, dangerous look," Nyx's mom said, giving her husband a fond glance.

Nyx shared his dad's lean build and prominent cheekbones, though Dad's hair was a shade darker than Nyx's amber blond. And Nyx had more muscles, from all his time in the dojo.

"Mom." Nyx could feel the top of his ears heating. "People just like to watch two guys joking around while they play old console games."

Though he had to admit they'd provided some fine entertainment. He and Durham had always been able to crack each other up. Add in the vintage gaming angle, and their channel had been surprisingly popular. And profitable.

It had started with an ancient Pac-Man machine Durham's dad excavated from the back of Dur's grandpa's garage. They'd decided to fix it up and play, and Nyx had suggested they do it live, on his Flail channel.

People had started to notice and send money, plus requests for other games and setups. Nyx and Durham had done some serious digging around on the 'net and in local junk stores to find outdated equip and obscure games. Their few dozen subscribers had turned to hundreds, and then thousands.

"Too bad your popularity has peaked," Emmie said, in a fake-sympathetic voice.

"Nothing lasts forever," Nyx said, taking a bite of salad.

"And you're on to the next project," his dad said. "I'm proud of you. You're going to learn a lot. Let me know if you need any more business advice."

It was a sincere—and valuable—offer. Charles Spenser had started and sold a lot of businesses over the years. Even though they didn't live extravagantly, Nyx knew his parents had over a million credits stashed away in investments.

"Thanks," Nyx said. "Your help on the initial plan was great. But I really want to do this on my own."

So here he was, standing in his new building, about to embark on an adventure even bigger than his dad suspected. Because how did you explain magical game interfaces on a business plan without sounding like a complete nerf? He'd glossed over those parts, saying stuff about state-of-the-art immersive tech, and mixed reality projectors and smoke machines and things.

At least Emmie had backed him up. For a price.

"Let me help," she'd said when he'd first told her what he was planning. Not that he'd intended to tell her, but she was relentless, and he'd ended up confiding his plans just to shut her up.

"No helping," he said.

She narrowed her eyes in that way that meant trouble. "If you don't involve me, I'll tell Dad that you're lying."

"I'm not lying," he lied.

"Do you really want him to know that your entire business plan is based on some magical overlap thing you can't even explain?"

"I can explain it." Sort of. Okay, not really.

She sniffed and tossed her teal-dipped hair over her shoulder. "Right. I'd like to see that show. Let me know, and I'll bring the popcorn."

"Great idea. I'll sell tickets."

"Really, Nyx." Her voice went serious as she dropped the annoyed-little-sister routine. "I can back you up about the fake tech stuff you're telling Dad. Plus it will be good to have somebody around who knows the actual truth."

He blew a breath out his nose and regarded her for a minute, but in his gut he knew she was right.

From then on she'd been helpful, down to the whole managing-the-juice-bar idea. Of course, she'd also made him agree to pay her way over minimum wage. He'd put up a token resistance and pretended to be outraged, but it was actually a good deal for him. There were financial loopholes around hiring a relative in a family business—loopholes their Dad had been using for years to employ his kids. Both Nyx and Emmie had learned a lot about business, whether they'd wanted to or not.

Tomorrow she'd come in and start getting the juice bar

ready. The club's grand opening was in just ten days. He knew that was pushing it, but he'd already printed up old-school flyers, and hired a digi-ad firm to send auto-notifications to all open messagers and tablets in the area and launch the club's social media campaign.

In addition to all that promo, Durham was fine with mentioning the club on their Flail channel. Nyx didn't expect all of their hundred thousand fans worldwide to attend the opening, but there were probably some locals who'd come check it out.

"Hello?" A woman in a brown jumpsuit stuck her head through the main warehouse door. "Delivery for Onyx Spenser. This the place?"

That must be the stuff he'd ordered for his bedroom.

Nyx went out to help unload the truck parked outside. The two delivery people handled the big boxes, and he directed them through the echoing space and through the hall leading to the living area.

"First room on the right, past the bathrooms," he called.

Ten minutes later, surrounded by empty cardboard and half-assembled furniture, he wished he'd made Emmie come in early. Assembling a bedframe by himself was a pain, and he didn't want to bother the construction guys. They had bigger jobs to take care of.

It took him way longer than he wanted, but he finally finished putting everything together. He scooted the mattress over and let it fall onto the frame, then opened the boxes of bedding and tossed the sheets and covers on his new bed. Nothing would stop him from spending the night in his own place, especially after he'd been so insistent about it with his mom.

Besides, he had some experimenting to do.

At first, he'd thought about embedding some of the Feyland leaves into the building itself, but quickly discarded that idea. He wanted to be able to change things around, not be stuck with the enchanted forest forever. Though it was a good place to start. The trick was going to be lining the anchors up correctly so that the forest started in the warehouse, facing the front door.

He'd figured out in his bedroom that no matter which way he positioned the forest, it never showed from the outside of his house. Once, though, he'd had a close call with the meadow spilling out into the hallway. He'd barely destroyed the blue flower anchor before his mom got to the top of the stairs.

Right now, though, the construction crew was still at work, and he was hungry. Nyx pulled on his black jacket and headed out, waving to the workers as he went. There was a good noodle shop a couple blocks north of him, on the edge of downtown. He had the feeling he'd be eating a lot of ramen in the coming weeks.

The air smelled of machine oil and the dusty end of a warm day. Ahead of him the skyline of Newpoint sparked silver and gold, the skyscrapers catching the setting sun. The Intertech building rose above them, dominating the view. He idly counted floors, until he lost track somewhere in the forties. What did they even do in there all day?

In middle school, his class had taken a field trip to the building. He didn't remember much about the trip except for long, clean hallways, a bunch of offices, and Durham getting in trouble for trying to sneak away from the back of the tour.

Dur hadn't gotten far, though, before the security cameras spotted him and a burly guy had escorted him back to the class.

"What'd you do that for?" Nyx had whispered.

"I wanted to see the whole thing," Durham had whispered back. "I hear there's like a city up on the top floors. Someday I want to work for Intertech."

"No way. Not me."

Already, Nyx had discovered a taste for running his own projects. An *entrepreneurial mindset*, his dad called it. The idea of going to work for a corporate behemoth and being enclosed in a giant building all day held no appeal.

Durham, though, had tried for the big-deal Intertech internship, but hadn't gotten in. Apparently they were notoriously hard to land. Nyx had commiserated, but in his opinion his friend would be better off heading to the fancy college he'd gotten into than shackling himself to a desk job at an early age. Even if there was a secret city at the top of the skyscraper.

Nyx gave the gleaming building a last glance, then ducked into the busy, cramped restaurant. The smell of garlic and a cloud of steam welcomed him as he took an empty chair at the counter.

It didn't matter what happened in the city's tallest skyscraper. Beyond keeping his tablet connected to the 'net, the doings of Intertech had no bearing on his life. He had much more important things to spend his time thinking about—like how he was going to install hidden compartments in the walls without the construction guys noticing.

CHAPTER 6

JUNE 22

By the end of the day, Marny's happiness was overlaid with a fog of exhaustion. Her mind felt stretched in all kinds of new ways from the brainstorming she'd done with the team and the possible projects they'd come up with for her to pursue.

She leaned against the elevator wall as it went up, her heels burning in the new shoes she'd bought yesterday. Hopefully, her duffel bag had arrived, or she'd be hand-washing her blouse and under things in the sink, and wearing the same clothes tomorrow. Classy.

In another week or so she could probably get away with her Converse high-tops and nicer new jeans, but for her second day on the job, she didn't want to risk it. Even though she generally didn't care much what people thought about her, at Intertech it was clear that employees—and interns—had to play by the corporate rules. At least until they learned how to bend them.

The elevator dinged and let her out on the fortieth floor. Marny slipped off her shoes and carried them down the hall, the carpet springy under her stockinged feet. She'd change, make a cup of tea, and enjoy some of the coconut bread her mom had sent with her. The thought of it warmed her heart, and she released a low breath. At least she could *taste* home, even if she wasn't there.

Loud, thumping music from Wil's room greeted her when she stepped into the apartment, followed by Anjah yelling at him through her closed door to turn it down. Maybe having roomies wasn't that different from living with her siblings, after all.

She glanced around the entry and living room, but there was no sign of her duffel. Damn.

It wasn't in her bedroom either. Not that she'd expected to see the lumpy green bag there, but still. How long was it going to take the bus company to find one misplaced piece of luggage?

She needed to call Intertech's front desk again to ask if it had come in yet, and also the bus people to ask them what the heck.

At lunch, she'd taken advantage of the hour-long break to run down to the retail store on the corner and buy a nice big mug for her tea habit, plus some specialty blends. She went into the kitchen, grabbed her fresh box of lavender mint tea, and kicked the kettle on to boil. The cheerful red and orange pattern on her new mug made her smile.

Wil's music got louder as he opened his door and ambled

out. He was wearing a worn T-shirt and sweats—clearly sharing Marny's impulse to shed her work clothes as quickly as possible.

"Hey there," he said. "Good day?"

"Yeah, I learned a ton. You?"

"It was great." He smiled, his eyes lighting up. "Man, I feel like I finally found my tribe. We speak the same language, you know?"

Marny nodded. Although she hadn't completely bonded with her supervisors, she already felt friendly with Angie and Ser Jellicoe.

"Want a cup of tea?" she asked, lifting her mug and inhaling the minty steam.

"Nah, I'm good. Had a snack earlier. I'll just grab a soda and get my simming on." He opened the fridge.

"Could you grab my coconut bread while you're in there?" Marny asked. "It's wrapped in foil."

"Uh." Wil closed the door and turned, soda can in his hand. "That was yours?"

"Yes." She didn't like the guilty look on his face.

"I'm sorry, dude. It's all gone."

"It's *what*?" She blinked at him, hoping that she'd heard wrong.

He gave her a sheepish smile. "It was really, really good, though."

"You ate my entire loaf of coconut bread?" A slow, angry burn kindled in her chest. No luggage, and now this?

"I'll buy you more—it's just that I was starving, you know?"

"That's no excuse. And it's not something you can just replace. That was extremely rude of you." What kind of people behaved so thoughtlessly? She glared at him. People like Wil, apparently.

"You could peel paint with that stare of yours," he said. "Anyway, sorry. You can have one of my Peps, if you want."

"Not the same thing." She folded her arms. "Never eat my food again without asking."

"Fine. Sorry." He stared at the floor a second, then opened his soda can and sidled out of the kitchen.

A minute later he was geared up and immersed in his sim machine. What a dud.

Frowning, Marny lifted the lid of the trash and peeked inside. Sure enough, a crumpled ball of foil shone back at her. With a last glare at Wil, she grabbed her mug of tea and went back to her room.

The hallway smelled like flowery perfume, most strongly in front of Anjah's door. Marny held her breath until she got inside her room, then let it out in a gust of annoyance.

At least the city was still there, shining outside her window. She wrapped her hands around her mug, absorbing the heat, and went to admire the view.

Slabs of shadow lay across the streets and smaller buildings, and the west-facing windows shone gold with the light of the lowering sun. A few wispy clouds smudged the horizon, maybe enough to hold on to a sunset.

Light glimmered in the corner of her vision and Marny leaned forward, craning her neck to the side. There had been something familiar about that flicker emanating from south of the downtown core.

It came again, a quick shimmer like a tiny firework, barely seen before it disappeared.

She tightened her grip around her tea mug. That had looked uncomfortably like a stray bit of fey magic; a wisp or pixie flitting over the mortal city.

No. Surely there was another explanation.

Somebody was setting off fireworks in a vacant lot or playing with lasers, or it was a reflection off a grav-car as it sped past. Nothing to do with the Realm of Faerie.

But there was no denying the game of Feyland was now everywhere, in worldwide release. Crestview couldn't be the only place the Realm crossed over into the human world. Why couldn't it happen here, in Newpoint?

She shivered, and took a quick swallow of her tea.

If something was going tweaked, her friends Tam and Jennet would know. They were the official Feyguard, after all, whereas she was just a normal girl.

Okay, maybe not that normal. She'd seen faeries and helped her friends battle them, as well as fighting by their side when necessary.

Despite the low-level worry winding through her, she smiled briefly at the memory of the fierce little changeling, Korrigan. He was an ugly guy with a mean streak, but brave and loyal when it mattered. If only all the fey folk were like that.

She watched as twilight dusted the city with ashes, but there was no more sign of the faerie light. If she'd even seen it.

Marny drank the last of her now-cold tea, then grabbed her messager and settled on her bed.

:You there?: she sent in group chat to Tam and Jennet.

:Sec,: Tam replied. *:In battle.:*

Marny scooched back against the pillows, wishing she had

her big Manu Samoa T-shirt to sleep in. She wasn't necessarily a rugby fan, but Grandma Harmony had brought it to her from her last trip to the islands.

:We're out. How was your first day?: Jennet sent.

:Good. Tiring.: Marny didn't bother mentioning her homesickness. *:Hey, is anything incoming on the Feyguard radar?:*

:Why?: Tam asked, and even from nearly a thousand miles away she could hear the worry in his question.

: Just saw something odd, and wondered. Nothing severe, just twinkly lights.:

:Strange noises?: Jennet sent.

:Like creepy hunting horns? No.: What she may or may not have seen wasn't the Wild Hunt—and she was grateful for that.

:Hm,: Jennet typed. *:Actually, I might need to go to India on Feyguard business—but we haven't been notified of anything around Newpoint. Pay attention if you have any strange dreams.:*

:And keep an eye out,: Tam sent. *:You have the power to see beyond normal reality.:*

:India?!: Marny was completely distracted by that news. Jennet was being sent to India? Poor Tam. *:For how long?:*

:Probably a few weeks. An interesting situation has come up. Dad's coming, too. Sort of like a family vacation.:

:Now with more faeries,: Tam added dryly.

:Ha,: Jennet typed. *:Listen, I agree with Tam. Trust your instincts about whatever you see, and stay in touch.:*

Not that Jennet could do a lot from halfway across the world. Nor Tam, since he was pretty much tied to VirtuMax with a summer internship the same way Marny was to Intertech. But if she ended up needing Feyguard help, surely it would arrive, in one form or another.

:Okay,: she wrote. *:I'll keep you posted. Goodnight you two.:*

:Hugs,: Jennet sent, along with a smiley emote.

:Night,: Tam typed.

Once they logged off, Marny's room felt cold and empty. With a sigh, she set her messager on the dresser, then went to stand in front of the window again. The lights of Newpoint filled the sky with orange city-glow, brighter than at home.

She watched for a long time, but there was no flicker of fey magic to be seen.

THE SPRITE CALLED Puck traveled deep into the misty dawn of the Realm of Faerie, swooping over dew-pearled meadows on the back of a snowy owl. His eyes glinted with mischief and merriment, and stalks of yarrow fluttered in his untidy hair. He wore a tunic of tattered leaves stitched together with cobwebs and his leggings were woven of emerald moss.

Ahead stood a circle of standing stones, the very tops catching the first rays of the rising sun. The granite glinted with mica, and in the center of the circle something stood, a pale blur, a creature whiter than the moon.

Puck grinned with delight. He had guessed well that he might find his quarry in this place, pining for the days when such a circle might open a doorway between the worlds. The sprite brought his owl to a silent landing just outside the stones and bade it wait for him. Then, mindful of the damp grasses, he floated up and into the circle.

The beast inside lifted its majestic antlered head and regarded him from eyes as deep and liquid as a forest lake.

"Greetings, walker between the worlds," Puck said, making the White Stag an elaborate bow.

"Puck. What causes you to seek me out? This is no simple visit."

"Ah, friend, you have always seen far too clearly." Puck settled himself cross-legged in the air. "Would you like to step over the boundary again, and bear a mortal upon your back for a time?"

"It is no simple thing that you ask," the stag said, his voice deep and sonorous, like the tolling of a bell. "Such things carry a price."

"A price that will be paid. I bring you the king's word upon it."

"Let me think upon it," the stag said.

A light breeze bent the meadow grasses, and the sunlight inched down the stones as the White Stag pondered. Puck sat patiently, bobbing a little upon the air and amusing himself by braiding and unbraiding the yarrow stalks in his hair. It was no great concern of his if the stag answered yes or no, although the great beast's agreement would certainly enliven things in the Realm, and beyond. If pressed, Puck would say that he was always in favor of a bit of bedlam.

Finally, as a sunbeam touched the ivory tips of the stag's antlers, the beast replied.

"I shall do this thing," he said.

At his words, a ripple spread out from the standing stones and shivered through the Realm. The bargain was struck. Puck grinned with anticipation.

"As it please you, come to the Bright Court and the king will set you on the path. Farewell, gentle hart."

"Be merry, wild sprite."

With a great bound, Puck leaped over the tallest stone and landed gracefully upon his riding owl. They swooped away over the brightening meadows, leaving the stag alone in the center of the stone circle, white as sorrow, pale as a winter moon.

CHAPTER 7

JUNE 23

Birdsong and waterfall woke Marny, along with a headache buzzing behind her eyes and the hazy tatters of a dream nagging at her. She shut off her alarm, which helped dial back the noise in her head, and lay there, staring at the ceiling a moment. It was important to pay attention to her dreams, Jennet had said. The problem was, all she remembered was a sense of urgency, the sound of bells, and some guy's face.

She squinted, trying to recall his features. Gray eyes, dark blond hair, and nice cheekbones. Too bad he didn't have an address flashing over his head. Had the dream been a warning, or just the usual random stuff that happened when a person was asleep?

Kicking off her covers, she got up and grimly pulled on the same clothes she'd worn the day before. They were still a little damp from her washing them out the night before, and she grimaced at the feel of the blouse against her skin. It would dry as she wore it, but not a fun way to start her morning. Her duffel had better arrive, and soon.

As for the dream, she'd keep an eye out for a gray-eyed blond guy, but that was about all she could do.

She stepped out of her room and met Anjah coming out of the bathroom in a cloud of perfume-scented steam. The other girl had a towel wrapped around her, and didn't seem self-conscious at all.

"Well." Anjah looked her up and down. "Not very creative in your wardrobe choices, are you?"

Marny tamped down her surge of annoyance. Anjah was shallow and conceited, and there was no point in letting that attitude spoil her own day.

"Maybe my luggage will show up today," Marny said. "Until then, it's rather petty of you to make fun of my nonexistent clothing options."

Anjah's cheeks colored. She didn't say anything, just gave a sharp sniff and stalked into her room, closing the door loudly behind her. Good. Hopefully she was embarrassed by her total lack of compassion—at least temporarily.

There was no sign of Wil, and Marny was glad. Stuck with an oaf and a princess for roomies. Welcome to the real world.

And what did they think of her?

She shrugged. It didn't matter, and it was only for two months. Grabbing her tablet, she headed for the dining room. Just because she lived with Wil and Anjah didn't mean she had any obligation to stick around and eat breakfast with them.

Halfway down the hall, she stopped. She'd gotten blisters yesterday, and her heels were already screaming at her in their new shoes. With a sigh, she turned back toward the apartment to put on her Converse. Limping through the rest of her day would be worse than getting a few funny looks because she was wearing canvas high-tops. Besides, she didn't think Intertech wanted their carpets stained with a trail of her blood.

Luckily, Anjah hadn't emerged from her room again to make more catty remarks about Marny's outfit. She shoved her pretty-but-painful shoes into her closet, laced on her high-tops, then hurried out again.

When she got to the dining room she paused by the door, scanning the tables. She didn't see anybody who matched the face in her dream.

"Marny—over here!" It was Brenna, waving from the side of the room.

Marny nodded and gestured to the cafeteria-style line, indicating she'd get her food and then join the liaison.

The breakfast offerings looked pretty decent. She chose a thick slice of banana bread, for a moment mourning her lost treat from home. Scrambled eggs, yogurt, and fruit rounded off the meal, plus a too-small mug of Earl Grey tea. What was it with these people and their fetish for tiny cups?

"Morning," she said, sliding her tray onto the table.

The Intertech dining hall was weirdly like being in the high school cafeteria—and yet worlds away. Instead of yellow linoleum, the floor was covered in a blue-patterned carpet. No long, institutional tables with attached benches, but clusters of round tables with comfortable chairs pulled up. The lighting was softer, too, not the glare of industrial-grade lights overhead, but warmer fixtures, with a few lamps scattered around the room. It even smelled better—like bacon and coffee instead of overcooked tomato sauce.

She sat down in a chair that was big enough—barely—to accommodate her large frame.

"Hey there." Brenna smiled at her. "Marny, meet my friend Quizley."

She pointed her fork at the guy seated to her right. His hair was brownish blond, his face lean, but his eyes were dark brown, not gray. Plus, he was about a decade too old; the face in Marny's dream had been somebody only a little older than herself. She nodded hello.

"Enchanté," Quizley said. "I understand you are the newest debutante to grace our halls?"

"Marny's with the Social Interfaces Design team," Brenna said. "Quiz here is a programmer."

"Yes." He drew the word out with a sigh. "I take everyone's foolish ideas and transform them to a more perfect form."

Whatever that meant. Marny raised one eyebrow. She couldn't decide if Brenna's friend was French or just eccentric. Maybe both.

"Nice to meet you," she said.

"Mm, indeed." The programmer turned his attention back to his omelet.

Brenna gave her a sympathetic look. "Quiz lives in his own little world. Don't take it personally."

"And a wonderful world it is, too," the programmer said, not bothering to look up from his meal.

"So, how're you settling in?" Brenna asked, pushing her empty plate to the side.

"Okay," Marny said. "My bag hasn't showed up yet."

"That's tweaked." Brenna frowned. "Did you check with the front desk?"

Marny finished chewing her bite of eggs. "Not this morning, no. I'll ask them after breakfast."

"Well, it's bound to turn up soon." The liaison picked up her coffee, then stopped, eyes going to the dining room entrance. "Uh oh. Somebody's in trouble."

Marny followed her gaze to where a muscular guy dressed in a black suit sauntered around the tables. Conversations hushed as he approached, then started up again once he'd passed by. All the man needed was a pair of mirrored sunglasses to complete the clichéd bodyguard look.

"Meh." Quiz glanced up. "Our esteemed leader has loosed one of his dogs to bring in a malefactor, I see."

"That's Mr. von Coburg's guard?" Marny watched the man as he got closer.

"They prefer to be called attachés," Brenna said. "Hey, Quiz, did you go rogue again? Because Bruno there seems to be heading right for us."

"Certainly not." Quiz sent her a haughty look. "Perhaps you are the one to incur the wrath of the CEO."

They got quiet then, as the man drew up to their table and stopped. Nearby diners craned their necks, and Marny swallowed. The air was suddenly heavy.

"Miss Fanalua?" the guard asked.

Brenna sucked in her breath, and Quiz slowly turned to regard Marny, brows raised high across his forehead.

"Um, yeah," Marny said. "That's me."

Her breakfast congealed in her stomach. Was the dress code

so severe at Intertech that she was being disciplined just for wearing her Converse?

"Dettwiler von Coburg would like you to attend him in his office."

Marny pushed her plate away and stood. She had the feeling it wouldn't be a good idea to ask if she could finish her meal—and besides, her appetite was totally gone.

"Good luck," Brenna murmured. "Chin up."

The guard gave Marny a curt nod. "Follow me."

Aware of the intense stares on all sides, she trailed the man, trying to look self-confident and serene. Inside, though, she felt like a little kid being called into the principal's office.

Or being sent to prison without trial.

CHAPTER 8

The guard, who didn't bother introducing himself, led Marny out of the dining room. Instead of turning right, toward the elevators, he went left.

"So," Marny said, "have you been working for Intertech a while?"

He grunted, and waved his card in front of a plain-looking door. For a second, she wondered if he was about to lock her into a janitor's closet in punishment for wearing non-regulation footwear. Maybe she should have gone for the bloody feet, after all.

The door led to an anteroom holding a single elevator. At their approach, the shiny gold doors slid open to reveal the gleaming wooden floors and richly paneled walls of what could only be von Coburg's private ride. The guard gestured her to enter, then followed her into the elevator.

There were no buttons inside. Completely voice activated, and no doubt coded to respond to only a few people.

"Top," the guard said.

Marny couldn't decide if the sinking sensation in her gut was due to the express elevator whooshing upward, or the doom that awaited her once she arrived. Would they actually kick out an intern for wearing the wrong shoes? She didn't think so—and, in fact, the other employees at breakfast had been wearing a wide array of footwear.

So maybe it wasn't her Converse getting her in trouble, after all.

Which left the even bigger question of why she was being summoned into the CEO's presence.

With a harmonious ding, the doors slid open. The guard—she might as well think of him as Bruno—strode out.

"This way," he said.

There was only one way to go, though. Straight down the wide hallway leading toward a large set of double doors.

Marny's feet sank into the carpet. It was at least an inch thicker than the standard-issue down below. The ceilings were higher, too. Perks of top-floor living, she supposed. Even the air smelled refined.

The big doors swung open as she and Bruno approached, revealing a large office. Another black-suited security dude stood just inside the threshold, and he and Bruno exchanged nods as she stepped into the room.

The far wall was one huge window looking out over the city, and Marny blinked at the view. She'd thought her own slice of Newpoint was prime, but this was amazing. Light flooded into the office and the city below gleamed and sparkled like a treasure hoard.

On the right side of the room, behind a vast expanse of gleaming ebony desk, sat Dettwiler von Coburg.

Bruno stopped and inclined his head. "Mr. von Coburg, here is Miss Fanalua, as requested."

"Very good." The CEO steepled his hands together and regarded her from his cold blue eyes.

Marny straightened her shoulders, resisting the urge to bow. He was the boss, sure, but he wasn't royalty or anything. She didn't think.

"Pull up a chair for Miss Fanalua," Mr. von Coburg said.

Bruno leaped into action, snagging a big, comfy-looking armchair from the other side of the room and placing it directly opposite the CEO. Slowly, Marny sat down. The desk stretched between her and Mr. von Coburg like an expanse of black ice.

Silently, the guard placed a glass of water at her right hand. Condensation beaded on the sides. She felt too cold to take a sip.

"Miss Fanalua." Mr. von Coburg leaned forward slightly. "No doubt you are wondering why you're here."

She cleared her throat. "The thought had crossed my mind. I didn't suppose you were in the habit of personally welcoming all the interns."

She surreptitiously tucked her feet under the chair. This still might be about her shoes, though now she really didn't think so.

"Not generally, no." He gave her a wintry smile. "But in reading over your file yesterday, I discovered you are from Crestview."

A stab of panic went through her. Was von Coburg aware of the faerie activity there? Did he know about Feyland?

"I am," she said.

"No doubt you're aware that VirtuMax recently made your small city its headquarters." He paused, waiting for her nod of confirmation, then continued. "I find myself curious whether you have connections at VirtuMax. Friends, family."

His pale eyebrows rose ever so slightly. He was fishing for information, but what?

"If this is about the nondisclosure agreement we had to sign for the internship, no worries," Marny said. "I know better than to leak anything I learn here to VirtuMax."

"So, you *are* acquainted with people high up in the company." He leaned forward. "The CEO's son, perhaps?"

A little shiver went through her. If he knew enough to ask that question, he'd done some digging. But still, he couldn't know about Feyland, right? She picked up her glass of water and took a sip, stalling for time, then wiped her damp palm on her pants.

"We go to the same school," she said. "But I wouldn't call us friends."

Not by any stretch, although they weren't enemies any longer, either. It was true Royal Lassiter had changed—heartbreak could do that to a person—but she still couldn't quite forgive him for his rotten manipulation of her.

"Hmm." Mr. Von Coburg tapped the smooth surface of his desk, and a display lit up.

She couldn't read it from where she was sitting, but she'd bet it had to do with her friends. His next words confirmed it.

"I see you are in close contact with a Miss Jennet Carter, whose father happens to be well placed within the company. And another of your companions, Mr. Tam Linn, has an internship with VirtuMax. In addition, your uncle seems to have had some experience beta testing for their game department."

A flare of anger heated the cold silence wrapping around her. Sure, this was the CEO of a major multinational corporation, but he had no business prying into her private life.

"Leave my family out of it," she said. Not that Uncle Zeg couldn't take care of himself, but still. "So I know people connected with VirtuMax. What are you getting at?"

"Pleasingly blunt." He stabbed at the display, and it faded. "You do understand that VirtuMax is one of our competitors."

"Is Intertech going into simulated gaming?"

The CEO leaned back, his stern expression revealing nothing. "I was hoping you might provide a little insight for me about the company."

Seriously?

"I don't have any secrets to spill—and even if I did, I wouldn't tell them to you."

The slow smolder of temper warmed her chest. The nerve of the man! Trying to pump her for inside intel about VirtuMax. He might be the CEO, but she refused to be bullied.

He regarded her, his eyes cold, and she tried not to squirm under his gaze. Dettwiler von Coburg made her feel like she was six years old and in deep trouble. It took all her courage to stand up to him, but she wouldn't let him intimidate her. Even if her internship was on the line.

"No need to take offense, young lady. I merely invited you up here for some friendly conversation."

Oh, yeah. If your idea of friendly included icy stares and demands for information.

"Well, I think our conversation is over." She said the words strongly, but couldn't help a twinge of fear. He was the CEO of a huge, powerful company, after all, and she was just a lowly intern at said company. But holding on to that internship wasn't worth being bullied.

"A pity," he said. "You could have a bright future here at Intertech, if you were so inclined. It would be unfortunate if anything marred your time with us."

Marny swallowed. That sounded like a threat, and she suddenly felt very alone. *When cornered, fight back,* her Uncle Zeg always said. *Don't be a victim.*

"Even if I knew something, I don't do corporate espionage, Mr. von Coburg. For anyone. So if that's all you called me in here for, we're done." She pushed out of the armchair and stood, glancing around for Bruno.

The guard waited impassively at the door, staring into space like he'd heard nothing of the conversation. Would he allow her to march out of the room? Even if he did, she wasn't cleared to use the executive elevator, and would have to wait for someone to come activate it for her.

The whole situation was tweaked.

Mr. von Coburg let her stand there awkwardly for a moment, then nodded to his guard. "Bruno, see Miss Fanalua out."

"Very good, sir." Bruno motioned her toward the door.

She looked at the CEO. His face was impassive, but there was a pissed-off look in his eyes. Seeing it made her glad and afraid at the same time.

"Goodbye, Mr. von Coburg," she said.

"It's been a pleasure." His tone implied the exact opposite.

Though Marny disliked turning her back on the CEO, she

did it anyway, suppressing a shiver as she strode away. Just as she reached the door, he spoke again.

"One more thing, Miss Fanalua. You might want to consider more appropriate footwear in the future."

Right. He couldn't resist that last jab, could he? She turned and gave him a sharp nod, then pivoted and followed Bruno out of the plush office. When the doors slid closed behind her, she released her held breath. That had been crazy.

And disturbing.

On one hand, she understood that the leaders of these huge tech companies were sharks. Look at Roy's mother, after all. CEO of VirtuMax and completely focused on that—to the utter detriment of her family. In that world, Marny supposed it was understandable to try and use every advantage. But to threaten a new intern if they didn't provide information about a rival company? That wasn't right.

Was there somebody she could report him to—some watchdog entity that kept big corporations in line? She'd have to find out.

Bruno silently escorted her into the elevator, which took them down to the twenty-eighth floor where the Social Interfaces Design team worked. The elevator door opened into a private foyer, but just past that was a hallway bustling with employees headed to their cubicles.

Time for work. Great.

Marny stepped out of the elevator without a backward glance. The guard wasn't her ally, and she doubted he'd speak a word against his boss, even if he'd witnessed the whole slimy interaction.

The second the elevator departed, taking Bruno with it, she

leaned against the wall and closed her eyes to regain her equilibrium. Her chest was tight with anger and something that felt suspiciously like tears. Dammit. Facing off against Dettwiler von Coburg had been one of the scariest things she'd ever done. But Uncle Zeg would have been proud of her for not buckling.

She wished more than anything that she could walk in the door of his simcafé, have him hand her one of his monster cookies, and tell him all about it. But she was on her own.

At least she knew her family loved and supported her, no matter how far away she might be. That knowledge would have to be enough to carry her through.

She pulled in a couple steadying breaths and let the tension flow out of her. Thankfully the little foyer remained empty, though conversation and the smell of coffee filtered into the quiet space.

Maybe she could talk to Brenna about what had happened. And for sure she'd write down the entire interview. Documentation was important, even if nobody ever saw it.

As was showing up to work on time.

With a last, rueful glance at her shoes, Marny pushed away from the wall and headed into the busy hallway. For now, she'd concentrate on her projects with the team—and hope that Mr. von Coburg's threats had been empty.

CHAPTER 9

JUNE 24

The smell of crushed oranges and coffee filled the warehouse, along with the high laughter of Emmie and her best friend, Sula. All afternoon they'd been running the juicer and espresso machine, coming up with concoctions and making Nyx taste them. Some of the drinks they'd invented had been surprisingly tasty. And some had been downright hideous.

Nyx counted his paces across the wide concrete floor, marking off the space for his "installation." He'd measured it twice already, but it never hurt to be extra sure. The orientation of the forest had to be just right, so people entering the club could see the expanse of magical trees but wouldn't be immediately engulfed in them.

"Hey!" his sister called to him, brandishing a glass of green liquid. "Come try the Goblin Blood."

Emmie had gone a little crazy with the theme—but maybe that kind of energy was exactly what he needed. And who wouldn't want to drink something called Pixie Dust (blackberry soda with cranberry sparkles), or exhale Ogre Breath (garlic, ginger, and carrot juice).

When he'd gone to get the permits, the guy at the city office had shaken his head.

"An all-ages club, huh? Tough to turn a profit on those. Last one folded after two months."

"Why's that?" Nyx had asked.

"Profit's in the alcohol, which you can't serve. Or the live music, but the licensing fees for cover bands will kill you." The man had given him a hard stare. "Unless this is a front for something illegal. Snow-vaping? Mutant dog fights?"

Nyx had let his distaste show in his eyes. "No. Just a place for people to come hang out with their friends, game some, dance. Feel like they're someplace else for a little while."

He hoped.

The man had grunted and let him finish filling out the paperwork on Club Mysteria without further trouble.

And in one more day, Nyx would know whether his venture would succeed, or be a complete failure.

The thought of the grand opening scared him more than anything. He'd never put so much on the line before. Not just the money, though that was substantial, but the dream, the vision. If the club was a flop, it would be very hard for him not to take it personally.

Luckily, Emmie was there, distracting him with her chatter and wild concoctions.

He joined her and Sula in brainstorming more names and

drinks, then directed their coffee-fueled energy to draping green gauze and hanging fairy lights. Though the enchanted forest was the main attraction, he wanted a sense of magic to extend to the entry, juice bar, and dance floor, which were all outside the boundary of the game.

Not really a game, his mind said. He shook off the shiver between his shoulder blades. Whatever it was, the various places he'd been able to recreate outside of Feyland weren't real. They only lasted a day or two, and popped like soap bubbles if the anchors were removed or destroyed. Besides, the forest wasn't endless, as he'd discovered.

The third time he created the enchanted woods he'd decided to test its boundaries. He'd called Emmie into his room and told her he was heading into the trees.

"What?" She'd given him a wide-eyed look. "What if you get lost in there? What if something eats you?"

"Then you can have my room." He'd punched her lightly on the shoulder. "I'm pretty sure it's going to be okay. But if I'm not back in, say, four hours, call Durham."

"Wake him up in the middle of the night so he can go in and get eaten, too? I don't think that's a great plan."

"For someone who was laughing at my 'fake' installation last week, you're sure concerned."

Emmie wrinkled her nose at him. "You might be an annoying big brother, but you're *my* annoyance. Whatever's going on in your room with that magical forest is creepy."

"Which is exactly why I have to go check it out. I told you, I'm in control of it." More or less.

"Three hours." She crossed her arms. "And then I'm telling Mom and Dad, too."

"Fine." He picked up the big knife he'd brought up from the kitchen, then turned and faced the shimmering forest.

"Do you think that knife will be enough?" Emmie asked, hovering at his shoulder.

"It's not like we have any guns in the house. Besides, it's more for cutting my way out of a trap or something. I *am* a third-degree black belt, don't forget."

"Like that's going to help when you meet a gigantic ogre who wants a human snack."

"Then I'll cut him." He waggled the knife at her.

"Ohh, so scary." Despite her tone, he could hear that she was frightened at the thought of him going in.

"Don't worry, Em." He tousled her bleached hair. "See you soon."

She batted his hand away. "I better."

He strode into the forest. The mossy ground cushioned his steps, and the underbrush smelled like pungent herbs as he brushed past. He turned and waved at Emmie, still visible through the pale-barked tree trunks. It was weird, seeing his messy bed and bright posters at the edge of the woods.

She waved back and he nodded at her, then kept going. A few more steps in, and he couldn't see his bedroom anymore. Apprehension tightened his breath. What if he really *did* get lost?

He should have brought something to mark his way: some bright string to tie on the bushes, or chalk to mark the trees. A trail of breadcrumbs. Something. Nyx felt in his pockets, but they were empty, and he didn't think pocket lint was going to do him much good.

With a mental shrug, he stripped off his faded red T-shirt.

Using the knife, he cut through the hem and tore a few long strips from the bottom of the shirt, then ripped them into smaller pieces. He put his shirt back on, now a midriff-baring T. He doubted that any forest creatures were going to start commenting on his abs.

As he moved further into the forest, he tied strips of his T-shirt to the branches every few paces. It wasn't a perfect system—he'd seen the vids where evil creatures followed the hero, undoing the markers or pointing them to lead back toward danger—but he'd have to take his chances.

The woods didn't seem that menacing, at any rate.

Liquid birdsong trilled from overhead, and a soft breeze stirred the silvery leaves. Shafts of sunlight illuminated the forest. It was more peaceful than scary.

Movement at the corner of his eye made him whirl, dropping into a defensive stance, but it was only a big orange butterfly flickering through the sunbeams. Nyx drew in a deep breath and kept going. There weren't any identifying landmarks, just trees and purple-flowered shrubs and a pale blue sky overhead with no clouds.

A spot of color ahead caught his eye, something red wrapped around a branch. It looked suspiciously familiar. Shaking his head, Nyx headed for it, weaving between the trees.

Sure enough, it was a strip of his shirt. Somehow he'd gone in a circle, which seemed kind of impossible. Admittedly, he'd grown up in the suburbs of Newpoint and wasn't a woodsman by any stretch. But he had a decent sense of direction and could have sworn he'd been headed in a straight line since he'd stepped into the forest.

"Fine," he said. "Are we playing games?"

The only answer was the rustle of silver leaves in the wind.

Nyx turned his back on the scrap of fabric and headed away, at a right angle from the direction he'd approached. A few steps later, he groaned. Ahead, a strip of his T-shirt dangled from another branch.

"Very funny." He had the feeling no one was listening.

The whole thing reminded him of an old kids' book his mom used to read out loud at bedtime. One of the stories had the animal characters going around and around a bush, following tracks in the snow and thinking they were tracking some kind of ferocious beast. But all along, it was their own footsteps. He suspected he was doing the same thing.

Intuition said his room lay behind him and somewhat to his right. Since he clearly was making no headway in the enchanted forest, maybe it was time to return to the normal world.

If he could.

Leaving the strips of shirt tied to the trees, he headed in the direction he hoped was out. In a surprisingly short time, he glimpsed the blue walls and gaming posters of his bedroom. Relief bubbled through him.

When he stepped onto his messy carpet, Emmie jumped up from his bed and gave him a hug. "You made it out!"

He squeezed her shoulders, then turned to look back into the forest.

"I ended up going around in circles. I think."

"What happened to your shirt?" She eyed the ripped hem.

"I needed the cloth to mark my direction."

He bent and snagged another shirt from the floor, a plain blue T with a hole in the side.

"Hold this," he said, handing it to her. "Stretch it out so I can cut off the bottom."

"I really don't think this is a good look for you," she said. "Are you planning to mutilate all your clothing?"

"I want you to go in with me." He set down the knife, then took the now-ruined shirt from her and started tearing it into strips.

"Are you sure?" She cast a wary glance into the woods.

"I have a theory, and if I'm right we'll be perfectly safe. Go into the forest and head left, tying these around the branches every few feet." He handed her the pieces of blue cloth. "I'll go to the right."

"You honestly think we'll meet in the middle? That doesn't make sense."

"Neither does having an enchanted forest in my bedroom, Em. The normal rules don't apply here, obviously."

"You don't have to be all superior about it." She made a face at him, but took the strips of T-shirt.

"If you get in trouble, yell," he said.

"Likewise. Ready?"

He nodded, and together they marched into the silver-shadowed woods. After a few steps he turned right, and Emmie headed the opposite direction. The peace of the forest settled over him, the dappled sun warm on his shoulders, the green scent of growing things rich in his nose.

"Can you hear me?" he called.

"Yep." Emmie didn't sound very far away.

"Okay, keep going."

Another minute or so, and Nyx glimpsed a scrap of red cloth ahead. He couldn't help smiling at the sight. Not only did it prove his suspicions correct, it showed he could bring things into the woods and they'd stay there. At least for a little while.

"Marco," he yelled.

"Polo," came the reply. His sister sounded even closer than before.

Up ahead something was moving, white and blue flashes between the pale tree trunks. He leaned forward, balancing on the balls of his feet, but wasn't too worried.

After a moment, he was sure. It was Emmie, moving through the trees.

She paused to tie a strip of cloth onto a nearby branch and he silently circled around, keeping a clump of bushes between them. When she turned to go, he leaped out.

"Boo!" he cried.

"Eee!" Emmie jumped back, her hand going to her chest. Then she glared at him. "Damn, Nyx. Give a girl a heart attack, why don't you?"

"Just checking your reflexes."

"You suck." She glanced around. "Were you following me this whole time?"

"No," he said. "Even though this looks like a forest, it seems to be just a sphere, and we're inside it. If that makes sense."

"Weird." She shook her head. "So what happens if we try to walk deeper in?"

"We go nowhere, I think."

"Then I'll see you in nowhere." She pointed at him. "And if you jump out at me again, I swear I'll put snails in your bed. Every night."

"Lucky me. Which direction do you want to go?"

She tilted her head, studying the slanting light falling through the trees, then nodded to her right. "That way."

"I'll stay here, then. Just for fun."

Nyx kept an eye on her as she went, the white of her shirt flickering between the tree trunks. It seemed like she was heading further into the forest. After a minute, he lost sight of her.

"Aha," she called. "I found a red cloth."

"Do you think you can find your way back out?"

"Pretty sure."

"I'll wait here, just in case. Yell when you're back in my room."

He didn't glimpse her again, but a short time later she called out.

"Made it!"

"Be right there." Nyx cast a last glance around the forest.

It was a weird, tricky place, but it was finite. He'd do a few more tests to make sure, but it was a relief to know that nobody could get lost and disappear forever into whatever magical world he'd conjured up.

During the following weeks he'd tried his hardest to lose his way in the forest, and even attempted it with the meadow, spinning himself around in the high grasses until he was dizzy. Every time he ended up walking around in circles a bunch, then wandering back into his room.

In fact, since that second time he'd conjured up the woods, he hadn't seen the golden mouse creature again. Maybe it had gotten smart and decided it didn't like being trapped inside a magical loop.

After thinking about it, Nyx had decided the landscapes were reflections—seemingly real, but only mirror images of the places inside the game of Feyland. Except that the trees felt solid enough to lean up against, and the moss was soft underfoot.

So, not reflections, but more like bubble worlds—little self-contained simulations.

How is it even possible? The question pricked at his mind.

He spent hours searching the 'net, looking for hints that he wasn't the only one who'd discovered this strange connection with Feyland. Nothing. Another several days was wasted researching VirtuMax, but they didn't seem to be planning any game theme parks, and there were no pictures or vids of the kinds of bubble worlds he'd experienced.

So, what to do? Was there something different about his particular version of Feyland? Or was there something tweaked about *him* that enabled him to carry things out of the game into the real world?

He shivered at the idea. None of it made sense.

Part of him thought he should tell his parents, maybe even get in contact with someone at VirtuMax, but then what? They'd confiscate his sim system for sure, and he might end up being the subject of weird experiments and testing. No thanks.

Mom and Dad would make him stop, and no doubt take away the game. Although, since he'd just turned eighteen, they couldn't legally control his actions. They could kick him out, though, and he didn't even want to start going down that road.

Silence seemed the best course. He'd discovered this ability, whatever it was, and he should be the one who decided how to use it.

The club idea had come to him one morning as he woke up and watched the enchanted forest fade away. Why *not* share it with other people? It was amazingly cool, harmless, and like nothing anyone had ever seen.

If he set things up right, people would think it was just an incredible simulation, the way Emmie had at first. Nobody could possibly guess the truth, and anyway, people wanted to believe things that didn't shake their worldview too much.

The more he thought about it, the more the idea felt right. He'd been needing something to do, and with Durham heading off to college in the fall, their Flail stream days were coming to an end. Plus, Nyx wasn't blind to the financial opportunities. He'd run with the concept until it was played out, or he lost the ability to bring items out of Feyland to create the bubble worlds.

So here he was, nervously pacing the warehouse floor two nights before the grand opening, and hoping he hadn't screwed up.

"I think we're done for the night," Emmie said, giving the juice bar counter a final swipe with a clean bar towel.

"Tomorrow afternoon we can write the menu up on the chalkboard," her friend Sula said. "This is going to be prime!"

"We hope," Emmie said. "Let's head—and get some good rest tonight."

She sounded so mature. Nyx gave her shoulders a squeeze. "Want me to come wait at the bus stop with you?"

"Nah." She shook her head. "It's still early enough that the skanks aren't out, and you're not the only one with the karate moves."

“Big talk for a blue belt.” He sank into horse stance and lifted his hands. “Bring it.”

“I’m not sparring with you.” She tossed her teal-dipped blonde hair back, then rolled her eyes at Sula. “Ready?”

“Message me when you get home,” Nyx said.

He wasn’t that worried—Emmie and Sula had taken the bus all over Newpoint for years, but it was a little later than he’d like. And his parents had given him the stern lecture about looking after his little sister whenever she was down at the club.

“Will do. Good night, bro.” She gave him a jaunty wave as she and Sula left.

He went to the door and stood outside, watching until the girls settled at the bus stop two blocks away. Lights were on in the tall skyscrapers, squares of yellow extending up into the twilight sky. He couldn’t see any stars.

The bus roared past, Sula and Emmie got on, and Nyx went inside and locked the warehouse door behind him. He made sure everything was secure, then went to fire up one of the sim systems in his spare room. Time to get to work gathering leaves. The enchanted forest wasn’t going to summon itself, and the clock was ticking down to the grand opening of Club Mysteria.

CHAPTER 10

JUNE 26

For the next couple days, Marny tried not to constantly look over her shoulder for Mr. von Coburg's guards. None of her supervisors said anything or treated her any differently, which suggested that her conversation with the CEO was just between the two of them. So far.

At least she finally had her duffel, but she wasn't sure she'd be able to forgive Anjah for how that had happened.

The morning of her third day of work, her luggage *still* hadn't shown up. She'd stared at her one outfit, then shook her head. Two days of wearing sweaty office clothing she could deal with, but she couldn't stand the thought of putting the blouse and slacks back on yet again. Even if it meant another scary interview with Mr. von Coburg.

If Intertech wanted to kick her out for breaking the dress

code, fine. Though her stomach knotted at the idea of going back to Crestview in disgrace.

But if the company booted her, who said she had to go home right away? Newpoint was a big city and she could probably find temporary work. She would get Brenna to help her, if it came to that. Failing her internship didn't mean she was failing her life, right? Still, the thought made her feel sick inside.

She pulled on the jeans and T-shirt she'd arrived in, but could only find one sock. Frustration grated through her, but she made herself slow down and check all the usual places—under the bed, balled up under her jacket. Nothing.

Marny padded barefoot to the front closet. Maybe she'd left a sock inside her Converse. She poked through the closet and finally discovered her sock lying under one of Wil's enormous, grubby athletic shoes. Thank goodness.

As she shut the door, a flash of familiar green caught her eye. Senses prickling, she leaned in and peered into the corner of the closet. Her duffel bag lay there, crammed behind a bunch of Anjah's coats.

What the actual hell? Nostrils flaring, she hauled her bag out. It was her duffel, no question. She unzipped it and gave a quick check of the contents, but everything seemed to be there.

How long had it been in the apartment, and who had stuck it in the closet and not bothered mentioning it to her? There were only two possibilities, and their names were Wil and Anjah.

"Morning," Wil said, ambling into the kitchen to start the coffee brewing.

Anger sizzling just under her skin, Marny grabbed her duffel and stalked over.

"Do you know anything about this?" she asked, hefting the green bag.

He blinked at it a second with sleepy eyes. "Hey—your luggage came? Congrats."

"Apparently it's been here a while—I just found my bag in the front closet. Any idea how it happened to get there?"

"No, that's weird. But at least you got it back, right?"

She watched him closely, but he didn't seem to be lying. Wil might be thoughtless and bumbling, but he wasn't malicious. Anjah, on the other hand...

"Right," Marny said.

She went to the bathroom door and opened it without knocking. The steamy air smelled like flowers and cream.

"Hey! Is respecting my privacy too much to ask?" Anjah turned from putting on her makeup and scowled.

She had a pink towel turban-wrapped on her head, and wore a fluffy white bathrobe, so it wasn't like Marny had walked in on her at an awkward moment. Though it would serve Anjah right if she had.

"Right now," Marny said, "I'm not sure you deserve any respect. I just discovered my duffel crammed into the hall closet."

Guilt flickered over Anjah's expression, and then she lifted one shoulder in an elaborate shrug. "I stowed it there while you waited for the rest of your bags to come, and must have forgotten to tell you."

Forgotten, her ass.

"There aren't any more bags," Marny said.

Anjah's perfect mouth opened a little in surprise. "That's all the luggage you have?"

"Unlike some people, I don't require an enormous wardrobe and tons of makeup to feel good about myself." It was mean of her, but Marny's temper was turned up way past simmer.

Anjah narrowed her eyes. "At least I have something worth showing off."

"It's too bad you're not proud of what's inside. I thought you were smarter than that. Shallowness is such an unattractive quality."

Marny didn't wait for Anjah to reply, but closed the door loudly, just short of a slam. She blew a breath out her nostrils, then went to change into something that wouldn't raise Intertech's eyebrows or make her a target for the CEO.

For the rest of the week, Anjah had pointedly ignored her, which was fine with Marny. Wil either didn't notice, or wisely didn't comment. They went to the dining room at different times, and Marny was glad she didn't have to sit with her roommates. Intertech was filled with interesting people, and she ended up hearing some fascinating conversations—stuff she probably wouldn't have otherwise been exposed to about future trends in media consumption and what was going on with Intertech's projects.

On Friday after work, Anjah was sitting in the living room when Marny came in.

"There you are," she said, flashing her tablet at Marny. "Have you seen this?"

Marny slipped her shoes off, then cautiously padded over to the couch. She drew the line at sitting next to Anjah, though.

As far as she was concerned, the girl still owed her a serious apology.

"What?" she asked, keeping her voice neutral.

"This ad for the new all-ages club opening tonight. It looks amazing."

Anjah held up her tablet so Marny could read the screen.

"*Club Mysteria, where enchanted wonders await.*" Marny shook her head. "I'm not really into the party scene."

Anjah gave her a little pout. "We should go together, to celebrate your first weekend in the city. Girls' night out."

"I don't think so." Marny wanted to make a cup of tea, watch some vids, and go to bed early. It had been a severe week.

"Please," Anjah said, sounding like she meant it. "My treat."

Marny studied her a moment. It was a peace offering, and the closest thing she'd get to Anjah saying she was sorry. Was she willing to accept?

"Is this a setup or prank of some kind?"

Anjah flushed. "I know you think I hate you—but this is real. I swear."

Marny glanced at the screen again, noting the little winged creatures dancing around Club Mysteria's logo. Faeries.

"Okay," she said. "But I don't want to stay out too late."

"Great." Anjah smiled, and it looked genuine. "We should leave around eight—I'll arrange for a cab."

"How far is it?" Maybe agreeing to go hadn't been such a good idea.

"Oh, the address is just south of downtown." Anjah waved her hand. "But I couldn't walk that far in my silver sandals."

Anjah's idea of sandals likely involved three-inch heels.

"I'm not getting dressed up," Marny warned.

"That's all right. I'll glitter enough for both of us." Anjah rose. "I better start getting ready. See you downstairs in the lobby at eight."

Marny stood in the living room, staring out at the sunlit rooftops and trying not to feel nervous. What had she just gotten herself into?

CHAPTER 11

Despite her assertion she wasn't planning to get all fancy, that evening Marny donned one of her nicer outfits. If black jeans and a top with a little lace around the edges counted as nice. But they were going to a club, it would be dark inside, and who really cared what she wore? Anjah would draw everybody's gaze in whatever outrageous dress she had on, anyway.

Marny laced up her high tops, then grabbed her red coat, Intertech ID, and debit card. If she couldn't stand Club Mysteria, she'd just walk back to Intertech or grab a cab. Anjah could look after herself.

Downstairs, Anjah hovered inside the front doors—and she hadn't been kidding about the glitter. Her dress was made of green and blue sequins that caught the light with every movement.

Marny glanced down at her basic outfit, then gave a mental shrug. She had no desire to dazzle.

"Oh, you *did* come," Anjah said, clacking over to meet her. Even in her heels, she didn't come up to Marny's chin. "I'm so glad. Come on, the cab's waiting."

Her evident relief made Marny warm to her a touch more. At least Anjah was making an effort to be nice.

"You went for the mermaid look tonight?" Marny said as she slid into the back seat of the cab after Anjah.

"This club we're going to is supposed to be magical," Anjah said. "I had to dress the part."

Magical. The word made the hairs on the back of Marny's neck prickle.

"How do you know about this place?" she asked. "Club Mysteria, right?"

"There's been serious buzz about it on the social webs. Plus all those ads." Anjah inspected her silver-flecked turquoise nail polish. "A local Flail channel star is supposedly involved—Nyx Spenser."

Marny shrugged. "Haven't heard of him."

"I hadn't, either—but then, I'm not a big gamer. He looks cute in the vids, though. See?"

Anjah flipped open her tablet and scrolled through a few pics, pausing when she got to a shot of a guy with dark blond hair. He seemed familiar. Marny studied his face.

"Wait," she said. "Isn't that one of the Retro Game-a-Thon guys?" She'd watched their channel a bit, two summers ago, before things started getting strange in Crestview.

"I think that's the name of their stream," Anjah said. "Anyway, isn't he prime? Apparently he does martial arts, too. A multiple black belt or whatever. I wonder if he has a girlfriend."

"I thought you liked that guy at Intertech."

Anjah shrugged, and her entire dress shimmered. "He's moving a little too slow for my tastes. Oh look, we're here."

The cab pulled up in front of what seemed to be a warehouse. The high upper windows were lit from inside, showing flashes of flickering green and gold. A heavy bass beat throbbed through the air, supporting a swirling synth and wild-sounding fiddle. Above the battered metal door the words *Club Mysteria* were written in curling gold script. And there was a line to get in.

"Maybe there won't be room for us." Marny wouldn't mind if they were refused entry at the door.

Anjah paid their fare and motioned her to step out. "I'm certain they won't turn us away."

"You, maybe. Me, I'm not so sure I'm their type."

Marny got out of the cab and scanned the people standing in front of the building. Some wore elaborate costumes complete with wings, while others had on outfits that would fit right in at a royal ball. That said, there were a few normally dressed people, too. They were just in the minority.

"Follow me," Anjah said, striding up to the door like she was queen of the world.

She headed for the front of the line, cutting a couple guys wearing hologram dragon shirts. Marny gave them an apologetic glance, but they seemed more bemused than offended.

"Hi," Anjah said to the big, brown-haired man manning the door. "I'm Anjah Lee. I reserved ahead."

"One sec." The guy consulted his tablet, then nodded. "Ms. Lee and guest. Go on in."

"How did you do that?" Marny asked in a low voice as the

crowd shifted so she and Anjah could get to the door. "I didn't know clubs took reservations."

Anjah looked smug. "Everything's possible if you know what kind of leverage to apply. In this case, a few extra credits and sweet words did the trick. They usually do, you know."

Marny lifted one brow. She'd never had extra money lying around to use as bribes, and using sweet talk to get her way wasn't in her repertoire. Nor did she want it to be.

"And guest?" she asked her roommate.

"I wasn't sure you'd come." Anjah's veneer of confidence slipped a notch.

"Well..." Marny lost her thought as they stepped into Club Mysteria.

Past the twinkling lights strung from the ceiling, past the gauzy hangings and juice bar on one side, past the colors strobing over the dance floor, lay the Realm of Faerie.

The sight of it stole her breath, and she stopped dead.

"Hey there." Anjah nudged her arm. "Haven't you ever been in a club before, small-town girl?"

Marny had to swallow to get her voice working. "It's not that. Just a second of *déjà vu*."

She was lying, though. That gut-stabbing familiarity wasn't a momentary sensation.

"Ooh." Anjah glanced around, a smile lighting her face. "It's so pretty. And that forest! What an incredible installation. I knew this place was going to be amazing."

Installation. Right. Marny blinked a few times, but there was no denying that the pale-barked trees were directly out of the Realm.

What the hell was going on here?

Panic scrabbled at the back of her mind, but she pushed it down. The Feyguard wouldn't let the Dark Queen come striding out of those woods and into the mortal world. Things were under control. Right?

"Let's go order something to drink," Anjah said, misreading Marny's shock. "You'll get used to this place in a minute. I'm dying to explore that forest, though."

That was what Marny was afraid of—but she couldn't voice her fears to Anjah. Nobody else would understand, except Tam and Jennet. She had to get a message to them right away.

Anjah towed her up to the polished wooden juice bar, where a couple girls in crazy makeup manned the machines.

"What'll you have?" the shorter girl with teal-edged blonde hair asked. Her blue eyeliner extended into feathers at the corners of her eyes, and tiny lights blinked in her hair.

"I'll take a Pixie Dust," Anjah said, then turned to Marny with an expectant look.

"Sure." Marny forced herself to concentrate. "Sounds good. Hey, is there a restroom nearby?"

"Through that doorway, then take a right." The server pointed to an opening draped with more of the green gauze.

"Be right back," Marny said.

She skirted the dance floor filled with stomping, gyrating bodies, and ducked through the doorway. The pounding beat muffled down, and she took a deep breath.

In the privacy of the bathroom stall, she pulled out her messager. She needed to try and reach all of the Feyguard. Even Jennet's dad. Maybe someone had pirated Feyland's sim code, and that was what she was seeing out there, not the Realm of Faerie. It was a thin hope, but she clung to it.

Because if that was actually a forest connected to the world of the faeries, they were all in deep, deep trouble.

:Mayday,: she wrote. *:Possible breach into the Realm.:*

A few seconds later, Tam's reply popped up on her screen.

:What's going on?:

:This new club in Newpoint has an enchanted forest in the middle of it,: she replied. *:Might be Feyland hack? Stolen sim code?:*

:Maybe.: That was Jennet. *:Let me wake up a little more, and go see if Dad knows anything. It's super-early in the morning here.:*

Right, the India thing. So much for Jennet riding to the rescue. And last Marny had heard, Spark and Aran were in New Zealand, still on the big FullD VirtuMax tour. Suddenly, Marny felt very much alone. And inadequate.

Uncle Zeg responded next. *:Are you in danger?:*

:Not immediate.: Marny hoped. It didn't feel dangerous, though. Just threatening, like dark storm clouds massing on the horizon.

Dammit, she wanted them here. She wasn't one of the official Feyguard, protecting the border between the worlds. She was just Marny. Sure, she'd had a few brushes with the fey folk, but she wasn't cut out to be a hero. That was her friends' job.

:Investigate. Carefully,: Uncle Zeg wrote.

:Okay.: What else could she do? She was the one on the front lines, whether she was qualified or not. *:I'll report back soon.:*

:Don't get yourself in trouble,: Tam typed.

Yeah, like she wasn't already. Marny tucked her messager into her bag, then went and splashed water on her face.

"All right," she said to the round-cheeked girl in the mirror. "Let's take care of this."

Luckily, there wasn't anyone else in the bathroom to overhear her talking to herself. She stepped out, then hesitated at the doorway back into the club.

The hallway continued on the other side of the bathrooms, but was blocked with a heavy curtain. Darting a glance at the dance floor to make sure she was unobserved, Marny pushed the curtain aside and stepped into the back hall. If she poked around a bit, maybe she could get some clues about what, exactly, was going on with Club Mysteria.

The first door she came to was locked. So were the next two. The fourth stood ajar, revealing another bathroom.

She slipped in and, by the light filtering in from the hall, made a quick inspection. Unlike the club's public bathrooms, this one seemed to be in personal use. By a guy, if the bulky razor, spice-scented shaving cream, and lack of makeup were any indication. Not to mention the damp towel on the floor. She resisted the urge to pick it up.

The end of the hall opened into a kitchen that was clearly more than just a break room. The cupboards were stocked with food, and a few dirty bowls cluttered the sink. Marny opened the fridge.

"Looking for a snack?" The low, dangerous-sounding voice behind her made her whirl.

A tall, lean guy stood there, something predatory in his stance. His gray eyes and strong chin looked familiar... ah, yes. Nyx Spenser. Anjah had been right—he was good-looking. Or would be, if his eyes weren't narrowed and his mouth set with anger.

"Sorry." Marny let the fridge door close. "I'll just go now."

She strode toward him, but he didn't move. Surprising,

since most people got out of her way once she was in motion. Though he wasn't a bulky guy, she could see the outline of muscles under his black T-shirt.

Finally she halted, way too close to him for comfort. Their eyes met, almost exactly at the same level. His gray irises held flecks of dark green. His breath smelled like mint.

Despite the sudden hitch in her chest, she wasn't going to budge. No way was she letting Nyx Spenser intimidate her. Even if she had totally been prying into his private space.

The knowledge made her drop her gaze.

"Sorry isn't good enough," he said.

She was so close to him she could almost feel the words vibrating out of his chest.

"It's all you're going to get." She made to move past him, but he reached and took her wrist in a surprisingly strong grip.

"I don't want this to turn physical," he said. "But unless you explain what you were doing back here, I'm calling the cops and charging you with trespassing."

For a second, she considered letting him do just that. But she didn't want any black marks on her name—not to mention what Intertech would think of one of their interns being taken in by the police. She was on shaky ground with von Coburg as it was. No need to make things worse.

"All right." She stepped back, and Nyx let go of her wrist. "I was..."

The intensity of his stare didn't fade, and somehow she knew he wouldn't take any lame excuses, like she was hungry and looking for something to eat. She wouldn't believe it herself, if their positions were reversed.

"I was looking around. I wanted to see how you'd set up your... installation."

One of his brows rose. "By poking through my fridge?"

"You never know." She gave him a small shrug.

"What's your name?"

"Marny." She wouldn't give him more than that.

He waited, obviously wanting a last name, but she remained silent, refusing to look away from his penetrating gaze.

At last he frowned. "Okay, Marny Noname. How my club is set up is none of your business, but I'll let it go this time. Since it's opening night. But if I ever find you creeping around again, I'll make good on that trespassing charge."

Marny leaned forward. "I don't *creep around*."

"Keep it that way." Nyx gestured toward the hall. "I'll escort you back to the club."

Marny studied him a moment, looking for any trace of faerie magic clinging to him. He didn't transform into a hideous goblin. Nothing glowed or shimmered at the corners of her vision, and she had to conclude he seemed to be an ordinary human.

One with a piece of the Realm of Faerie in the center of his club.

Then realization shocked through her, like she'd been doused with a bucket of freezing water, and she sucked in a quick breath. She'd been an idiot. The reason he looked so familiar was because *his* was the face in the dream she'd had. Which, added to the magical trees out front, made perfect sense.

"Tell me about the forest," she said, slowly walking out of

the kitchen.

"It's a proprietary technique."

"Does VirtuMax know you've stolen part of their Feyland game?"

Sometimes the best defense was a strong offense. And she couldn't tell how much he knew about the Realm, or the existence of magic. It was a tricky subject to bring up.

His expression remained impassive, but his eyes widened slightly.

"Are you some kind of corporate spy?" he countered.

"I have connections." Let him stew on that. "I'm sure the company would be very interested to find out you've appropriated their images."

Something flickered in his eyes—guilty secrets. "If they can prove I've stolen something under trademark or copyright, more power to them. I don't think you'll find a forest exactly like this in-game."

Thinking it over, Marny nearly missed a step. Was he right? She couldn't remember whether the silvery-leafed trees appeared in the basic game of Feyland, or only when a person entered the Realm.

Nyx held open the heavy curtain, then followed her into the crowded warehouse. The music was too loud to continue their conversation, but that was fine. She hadn't yet figured out how to crack his cool façade. Not to mention determining if they were all standing on the brink of unspeakable disaster.

Thoughts whirling, Marny headed to the juice bar where Anjah sat waiting for her. Nyx followed right behind, quiet and dangerous.

"There you are," her roomie said, setting down her half-empty glass of fizzy pink liquid. Then her gaze went to the guy standing at Marny's shoulder and a sly smile crossed her face. "Well, look who you found. Nyx Spenser, I presume?"

She held out an elegant hand, and Nyx took it, bowing slightly. "Charmed. And you are?"

"Anjah Lee." She batted her eyelashes at him.

"Welcome to Club Mysteria," he said. "Excuse me a moment."

He headed to the end of the bar, where the light-haired girl joined him. They began a low-voiced conversation, and Marny could feel Nyx watching her.

"My goodness." Anjah gave her conspiratorial look. "I see I've underestimated you, Marny. Not even here for five minutes, and you managed to drag the handsome Mr. Spenser out of hiding. You must have hidden talents."

"I suppose." Many picked up the drink waiting for her on the bar.

The glass was cold, the pink liquid bubbling slightly. She took a sip, then set it back down, the too-sweet flavor lingering on her tongue. Glancing down the bar, she saw that Nyx was gone and the barista girl had returned to making juice. Still, she knew he had her under surveillance.

"Too bad," Anjah said, noticing the club owner's absence. "Are you ready?"

"For what?"

Anjah slid off the barstool she'd been perched on and shot Marny a grin over her shoulder. "To enter the magical woods, of course. Come on."

It was the only thing left to do. Squaring her shoulders, Marny followed her roomie straight into the enchanted forest.

CHAPTER 12

From the dark corner he'd claimed as his vantage point, Nyx watched Marny Noname and her shiny friend Anjah Lee head into the enchanted forest.

He should've known a simple curtain wouldn't keep people out of his private space. Closing the hallway off had just moved from the bottom of his priority pile to the top. First thing tomorrow, he'd get the carpenters to install a real door.

What had she been doing back there, anyway? What was she hoping to find? She didn't give off a criminal vibe. But she hadn't denied being a corporate spy, either.

After the club closed, he'd do some serious digging and discover everything the 'net would yield about the mysterious Marny.

Other than that one incident, though, the night was going well. The club was hopping, and he'd told the hired doorman/bouncer to be careful not to let in more people than the fire code allowed. That would be the quickest way to get shut down, and Nyx was sure a couple plainclothes police mingled in the crowd. It only made sense, and the Newpoint chief of police was generally acknowledged to be a smart lady.

Emmie's pale hair shone as she came over to where he stood.

"So, who's the girl you told me to watch?" she asked.

"Not sure yet." Nyx folded his arms and searched the trees for a glimpse of her.

For a big girl, she moved well—balanced on her feet and graceful, like she knew exactly where her body was in space.

"What was she doing back in the living area?"

"Looking around."

He'd been an idiot to ignore the fact that VirtuMax would want some hefty licensing fees once they discovered he was using their images. Or at least that was how they'd perceive it.

Better to beg forgiveness than ask permission though, right? He could probably afford it, judging by how well the opening seemed to be going. And frankly, what he'd told Marny was true; the enchanted forest he was using was subtly different from what lay inside the game of Feyland.

His mind skidded away from why that might be.

"Are you okay?" Emmie scanned his face.

"Just thinking. There's a line for the juice bar—you better get back."

"Slave driver." She gave him a look, but there wasn't real heat to it.

They both knew she was loving every minute of being a juice jockey. Not to mention he was paying both her and Sula a more-than-decent wage.

"Well, don't think too hard," she said. "Don't want to strain your brain."

Without waiting for his comeback, she headed to the bar, and Nyx returned to scanning the forest. Bright green flashed between the trees, and pretty soon the short woman Marny had come with stepped out, smiling.

Marny followed right behind. She sent a thoughtful glance back into the woods, her expression a little less tight about the eyes than when she'd gone in. What had she been afraid of finding in there?

She'd recognized the forest as being associated with Feyland, so obviously she was a gamer. Well, that or she worked for VirtuMax, but he doubted the corporation would be sending spies to his club on opening night. They had no reason to.

He'd never leaked any vids—plus he had jammers on in the warehouse. Nobody was going to be able to film anything inside the club unless they had government-level tech.

So, her arrival tonight was just coincidence, and he was jumping to conclusions. Marny was only a nosy girl who had gotten caught.

Maybe.

He spent the next hour keeping an eye on her. She talked some with her friend, and then the shorter girl hit the dance floor with two interested guys. Slowly, and so casually that it wouldn't be obvious unless you were watching her, Marny made her way around the entire perimeter of the warehouse. At least, she tried.

It wasn't nice to laugh, but he couldn't help smiling when she kept entering the forest at one point and walking out in nearly the same place, an annoyed look on her face. Finally she settled for going along the side walls, stopping when she hit the trees, and looking all around.

There was nothing to see. He'd hidden the anchors in secret compartments he'd managed to install. Nobody except him even knew they were there.

At last Marny gave up and went back to the juice bar. There was a stubborn set to her face that didn't bode well for him, but he still wasn't sure what sort of trouble she might cause. After sipping at her drink for half an hour, she went to talk to her friend. The other girl shook her head, and Marny didn't spend too much time arguing with her, merely nodded and headed for the door.

Nyx fought the urge to follow her as she left. It was opening night of his club, for sim's sake. He couldn't just walk out on his grand achievement.

Besides, he had the feeling she'd be back.

Around two in the morning, the crowd quieted down. Nyx had his doorman shoo everybody out and lock the door as he left. Emmie and Sula cleaned up the juice bar while Nyx counted the take. It had been a good night.

"Great job," he told the girls. "You guys head to bed."

He'd set up one of the extra offices as a guest room as soon as he realized Emmie would be working for him. It wasn't reasonable or safe to send her home on the bus in the middle of the night. He'd made it a condition of her employment that she, and any of her friends on the late night shift with her, stayed over at the club and went home in the morning.

"Won't that cramp your style, big brother?" Emmie had

asked. “You know, hot dates with all the ladies who fall at your feet.” Then she’d laughed at him.

“Shut it. I’m not opening Club Mysteria so that I can be a stud.” Not that he would say no if he made a connection with somebody—but the type of people on the club scene weren’t necessarily the type he wanted to date, so he figured it wouldn’t be an issue. At least not right away.

“Sula gets her license in a few months, anyway,” Emmie said. “So I guess it’s okay. It’s not like you’ll be open late every night of the week.”

He’d decided—for his own sanity, mostly—that the club would only be live Tuesday through Saturday, closing at nine on the weeknights. Maybe it was a terrible business ethic, but he wasn’t interested in chaining himself to his work. And on paper, when he ran the numbers with his dad, it had penciled out.

“Don’t stay up too late,” Emmie said.

“It’s already too late.” The adrenaline that had lifted him through the evening was fading, and tiredness tugged at his brain. But he had some research to do before he let himself sleep.

After checking that the warehouse was secure, he headed to his room, ignoring his bed in favor of the netscreen. He needed to find out more about this Marny girl. Was she really a threat to the club?

It was ridiculously easy to track her down. Two keyword searches later a press release from Intertech popped up, announcing their new interns. One of the chosen three was a certain Marny Fanalua, from Crestview. He flicked to images, and found a picture of the Crestview High Gaming Club at a tournament. Though the image was fuzzy, there was no doubt the girl pictured staring at her screenie game with grim concentration was the same Marny he'd met that night.

Crestview... Something about the name niggled at his memory.

He keyed in a few more search words, then sat back, a chill gripping his neck as he read. Crestview—the new home of VirtuMax corporate headquarters.

Ah, crap. When Marny said she had connections, she'd been serious. VirtuMax *and* Intertech, in one big, intense package.

Okay, relax. She was only an intern, and even if she lived in Crestview, that didn't mean she was all in with VirtuMax. A senior in high school didn't have that much power, right?

He knew he was lying to himself, though. After all, he'd amassed a fortune as a high school student, and the second he left school he'd gone on to bigger projects. It would be foolish to underestimate Marny.

Know thy enemy. It was a quote from Sun Tzu, an ancient Chinese general his dad had made him study before going into business. Thousands of years later, the advice was still sound.

The next time Marny Fanalua set foot in Club Mysteria, Nyx was going to know everything about her, down to her game high scores and her favorite kind of peanut butter.

MARNY GRABBED a cab back to the Intertech building, relieved that Anjah wanted to stay and dance. It would be too hard for Marny to try and process the events of the night and hold a conversation at the same time, even though Anjah was pretty good at keeping a one-sided chat going without much input.

As soon as she was in her bedroom, Marny locked the door, turned on the bedside lamp, and pulled out her messager.

:So? What's going on?: Tam asked the instant she activated the group chat.

:Wish I knew. It's like the Realm, but not. Hard to explain.:

:Are you in danger? Should we come?: Uncle Zeg asked.

Marny thought for a minute. Although the forest inside Club Mysteria looked magical, she was pretty sure it didn't lead directly into the Realm of Faerie. Despite trying for the better part of two hours, she hadn't been able to go anywhere except around in circles. She'd walked past the same couple making out about seven times, and kept ending up where she'd started.

That didn't mean the forest was safe or that the fey folk couldn't use it as a gateway, but wouldn't the Elder Fey alert the Feyguard if they did?

:I think the situation's stable for now,: she wrote. *:Have you guys gotten any warnings?:*

:No,: Jennet replied. *:Dad says there hasn't been any security breaks in terms of VirtuMax code. Spark and Aran haven't checked in yet, though.:*

:They're even farther away than you are,: Tam typed. *:But they should be waking up soon. I have a message in to them.:*

:Do you want me to come to Newpoint?: Uncle Zeg asked.

He was pretty much the only one who could. And Marny had to admit she'd like him there, but...

:Isn't Grandma Harmony arriving in two days?: Without proof of danger, Marny couldn't haul her uncle a thousand miles away—not when he had more pressing family obligations. And

a business to run, on top of that. *:How about once she's settled, you come. I can handle things until then.:*

:You sure?: her uncle typed, but she could tell he was relieved. Also, that he trusted her to fly into the wide world on her own, and handle whatever came up.

:Yeah. For now, things seem okay. Tell Spark and Aran to message me if they know anything.:

Having the Feyguard spread all over the world in different time zones was frustrating. On the other hand, it meant there was always a Feyguard awake somewhere. Not that it did Marny much good at the moment.

She said good night to everyone, then turned off her messager and flopped back on her bed. The lamp cast a circle of light on the ceiling and she stared at it, trying to still her whirling thoughts.

All she knew for sure was that Nyx Spenser was messing around in matters he didn't understand. Even if the forest seemed benign at the moment, faeries were tricky creatures.

With the rest of the Feyguard unable to come to Newpoint right away, it was up to her to keep an eye on things. She desperately hoped that all hell—or Faerie—wasn't about to break loose.

Perched on his golden throne, grasses glimmering beneath his feet, the Bright King watched as something pale approached his court. A creature the color of moonlight, its nine-pointed rack of antlers made of purest ivory. The White Stag.

The gemmed trees twinkled more brightly as the stag

passed, and the pixies chimed with laughter, swooping about the creature in a dizzying display.

Satisfaction moved like a wave of deep amber through the king, and he leaned forward with a gesture of welcome.

Long it had been since the stag had set foot in either court. Longer still since it had borne a human between the worlds on its broad back. But all of that was about to change...

CHAPTER 13

JUNE 27

The next night, Marny Fanalua showed up again at Club Mysteria. Nyx nodded in satisfaction when she stepped through the door. Not that he'd been a hundred percent certain she'd come, but the odds had been high.

She was wearing jeans and a purple top made out of some flowy material, and this time she didn't have her glammed-out friend with her. When she went to the juice bar to order a drink, Nyx could tell that Emmie totally recognized her, but his sister stayed calm and professional. From the sharp look in Emmie's eye as she set a dark blue concoction in front of Marny, though, he'd have to answer some questions from his inquisitive little sister later on.

But first, he had questions of his own for Marny. She was a smart one, and he was looking forward to verbally sparring with her again—though not quite yet. He wanted to observe her in his club a little longer and see what she did.

As she had the night before, she prowled the boundaries of the enchanted forest. She stepped in and out of the woods, her expression growing more thoughtful every time. Although the club was crowded, Nyx angled his way around people and never lost sight of her.

Finally, she stood against the wall, arms folded, and watched as brightly dressed people flowed into the forest. The patrons of Club Mysteria exclaimed in wonder at the silver-leafed trees and soft mosses underfoot. Happy voices and laughter drifted between the pale trunks.

It was the reaction he'd been looking forward to ever since he first got the idea to open the club, but he couldn't fully enjoy it. Not with the distraction of a certain large-boned girl whose eyes were filled with suspicion.

Marny Fanalua was a puzzle. One he was going to solve.

Quiet as a shadow, Nyx moved to stand beside her. She smelled faintly of coconut and flowers.

"You don't like my forest?" he asked in a low voice.

She didn't jump, only turned her head like she'd been aware of him all along.

"I'd like to know where it came from," she said.

"Trade secret."

Her gaze narrowed and she regarded him for a long moment. Not admiringly, not angrily, just with an assessing stare that made him uncomfortable. He didn't know what to do with it. Flirting with her wasn't going to work, which left confrontation.

"I understand you're from Crestview," he said.

That made her look away for a second, but not before he saw surprise flash across her expression.

"So?" She shrugged.

"So, you're working for VirtuMax."

"Actually, no." There was a touch of irritation in her voice. "Why does everyone assume that?"

Good. Emotion was leverage he could use to crack her calm façade. He'd never met anyone so self-possessed. Even after he'd caught her snooping around last night, she hadn't seemed frightened or intimidated by him. Annoying as that might be, he also admired it.

"I know you're working for Intertech," he said. "So don't bother trying to deny that one."

"I'm not a corporate minion, here to slap you with fines or sue you for infringement. Even if it's warranted." She glanced at the enchanted forest. The silver light illuminated the round curve of her cheek.

"Why are you here, Marny Fanalua?" He moved to stand in front of her.

She met his gaze, only having to tilt her chin up a fraction.

"Because even if you deny it, I recognize your forest," she said. "And you might be a badass, but you really have no idea what you're messing around with."

"Then why don't you tell me."

She looked over the crowded club, the strobing lights of the dance floor, the noisy juice bar.

"Not here," she said.

From any other girl, he would have thought it was a ploy to get him alone. But Marny seemed impervious to the fact he was a Flail star and owner of the club, and that made him like her a bit better. She judged people on her own terms, which was refreshing. Though he still didn't trust her.

"All right." He tilted his head, indicating she should follow him over to the bar.

He strode to the side of the counter, and people nudged out of his way. Some of them knew who he was, and some of them simply responded to his air of assurance.

"Hey, Emmie." He caught his sister's eye. "I'll be in back for a bit. Buzz me if you need anything."

Emmie's teal-colored eyebrows rose almost high enough to touch her bangs. She glanced from him to Marny, and he could see her matchmaker antennae unfurl.

"What—"

"Later. Hold the fort."

"Mmkay." Her tone told him there'd be no avoiding her interrogation after the club closed.

He'd deal with that issue when it came. He could always tell her Marny was an inspector of some kind—which almost felt like the truth.

"Come on." He beckoned to Marny, felt her following as he cut across the corner of the dance floor.

They ducked under the green swag of gauze, and Marny made a low sound of surprise when she saw the new door installed in the hallway.

"Yeah," he said. "Learned my lesson last night."

A flush of pink washed her brown cheeks—so faint he wouldn't have seen it if he hadn't been looking for a response. Good. She was embarrassed, either about spying, or about getting caught.

He pressed his thumb to the keypad, and the door slid open.

"I'd say welcome, but you've already seen the place." He led her in and closed the door behind them.

She glanced at the closed doors lining the hallway as they headed toward the kitchen. "Not much to see."

"If that's an attempt to get me to open the other doors, it's not going to work."

"I expect I'd find a sim system or two," she said.

He blinked, but really, it was a reasonable assumption to make.

"Since I'm a gamer, I'd hope so." He pulled out a chair for her at the small table. "Glass of water?"

"Sure." She sat, hands folded loosely on the table in front of her. "So, you've played Feyland."

It wasn't a question.

He set two glasses of water on the table, then snagged the other chair and sat across from her.

"Who hasn't played Feyland?" he said. "It's only the biggest game release of the century."

She leaned forward. "Have you ever experienced anything strange while you played?"

His heart clunked at the question, and he had to force himself to stay relaxed, legs outstretched, voice easy.

"You mean like glitches? The game hasn't bugged out on me, no."

While part of him wanted to answer her honestly, he had *way* too much on the line to just hand out information to anyone who asked.

Her mouth twitched, but she didn't come right out and accuse him of lying.

"Are you sure they were only *glitches*?" she asked, her intense brown eyes focused on his face. "Because the forest out there suggests otherwise."

He took a sip of water, thinking how best to answer her.

"Okay," he finally said. "I admit I was inspired by the graphics in Feyland to create my installation. Are you here to sue me for trademark infringement?"

"I wish," she said. "I told you before, I'm not an employee of VirtuMax."

That was an interesting way to put it—and open to a bit of interpretation. She hadn't denied any connection to the company, after all.

"Then you're Intertech's mole."

"Nope." She pushed her glass away, the water slapping up against the sides.

"Why are you interested in my club? Seems to me it's none of your business, since you're so *unaffiliated*."

"I just think you need to be careful," she said.

"Of what?" He made an exaggerated show of peering down the hallway. "Thugs after me? The copyright police taking away the fruits of my labors?"

"You have no imagination," she said. "That forest isn't safe."

"Come on. You're telling me some scary creatures are lurking in the woods? The big bad wolf, ready to jump out and eat me? You have too much imagination, Marny Fanalua. Besides, I've seen you go in and out of my enchanted forest over a dozen times. You know it doesn't go anywhere."

"You better hope it stays that way," she said.

"How about, instead of telling me you're afraid of monsters, you go back to your comfy Intertech apartment and let me run my club the way I want." It was cold, but her words had kindled a faint dread deep inside him.

The last thing he needed was some meddlesome girl making him second-guess all his decisions about opening Club Mysteria. It was fine. He'd been in and out of the forest hundreds of times. Nothing creepy was going to come out of the woods. He didn't know why Marny was trying to freak him out, but she had to have some ulterior motive.

Her expression hardened. "If that's how you want to play it, don't say I didn't warn you." She shoved her chair back and stood.

"Right." He rose to face her, once again surprised he didn't have to look down to meet her gaze. "If it tweaks you so much, how about you just stay away. Permanently."

He didn't have the time or energy to deal with her head games. Whatever she was after, she wasn't going to get it.

"Are you banning me from your club?" she asked.

"Now that you mention it, yes."

He took her elbow to steer her back down the hall, but she neatly pivoted away from him.

"You really are as dumb as you look," she said, shaking her head.

He didn't expect the words to sting, but they did, like a small yet annoying insect. "What does that even mean?"

"You handsome guys are so full of yourselves you can't see what's right in front of your faces. Expecting the world to fall at your knees, when it's really just sharpening its knives."

"Wow, that's grim." He made a guess, the words out of his mouth before he could check himself. "So, you were dumped. I'm sorry—but coming into my club and throwing around crazy suspicions isn't going to fix your broken heart."

"Ha. My heart has never been dented, let alone damaged." Her words were fierce and sincere.

"If you say so." He motioned toward the door. "After you."

She turned on her heel and strode forward, hitting the hallway door button with a bit more force than necessary. As soon as it opened, she stalked into the club. He followed, fighting the urge to apologize. There was nothing to apologize for. The bass beat thumped in his chest, and the flashing lights on the dance floor seemed garish after the quiet kitchen.

As Marny strode past the bar, Emmie looked up, her face full of questions. Nyx shook his head. He'd explain later. Though what was there to explain? A girl with tweaked theories and ties to big gaming corporations had been nosing around, and he threw her out. No big deal.

Marny paused near the exit and turned to face him. At the door, his bouncer raised an eyebrow, and Nyx held up one hand. Everything was under control.

"I hope you're right, Nyx Spenser," she said. "I really do. Otherwise, opening this club could be the biggest mistake of your life."

"Because terrible monsters are going to come rampaging out of the forest, eat up everyone on the dance floor, then take over the world." It was a ridiculous notion.

She frowned at him. "Find me when things start getting tweaked."

"Yeah, right. I'll be sure to do that." He folded his arms. "Goodbye, Marny Fanalua."

And good riddance.

For a second more, she regarded him steadily. Then she gave a small shake of her head and took her leave. The open door let in the smell of exhaust and warm concrete.

"Everything okay?" his bouncer asked, pulling the door shut behind her.

"Sure. No problems."

Then why did the back of his neck prickle when he glanced at the glimmering forest?

Marny was too mad to slow down and try to catch a cab. She leaned forward into the night, not quite running but moving fast, her shoes slapping the sidewalk. Ahead of her, the skyscrapers rose, bright beacons shedding so much human light they washed the stars to invisibility.

Although she wanted to think Nyx Spenser was a stubborn idiot, she had to admit there was no reason he should believe her. If she hadn't seen the fey folk with her own eyes, she wouldn't believe herself, either.

Damn, she hoped he was right—that the enchanted forest was safe, just a small enclosed mystery brought into the world. Because no matter how much he might deny it, or claim it was some kind of virtual installation, she knew the woods were directly out of the Realm of Faerie.

But maybe unconnected.

It was the *maybe* part she was worried about. She'd

explored the forest, tried to trace the boundary, and ended up either going around in circles or stepping back into the warehouse. For now, it seemed Nyx was right. How long that would last, though... She shivered, despite the warm city air.

"Hey, babe!" Two guys cruising by in a grav-car waved their drinks at her. "Come party with us."

Marny ignored them. After a few more catcalls and a burst of laughter, they drove away.

She wasn't nervous about being alone at night—at least not in that part of Newpoint. Because of her size, people generally didn't bother her. Plus, she had her knife strapped to the side of her calf. Uncle Zeg had showed her how to aim for the vulnerable parts, but her blade offered more than just protection from humans.

Faeries disliked being around cold iron, and the touch of it was severely painful to them. She'd put her knife to good use in the past, and with the enchanted forest currently growing in Club Mysteria, she might need it in the future, too.

It was going to be harder to keep an eye on things now that the infuriating and stupidly handsome Nyx Spenser had banned her from his club.

But since when did she let a little thing like that stop her?

CHAPTER 14

Nyx kept an eye on the enchanted forest the rest of the night, watching while club goers wove in and out of the trees. Everyone came back out just fine, and nothing freaky emerged.

Still, when it was time to close he felt his shoulders relax a little. Stupid, to let Marny's wild speculations catch hold of him.

What if she's right?

He pushed the thought away and went to check in with Emmie at the juice bar.

"Did you guys have a good night?" he asked, although he'd seen how busy she and Sula had been.

"Great. A couple cute boys left us big tips." She finished stacking up the glasses, then shot him a look. "You didn't seem to be having much fun, though. What's with the girl who keeps showing up?"

"She won't be back."

He didn't feel like explaining anything more. No need to give his sister weird ideas about the forest. They'd both been in there, after all. It was perfectly safe.

"Worried she's going to kick your ass?"

"She doesn't have the training for it," he said.

"Oh?" Emmie's eyebrows went up. "You two spent some private time in the back, I noticed. She's cute, in a stern kind of way, but I didn't think she was your type."

"What is my type?" he countered. Marny Fanalua wasn't his problem anymore, and he was done talking about her.

"Well now, that's a good question. For a while, I thought it was those tall, leggy girls with too much hair. But now, I'm not sure."

Neither was he—not that he'd admit it to his little sister.

"You and Sula finish up and get to bed," he said.

"I'm ready for a couple days off," Sula said, giving the bar one last polish with her towel. "This has been a lot of work."

"Worth it, though." Emmie shot her a grin. "Plus, next week Nyx is giving us a raise."

"I am?" He tried not to smile at her audacity.

"Sure you are. We all know you started us low. But now that the club is a big success, you can afford to pay us what we're worth. Plus, we've got experience."

"I'm not sure two days counts—either in the experience or the solvency department."

"Pessimist." Emmie rolled her eyes at him, then beckoned to her friend. "C'mon, Sules, this tightwad can close up by himself."

He shook his head, but Emmie was right—he *was* planning to give them a raise. Next month, though, not next week. He finished locking up, then stood in the warehouse, studying the forest.

It looked peaceful and serene, unchanging, but it was almost time for him to go in-game and get some more anchor points. The longest that one of his bubble worlds lasted had been three days, so this one was due to dissolve tomorrow. Which was fine, since the club would be closed until Tuesday evening.

He almost went to the hidden compartments and took out the anchor points, but a yawn grabbed him, so big it made his eyes water. Damn, he was tired. The forest would fade away soon enough, and he was suddenly so weary he wanted to lie down right there on the floor and sleep.

Luckily, his bedroom wasn't far. He trudged into the hall and opened the door, hearing Emmie and Sula giggling in the guest room. Tomorrow they'd leave, and he could fire up his sim system and grab some more leaves, or maybe change over to the meadowscape instead of the forest.

But first, sleep.

FRANTIC BANGING on his door wrenched Nyx to consciousness out of weird, silver-lit dreams.

"Nyx! Wake up!" It was Sula's voice, shrill with fear.

He rolled to his feet, alertness washing over him like he'd been doused with cold water.

"Coming!" he called. He flicked on his light, then swiftly pulled on his jeans and a T-shirt.

The alarms around the perimeter of the warehouse hadn't

been tripped, or he'd hear the blare of sirens. Maybe Emmie was sick? He yanked open his door.

Sula stood there, her eyes wide and scared, her arms wrapped around her ribs.

"What is it?" he asked.

"Emmie's gone," she said. "At first, I thought she was just pranking, but when she didn't come out, I tried to find her. And she wasn't there at all."

"Wasn't where?" Ice clutched his chest.

"In the forest."

Damn, damn, damn. He was such an idiot.

Why hadn't he removed the anchors? Why hadn't he listened to Marny?

Maybe it was all a mistake—a misunderstanding. Maybe Sula had a bad dream and Emmie was in the bathroom.

He strode down the hall, checking each room, but there was no sign of his sister. The forest stood serene and shining in the main warehouse.

"Emmie!" he cried, senses straining.

"She's not there," Sula said behind him, sniffling loudly.

He wanted to dash into the trees—but first he needed to know exactly what Sula had seen. Or thought she had seen. Information first, then action. Forcing himself to breathe more slowly, he turned to Emmie's friend.

"Come into the kitchen," he said, "and tell me what happened."

Pushing down the dread swamping his thoughts, Nyx led Sula into the back. She perched on a chair, but he couldn't sit. He leaned against the counter and folded his arms, regarding her.

"I woke when Emmie got up," Sula said. "She opened the bedroom door and there was this noise like bells chiming. Something about it made me want to follow that sound. It was coming from the club—from the forest."

Nyx nodded, a sick feeling crawling through his gut. He was supposed to protect his sister, not let her stumble into danger.

"Then what?" he asked.

Sula's brows drew together. "There was something in the forest. Some kind of white creature, moving through the trees. Emmie went in, and it went right up to her."

Hell. Nyx clenched his hands into fists. He should've paid attention to what Marny had been trying to tell him, but he'd been so sure the enchanted forest was safe. Nothing could come out of it.

Except something had.

"What did it look like?" He was half expecting Sula to tell him a unicorn had come and stolen his sister.

"It was a big white deer," she said. "Big as a horse, with antlers. It bent down, and she got on it and rode away."

"Why didn't you follow her?" The words came out harsher than he wanted, but this was his sister they were talking about.

"I tried!" Sula gave him a wounded look. "Do you honestly think I'd just stand there while my best friend was kidnapped by some freaky animal that appeared from out of nowhere?"

"Okay, sorry." He held up his hands. "I know you care about Emmie. So you went after her."

"I ran right into the forest, but the white deer was gone. I called and called her name, and kept running, but I was just going around in circles. After a while I gave up and came to get you."

He only wished she'd done so sooner.

"Hey, don't cry," He handed her a paper towel, though he felt like crying himself. Stronger than tears, however, was anger —at himself, at the forest, at Marny, who had tried to warn him. "I'm going to take another look in the forest."

"Don't leave me alone," Sula cried, jumping up. "This place is tweaked."

He didn't try to deny it, or calm her down. Instead, he lengthened his stride until he was almost running down the hall.

The trees remained quiet. A breeze stirred the leaves, but there was no flash of white between the pale trunks, no glimmering stag carrying Emmie on its back.

Though he knew it was useless, Nyx plunged into the woods, calling her name until he was hoarse. He caught glimpses of Sula standing tensely just outside the boundary of the forest, refusing to set foot on the velvety mosses. He couldn't blame her.

Forty-five minutes later, he had to admit defeat. He'd been in and out of the trees a dozen times, and there was no trace of Emmie.

"Now what?" Sula asked, her eyes red from crying. "Call the police?"

"And tell them what? My sister disappeared into a magical forest riding on the back of a white stag?" Nyx sank down on one of the barstools and rubbed his forehead.

"As soon as it's light, I want to go home," Sula said. "This place is way too freaky for me."

"All right." Good thing the club was closed for the next two-plus days. Though he had no idea how to get his sister back. He swallowed down the panic rising in his throat.

There was one person he could go to, who might know what the hell was going on. Marny Fanalua. If only he'd been smart enough to get her messager number—but he could sleuth it out.

Two hours later, the sun was rising, his eyes were gritty from too little rest and staring at the screen, and Sula was asleep, curled up on top of his bed. He hadn't found any answers to where Emmie might have gone, other than some old Celtic myths about the White Stag. They couldn't possibly be true, though—could they?

He also hadn't been able to ferret out Marny's contact info, but he knew where to find her. Intertech.

Now that it was morning, he'd head for the immense skyscraper and track her down. Failure wasn't an option.

Where was Emmie? The question scraped him until he wanted to yell with frustration—but that wasn't going to help anything. Instead he shook Sula awake, helped her gather her things, then called a cab to take her home.

"Let me know as soon as you find Emmie," Sula said, her voice strained.

"I will. Until I do, try not to say anything." The last thing he needed was his parents freaking out all over him, on top of everything. He could solve this. He had to.

"Okay." Sula nodded. "I know you'll find her."

Her faith in him made him feel a little ill. What if he couldn't find his sister? But he kept his expression confident. Sula was freaked enough without seeing him fraying at the edges.

The cab carrying Sula pulled away from the curb outside the warehouse, headlights dimming as the day dawned. To the north, the tall Intertech building was outlined in red-tinged light. He tried not to compare it to the color of blood.

It was only the sunrise.

CHAPTER 15

JUNE 28

An irritating buzzing noise woke Marny, coming from outside her room. She blinked at her tablet, trying to wake up enough to figure out what was going on. Six forty-five in the morning—way too early for a Sunday. She'd planned to sleep in. Grimacing, she pulled the extra pillow over her head and hoped that one of her roommates would deal with the noise.

It stopped and she let out a sigh of relief, only to toss the pillow aside a minute later when the buzzing started up again.

"What?" she mumbled.

It didn't sound like a fire alarm or anything too urgent. Had Anjah set her clock to go off, and then forgotten about it?

Marny pushed back the covers and got up. She didn't care if Anjah or Wil saw her in her garish tropical-print nightgown. It would serve her roomies right for waking her up.

A quick check of Anjah's room showed her neatly made bed, and no alarm ringing. Either she was up way early, or hadn't yet come home. Marny shook her head, but it wasn't up to her to police her roommate's behavior.

Wil was sound asleep, snoring with one arm hanging off the bed. The buzz wasn't coming from his room either, but from the front of the apartment. From the intercom by the door, to be exact.

She tapped the button. "Yes?"

"Front desk calling. Is Miss Fanalua there?"

"Speaking. What is it?"

"There's a Mr. Nyx Spenser here, insisting he needs to see you immediately."

Adrenaline jolted through her, waking her up quicker than a strong cup of tea. "I'll be down in a minute."

If Nyx was there, after summarily throwing her out of his club the night before, then something had gone very wrong.

"Can't I go up?" Nyx's voice filtered through the connection. "It's important."

"Sir, wait. You can't access the elevators without an escort. Mr. Spenser!"

"I'll be right down," Marny said into the intercom. But not dressed like a Samoan grandma.

She hurried back to her room, pulled on jeans and a T-shirt, and slipped her feet into a pair of sandals. A quick detour to the bathroom to brush her teeth. She stared at her hair in the mirror for a second, but it was pretty hopeless, so she just smoothed it back with her hands.

At the front door, she pivoted and dashed back to grab her badge. It wouldn't do for both of them to be stuck downstairs.

The elevator seemed slower than usual. She watched the numbers count down, trying not to fidget with tension. When it finally reached the lobby level, the door slid open to reveal Nyx standing there, his mouth set in a tight line. A security guard hovered behind him—not one of Mr. von Coburg's pets, she was relieved to see.

"He's okay," she said, waving her badge at the guard. "Guests are permitted, right?"

"Usually you need to notify the front desk in advance," the security guy said.

Nyx gave her an imploring look. She could tell he was doing everything possible to contain the tension coiled through his body. His fingers were curled into fists and he balanced lightly on the balls of his feet, as if he were about to explode into action. He looked like a fighter—which she supposed he was, with his black belt in judo or whatever.

"Next time, I'll do that," she said. "Can he come up now?"

"All right," the guard said. "But follow protocol in the future."

"I will. Thank you."

Nyx practically bolted into the elevator. Marny kept a pleasant expression on her face for security's benefit, but the second the door closed, she turned to Nyx.

"I can tell it's not good," she said, then glanced at the camera mounted in the upper corner of the elevator. "But hang on just a minute."

Nyx gave her a terse nod and stared at the glowing readout as the numbers flashed by. He stayed silent as she led him down the hall to her apartment, his footsteps quiet and deadly, like a lion on the prowl.

"Is it safe to talk?" he asked softly as the apartment door slid closed behind them.

"Maybe. I'll put the water on to boil, and then you tell me what's going on."

The sound of the electric kettle wouldn't completely mask their conversation, but it might discourage any casual listener manning the security boards.

Nyx followed her into the kitchen, and as soon as the hiss and gurgle of heating water filled the space, he spoke.

"My sister's missing. And I owe you a huge apology." He glanced down at his hands, then back at her. The edge of panic lurked in his eyes. "I should have listened when you told me the forest was dangerous."

She bit her tongue. *I told you so* wouldn't help anything, and Nyx was clearly paying a high price for not heeding her warnings.

"Your sister—the blonde-haired girl at the juice bar?"

"Yeah. According to her friend, a creature came out of the woods and carried Emmie away."

"Crap. What kind of creature?" This was severely bad. If the Dark Court was involved—well, Nyx's sister might be next in line for blood sacrifice.

"A white deer. I did some research, and in Celtic mythology, the White Stag is some kind of messenger between the worlds or something."

"Okay. That makes sense."

"How?" He reached out and grabbed her arm. "How does any of this make sense? Tell me what you know. Please."

She gently pulled away and took a breath. Honesty time. Hopefully the sound of the bubbling electric kettle would be enough interference. What she was about to reveal could get all of her friends in trouble—plus put way too much power in the hands of Intertech, if anyone overheard. Well, overheard and believed her wild tales.

"The game of Feyland opens a gateway to the Realm of Faerie," she said, leaning forward and keeping her voice low. "Not like happy-happy fairyland, but the place of the old tales and ballads. Magical, and dangerous."

He didn't scoff at her, to his credit. Instead he blinked a couple times, processing the information, then focused back on her. "So how do I go to this Realm place and get my sister back?"

"Yeah—that's the question. Usually people go in-game and then transition into the Realm. I think you've been doing that without realizing it." Or perhaps he'd known something was off, but not understood the peril.

"So I can log in to Feyland, play the game, and find my sister that way?"

"Maybe." She frowned, thinking. "But your sister didn't get sucked in by playing a sim game. She went into the Realm via the forest in your club."

"Dammit." He began to beat his fist softly against the counter. "It was supposed to be safe."

The kettle shut off with a loud ding, and the sound of boiling water subsided to a quiet simmer.

"Dealing with the fey folk is never safe," Marny said. "We need to go to your club and figure it out from there. Maybe the forest will let us through."

She still had plenty of questions for him, but this wasn't the place.

"Right," he said, some of the desolation leaving his voice. "Come on."

"Let me put on some real shoes and grab my jacket. Give me a minute."

It wasn't quite cold enough to warrant her coat, but she felt like she needed the extra layer of protection. She didn't mention her knife, but she took the time to grab it out of her underwear drawer and strap the calf sheath on under her jeans.

As she and Nyx stepped out of the apartment, Marny caught sight of a black-garbed figure at the end of the hallway. One of von Coburg's guards. He stood with his hands clasped behind his back, obviously staking out the elevator. She hoped it wasn't on account of her and Nyx, but the cold feeling in her gut suggested otherwise. Nyx must have felt her tense up, because he shot her a look.

"What is it?" he asked, leaning close. His breath tickled her ear.

"Top-dog security," she replied. "Your early morning visit is a little... unusual. Made them suspicious."

The proof that Intertech was watching her so closely made the hairs on her arms prickle, but there was nothing to do except brazen it out.

Nyx put his hand on the small of her back. "Keep walking. And trust me."

She made herself stride forward. Nyx kept pace, still touching her. It should have felt annoying, but instead the light pressure of his hand was oddly steadying.

A few paces from the elevator, the guard straightened and gave them a fake-looking smile. "Good morning, Miss Fanalua. A bit early to be having guests, don't you think?"

She didn't bother replying, but kept heading for the gleaming doors.

"Not so fast." The guard moved directly in front of them. "The boss wants to know what brings Onyx Spenser to Intertech."

Onyx, was it? She sent him a sidelong glance.

Nyx wore an easy smile that made his face look even more handsome. He slipped his hand around her waist and snugged her up against him.

Half of her wanted to bolt out of his grasp, but she went with it, guessing where he was going. And, though she was reluctant to admit it, he felt good—all lean, hard muscle. He smelled like coffee and salty skin, and she breathed shallowly, trying not to inhale too deeply of his scent. Something inside her flopped around like a fish at the end of a line, and she tried to ignore the bright and flailing sensation.

"I had to come," Nyx said. "I met this girl at my club, and she ran off like Cinderella, so I tracked her down. Lucky me, she agreed to come out for breakfast."

He gave her a warm smile, and she glimpsed the spark of mischief in his eyes. He was enjoying this! She almost pulled out of his embrace, but they had to continue this little charade until they got out of the building and away from the surveillance cameras.

The guard narrowed his eyes. "She doesn't seem like your type."

"And you seem like a judgmental ass," she said under her breath.

Nyx squeezed her in warning. "Sometimes, when you meet the right girl, you just know."

Way too sappy. She elbowed him a little, and his smile widened.

"So," Marny said to the guard. "Can we go get our omelets and coffee now, or what?"

"There's a great waffle place a few blocks down." Nyx lifted his hand and smoothed her hair back behind her ear, like he really was falling for her.

She resisted the urge to bat his fingers away. It was irritation she felt, not attraction. Right?

"Sounds good," she said. "Do they have fresh berries and whipped cream?"

Her stomach gave an embarrassing rumble, which added to the veracity of their banter about breakfast.

The guard glared at them and made an annoyed sound in the back of his throat.

"Fine," he said at last, stepping back toward the wall. "You two *lovebirds* enjoy your day."

He gave the word a sarcastic slant, and Marny pushed down her stab of annoyance. Was it really so unlikely that someone like Nyx would find her attractive?

As they waited for the elevator, Nyx kept his arm around her. The doors slid open, and she stepped inside first. The warmth of his touch lingered, and she tried to forget how nice it had felt. Instead, she crossed her arms and leaned against the brushed metal surface of the wall.

"Hey." He settled beside her and nudged her shoulder with his own. "Don't go all hedgehog on me."

"Do I look blue to you?" She slanted him a look, wondering if he'd pick up on the old game reference.

He laughed and leaned comfortably closer. "Did you watch

our Flail stream, that time we played Sonic and kept drowning for a week straight? That was so tweaked."

"It made me like you more," she admitted. "You could fail and still laugh at yourselves. Not that I followed your stream all that much."

"Of course not. Watching two decent-looking guys play old-school games is so boring."

"Some of us have better things to do," she said, as her cheeks warmed. "Although I guess that friend of yours isn't too hard to look at."

She felt his laughter, but any reply he might have made was cut off by the ding of the elevator arriving at the lobby. The doors slid open, but before she could step out, he linked his arm around hers. It was just for show, of course.

Damn the warm glow that filled her. She wasn't supposed to react like this to a guy. She was Marny—strong, capable, independent. Not a girly-girl who was dependent on some man to make her feel good about herself. *Pfft* to that.

"So your full name is Onyx?" she asked as they headed past the front desk.

"Yeah. Named after a gemstone. My sister's name is Emerald. Emmie." His voice tightened.

"What, are your parents mineralogists or something?"

"No, but my mom's name is Opal. I guess they decided to go with the theme." He held the door open, then followed her onto the sidewalk.

The air felt heavy, and Marny glanced up. Although the sky overhead was blue, clouds massed at the horizon. A storm was coming.

"I hope you don't mind a rain check on breakfast," Nyx said.

"I've got some fruit and stuff at the club. I know you haven't had anything to eat."

Now that they were out of the Intertech building, the urgency had returned to his voice. He leaned forward, scanning the street for a cab.

"That's fine," she said. There were way more important things at stake than waffles.

It didn't take long for them to grab a cab and make it down to Club Mysteria. Nyx unlocked the door and Marny stepped into the hushed cavern of the warehouse. Dim sunlight sifted through the high windows, and without the strings of fairy lights and the flashing dance floor strobes, the place seemed almost drab.

Especially since there was no sign of the enchanted forest.

"Dammit!" Nyx's shout echoed across the stained concrete floor and bounced off the blank walls.

Whatever magic Club Mysteria had hosted was gone.

CHAPTER 16

Nyx balled his hands into fists. He wanted to punch something: the walls, the bar, the empty air where the forest should have been.

It was gone, and so was Emmie.

Panic and self-loathing clogged his throat and he bent over, the pain of losing his sister slicing through him.

"Hey. Breathe." Marny put her hand on his back, and he realized he'd been making an ugly choking noise.

With effort, he straightened and hauled in a breath.

"I know it seems dire," she continued, her voice steady and calm. "But your sister isn't the first mortal to stray into the Realm."

"What do you mean?" He shrugged off her touch and glared at her. "You actually know of other people who have disappeared like this? Why didn't you tell me?"

If only she'd forced him to believe her, none of this would have happened.

"You weren't listening," she said. "And all of the people I know who were sucked into the Realm returned and were fine, okay? We'll get your sister back."

"How?" He waved an agitated hand at the empty warehouse. "You said we had to go in through the forest. And it's gone."

"Then we start by re-conjuring it. You know how to do that, right?"

"Yeah. I can. But what if it's not the *right* forest?"

Damn, he was sounding like a whiny kid. He closed his eyes for a second and let out a deep breath. *Calm down, idiot.* Marny was there to help, and she didn't deserve to be on the receiving end of a tantrum. No matter that there were good reasons for him to be on the edge.

"Then we deal with that when we get there," she said. "One step at a time. Now, what do you need to do to create the forest again? Cast a spell?" She wiggled her fingers.

"It's not magic. Not really. I have to go in-game and get some stuff."

"Get some stuff?" Her voice rose in surprise. "You mean, out of Feyland?"

"Yeah. I know it sounds crazy—"

"We've already established you're not crazy." She gave him a thoughtful look. "It's not normal for players to be able to bring things out of the Realm. But it's not impossible."

"There's a lot I wish you'd told me, Marny Fanalua."

She opened her mouth to reply, and he held up one hand, forestalling her from speaking.

"But you're right," he continued. "I couldn't believe you last night. I'm sorry for that. And for freaking out on you. It's just..."

"I know. I'd be losing it, too. But we're not in this alone. Those people I mentioned that have gone into the Realm and come out again? They're my friends—and my uncle, Zeg—and they're called the Feyguard. Their job is to help with exactly these issues. Let me get ahold of them."

"Okay." He clung to the thought that help would be on the way while Marny typed on her messager.

After a minute, she tucked it away, her expression a little unsettled.

"Are they coming?" he asked, not liking the look in her eyes.

"I could only reach Roy and my uncle. They'll try coming to help us via the game—but they haven't gotten any alerts about anything going wrong, which may make it hard for them to find us. Not that it's a perfect system, but still..." She gave herself a little shake and refocused on Nyx. "So—you need to enter Feyland. Where's your FullD setup?"

"Spare room."

He turned and headed for the back hallway, Emmie's loss echoing through him with every step. Marny followed, quiet and light on her feet. Her steady acceptance of what was happening helped center him, and he pushed away the corroding blame. First, get Emmie back. He could deal with his own stupidity later.

"Good thing I have two sim systems," he said, holding open the door. "We can go into Feyland together."

She shook her head, her thick black hair bobbing. "No. I don't sim."

He paused and gave her a hard look. "I thought you were a serious gamer."

"Screenie only. Simming makes me claustrophobic." She

glanced at the two rigs in the room, and her shoulders hunched a little.

"What if I get into trouble in there?" he asked. "What if everything has changed, or your theory about going through the enchanted forest is wrong, and I *do* get a chance to rescue Emmie?"

Her mouth set in a grim line. "I really don't—"

"Please. I need you." He couldn't keep the desperation from his voice. Marny was his lifeline—the one person who knew what was going on, who had a clue how to save his sister. He didn't want to go anywhere without her. In game, or out.

Indecision was clear in her face, and he could see the flash of panic in her eyes when she looked over at the equipment again. She really was afraid of gearing up.

Dammit. He wasn't the kind of guy who'd force somebody past their comfort level. No matter how much he wanted to *make* her come. She'd already said no. He took a deep breath.

"I'll try going in by myself," he said, though the words stung his tongue. "I mean, maybe your friends are on the way, right?"

He didn't want to game alone, especially since now he knew how dangerous Feyland could be. And he was half hoping that she'd relent, give him that rare smile, and say of course she'd come.

But she stayed put as he went over to the sim chair and started pulling on the gloves. Her expression was tense, and her clenched hands were a dead giveaway.

"I..." she began, then trailed off, her voice croaking a little.

"It's okay," he said, though it wasn't. "If I see anything strange, I'll come back out."

She nodded tightly.

Nyx flexed his fingers inside the gaming gloves, then settled in the chair. Swallowing the words of entreaty clogging his throat, he pulled on the sim helmet and carefully didn't look at Marny. She hadn't moved from her post by the door, and disappointment and anxiety churned in his stomach.

Churned worse when he entered the game, the golden light triggering a bout of nausea he fought down. Then he was in, standing in a circle of white-spotted red mushrooms.

The air smelled like dusty mint, and warm sunshine spilled into the clearing. The light danced off the silver-leaved trees, a bird sang nearby, and despite himself, Nyx's clenched jaw relaxed. Not that he was completely safe, but he knew from experience that fear could tighten a competitor up so much they lost their edge.

Time to focus on his main objective: get some leaves so he could re-conjure the enchanted forest and go after Emmie.

Although if he caught even a hint of his sister in-game, or saw anything white moving in the forest, he was so going after that.

One step at a time.

He slipped an arrow out of his quiver and nocked it on the bow, then quietly stepped out of the mushroom ring. The path winding through the trees looked clear, but he didn't trust it to stay that way. Feyland was a tricky place.

Dappled shadows fell over the purple-flowered bushes and ferns growing beside the path. Ahead, something moved, and he halted, lifting his bow.

It was just a branch swaying in the breeze. Nothing to jump at. Swallowing, Nyx kept going. Marny and all her talk of how dangerous Feyland was had really hyper-tuned his nerves. He passed a pile of sticks lying near the path, and couldn't help glancing into the deeper shade under the trees. Had something white flickered there, between the pale-barked trunks?

The scrape of wood on wood made his whirl. He raised his bow, only to have it whacked out of his hands by an oaken staff. The wielder stood before him—a twiggy creature with long limbs made of branches. Around its face was a halo of green leaves, and its eyes were dark and unfriendly.

It lifted one gnarled hand and blew a puff of sparkling dust into Nyx's face. He coughed, then whirled, searching for where his bow had landed in the underbrush. He needed to snatch his weapon, then sprint up the path for a clear shot...

The path was blocked by another treelike creature on the other side of him, this one covered in green needles and carrying a pointed spear. Dammit. Nyx fumbled for the knife at his belt with suddenly clumsy fingers, only to have the first creature grab him and whip vinelike ropes around his torso.

No! How could he have been caught so easily? He was failing Emmie.

He scrabbled at the bindings, trying to find a spot he could wriggle an arm free. His body felt sluggish and unresponsive. Had that dust been some kind of drug?

"I told you the mortal would be easy pickings, Pinebough," the first creature said in a voice that creaked like branches rubbing together.

The needle-covered creature gave a slow nod. "Not much of a fight in it."

"Not supposed to fight it. Just capture the human and bring it to the court. Simple."

"Simple—if you cheat," Pinebough said. "Nightshade dust is for cowards and puny brambles."

The first creature narrowed its eyes. "Are you calling me a bramble bush? I'll poke you."

Pinebough's needles rose, puffing up his size. "Everyone knows your grandmother was nothing but a briar rose. Barely worthy of being called a spriggan."

Nyx blinked sleepily. Part of him knew the argument was a perfect chance to try and escape, but somehow he couldn't get that part of his brain to talk to the rest of his body. Idly, he noted the bushes beside the path moving, though there was no breeze. The ferns dipped and swayed, as though something had just walked through them.

"You poked me!" Pinebough glared at his companion and raised his pointed spear. "Prepare to battle!"

The first creature shoved Nyx behind him and lifted his staff. "I'll scatter you to the winds, rootbrain."

Nyx stumbled, his feet feeling like they were stuck in cement. Something grabbed his elbow, steadying him.

"Who...?" He blinked, his vision blurry, but couldn't see anything.

"Shh. I'm going to cut you loose, but as soon as I draw my blade, I'll become visible," a soft voice whispered in his ear. "Get ready to grab your bow. I think we can take them out."

"Marny?" Relief rushed through him, clearing his mind a bit. "I'm drugged—not sure I can shoot." Or even walk.

"Crap. Okay, let's figure out plan B."

He could hear her breathing, could faintly sense the reassuring bulk of her body next to him. Part of him was embarrassed that he needed rescuing like some damsel in distress, but mostly he was profoundly glad she was there.

The branchy creatures were still fighting and paying no attention to Nyx, but judging by the amount of needles and twigs littering the path, their battle would be over soon. Then they'd get back to taking him to the court, whatever that was. It didn't sound good.

"Start moving toward the clearing," Marny said. "Hopefully the spriggans won't notice for a bit. Go slow."

He nodded. Slow was about the only setting he could manage.

"What about you?" he whispered. It went against his instincts to leave the fighting to Marny and just run away. Besides, she was his only ally. What if she got captured, too?

"As soon as you're at the faerie ring, I'll join you," she said.

Carefully, so he wouldn't face-plant into the shrubbery, Nyx began shuffling away. He'd made it about halfway back to the clearing when Pinebough let out a shout.

"The human is escaping!"

Nyx broke into an awkward trot, biting his lip hard so the pain would clear his head. *Don't fall. Don't look back.* His job was get to the mushroom ring, and trust that Marny would make it, too.

His pursuers clacked after him, and then he heard a thud.

"You tripped me," the first spriggan cried. "You underhanded spawn of a thistle! You think to deprive me of my fair share of the bounty?"

"I never touched you," Pinebough replied. It lifted its pinecone-like nose and sniffed. "I smell another presence!

Some sneaky magic is at play. An invisible foe stands in our way."

Nyx heard the sound of thrashing branches, and then a grunt of pain. Marny.

"Aha—the rogue is discovered," the first spriggan said.

"Another human. Our bounty has doubled." Pinebough's voice was full of glee. "Grab her, quickly."

"I don't think so," Marny said. "Nyx, run!"

It was hard, with his arms bound against his body, but he forced himself to go faster. Ahead, the mushroom ring glowed scarlet in the sunshine. Almost there.

He stumbled over an exposed root and lost his balance. No, dammit. He went to his knees, and then Marny grabbed him and hoisted him to his feet.

"Cut me free," he gasped.

She glanced over her shoulder, then used the knife already in her hand to slice through his bindings. Blindly, Nyx reached out and tore a handful of leaves off a nearby bush.

"Go, go," Marny said, grabbing his arm and propelling him forward.

The two of them careened into the clearing. Marny practically threw him into the center of the faerie ring, then leaped in herself.

"No!" Pinebough cried.

The spriggan lunged, stabbing with his spear, and hit Marny in the upper arm just as brilliant golden light began swirling around them. She cried out, and then the world turned upside down.

CHAPTER 17

Pain drilled through Marny, accompanied by the horrible queasy sensation she always got going in and out of Feyland.

She squeezed her eyes shut and concentrated on breathing through the nausea. Getting sick all over Nyx's equip was not an option—although she had the feeling she'd already gotten blood on his sim chair. Stupid, to let that spriggan get close enough to spear her.

The golden light stopped spinning, then cleared to show the room where Nyx kept his sim systems. They'd made it.

And she could not wait to get out of the constricting dimness of the gaming helmet.

She sat up, then gasped and fell back into the chair as fire ripped through her arm and seared along every nerve ending. Tears sprang to her eyes and she blinked them away. *Just a little poke*, she told herself. *I'm okay.* The warm liquid oozing down her arm wasn't a good sign, though.

"Marny!" Nyx pulled off his gear and hurried to her side.

Before she could ask him to, he lifted off her helmet then carefully removed her gloves.

"Is it bad?" she asked.

"Bad enough." He looked shaken. "We need to get you medical attention."

Gritting her teeth, she glanced at her arm. There was a hole in her body, partially obscured by her torn T-shirt. What she could see of the wound looked very red—and was that bit of white her *bone*? As she watched, blood trickled down her arm and dripped off her elbow onto the carpet.

"Sorry about your stuff," she said.

"That doesn't matter. Hang on, I'm calling the med techs, and grabbing my med kit from the bathroom. We need to stop this bleeding."

She nodded, and concentrated on breathing until he came back. Probably better not to sit up until they stanched the flow of blood.

"This is going to hurt," he said, reaching for the sleeve of her shirt. "Sorry."

It did, but the pain was an ocean she swam in. The trick was not to let the waves crash over her head. And not to watch what Nyx was doing. She concentrated on his face instead.

He peeled back the cloth and went a bit pale, but his hands remained steady as he held gauze against her shoulder. After a few moments, he pulled it off and sprayed something on her skin. The wound instantly felt somewhat better, the pain notching down to an almost bearable level.

She still couldn't look at it, though. Only him.

Funny—she couldn't see the handsome guy, the Flail star,

the cocky club owner any more. He was just Nyx, and weirdly, it felt like she'd known him for ages.

"Are you all right?" she asked. "You seemed pretty woozy in-game."

He gave her a crooked smile. "Either the transition back out or, you know, the medical emergency, cleared my head."

"How long until the medics come?" she asked.

"About five minutes."

That didn't give them much time. And though he wasn't thinking things through, she was.

"We need to get me out of the chair," she said. "And figure out a reasonable explanation for how I got hurt."

"Oh. Right." He stared at her a second. "Speaking of which —how can you get stabbed in-game and then be sitting here in the real world, bleeding? That makes no sense."

"You have to be careful in Feyland. I told you it was dangerous."

"The hell with that!" His voice rose, echoed through her head. She winced, and he instantly looked sorry. "You got hurt, and it's my fault."

"Strategy first," she said, suddenly exhausted. "Argue later. Now help me up."

He put his arm around her waist, supporting her while she got unsteadily to her feet. It was all she could do not to lean heavily against him. Instead, she concentrated on balancing upright, despite the throb all down her left side.

"Sling your arm around my shoulders," he said. "We're going into the warehouse."

There was a confidence in his voice that meant he'd come up with a plan. Good, because she had no idea how they were going to finesse her injury. Getting stabbed in-game was certainly not an explanation the med techs would believe—even if she had wanted to try the truth, which she didn't.

The trip down the hall and out into the cavernous space seemed to take forever. Each step jarred Marny's wound, sending missiles of hot pain through her. Nyx was patient, his grip around her waist steady.

He led her to one of the clusters of furniture near the dance floor and she managed to sit on a small couch without keeling over.

"Put your feet up," he said, already moving away. "I have to set the stage."

He disappeared into the back, and she could hear him rummaging about. A few moments later he returned with a pair of long spears. They were made of white wood, with red tassels on the bottom and a sharp-looking metal point on the top.

"Handy, that you have those lying around," she said.

"Part of my martial arts weapons collection." He glanced at the spears. "At first I thought I'd display them on the walls, then realized that was a dumb idea. I can't screen everybody who walks into the club, and there are too many idiots in the world to risk them being taken down and used. Anyway, we can say I was showing you some moves, and the spear slipped."

"Yeah, right into my arm." Marny brought her hand up to her wound. "Come here so we can get one bloody."

Nyx laid one of the spears down, then brought the other one over. He eyed her arm.

"The plas-skin has stopped the bleeding. I'm not sure we can get enough onto the spear to look realistic."

"Then stab me again," she said, bracing herself.

"Don't be ridiculous." He sounded horrified at the thought.

"Squeamish? We have to make this look good." Besides, what was more pain? She was already living inside the red hole in her body.

"I am not reopening your wound. Sorry."

The sound of sirens drifted down the street. Marny made a grab for the haft of the spear, and he yanked it out of reach.

"Nyx," she said.

"No."

He glanced around, his face tense, then sprinted over to the juice bar. Glass clinked on glass as he rummaged around. The sirens got louder, then cut off abruptly as the med techs arrived. They were out of time.

Moving fast, Nyx lifted a bottle of something from the bar, then gathered up both spears and ran to the center of the room. He tossed one weapon behind him, then knelt and poured red liquid from the bottle over the point of the other spear. For good measure, he smeared some of it down the white wood. It looked dark red and sticky.

The smell of berries drifted into the air, and Marny hoped that in the excitement the ambulance crew wouldn't notice that the apparent scene of her injury featured raspberry syrup instead of blood.

Somebody banged on the door.

"Coming!" Nyx yelled.

He made a quick detour to deposit the bottle of syrup back on the bar, then opened the warehouse door. Two white-garbed med techs stood there, one male, one female.

"You have an injured person here?" the man asked.

"Yes, my friend, Marny." Nyx gestured to where she slouched on the couch. "We were sparring and my spear slipped and got her in the arm."

The female tech gave the spears on the floor a cursory glance, then hurried to Marny's side.

"Good, you got plas-skin on the wound right away," she said. "How's the pain?"

"Bearable," Marny lied.

The tech narrowed her eyes. "Can I administer some pain medication? It's going to help while I take a look at your injury. Okay?"

Not worth arguing over. Marny nodded, and the tech pressed a dispenser against her wrist. A few seconds later, blessed coolness spread through her. She took a deep breath and let it out, grateful that she could breathe without feeling like she was swimming through lava.

"Good," the woman said. "Timmo, got the scanner?"

"Right here," her partner said, lifting a slim piece of equipment. "Before we treat any further, we need some information. If you'd fill this out." He handed his tablet to Nyx.

"How old are you?" the woman asked Marny.

"Eighteen," she said. She'd be eighteen in four months, so it was only a small lie. Besides, claiming she was an adult was going to save all of them a world of hassle.

Nyx shot her a quick look, his fingers flying over the tablet, and she wondered exactly how much he knew about her. More than she knew about him, that was for sure.

The tech held the scanner up to her shoulder. "Relax—I need to lift your arm."

Marny tried to stay loose as the woman raised and lowered

her arm. There was an unpleasant tugging sensation, but it wasn't excruciating.

"It's clean, and luckily the bone didn't get chipped," the med tech said. "You've had some blood loss, so take it easy for the rest of the day. You should heal up pretty quick. Keep plas-skin on it, keep it clean and immobilized, take a pain med when you need to."

"All right," Marny said—although the part about taking it easy was *so* not going to happen. She and Nyx had to go rescue his sister, which wasn't going to be an easy-mode quest by any stretch.

"If you get a fever or the wound swells up, numbness, redness, or shooting pains down your arm, or any other complications, seek medical attention right away. Here's a sling—wear it for at least a week."

"Okay." Marny sat up a little so the woman could put the sling on her, then signed the tablet the other tech stuck in front of her.

The two med techs conferred with Nyx for a minute, but for some reason the dust motes sparkling in the light from the high windows were way more interesting. She heard the techs heading for the door, their footsteps reverberating almost visibly through the air.

The pain meds were doing strange things to her head. She felt like she was floating a couple feet in the air, as if she was a grav-car. The thought made her laugh.

Nyx came back from seeing the med techs out, and gave her a funny look.

"You doing okay?" he asked.

"Just great. Ready to go find your sister?"

"There's one problem—besides the fact that you're hurt."

"I feel fine." She waved her hand in front of his face. "See?"

"That's the wrong arm." His voice was edged with exasperation. "You need to sober up."

"Your eyes are the color of mist," she said. "But warm, you know, like the clouds just after sunset. Wait—I'm babbling, aren't I?" Somehow, she wasn't too concerned about the fact that her mouth and her brain didn't seem very connected.

"Stay right here," he said, as if he didn't trust her to not move from the couch.

It was a comfortable place, though. She yawned, remembering that Nyx had woken her up painfully early that day.

"Here." He was back, pressing a cold can into her hand. "Haydeez energy drink. Favorite of gamers everywhere."

"That stuff is terrible for you. Corrodes your insides. I got Tam to stop drinking it years ago."

"Fine—but right now it's what you need. Come on, take a sip. I need the real Marny to come back now."

"You're trying to poison me." She sent him a sideways glance.

"I'm not, I promise." He settled next to her on the couch and wrapped his hand around hers, holding the drink in place, then lifting it to her lips. "Please."

"You first."

He took the can from her and drank, then handed it back, his gaze never leaving hers. Damn, the look of entreaty on his face could melt a rock. She set the can to her lips, the metal still warm from his mouth, and sipped. The drink was sweet and cool, and tasted surprisingly good.

"The whole thing," he said, when she lowered the can.

"Let a girl breathe."

Still, she went back to drinking, tipping the can up to get the last sip. A drop slid down the side of her chin. Before she could wipe it she felt his thumb there, gently smoothing the liquid away.

"I'm not some little kid you have to clean up," she said.

"Believe me, I know you aren't."

There was something in his voice, his eyes, that she couldn't read. Or maybe she could, but it confused her. She filed the sensation away to figure out later.

His hand lingered against her face for a moment, and then he slid back, his expression turning businesslike. "Feeling better?"

She frowned. How did she feel, other than totally thrown by his attention? Her body buzzed, weirdly attuned to where he sat next to her. The floaty sensation in her head was dissipating, and her arm throbbed, like a drumbeat turned way, way down. She suspected the volume wasn't going to remain that low, but for now it wasn't a problem.

"Yeah," she said. "So—do we have to go back in-game?"

He tilted his head. "You'd go into Feyland again with me? After what happened, and your claustrophobia and everything?"

"Not that I'd want to, but yes." She'd hate it, of course, but she'd fought that battle for him already, wrestled her fear down and survived.

When Nyx had geared up and gone into the game, she'd been paralyzed. For several minutes she'd just stood there, her sick apprehension at the thought of putting on the sim helmet warring with the fact that he really *did* need her. Despite knowing that his sister had disappeared into the Realm of Faerie, Marny could tell he still wasn't taking the game seriously enough.

Part of the churning in her gut was the intuition that he could get himself in severe trouble—that, in fact, he was heading straight for it. And there was no guarantee the Feyguard would reach him in time, whereas she was right there.

Deal with it, she'd told herself. *You're so damn proud of being strong—so be strong already.*

She needed to force herself to play, despite the clammy sweat breaking out all over her body, and her racing heart that felt like it was going to smash itself to a pulp against her ribcage.

So she'd moved her feet, one step at a time, over to the sim chair. She'd almost choked up completely while she put on the helmet, but clung to the sound of his voice telling her he needed her.

He needed her.

It got a little better once she was interfaced with the FullD equipment and logged on with her Rogue character. Once the nausea passed and she stood in the faerie ring, with the warm air against her face, she felt almost functional.

Then she'd heard the raspy voices of the spriggans gloating over capturing a human. The last vestiges of her panic had fled as she went invisible and hurried to Nyx's rescue.

"Hey." He set his hand over hers, his touch warm. "I'm not asking you to do that. You came in to help me, and got hurt. I owe you for that."

It was true, and she didn't bother denying it.

"So now what?" she asked.

It wasn't a good idea to go back into Feyland, anyway. No doubt the spriggans, plus reinforcements, were camping the entry point, waiting for them to show up again.

"I might have another solution," he said.

"What other solution?" She ignored the fact of his hand over hers, and how it made her feel. "We barely set foot into Feyland before we had to run out again."

"Yeah, but I got these." He reached into his jeans pocket and came out with a handful of leaves.

They were shiny dark green, with lavender undersides. A faint sheen of silver caught the light as he tipped his hand.

"Will they work?" she asked.

"I hope so." He peered down at the foliage. "I've never collected these kinds of leaves before, so I don't know what place they'll conjure up, or where it will take us."

"As long as it's in the Realm somewhere, we can figure it out." And they wouldn't have to use the interface of the game. Which probably wouldn't work anyway, since Emmie hadn't disappeared while playing Feyland. Right?

He stood, then gave her a wary glance. In the dimness of the warehouse he looked suddenly vulnerable.

"Want me to leave while you do your magic spell?" she asked, scooting to the front of the couch. Her arm twinged, but she didn't flinch.

He regarded her a moment, then shook his head. "You're already in deep—we both are. Might as well watch."

With a loose, easy stride, he went to the wall near the back of the warehouse. She couldn't quite see what he did, but it looked like there was a built-in compartment. He moved to the right-hand wall and pressed an invisible button. Sure enough, a small drawer slid out, and he tucked some of the leaves into it.

He repeated the action on the other side, and the remaining leaves went into a secret spot in the floor. Empty-handed, he came back to the couch.

"Now what?" she asked. "Don't you have to wave your hands and chant some mystical words?"

"Nope," he said, settling on the cushions beside her. "We wait a few minutes."

"You missed an opportunity to be dramatic, you know. Some fancy moves and a fake spell could have totally impressed me."

He gave a faint snort. "Yeah—somehow I don't think you're that easily impressed, Marny Fanalua."

She admired him more for knowing that, and not playing things up. His calm confidence was one of his more appealing qualities. That and the way he so clearly cared about his sister. Not to mention—

Oh, dammit, she was *not* falling for Nyx Spenser.

Marny resolutely turned her attention away from him and stared into the dim cavern of the warehouse. She didn't need a boyfriend, and for sure she didn't need a useless attraction to a guy who lived hundreds of miles from her hometown.

But you're both here, in Newpoint, a treacherous part of her whispered.

Maybe so—but they had a job to do, one that couldn't afford any complications like messy feelings.

Something glimmered at the back of the warehouse, a silvery light that slowly brightened. As if it were a holograph coming to life, a forest of pale-barked trees appeared, first the outlines, then filling in until a stand of woods populated the entire back third of the space. Leaves stirred in an unfelt breeze, and dark green bushes with lavender-tinged leaves filled in the spaces between the trees. The last part to appear was a carpet of emerald moss studded with tiny white flowers.

Beside her, Nyx let out a relieved breath. "I wasn't sure it was going to work."

"Well, it did. Good job, magician."

"I dunno—the only magical thing I can do is bring things from the game into the real world. I'd rather be able to cast fireballs and levitate."

"Wouldn't we all." She slid to the edge of the couch. "I guess, now that your forest is back, we go into it."

"Not so fast." He gave her a long, level look.

"If you're about to tell me I'm not in any shape to do this, you can just shut it. We go in—together."

He closed his mouth on whatever he was about to say, and turned his head toward the forest. The trees looked innocent, but beyond them were deeper shadows. Malevolent shadows, waiting for them.

CHAPTER 18

Nyx clenched his fists, then made himself relax. Marny was hurt, and he was pretty sure the med tech's command for her to rest didn't include exploring enchanted forests, fighting magical foes, and helping to rescue his kid sister.

But the determined light in Marny's eyes warned him he couldn't dissuade her from coming, and the fact remained that he needed her help. She'd saved his ass in Feyland, and he was beyond grateful she'd shown up when she did. It had taken a lot for her to overcome her fear and enter the game. His respect for her—already high—was now practically off the charts.

"We'll need to get some supplies together," he said, glancing again at the glimmering trees.

"I need to let my friends know what's happening. And see why they couldn't help us last time." She pulled her messager out of her pocket and began to write awkwardly, using one hand.

He knew better than to offer his help, plus he had the feeling she didn't want him to see who she was contacting. If she wanted assistance, she would ask—it wasn't like Marny to play coy games.

And how do you know what is and isn't like her? He shrugged the question away. In the few short days he'd known her, they'd already shared secrets, not to mention an experience way outside reality. With more to come.

"I'll be in the kitchen," he said, getting off the couch.

They needed to eat, and not just a protein bar and energy drink. It would be stupid to dash off into the woods hungry and unprepared. No matter how impatient he might feel, breakfast came first. Then he'd gather provisions: food, water, weapons. Pain meds. Who knew how long it would take for them to find Emmie?

What if you only wander around in circles, like always? his mind said. He refused to listen. Besides, he had Marny with him this time. She was his secret weapon. Maybe by themselves neither of them had managed to cross into the Realm, but together, he felt they were unstoppable.

Or maybe he was just deluding himself. They'd find out, soon enough.

In the kitchen, he rummaged around in the fridge, assembling the ingredients to make omelets. There was something soothing about chopping up scallions and tomatoes, cracking the eggs and beating them. Little tasks he could concentrate on to keep the edge of panic at bay.

He put water on for coffee, too. Nerves were keeping him wide awake, but he could feel the effects of too little sleep pulling on his brain.

Marny came in just as the toast popped and he was sprinkling grated cheese over the cooked eggs. She snagged the bread out of the toaster, one-handed, and buttered the pieces while he slid their omelets onto plates.

"Smells good," she said, sitting at the table. "I'm starving."

"I still owe you a waffle breakfast." He set her plate in front of her, then settled in the other chair and began to eat. She wasn't the only one who was hungry—the eggs tasted delicious. He was going to have to make seconds, for both of them.

"After we rescue your sister, I'm holding you to that," she said, finishing off her toast.

She sounded so confident. Half of him wanted to lean into her quiet strength, but the other half was beating its fists desperately, about to freak out. *Stop it,* he told himself fiercely.

"Another egg?" he asked. "I think I'll just scramble this time."

"Sounds good. And I'll take a cup of coffee, too. Hey, don't look at me that way." She gave him a faint grin. "It's not poison, like that Haydeez stuff."

"I thought you were a tea drinker." He filled a mug for her, then grabbed the carton of cream and set it on the table.

"Mostly. But coffee has its time and place." She poured a splash of cream into her coffee. "Anyway, I got ahold of my Uncle Zeg. He'll keep trying to get to us in-game."

Nyx heard a trace of doubt in her voice. Her friends hadn't shown up when he was in trouble, after all.

For a second, he thought about asking Durham to come with them—but no. The amount of explanation needed would take too long. It was just himself and Marny.

"Will that work?" He gave the eggs in the pan another stir.

"I thought you said we wouldn't be able to rescue Emmie unless we followed her into the forest."

"Maybe." Marny didn't sound too sure. "Thing is, I'm not a Feyguard, not officially. I can't move across the boundaries between the worlds like they do. So it's possible they can come help—but it might also be entirely up to us. It depends on where they took Emmie."

She trailed off, staring into her mug.

"Meaning?" He dished them up the scrambled eggs, and put more toast on while he was at it.

Marny swallowed. "Meaning if Emmie's in the Dark Court, it's going to be incredibly dangerous to try and get her out."

He *so* did not like the sound of that. "And if she's not there?"

"Then she'll be in the Bright Court—which, frankly, isn't that much better. The fey folk don't play by human rules."

"So either way, my sister's in trouble." He pushed the last few bites of egg around on his plate, appetite gone. "How do you know so much about the Realm of Faerie?"

"My friends, and some research on folklore on the 'net. And most of all, this ancient paper book of Jennet's that's full of information. It's basically become the manual to use when dealing with the fey folk."

"Sounds useful."

She made a face. "It's a start, but that's about it. There's a ton I don't know."

"Well, that's more than I do. You ready?"

"Yeah." Marny got up and rinsed off her plate. "Do you have any cloaks lying around? They could be useful disguises, not to mention help keep us warm."

"Actually, I do." He and Durham had gone through a hard-core cosplay period, and for some reason he'd brought the box of costuming stuff when he'd moved into the warehouse.

Ten minutes later, each of them cloaked and carrying a backpack of supplies, they stood in the warehouse and faced the enchanted forest.

Marny had one of his Shaolin spears—the one not covered in raspberry syrup—and he'd decided on an array of throwing stars, a long knife, and a pair of nunchaku tucked through his belt for good measure. She'd watched him assemble his arsenal from his weapons collection, one brow raised.

"How come you don't play a Fighting Monk in-game?" she'd asked.

"I've been practicing martial arts for over ten years. Doing something different for a change sounded fun."

"Well, I'm glad you're a black belt in real life. I hope those moves work on fey creatures."

"They should."

He refrained from mentioning he was actually a third-degree black belt. No point in boasting. Either his skills would be up for the task, or they wouldn't.

They'd find out soon enough. He glanced at Marny standing beside him, her face partially shadowed by the hood of her cloak. The curve of her cheek was illuminated by the soft silver light coming from the forest, and her expression was determined.

"You'll tell me if you need a rest," he said.

"That's what we packed Haydeez for." She sent him a wry look. "I don't intend to slow us down."

"Yeah, well, you falling over would do that, so don't push

yourself too hard. You're recovering from a stab wound, remember?"

"I've got my trusty walking stick." She lifted the spear a few inches.

He'd shown her a couple moves, though she didn't have a lot of power one-handed. Still, she could poke things, and use the haft for support and balance.

"Ready?" he asked.

"Yes." The clarity in her voice steadied him.

He gave the quiet warehouse one last glance, then strode into the forest. The moss cushioned his steps, and he could barely hear Marny following close behind. Overhead, the silvery leaves stirred. It seemed to be the same enchanted woods as ever—which was a bad thing if it meant they'd be stuck in a bubble, going around in circles.

And after several minutes, he felt like that was exactly what they were doing. Marny didn't say anything, but her expression grew more and more serious.

Finally, Nyx stopped. Through the trees, he could just glimpse the inside of the warehouse—the silent dance floor, the empty bar.

"This isn't working," he said, despair rising up from his belly.

"It has to." She sounded fierce. "If a creature could come out, then we can go in. We've got to keep trying."

Her words nudged something in his brain, a memory of his early days when he first conjured up the forest...

"Okay," he said. "Maybe there's one thing I could try."

It was the only thing he could think of. Not letting himself dwell on what would happen if it didn't work, Nyx reached into his pack and rummaged through his provisions. Careful to avoid the edges of his extra shuriken, he pulled out a protein bar.

"Ah," Marny said, like she knew exactly what he was doing.

He went a few more paces into the forest.

"Um, hello," he called, breaking off a piece of bar and setting it on the velvet-green moss. "Want to come out for a treat?"

He straightened and backed up a step, and Marny waited silently beside him, her expression wary.

A shiver of motion, deep in the forest. *Please, don't be spriggans.*

The bushes rustled, closer now, and he loosened his knife in its sheath. Just in case. From the corner of his eye he saw Marny take a tighter grip on her spear. Whatever was approaching was almost upon them.

A golden blur darted from the shadows and halted a pace in front of him. Nyx sent up a quick prayer of gratitude. It was the mouselike creature he'd seen the very first time the forest had appeared in his bedroom.

"Hey, guy," he said softly. "Sorry I don't have more pizza crusts—but you're welcome to this protein bar."

The creature tilted its head, like it was listening, then snatched up the hunk of bar and devoured it in two bites.

"Ask it to lead us into the Realm," Marny said.

Nyx nodded, then reached forward and set down another piece of protein bar, keeping his movements slow and careful.

"Happy to give you more of this, if you'll show us the way into the Realm of Faerie," he said.

With a quiet squeak, the creature darted forward and

grabbed the food, munching it down so quickly Nyx didn't even see its mouth move.

"I hope that's a yes," Marny said.

The golden mouse turned and whisked away, disappearing back into the underbrush. It didn't come out again. Dammit.

"Well," he said, after waiting what felt like an endless few minutes. "I guess that's as good a way as any." He gestured in the direction the creature had disappeared.

"Fair enough," Marny said.

They tromped silently for a while, the scenery unchanging, and he kicked himself for not marking the trees where they first came in. This was a stupid plan, and he was an idiot to ever believe it could work.

"Look," Marny said, nodding to their left.

The little creature sat under a purple-edged shrub, watching them with curious, intelligent eyes. Keeping his gaze on it, Nyx broke another piece off the bar and held it out.

Instead of running up to get it, the golden mouse turned and scampered under the bushes. Nyx gave Marny a questioning look, and she nodded. Looked like they were playing follow-the-mouse.

They pushed through the green-leaved bushes, and he kept an eye out for flashes of bright fur. Just when he thought they'd lost their guide, the creature would reappear and cock its head, as if impatient with their slow mortal feet.

"Hey," Marny said after a while. "The forest has changed."

He'd been so intent on following the little mouse that he hadn't noticed, but now he saw that the trees had gotten taller, the sky a brighter blue overhead. Pink and purple flowers dotted the bushes, and orange butterflies darted in and out of shafts of sunlight.

The air smelled different, too, green and moist. A bird sang nearby, a liquid trill of notes ascending.

"Did we do it?" he asked.

"I think so, thanks to your little friend."

Nyx quickly unwrapped the rest of the bar, then looked around for the mouse. "Where'd it go?"

They scanned the bushes, and then Marny lifted her head, a smile curving the corners of her mouth. "There."

The golden creature had sprouted feathery dark blue wings and was hovering in a small clearing just ahead. Its fur glinted in the sun and there was a look of faint amusement on its pointed face.

Nyx stepped forward and held out the protein bar.

"Tha—"

"Your help is much appreciated," Marny interrupted. In a low voice she said to him, "You're not supposed to thank faeries. It's a thing."

"Okay." He made the creature a little bow, then held up the bar again. "Please accept this token of our, um..."

The creature regarded him from its bright eyes, then swooped over. It took the bar between its tiny paws, then bent its head. He felt the soft brush of its fur and then a sharp sting that made him jump back.

"Hey! It bit me." He held up his hand. A single drop of blood welled up on his index finger.

The flying mouse gave a high trill, like it was laughing, then beat its wings. Up it went, ascending almost to the treetops. Nyx squinted against the light, but the creature was gone.

"Be careful with that." Marny nodded at his finger. "Make sure you don't smear any blood around."

He nodded and stuck his finger in his mouth, sucking the blood away. The metal tang quickly faded.

"Why'd it do that?" he asked, inspecting his finger. The bleeding had stopped.

"Because it's a faerie. They're completely unpredictable. Don't think they're your friends. And don't necessarily assume they're your enemies, either."

"Except mostly they are."

"Yeah. Mostly." There was something in her voice that made him think she spoke from experience. "Anyway, I'd say we made it into the Realm."

He nodded, a sudden cold fear gripping him. They had managed to enter the Realm of Faerie—but how were they supposed to get out again?

CHAPTER 19

Nyx looked over Marny, but didn't voice his fear.

The Realm wasn't going to conveniently dissipate around them like one of his bubble creations once they rescued his sister, but somehow they'd find a way out. Those Feyguard friends of Marny's would help, right?

In the meantime, they were, once again, stranded in a magical forest.

"Now what?" He glanced around, but the golden mouse seemed to have disappeared for good. "I think we lost our guide."

"Hmm." Marny met his gaze, her brown eyes full of the usual determination. "You said your sister rode off on the back of a white stag?"

"According to her friend, yeah."

"That doesn't sound like something out of the Dark Court." She turned in a slow circle, peering into the trees, then stopped and tipped her spear forward. "I say we head over there, where the light is stronger. And if Emmie isn't in the Bright Court... Well, we can deal with that later."

"Tackle the easier enemy first." He nodded. "So, we just keep going toward the sunshine?"

"I think." Marny took a tighter grip on the haft of her spear. "And hope we don't have to do too much fighting along the way."

Nyx settled his pack and began picking a path through the bushes, careful to do as little damage as possible. Marny followed, her steps as vigilant as his. Once again, her light-footedness struck him, especially with one arm bound up in a sling.

"Have you had dance or martial arts training?" he asked. "You move well."

"My grandma taught me the Taualuga when I was young," she said. "That was pretty intense, even though I never had to perform it."

"What's that?"

"A traditional ceremonial dance. My family's Samoan."

"Cool." He'd figured it was something like that. "Do you visit the islands regularly?"

She let out a snort. "The only one who can afford that is Grandma Harmony. Newpoint is the farthest I've ever been from my hometown."

He didn't know whether to offer his commiserations or congratulations, so he just kept quiet. They walked silently for a bit, and he noted the trees were thinning out, showing glimpses of the sky beyond.

"Do you hear that?" Marny asked.

He paused. Barely audible beneath the hushing of the wind in the leaves was the sound of running water.

"A river, maybe?" he said.

She nodded. "That reminds me—we shouldn't eat or drink anything while we're in here, no matter how good it looks. Only the food we brought, otherwise we could end up trapped in the Realm of Faerie for years."

"Right." He dimly recalled some old tales about the negative consequences of eating food in magical lands.

The forest changed, the pale-trunked trees turning to shorter willows, the flowers now trumpetlike yellow bells on fleshy stalks. The noise of running water was loud. Nyx pushed through a stand of willows, and only his quick reflexes kept him from tumbling into a clear, rushing river.

It was wider across than they could jump. Glancing up and down the bank, he saw no sign of a bridge spanning the water.

"Maybe we can follow it downstream," Marny said, coming up beside him. "Surely it leads somewhere."

"Looks fairly deep." He peered at the current. "If the bank gets impassable, I'm not sure we can wade it."

"I'm not sure we'd want to. All kinds of creatures could be living in there."

"Um, yeah." He took a step back. "I think I see one now."

Something was rising in the middle of the stream—a head topped by swirling green hair. Two bulbous eyes peered above the water, regarding them the way a frog looks at a fly.

"Tasty morsels, come a little closer," the creature said in a burbling voice. It began humming, a wordless tune that floated and twined like weeds in the current.

"Water hag," Marny said in low voice. "Time to go."

She moved into the willows, but Nyx stood there, reluctant to turn around. He imagined he could feel clammy hands grasping him, pulling him down...

"Come on." Marny grabbed his arm.

He blinked, his thoughts slow and sludgy. Wouldn't the water feel cool and nice, the mud so silky between his toes?

Without meaning to, he moved nearer to the river.

"Not okay." Marny pulled at him, but he turned his wrist and broke her grasp.

The creature smiled and drifted closer. One moment she was a green-haired hag, and the next she transformed into a beautiful maiden with promises in her eyes.

"Dammit. Come *on*. I can't drag you out of here one-handed." Marny's voice buzzed annoyingly in his ears. He swatted the air, trying to drive it away.

The water maiden's song almost resolved into words. If he stayed a little longer he would hear them. He would *understand*.

"Ow!" A sharp pain in his back made him whirl.

Marny stood there, pointing the spear at him. Her eyes shifted to the left.

"Duck," she cried.

He did, and she jabbed awkwardly at the hideous, green-slimed creature emerging from the river.

"Arghh," the hag cried. "What cold iron befouls the air?"

"The kind that will hurt you," Marny said. "Now, get away."

The creature grabbed the haft of the spear, keeping the point from touching her. With her other hand she reached toward Nyx. His vision flickered, the hag strobing from lovely to ugly with every blink.

It was too freaky. He bounded to his feet and pulled his knife out.

"Begone!" He shook the point at her.

"We mean it." Marny tugged at the spear.

"Iron, fly," the water hag screeched. "Say goodbye, up and down, then you drown!"

On the last word, she ripped the spear from Marny's grasp and swung it hard at Nyx. He got his arm up for a block and the sudden impact knocked the knife from his hand. It tumbled through the air, glinting, then hit the water with a splash and disappeared.

"Run!" Marny cried, already scrambling away.

Nyx turned and bolted through the willows, mourning the loss of their best weapons. But no way was he going after the creature for his spear, or diving into the river to get his knife. They'd just have to keep going with what they had left. He shot a look over his shoulder.

The water hag had transformed to a maiden again, her long blonde hair shading down to green at the tips.

"Alas!" She gave him a beseeching look from eyes like clear blue pools, and held out her arms. "All I beg is but a single kiss from your lips."

"That would be a no." Nyx turned his back on the creature and followed Marny.

The smell of crushed willows filled the air, as behind him the water hag sobbed and pleaded. Marny reached back and caught his hand, like she was worried he planned to turn around. No chance of that—he'd seen the sharp tips of the creature's teeth and knew all she wanted him for was lunch.

Together, they plowed back under the trees.

"It's safe," Marny said, stopping and sucking in a breath. "Pretty sure the hag can't come this far out of the water."

"If you say so." He squeezed her hand, then let go. "Are you all right? Sling holding up?"

"Well enough. Sorry about poking you back there."

"It had to be done." He shivered at the memory of how easily the water hag had cast her spell over him. "How come you weren't affected?"

"I have some protection against faerie glamour."

He opened his mouth to ask, and she shook her head.

"It's a long story." She glanced around at the quiet forest. "And not one I want overheard. When we get out of here, I'll tell you."

"You better."

There were a lot of things he wanted to hear from Marny, and not all of them had to do with the obvious adventures she'd had dealing with the fey folk. She was one of the most interesting people he'd ever met.

"So much for following the stream," she said. "I guess we keep going through the woods."

He was about to reply, then held up his hand. Something deep in the forest crashed through the underbrush. The ground vibrated with the sound of hoofbeats.

"Crap." He glanced around, looking for a hiding place. A nearby cluster of bushes had branches that swept the ground. "We can take cover under there."

Marny made a face, but hurried over to the shrubbery. "I wish we were here as our in-game characters. Sure would be nice to turn invisible about now."

"We'll have to do the best we can as ourselves." He pulled a few of the branches aside, careful not to break them.

Marny got down on all fours—well, three, since she couldn't use one arm—and started wriggling into the small hollow at the base of the bushes.

The sling and her pack made her awkward, and he tried not to urge her to hurry up as the sound of approaching riders grew near. Just when he was about to give her a push, she pulled her legs in. A heartbeat later he slid in after her, practically ending up in her lap.

Her body was softness laid over solidity. The line of her thigh and hip and arm pressed against him, but he could feel the strength under her curves. Her lips were full, and for a second he wondered how it would feel to kiss her.

"Sorry it's so tight in here," she whispered, holding his gaze.

He shot her a quick smile to show it was fine, then pushed all thoughts of kissing out of his mind. This was *so* not the time.

The sound of hooves pounded the earth outside their hiding place, and they both stilled.

To his dismay, the hoofbeats slowed. The cold chill on the back of his neck told him that he and Marny were about to be discovered.

CHAPTER 20

Marny watched from between the overlapping leaves as the riders approached. Through the foliage she glimpsed two horses bearing armored figures. One wore silver mail, the other golden.

Her breath caught. Surely the Bright King himself wouldn't be out riding around the forest looking for them? For the first time in a long while she wished she were smaller, so that she could slip further back into the concealing shrubbery.

"The scent of humans is strong here," a cold voice said. "They must be nearby."

With a chiming of bells, one of the riders dismounted. His armor shone pale in the light, and the glimpse she caught of his face showed high cheekbones and green eyes slitted like a cat's. His long, dark hair fell in a single braid down his back, and a deadly looking sword hung at his side.

"There was a commotion by the water," he said. "Shall I investigate, Bright Lance?"

"Do so. I will search this portion of the forest. Should you discover the humans, call out, and I shall do the same. We will present these mortal pests to our liege lord in good time."

"As you say." The silver-armored faerie turned and led his mount toward the stream.

The remaining rider turned in a slow circle, sunlight gleaming off his golden-hued armor. Then, excruciatingly slowly, he urged his mount to walk directly toward their hiding place.

Beside her, she felt Nyx tense. He wasn't planning to fight, was he? But what else could they do? She didn't think they could outrun a mounted faerie knight, especially when he had magic at his disposal.

The horse halted in front of their bush, and the rider dismounted. Marny swallowed, her spit sour with fear.

The Bright Lance's gauntlets glinted as he reached to pull aside the branches of their shelter. Nyx shifted forward, his expression fierce.

Something pulled her from behind, a sudden tug as the air gave way to emptiness. With a stifled yelp, she fell backward. A confused blur of leaves and branches, the smell of freshly turned soil, and then she landed with a thump on hard-packed earth. Her backpack cushioned her fall, but her arm twinged sharply and she gritted her teeth against the pain.

Nyx tumbled on top of her, and there was a confused moment as they sorted themselves out. By the time they sat facing each other in the dim light, her wound was hurting in earnest.

"Where are we?" he asked. "And where's that faerie guy?"

Marny glanced around the earthen hollow, which appeared

to be a shallow cave. Daylight filtered in from an opening between two raised stones, with a third laid across the top, forming a small doorway. It looked big enough for her to wriggle through. Probably.

"No idea about where," she said. "And I don't think the knight followed us."

"Yet. I have the feeling he's not going to give up."

Marny had to agree—this was a temporary reprieve. She was about to suggest they leave, when the far side of their small shelter began to glow, a sphere of brightness forming there. The strength of a candle flame at first, the light grew more intense until she had to squint. Inside the sphere a fey creature capered.

"Company," Nyx said, rising to a half-crouch.

Marny reached for her knife, setting her fingers on the handle.

"Foolish mortals," a high-pitched, familiar voice said. "You are safe for the moment, but do you truly think you can stumble undetected about the Realm?"

"Puck?" Marny raised her hand to shade her eyes.

The glowing sphere faded, leaving behind a grinning sprite sitting cross-legged in the air. His tattered tunic was stitched with leaves, and he had feathers woven into his hair.

"Indeed, Mistress Marny." Puck bounced up and made her an elaborate bow. "Pray, introduce me to your companion."

She hesitated. Jennet had told her that names held power in the Realm of Faerie. But Puck already knew all the Feyguard by name, and besides, "Nyx" wasn't an actual birth name, but a nickname. It was probably safe enough to make the introduction.

"Puck, this is my friend, Nyx," she said.

"Indeed." By the twinkle in his eye, she suspected the sprite had known that, and had tested her in some way. "Well met, Master Nyx. Tell me, what brings you two mortals faring so far?"

"We're looking for my sister," Nyx said, a challenge in his voice. "Have you seen her? And how come you know Marny?"

"Questions upon questions." Puck turned a lazy somersault in the middle of the air. "What will you give for the answers, I wonder?"

Right—there was always a catch where the fey folk were concerned. However, since she and Nyx had actually come into the Realm as their physical selves, with items from the real world, maybe they had something to bargain with.

She dug in her jeans pocket. A tissue, a mint wrapper, some lint. Ah, a dollar coin. They weren't made with iron, were they? She pulled it out.

The metal gleamed softly in the palm of her hand, the embossed symbol and numbers on it looking suddenly strange and foreign.

"How about this?" she asked.

Nyx shot her a glance, as if he thought info about his sister was worth way more than a dollar. Which, of course, it was—except that anything from the mortal world was special here.

"It's like your crossover leaves," she said to him.

She hoped that any power the coin had in the Realm wouldn't ultimately prove dangerous to humans.

His expression cleared. "How about it, Puck? What can you tell us?"

The sprite flew over and flicked the coin with his fingernail. It let out a ping, and Puck nodded, apparently satisfied.

"You shall find what you seek in the Bright Court," he said, plucking the dollar from Marny's hand.

"Hey, not so fast." She swiped at it, but Puck swooped away, laughing.

She'd look dumb trying to chase him around in the little cave, so she settled for scowling and settling back onto the dirt floor.

"The Bright Court," Nyx said. "How do we get there?"

"You are well on the way," Puck said. "Your intent aligns with the wishes of the Bright King, allowing me to transport you to this passage."

"Why help us?" Marny asked. She knew better than to take the sprite's assistance at face value. The fey folk always had an ulterior motive. If only she knew what Puck's was. "I mean, those guys after us were the king's guards or something, right? Maybe we should have let them capture us and take us to the court, if that's where Nyx's sister is."

"We didn't know that at the time," Nyx pointed out.

"Yeah, but why not let us get taken?" She gave the sprite a narrow-eyed look. Maybe Nyx had missed the fact that Puck hadn't actually said Emmie was in the Bright Court, but she hadn't.

"Should you hope to be successful, you must bargain with the king from a position of strength," the sprite said. "Captives in his court have little recourse."

"So, you want us to rescue her?" Marny asked.

"The balance must be restored," the sprite said.

Which was another of his maddening non-answers.

"We appreciate the help," Nyx said. "But it would be nice to have a little more to go on."

"You are fortunate to have even this much assistance," Puck said, cocking his head to one side. "I have told you everything you need to know, and more."

"Fine," Marny said, shifting to find a more comfortable position on the packed dirt floor. "We get to the Bright Court, find what we're looking for, and make a bargain with the king. Do I have that right?"

Puck waved one hand through the air, leaving a glittering trail. When he smiled, his teeth glowed in the light. "Indeed, Mistress Marny, you do."

Unfortunate. Bargaining with the fey folk was always a bad idea—but how else could they get Emmie out of the Realm of Faerie?

Speaking of which...

"Do you happen to know a quick escape spell we could use?" she asked Puck. "We'll pay you for it."

Nyx nodded, clearly sharing her thought that once they got his sister they'd need to leave immediately. It wasn't a good idea for humans to hang around in the courts of the fey.

Puck tilted his head and screwed up his face, making his chin look even more pointed.

"Perhaps," he said. "But no mortal escapes unscathed from the Realm of Faerie. Are you willing to pay the price?"

"If that's our only ticket out of here, then yes," Nyx said.

Marny frowned—but really, what choice did they have?

"Mistress Marny?" Puck turned his bright eyes on her.

"What kind of price are we talking about?"

She thought of her friends, who bore their own scars from

the realm. Jennet had nearly died. Tam had been willing to sacrifice himself to save her, and had almost lost his brother to the Dark Court, too. Roy's heart had been broken and she still wasn't sure he'd recover fully, despite the fact that he could see Brea, the girl he'd fallen in love with, once a month.

But it was far too late to choose any other path. Marny was here with Nyx because his sister needed rescuing. Even though she wasn't a Feyguard, she knew what was right. What had to be done.

Puck nodded, as if he could hear her thoughts. "You have a brave soul, Mistress Marny. Sometimes, the price is not something taken away, but accepting a new burden. I cannot tell you what it might be."

"Why not?" Nyx demanded. "I'm not a fan of all this vague talk."

The sprite slowly rose into the air and floated above their heads, just below the earthen ceiling. His next words carried an edge of darkness Marny had never heard in Puck's voice before.

"When you brush up against magic, the path of your life is changed. I have neither the skill nor the desire to peer deeply into Fate's web to see what awaits you. But you are here, two mortals in the Realm of Faerie, and that will mark you both. Forever."

He gestured, his long fingers scribing runes into the air. The symbols hung there, first glowing white, then shading to gold, then to deepest indigo. The sound of chimes filled the small cave. Despite herself, Marny scooted a bit closer to Nyx, grateful for his warmth. He reached out and set his hand on her knee.

The runes dissolved into a rain of glitter, falling over them.

It felt like cold droplets, like fire, like regret. Something flared in Marny's injured arm, and she inhaled sharply.

"What?" Nyx asked, his eyes concerned.

"I have healed Mistress Marny of the injury she sustained from the spriggan guard," Puck said.

He drifted down to settle cross-legged before them. Although there was still a touch of purple glow in his hair, his grin was the same as ever.

"What else?" She peered closely at the sprite.

"Imbued you both with the magic to leave the Realm. In order to trigger the spell, I need a lock of hair from each of you, a bit of mortal food, and something you wear about your person."

"Sounds creepy," Nyx said.

Puck simply shrugged.

"All magic is creepy," Marny said. "But what else can we do?"

She dug through her sack and pulled out a protein bar. For a second, the image of Korrigan flashed before her eyes—the hideous changeling creature she had volunteered to babysit, and ended up strangely fond of.

"You are not without allies in the Realm," Puck said, again seeming to read her mind.

"I thought Korr was a creature of the Dark Court," she said. "Aren't we headed into the Bright?"

The sprite gave her a conspiratorial wink as he took the protein bar. "Who knows?"

She rolled her eyes. There was no getting straight intel from Puck.

Nyx fiddled with something at his neck, then offered Puck a cord with a Chinese character hanging from it.

"Here," he said. "I basically never take this off. Will it do?"

"Indeed." Puck grabbed the cord and held it up, studying the symbol.

"What's the character mean?" Marny asked.

"Luck." Nyx gave her a sideways smile. "Appropriate enough, given the circumstances."

They'd need more than just luck, of course. Magic, and smarts, and certainly his fighting skills into the bargain. She was not looking forward to whatever came next.

Marny pulled off her sling, glad to find the movement didn't hurt. She stretched her arm back and forth a few times, but Puck had spoken the truth.

"I don't suppose you'd take this?" She indicated the useless sling.

Puck's response was a sniff of disdain.

"Okay then." She held her now-healed arm out to Nyx. "Could you untie my bracelet?"

It had been a gift from Grandma Harmony, the last time she'd gone to Samoa. Marny suspected the woven band decorated with seashells had been a cheap tourist souvenir, but she'd still loved it.

Nyx's nimble fingers made short work of the knot, and Marny slipped the bracelet off and handed it to Puck.

Another sacrifice. Another tiny scar.

"Now, your hair," the sprite said.

"You might want to shield yourself," she told Puck. "Cold iron, coming right up."

"Your warning is timely." He tucked their jewelry away, then flicked his fingers.

A crystalline cocoon folded about him, and he nodded to Marny. She pulled the knife from her calf sheath and the sprite flinched a bit, but other than that seemed fine.

"So," Nyx said. "I notice you've got a knife. Know how to use it?"

"Yes, my uncle insisted on it. Here, bend your head and I'll get some of your hair."

He didn't seem at all nervous about letting her wield a blade right by his neck. Still, she was extra careful as she lifted a strand from the back of his head and neatly sheared it off.

"I think it won't be too noticeable," she said, handing him the lock.

"No worries. It'll grow back, and I'm not one of those super-vain guys."

"Only medium-vain?" She sent him a wry smile to take the sting out of her words.

He merely raised an eyebrow, which, dammit, made him even cuter. Trying to ignore the pull in her stomach when she looked at him, she grabbed a piece of her own hair from behind her ear and sliced it off. Compared to his smooth strand, her hair seemed wild and frizzy.

As soon as she slipped her knife back into its sheath, Puck dissolved the crystal shield around him. Nyx handed his hair to the sprite, but Marny hesitated.

"Are you sure you need it?" she asked. "And it's not going to be used to harm us in any way?"

There had been some issue with Jennet having to give the

Bright King a lock of her golden hair, which later he'd used to summon her to the Realm. Marny wanted no part of that.

Puck gave her a serious look, his face suddenly wizened and old. "On the moon and stars, the sun and rain, I swear that the trinkets I am about to craft cannot be twisted to do harm to either yourself or Master Nyx."

That was reassuring, as far as fey promises went.

Puck waved his hand and two wooden bowls appeared, so finely crafted they almost seemed made of porcelain. One was paler than the other, with a wavy grain. Puck held this bowl out to Marny, and she dropped her hair in.

Her bracelet joined it, and then he crumbled a bit of the protein bar into the mix. When he was done he set the bowl to one side, where it hung motionless in the air, then used the second bowl for Nyx's items.

"Now I create the spell." Puck handed her back the unused portion of the bar. "Speak not while I perform this magic."

"Got it," Nyx said, and Marny nodded her agreement.

The sprite placed Nyx's bowl in the air beside hers. From somewhere he produced a thin, thorny stick that looked like a rose stem without the flower. He snapped it in half and added it to the bowls, then with a touch of his fingers sent them spinning.

"Widdershins turn, a lock and a key," he chanted. "These mortals return to their world in safety. Ash and oak, sup and briar, the portal opens into fire."

Bright golden-green light flared up from the bowls. The light flickered in the cave, and for a second Marny saw an arched doorway outlined against the back wall.

As quickly as it had appeared, the brilliance faded. She blinked, spots of fire imprinted on her retinas.

"Did it work?" Nyx leaned forward to peer into his bowl.

"Indeed." Puck lifted the cord. "Your talisman is complete."

The Chinese character for luck had been replaced by a twining Celtic symbol fashioned of wood and metal. It gleamed softly, flickering green and gold around the edges.

"Wear these until the proper time." Puck handed the necklace to Nyx, then plucked up Marny's bracelet and gave it to her.

The seashells had been turned to the same twisty Celtic talisman as Nyx's charm. Despite a lingering glow, the bracelet was cool in her hands.

"What *is* the proper time?" Nyx asked, slipping the cord over his head.

"And are these things safe to wear?" she added, though mostly just to annoy Puck.

At Nyx's gesture, she held out her wrist and he fastened her bracelet back on. It struck her how in accord they were, both of them understanding what needed to be done without having to talk about it. It was comfortable and a little scary all at once.

She wasn't sure if their connection—and there was one, she couldn't deny it any longer—was a threat to her self-sufficiency. While they were in the Realm of Faerie, though, it was definitely a good thing that they were on the same screen.

"Best if you tuck the trinkets out of sight," Puck said. "They will remain quiescent until you need to return to the mortal world. Then throw them into the fire, and you will be transported home."

Marny shot the sprite a look. "One problem. What fire?"

"Another problem," Nyx said. "What about my sister?"

Puck let out an exasperated sigh. "You mortals are so prosaic. There is always a fire at court—Bright or Dark, regardless. Anything you are holding fast to will be taken with you when you cross between the worlds."

"So, find my sister, grab her, throw the trinkets in the fire," Nyx said.

"It sounds simple," Marny said. "But it won't be that easy. These things never are."

"Hey, I'm a gamer. I know my boss fights. There'll be adds and unexpected twists."

"The Realm of Faerie is no game," Puck reminded him. "But the metaphor is apt enough."

The faint sound of silver bells drifted on the wind, and the sprite glanced up at the stone-enclosed opening of their hideaway.

"I must depart," he said. "Fare well, adventurers. I wish you luck upon your quest."

He sprang into a handstand, then tumbled into a flip and was gone.

"Wait—" Nyx said, but it was too late. He turned to Marny, frustration clear in his gray eyes.

"That is so like Puck," Marny said. "Abandoning us to our own devices."

"I'll take your word for it," Nyx said. "Now what?"

The thud of fast-approaching hoofbeats vibrated though the little cave, and Marny felt her pulse accelerate in response. The faerie guard had found them again.

"Now," she said, "we've got trouble."

CHAPTER 21

The sound of silver bells drifted into their small shelter. Marny glanced at the light filtering through the stone-capped opening—their only escape route. Too late now. They were trapped.

"Ah, crap." Nyx flexed his fingers and rose into a fighting stance. "Get your knife out."

Marny reached for her blade, but hesitated. Could the two of them really defeat the Bright Lance and his companion?

She glanced around the shallow cave. They could stand and fight—which, considering they were mere humans against armored magical faeries, could go badly—or they could get the hell out. Hadn't Puck said this was the beginning of a passageway? She'd even seen the outline of a door...

"One sec." She scooped up her sack and went to the back wall.

Moving on instinct, she lifted her wrist and touched her enchanted bracelet to the granite. A green-gold light flickered over the surface of the stone, illuminating the edges of the arched doorway she had glimpsed earlier.

Quickly, Nyx joined her and pressed his talisman against the rock. The light from the entrance to their cave dimmed as a body blocked it. *Come on, open.*

With a single, clear chime, the door swung wide. Marny ducked through, Nyx right behind her.

The second they were over the threshold, the passageway thudded shut, cutting off the Bright Lance's shout of rage. That had been close.

The passage was dark and cool. She strained her eyes, searching for any glimmer of light, but saw nothing. The sound of her breathing grew loud, louder. She tried to quiet it, but claustrophobia pressed in from all sides. She could feel the first turn of panic screwing into her chest.

"Hey." Nyx found her hand unerringly in the darkness, and squeezed. "It's okay."

"Dammit." Her voice was tight.

"One sec. I need both my hands."

He guided her fingers up to his shoulder, and she tried not to clutch at him, grateful beyond words that he hadn't just let go and left her alone in the dark. She heard him rummaging through his sack, the clink of plasmetal. A moment later he clicked on a flashlight, and her knees went soft with relief.

The small white light showed they were standing at one end of a passage hewn from the rock. Bits of mica glittered in the stone, and the air smelled of dampness and roots.

Thankfully the tunnel was big enough for them to stand in. She didn't know if she'd be able to hold it together if they had to crawl through the earth, tons of soil and rock overhead, waiting to collapse and smother the life from them...

Stop it. She squeezed her eyes shut for a second, forcing back the urge to vomit. Nyx took her hand again, and that helped. Though she hated him seeing her weakness.

"I'll lead," he said.

She nodded, not trusting her voice. As he stepped forward, she concentrated on the warmth of his hand in hers, the way his amber hair curled under at the back of his neck. When the panic threatened again, she began counting their steps. She was concentrating so hard on not freaking out, she didn't notice that Nyx had stopped until she ran into him.

"Sorry," she said, glancing up. "Whoa."

The tunnel opened into a misty hallway full of arched openings running along one side. Ornate lamps hung suspended on golden chains, shedding a soft radiance that made Nyx's flashlight look harsh in comparison. Even as she noted the contrast, he shut his light off.

"This is interesting," he said.

Marny took a deep breath, steadier now that there was light and space ahead.

Behind them, from the darkness of the stone tunnel, came a thud. How long would it be before the Bright Lance got the door open?

She traded a glance with Nyx, and they hurried forward.

The first archway they passed showed a manicured lawn stretching to the edge of a lake. A stone castle rose above the water, blue pennants flying in the breeze.

The next doorway opened onto a garish scene where a

multi-armed blue deity threw marigolds at a horde of screaming demons. Marny shuddered and picked up her pace.

At the third arch, she paused.

"*What*?" A sense of incredulity washed over her.

Mr. von Coburg stood at the head of a meeting table where the Social Interfaces Design team sat, looking unhappy.

"It's unfortunate your intern chose not to come to work today," the CEO said. "Especially as this progress meeting is mandatory."

"I'm sure there's a misunderstanding," Angie said, and Ser Jellicoe nodded his agreement. "Maybe she's sick, or had an accident."

"I shall investigate," Madame Fontaine said, her voice cold. "Now, about the newest research..."

"Hey, we have to go." Nyx tugged at Marny's arm.

"But I'm missing a crucial meeting." Damn. Was she going to lose her internship over this? Dismay pressed like a fist into her stomach. "It's Monday morning already in the real world."

"How can that happen?" There was an edge of panic in Nyx's voice.

"Time moves differently in the Realm. At least, according to my friends, and Jennet's book of lore."

If she stepped through that archway, would she magically arrive at Intertech in time to salvage her job?

She glanced at Nyx and immediately ditched the idea. They were in this together, and she'd promised she'd help. Whatever the consequences, she wasn't the kind of person who broke her word. Especially since she had the feeling Nyx wouldn't be able to rescue his sister without her.

Two mortal souls trapped in the Realm of Faerie, versus her future.

It was a crappy choice, but easy enough to make.

"Come on." Marny shot one last glance at the meeting room, then made herself walk past.

There was no way she could explain why she hadn't shown up at work. She could feel her internship, and everything that it represented, slipping away.

Living at home for years and working a minimum-wage job, coming right up. She swallowed the salty taste of failure.

"Are you sure?" Nyx asked. Clearly he could tell it was important.

"I'm not abandoning you. And I'm not arguing about it. Your sister is here somewhere, so let's go find her."

That shut him up. Looking grim, he strode down the hall beside her.

As they passed the next opening, Marny glimpsed a shining expanse of lake with mountains rising at the far horizon. A graceful boat lay upon the waters, manned by a hooded figure who began to turn as if sensing their presence.

A chill running down her spine, Marny quickened her pace. She held her breath until they were safely past that archway.

The one beyond opened onto a midnight forest, the light of a purple bonfire glimmering between the trees. As they drew even with the door, a long, eerie howl sounded, and she shivered. Their choices seemed to be getting worse.

"Let's not go in there," Nyx said.

She nodded. By then they were practically running. She had the cold suspicion they'd just passed the Dark Court.

But if that had been the Dark Court, could the light spilling from the opening ahead be the Bright one?

“There they are!” a voice called.

Marny looked over her shoulder to see the Bright Lance appear out of the mist at the end of the corridor. He drew his sword and charged toward them.

“I think this next doorway is the last one,” Nyx said.

“Then wherever it leads, we’re going in.”

No way did she want to go back to any of the other portals, except maybe the very first one—but that would take them right into the arms of the faerie guard.

They sprinted for the opening. The air was filled with radiance, and she glimpsed trees of gold and silver with shining leaves. Music lilted through the grove and glowing pixies darted among the trees, their light glinting off flowers made of garnets and sapphires, topaz and amethyst.

This was it. It perfectly matched the description in Jennet’s book.

“Ready?” Nyx asked, grabbing her hand.

She squeezed in answer, and together they dashed over the threshold into the heart of the Bright Court.

CHAPTER 22

Although Nyx had explored his own enchanted woods plenty of times, the forest of the Bright Court held so much magic he *felt* it, like a current running over his skin.

He pressed Marny's hand, then let go so he'd be ready to act at a moment's notice. Herb-scented air wafted around them, and before his eyes the metallic trees shifted, creating a wide pathway leading toward a clearing.

He glanced at Marny. She seemed nervous, but strong. There wasn't anyone else he'd rather have at his side.

Together, they strode forward. His heartbeat thumped in his chest, but he stayed light on his feet, primed to attack or defend as necessary.

As they approached the clearing, Nyx blinked at the sight of the creatures gathered there: ethereal maidens with gossamer wings and scary-looking eyes, stubby gnomes wearing pointed hats, fur-covered things with human faces and hands, tall twiggy creatures armed with pointy spears—including the spriggan called Pinebough.

Some of them were dancing, some feasted at long tables filled with food and drink, some reclined on couches of velvet moss.

In the very center rose a dais covered in glimmering grasses. Upon the dais stood a throne made of gold, and upon that throne sat the Bright King. His armor shone like the sun, and a circlet of dazzling light sat upon his head. Pointed ears emerged from his long, pale hair, and his face was full of sharp angles.

Slowly, the king turned his head and looked at them. Nyx felt that sapphire gaze like a blow. The Bright King's eyes were filled with knowledge and raw power—inhuman and incredibly ancient.

"Don't look," Marny whispered.

Hastily, Nyx turned his eyes away.

The music stopped, the dancing stopped, the creatures at the feasting tables set down their goblets, and the entirety of the court turned to regard the two mortals who dared to enter the Bright Court.

Never in a million years had Nyx imagined something so far outside normal reality. With Marny beside him, he walked up to the dais in the center of the clearing. Part of his mind was freaking out, pointing at the faeries and screaming, but the other part stayed calm, focused.

"Your Majesty," Marny said, bowing to the king.

Damn, she was amazingly fearless. Following her lead, Nyx bent at the waist, pack shifting on his shoulders.

"Greetings, mortals." The king sounded amused. "You

arrive in the flesh, instead of wearing the guise of avatars. How unusual. And foolhardy."

"Sometimes you have to take risks," Marny said. "We've come in search of someone."

"Yeah," Nyx said, at last finding his voice. "We're looking for my sister."

"I know well enough what you seek," the king said. "Did you think you could enter my Realm and take pieces of it away with impunity, Nyx Spenser?"

He couldn't answer that. Pleading ignorance wasn't going to get him very far, he could tell that much.

"Is she here?" Marny pressed.

"Quiet, Mistress Marny," the king said. "You are not the one who owes the debt."

She scowled at the king, but didn't say anything more.

"I'm not letting you keep my sister in exchange for a few leaves," Nyx said, anger clearing his head. "That's hardly a fair trade."

"Who said it must be fair?" The king gave him a sharp smile. "However, your words have merit. You may win your sister back—but payment is still owed."

He gestured, and in the depths of the shining trees something moved. Something white, with tall branching antlers of pure ivory. As it paced forward, Nyx saw a girl upon its back.

"Emmie!" he cried.

She swayed slightly as the White Stag entered the clearing, her gaze unfocused. It was disturbing, the way she looked right past him.

"What have you done to her?" he demanded, wanting to dash up and deliver a solid roundhouse to the king's jaw.

"She remains woven in dreams," the Bright King said. "Would you prefer she wakes and sees that all of this is real?"

He swept one long-fingered hand over the court, and the creatures cackled and giggled. A nymph with dripping hair bared needle-sharp teeth at Nyx, and Pinebough growled menacingly and shook his spear.

"Maybe not," Nyx said.

What next? Could he run over and grab Emmie off the stag? He scanned the court, seeing way too many armed creatures who wouldn't hesitate to fight at the king's command.

Marny caught his gaze and tipped her head to the bonfire at the edge of the clearing. Its rose-colored flames reflected warmly off the metal-barked trees. Too far away for them to reach, especially if he was lugging his sister. Which meant the king had to let Emmie go.

"Well, mortal, have you anything to propose?" the king asked.

"I do." Nyx drew in a breath through his nose. "Trial by combat. If I win, Marny and I take my sister back to the mortal world."

"*Safely* back," Marny added, then turned to look at him. Worry and hope sparked in her warm brown eyes.

"It's okay," he said, though of course it wasn't. There were any number of ways this could go severely wrong.

The king laughed, the sound chiming like a clear bell over the court. "Do you think to challenge me to personal combat?"

"No." Nyx wasn't that stupid. "I thought I'd fight a champion of your choosing."

He glanced over the gathered creatures, weighing his options.

Pinebough and the other spriggans were formidable, but breakable if he could get in past their guard. The sharp-teethed hairy things could be a problem, but Nyx was fast on his feet, and any living creature had its weak points. He didn't see any elfin knights standing around, which was fortunate.

"Ah. Clever enough." The king nodded. "Very well. I choose as my champion—"

"Me!" The voice rang through the clearing.

The Bright Lance strode forward, eyes narrowed, mouth set in a hard line. When he reached the dais, he went down on one knee before the king.

"My liege," he said. "I beg you, allow me to fight this upstart mortal. He must pay for his many slights to the Bright Realm."

"Including the fact that he so ably eluded you?" The king's voice held a cutting edge.

"He had aid," the guard said. "That annoying sprite—"

"Speak no ill of Puck in my court," the king said. "Annoyance or no, he serves his purpose and it is not for you to judge him."

"I stand reprimanded." The Bright Lance bowed his head. "Still, will you choose me for your champion, my king?"

A heartbeat of silence fell over the clearing, and Marny shot Nyx a scared look. Too late to back out now. He'd said he would fight whomever the Bright King chose.

"I choose you," the king said, and the watching fey folk cheered. "Nyx Spenser, I agree to let you battle my champion, the Bright Lance. Should you win, you may retrieve your sister and, along with Mistress Marny, safely pass from my court.

Should you lose, I will keep your sister in payment for your meddling in the Realm of Faerie."

Oh, crap. There was no way in hell he could afford to lose. Nyx studied the imposing figure of the Bright Lance. But how could he win?

Expression taut, Marny took his hand. "You can do this. I have faith in you." She lowered her voice. "And I won't just be standing there watching, if you know what I mean."

He nodded. Marny knew better than to try to interfere in the fight, but she would be alert for any opportunity. And trying to reach Emmie while the court was distracted.

"Good luck," he said, shrugging out of his pack and handing it to her.

"You too."

"Clear a space," the king commanded.

The creatures of the court sprang to do his bidding, moving the tables and couches aside, then gathering in a rough circle. Marny, a pack slung over each shoulder, edged toward where the White Stag stood. Emmie remained quiet and unresponsive upon its back.

It hurt Nyx's heart to look at his sister, so he concentrated on running through a quick set of warmups, trying to loosen and limber his muscles.

The Bright Lance paced into the center of the cleared space. He was taller than Nyx, his breastplate engraved with swirling designs. At his side hung a slender sword, and he had a small round shield upon his back.

"Um, don't I get to choose my weapons?" Nyx asked.

The court laughed, and the king's champion smiled.

"I believe the choice is whether or not to use magic," the

Bright Lance said. "Which do you prefer?"

Ah, dammit. Nyx shook his head. They'd boxed him right into that corner, hadn't they?

"No magic," he said.

The Bright King raised his hands, sketching strange symbols in the air. A moment later, a ring of knee-high scarlet flames encircled the two combatants.

"Fighters must remain in the circle of fire," the king said. "No magic may pass the barrier. At first blood, the combat is ended. Make a fine sport of it."

Clearly that last comment was for his champion, who looked more than ready to draw his sword and cut Nyx that very instant.

Great—on tonight's entertainment bill was "bait the human." It was obvious everyone in the court expected the Bright Lance to win. Well, except for Marny, who was making her slow, imperceptible way over to the White Stag.

Time for him to provide some distraction. He cracked his neck, went into a defensive stance, and beckoned to the Bright Lance.

"Come at me, bro."

"Gladly."

With no further warning, the faerie knight rushed forward, blade already in motion.

Nyx waited until the last possible second in order to take his opponent by surprise, then dropped and swept his leg out, hoping to bring the knight down. The Bright Lance's sword swished just past his ear, but his opponent was too nimble, and leaped over Nyx's outstretched leg. Still, he'd missed his strike. As he overshot, Nyx danced back.

Despite the fancy armor, the faerie moved quickly and easily. He didn't equip his shield, which meant he still didn't think Nyx was much of a threat.

Okay, first order of business was to disarm the Bright Lance. Nyx pulled out his nunchaku, gave them a quick twirl, then dropped into a ready stance.

"You consider two sticks an adequate weapon?" the faerie scoffed.

Nyx didn't bother replying, just kept his eyes on his opponent's blade. In order to entangle the sword, he'd have to let it get close enough to cut him. Good thing he'd spent years sparring, watching angles of attack and training his body to react quickly.

Life wasn't just about playing video games, after all.

The Bright Lance pulled his sword back and charged. Adrenaline sizzling through him, Nyx sidestepped and flung the nunchaku out. The chain slung around the hilt of the sword with a satisfying clunk, and he caught the flying end of the stick as it wrapped back, landing in his palm with a hard slap.

He wrenched and the sword flew out of the Bright Lance's grasp. Nyx pivoted, letting the momentum carry the blade away. Regretfully, he had to release his nunchaku, too. Both weapons sailed through the air, clearing the circle of flame.

The faerie let out a cry of rage as the watching creatures scrambled to avoid the sword and nunchaku. From the corner of his eye, Nyx saw Marny grin. She was nearing the stag—but still not close enough to snatch Emmie from its back.

"Clever," the king said from his vantage point upon his throne. "You humans can be the most surprising creatures."

The Bright Lance bared his teeth. “Cleverness will not win you this match.”

Quicker than thought, he rushed forward. Nyx threw his arms up into a block, but the faerie bore him to the ground. Damn, the guy weighed a ton. Was he able to adjust his body mass at will?

The Bright Lance got one arm across Nyx’s throat and began to press.

I don’t think so.

Grabbing the top of the faerie’s breastplate, Nyx pulled hard. Overbalanced, the Bright Lance tumbled forward and Nyx slithered out from under him.

Time to get serious. He scrambled up and reached under his sleeve for one of his sheathed throwing stars. As the faerie knight rose, rage burning from his silvery eyes, Nyx flung the sharp-edged shuriken.

The star blurred, and the Bright Lance ducked aside with quicker-than-human reflexes. Instead of hitting his neck, the weapon pinged off the faerie’s armor and spun away to land outside the scarlet line of flames.

Dammit. Nyx only had one more in the sheath—the other shuriken were tucked in his sack. Stupid.

The Bright Lance rushed him again. Nyx leaped to the side, almost stepping outside the circle of flame. The watching fey folk murmured, their eyes bright with anticipation.

Quickly, Nyx pulled out his remaining throwing star and held it between his fingers. The goal now was first blood, and he literally couldn’t throw away his last chance. He’d have to wait for his opponent to get close.

Too close. But it was necessary.

CHAPTER 23

The scarlet flames surrounding Nyx and the Bright Lance flickered, painting red reflections on the faerie's armor.

"Enough of this foolishness, mortal," the Bright Lance said. "I am here to fight you, not dance with you."

"Okay, then." Nyx rushed forward, foot lifted to deliver a double kick.

The feint worked. The knight focused on the first, weaker kick while Nyx rebounded into a roundhouse. His right leg whipped out, the top of his foot connecting with the Bright Lance's temple, but instead of going down, his opponent only staggered backward a pace.

As Nyx whirled back into his stance, the faerie rushed him, one bare hand outstretched. The Bright Lance's nails were filed into points, easily sharp enough to pierce the skin.

Ah, crap.

Feeling like he was moving in slow motion, Nyx stepped to the side, prepared to use his opponent's momentum to send him flying past—ideally, all the way out of the circle. But the Bright Lance corrected, and Nyx had to drop to his knees on the grass to keep those fingernails from slicing across his cheek.

The faerie pivoted, too fast for the human eye to see, and lunged, bearing Nyx down and pinning him to the ground. His breath went out in a huff of pain. Dimly, he heard Marny call out, but all his attention was on the icy rage in his opponent's eyes.

"And so it ends," the faerie hissed, raising his fingers into claws above Nyx's face.

"Yep," Nyx gasped.

The knight had gotten a knee right into his solar plexus—but though he might be down, Nyx wasn't done.

Holding the Bright Lance's gaze, he whipped his hand up. The edge of the throwing star sliced the side of the faerie's hand, and he gave a howl of pain. In that moment of distraction, Nyx threw his opponent off.

He scrambled to his feet and sucked in air, trying to get his breath back. His ribs ached where the knight had landed on him, and would probably hurt a whole lot more once the adrenaline surging through him subsided.

"Hold," the Bright King said as his champion gathered himself to attack. "First blood has been drawn." He nodded to the trickle of purplish blood encircling the Bright Lance's wrist.

"But, my liege—"

"Silence. The terms of combat have been fulfilled. Much as it pains me to say it, the human has won." The king sounded unhappy, but not as pissed as he might be. Maybe he'd enjoyed the show after all.

The monarch snapped his fingers and the scarlet flames

vanished. Slowly, the White Stag paced forward, bearing Nyx's sister. Marny walked at its side, one hand protectively on Emmie's leg. Her gaze met Nyx's, full of approval and unwavering confidence, and he let out a long breath.

They'd won. Barely, but he'd rescued his sister.

Although they weren't safely home yet. He wouldn't put it past the Bright King to pull some last-minute shenanigans.

"I claim victory," Nyx said. "Now give me my sister."

The king regarded him, endless ages echoing in his eyes. A deep sorrow and joy whirled there, and for a moment Nyx swore he glimpsed stars.

"I release your sister from the Bright Court," the king said. "The White Stag has agreed to bear the three of you safely from my domain. Will you accept?"

"Yes," he said.

"No," Marny said, sending him a panicked look.

Nyx frowned as she shook her head at him, but it was too late. He'd accepted the king's proposal—and really, safe passage out of the Realm was a good thing, right?

"Mount yourselves upon the stag," the king said, gesturing. "He is strong enough to bear three."

The White Stag gracefully went down on the gold-tinged grasses and gave Nyx an expectant look from its dark eyes.

"Nope," Marny said. "I'm not taking this ride."

"Get on." Nyx slung his leg over the stag. Its hide was soft as velvet. "It's our ticket out of here."

"Yeah, but to where?"

"Mistress Marny," the Bright King said, and there was a low tolling in his voice, a bell warning of an approaching storm.

"Do you wish to remain here in my court? You are most welcome to do so."

"Not really." Marny edged closer to the stag.

"Then mount and depart. Or stay and revel among the fey folk for centuries, leaving your mortal cares behind. The choice is yours."

"Crap," she said. "Frying pan, meet fire."

"Get on, already," Nyx said.

It worried him that Emmie was still so unresponsive, but if he had to, he'd send her off with the White Stag while he and Marny stayed behind to battle their way out of the Bright Court.

Why did Marny have to be so stubborn?

Finally, she handed him his pack, then set her hands on his shoulders and seated herself behind him on the stag. She leaned forward, her warmth pressing against him, and whispered, "Think we could steer this thing over to the bonfire?"

"I'll try."

Though without any bridle or reins he wasn't sure how. Maybe the deer would respond to a few kicks in the side.

"Excellent," the Bright King said. "Your visit has been most entertaining. Fare thee well, mortals."

The White Stag rose, jolting them a little, and Nyx held on to his sister.

"Emmie," he said. "Wake up. Are you there?"

She made no response—which was probably a good thing. Once they returned to the human world, though, if she didn't snap out of it he was going to come back to the Realm and kick some faerie ass.

The king waved his hand in dismissal, the harp struck up a

jaunty tune, and the stag turned regally and began pacing out of the court. To their left, the bonfire glittered with rosy flames.

"Turn, please." Nyx kicked his heel against the beast's side, softly at first, then harder.

The White Stag ignored him, and he didn't want to make it buck or rear by bashing too roughly at its ribs. Marny added her prodding, then leaned hard in the direction of the bonfire.

"Come on," she said. When the stag refused to turn, she let out a frustrated breath. "We have to jump off and drag Emmie over to the fire."

Nyx nodded. "On three. One. Two." He tightened his grip on his sister and prepared to leap off. This was going to be a little tricky.

"Three."

Neither he nor Marny budged. Their legs were stuck fast with magic to the sides of the White Stag. He cursed under his breath and tried to pry at least one of his legs free. Marny huffed out a sound of annoyance, and he could feel her attempts to twist off the deer, too.

"Stupid faeries," she said bitterly.

"Dammit." He craned his neck as the bonfire receded behind them.

They needed flames to activate their talismans, and he hadn't brought a lighter or anything. Would they have to wander around the Realm aimlessly until they found another source of fire?

The laughter of the fey folk followed them as the White Stag, seemingly oblivious to the struggling humans on its back, entered the forest of gemmed trees. Glowing balls of light chased them, zipping over their heads and twirling in the air.

Two of the pixies descended, whirling about the humans with dizzying speed. One landed on his shoulder, then dived into the sack he carried.

"Get out." He beat at the sack, half hoping he'd squish the creature.

After a moment it emerged, and Nyx swore it laughed at him, high and annoying like the whine of a mosquito.

Marny swiped at it, but the pixie zipped into the air and rejoined its companions. The glowing creatures whirled once more around the stag, then careened back toward the Bright Court.

"I hate this place," Marny said matter-of-factly.

"Seconded." He tried once more to dismount.

No luck, of course. The White Stag bore them steadily through the trees, the radiance of the court dimming as they went further into the forest.

"At least we got Emmie out," Nyx said. "That was tweaked."

"No," Marny said. "That was too easy."

"Are you kidding me?" He swiveled so he could see her face. Her expression was dead serious. "You weren't the one who had to fight a fully armed faerie knight. Are you saying they let me win?"

"I'm not saying that—don't look so insulted. I'm sure the king wanted you to lose, and the Bright Lance didn't strike me as the sort who'd agree to throwing a fight in favor of a human. But they let us leave—and I'm worried about the agreement you made."

"The king said we'd get home safely."

"Actually, no." She raised her head and looked at the forest, then glanced at the sky above. "He only said we'd pass safely out of his court. And I'm very much afraid this isn't the way back to our world."

Nyx surveyed the trees, which had changed from gold and silver to the familiar white-barked ones. Overhead, the sky turned a dim lavender color. As he watched, a single star appeared, and then another.

"Where do you think we're going?" he asked, though the chill in his chest told him the answer before Marny spoke.

"I think the stag is taking us... to the Dark Court."

CHAPTER 24

A wave of despair-tinged exhaustion rolled over Marny as she said the words. The Dark Court. The last place in the universe they should be, so of course it was where they were headed.

She should've trusted her instincts—but there had been no point at which she could have made any other choice, aside from not entering Nyx's enchanted forest. Refusing to help him hadn't been an option.

So here they were, stuck on the back of a magical deer carrying them relentlessly toward the Dark Court.

The trees around them turned to gnarled oaks, and overhead the sky grew darker. The stars shone, brilliant sparks forming strange constellations.

"I'm so sorry," Nyx said, turning partway around so he could see her. "I should've listened to you."

"I suspect we would have ended up in exactly the same place," she said.

The events had unfolded inexorably, each step forcing them onto the path the faeries wanted them to take. She and Nyx weren't without resources, however.

Slowly, Marny slid her hand down her leg, until she touched the calf sheath holding her knife. Hoping the stag didn't notice, she bunched her jeans up enough to get her fingers around the handle.

When she tried to pull it out, though, the knife stayed put, like it was super-glued into the sheath.

"Stupid deer magic," she said. "I can't get my knife out."

A thoughtful look crossed his face. "Can you reach into my pack? Find the throwing stars? They're wrapped up, but still sharp, so be careful."

He swiveled back around so she could open the bag slung over his shoulder.

She reached inside the pack, her fingers brushing over a can of Haydeez, a couple protein bars, and his flashlight before she felt a folded piece of silk.

"This it?" She pulled out the small bundle and handed it to him.

"Yeah, although..."

The frown on his face deepened as he folded back the silk. Instead of two plasmetal shuriken, two bright flowers lay upon the silk, their petals gaudy orange and red—and completely harmless.

"That pixie," Marny said, irritation flooding through her. "I wish I'd had a bug swatter."

"Oh man, they're fading." Nyx poked at the flowers with one finger.

Sure enough, the petals were shriveling before their eyes,

disintegrating to dust. A sudden breeze blew up, whirling over the cloth, and moments later all trace of the former throwing stars was gone.

"So much for our weapons." Nyx grimaced, then balled the silk up and stuck it in his pocket. "This place seems determined to disarm us."

The Realm of Faerie pretty much sucked, but talking about how tweaked it was would just make things worse.

"At least I still have my knife," she said. If she could ever get it out of the sheath. "Do you want a Haydeez?"

"Sure. We might as well meet our doom wide awake, right?"

Marny handed him a can, then dug out one for herself. Nasty stuff. She made a face at the super-sweet taste, but kept drinking. They both needed the energy jolt.

Darkness folded around them, the way ahead lit by a pale glimmer emanating from the White Stag itself. A sickle moon cut the sky overhead and white moths fluttered in the branches of the shadowed oaks. Then, faintly, the silence was broken by the sound of music.

Not the jaunty harp tunes of the Bright Court, but a forlorn keening of bagpipes, the low throb of a drum, a minor chord strummed from a sad guitar. Through the screen of trees, Marny glimpsed purple flames flickering, where strange, oddly jointed creatures with glistening wings capered about a bonfire.

The trees encircled a clearing, where nightmares laughed and coiled in the shadows. At the far side rose a throne made of tangled vines, and Marny's spit dried in her throat.

They were almost to the Dark Court.

"Fire," Nyx remarked.

"Yeah." She didn't hold out much hope of being able to get the stag to walk conveniently past it, however.

"Game plan?" Nyx asked, his voice tight.

"At some point this stupid deer has to release us. When it does, we grab your sister and run."

She didn't elaborate. No point in informing any listening creatures of the exact details, but Nyx knew as well as she did that they had to get Emmie and themselves over to the purple bonfire. And then hope Puck's trinkets worked as advertised.

The White Stag bore them into the clearing and halted directly before the Dark Queen. Marny's brain froze. She was dimly aware of the beautiful and hideous denizens of the court, the musicians playing softly from the shadows, the gossamer-winged maidens gathered behind the queen's tangled throne.

But the queen herself stole all thought, all breath.

Black hair framed a face of ethereal, deadly beauty. In her midnight gaze secrets swam, and Marny made herself look away. Getting trapped in the queen's eyes was most definitely not a good idea.

The Dark Queen wore a gown of shade and starlight, the edge of it trailing upon the ground and curling up like smoke. She regarded the humans a moment longer, and then she smiled. Marny shivered at the bitter frost in her expression.

"Well." The queen leaned forward. "What a sorry trio of mortals have landed upon my doorstep. One wrapped in dreams, one wracked with guilt, and one afraid of her own softness. You shall do well here, among the shadows."

"We're not staying," Marny said.

The queen laughed, the sound like ice cracking on a frozen

lake. "Amusing as ever, you humans. Of course you will remain. You have no other choice."

She flicked her long, pale fingers and the White Stag knelt gracefully on the velvet mosses before the throne. Marny tensed, and felt Nyx do the same. The bonfire was several yards away, and she forced herself not to glance over at it.

"My queen." The guitar-playing minstrel stepped forward, and Marny saw with relief that it was the former human named Thomas. "Might you not reconsider? You only need one of these humans to open the gateway, after all."

Once a mortal man, Thomas Rimer had made a bargain with the Dark Queen. Marny had never encountered him, but Jennet talked a lot about the guy, who had been her dad's best friend and a lead programmer at VirtuMax. Now, however, he was bound to serve as the queen's Bard in the Dark Court —forever.

An eternity spent in the Realm of Faerie. Marny shuddered at the thought.

"Bard Thomas." Displeasure shaded the queen's voice. "Once again you overstep. Silence—I will hear no more of your counsel on this matter."

The bard nodded, his weary eyes meeting Marny's. She pressed her lips grimly together and gave him a nod. At least he'd tried.

Now what? She swallowed back her fear and tried to focus, but her thoughts kept darting aimlessly around like the moths in the trees.

"So, can we get off this thing?" Nyx asked, voice full of bravado. "I need to pee."

A group of nearby goblins cackled, and Marny shot them a

look, hoping that Codcadden wasn't among them. That was one nasty redcap, and she was relieved he didn't seem to be present at court. Probably off somewhere ripping the legs from pixies or something equally vicious.

Of course, there were plenty of other horrible creatures she and Nyx would have to face as they dashed for the fire: a black-mouthed banshee, an ogre wearing a belt festooned with wide-eyed, decapitated heads, and any number of clawed and fanged faeries that looked eager to take a bite of tasty human flesh.

Dammit.

"White Stag," the queen said. "You have fulfilled the bargain struck with myself and my brother. Divest yourself of your burden and rise. I grant you the freedom of the Realm. Both courts are equal in your demesne, and none may harm you without due cause."

At the edge of the clearing, a red-eyed hound growled. The queen shot a glare in that direction. Marny followed her gaze, and shivered to see the horned silhouette of the Huntsman lurking within the trees. Lean hounds with wicked teeth swirled about his feet like fog, and two elfin knights mounted on flame-footed steeds stood at his side.

"Leash your dogs," the queen said. "This is no quarry of the Wild Hunt."

The Huntsman made a gesture of assent and his hounds slunk away, back into the darkness beneath the oaks. He and his riders turned and went with them, and Marny was glad to see them go.

Not that she and Nyx didn't have enough other enemies to deal with.

"Mortals, you may alight," the Dark Queen said.

Marny exchanged a quick glance with Nyx, then slung her leg over the stag and gratefully stepped off. She did not *ever* want to be stuck on a magical mount again. Beside her, Nyx stretched his legs and dismounted.

He tucked an arm around his sister and coaxed her off the White Stag. For a second she swayed, and Marny worried the girl was going to topple over, but Nyx steadied her and she remained standing. Emmie didn't look very present, though. She blinked and smiled dreamily at the faerie maidens hovering behind the queen's throne. Good thing she wasn't looking at the goblins.

The stag leaped gracefully to its feet and bowed to the queen over one outstretched foreleg. Then, quick as a moonbeam, it whirled and bounded out of the Dark Court. Its pale hide glowed against the blackness of the trees, growing ever more distant until it was a speck of star in the velvety dark.

CHAPTER 25

As the denizens of the Dark Court watched the White Stag disappear into the woods, Marny bent and checked her knife. It was loose in the sheath again, and she let out a quick breath of thanks.

Question was, when should she use it? She wasn't foolish enough to think she could attack the queen. And they were still too far from the bonfire to make a run for it—especially if Nyx had to carry his sister.

"Well now, mortals." The queen's fearsome midnight gaze settled upon them once more. "What a lovely offering you three shall make. Alas, my preparations are not yet complete. Until they are, I offer you the hospitality of my court."

The watching fey folk laughed, a cacophony of rasping and shrill mirth, overlaid with a silver ripple of chimes.

"We'd rather just be going," Nyx said. "Thank you so very much for the offer."

The queen winced a little at his words, but simple thanks were not enough to wound so powerful a faerie.

"Nyx Spenser," she said. "By your name I bind you to my will. Look into my eyes, and know the enchantment of the Realm."

"Um, that's a no," he said, blinking rapidly.

"Once I call you." The Dark Queen reached out a long-fingered hand. "Twice again, Nyx Spenser, for none can resist my sway."

Marny darted a panicked look at Nyx, who was staring at the queen, his expression going slack. This time, he didn't make a sassy comeback.

"Stop looking at her," Marny said.

She grabbed his hand and tried to make him turn to face her, but he resisted, his gaze focused upon the queen.

"Thrice I name thee, Nyx Spenser. And the deed is done." She set one finger under his chin, and he swayed forward at her touch, his gaze unfocused.

"No!" Marny cried. "You can't have him."

The queen turned a searing look upon her. "I grow weary of meddlesome mortal girls who think they can snatch their presumed beloveds from me. This one is mine, and his sister as well. But you, Mistress Marny, shall be the first sacrifice."

Oh, crap. She was in deep trouble now.

And where the hell were the Feyguard? Wasn't this the very thing they were supposed to prevent from happening?

"Bard Thomas." The queen snapped her fingers, purple sparks flying from her hand. "Take these humans to your quarters and tend them well until I call for them."

Expression strained, Thomas stepped forward. "As you command, my queen."

"Can't you help us?" Marny asked him, desperation squeezing her chest. She glanced at the bonfire, then back to him, hoping he could read her mind.

Although she wasn't going to use her talisman and return home, not without Nyx and his sister, so what good would it do to walk past the flames?

"I am sorry." Thomas shook his head, his eyes filled with sorrow. "I am bound to do the queen's will, much as it might pain me. Now come."

Thomas took Emmie by the elbow and began leading her away from the throne. Nyx turned and followed, moving like he was half-asleep. For a moment, Marny hesitated. The knife strapped to her leg burned in its hidden sheath, but without Nyx's help, there was no way the three of them could escape.

A cold wind stirred the branches of the oaks, and despair settled over Marny like a black cloak, muffling her in its folds.

"Mistress Marny," Thomas said. "Follow."

There was nothing else she could do, short of throwing herself at the Dark Queen, which could only end in disaster. Steps heavy, Marny went to join the others. They were moving slowly, due to the enchantments laid on both Nyx and Emmie, which let Marny catch up quickly, but also allowed the watching fey folk plenty of time to jeer and chitter at them as they passed.

To her surprise, Thomas seemed to be veering toward the bonfire. Maybe he'd gotten her message after all. Not that it would help. Both Nyx and Emmie were zombies, and Marny couldn't save the three of them single-handedly.

Do something! a frantic voice inside her insisted. *Before it's too late.*

But what?

She cast her mind back, trying to recall the queen's words. Something about meddlesome mortal girls saving their—how had she put it? Presumed beloveds.

Swallowing hard, Marny glanced at Nyx walking in front of her. Despite the thousand reasons why it was a bad idea, she had to admit she was starting to fall in love with him.

Was that the answer?

Ahead, the purple flames of the bonfire leaped, smearing the air with violet light. She had to act. Now.

"Nyx." She caught his arm and tugged. "Nyx Spenser, listen to me."

He paused a moment, then kept walking. Dammit.

She hurried ahead and blocked his way. The eerie purple fire cast shadows flickering over his face. He tried to sidestep her, but she spread her arms wide and pulled him into her embrace. Thank goodness for her size and strength. Although he struggled, she was able to hold him for long enough to lean forward and whisper in his ear.

"Onyx Spenser," she said. "I love you. Come back to me. Please."

He went rigid in her arms, but the look in his eyes remained blank.

"Onyx," she said. "Onyx."

There was no sense of recognition in his gaze. Desperately, Marny thought of all the faerie tales she'd ever heard of.

Couldn't evil spells be broken with a kiss?

Desperate hope trembling through her, she tilted her head

and pressed her lips against Nyx's, willing him to respond. His mouth was cold and set, but a heartbeat later she felt something change.

A shiver went through him, and his lips warmed beneath hers. His arms went around her, and she felt as if someone had just set off a firecracker inside her chest, a sudden explosion of sound and light.

"No!" the Dark Queen cried. "Stop them."

Cackling, the redcap goblins thronged forward, first among the terrible creatures of the Dark Court.

Marny tore herself away from the kiss and took Nyx by the shoulders. "Wake up—please."

He blinked, and awareness returned to his eyes. With one glance she saw him take in the clearing, the approaching faeries, his sister. The bonfire.

"Go," Marny said, giving him a little shove. "Grab Emmie. I'll buy you a couple seconds."

She grabbed her knife, just in time to stop the first surge of goblins. They drew up short at the sight of the cold iron and hissed at her, baring sharp teeth. She thrust the knife at them and slowly backed toward the fire.

From the corner of her eye she saw Nyx grab his sister, then pull the talisman from his neck. Thankfully, Thomas did nothing to stop him. She supposed the bard was trying to help in whatever small way he could, without directly opposing the queen.

"Ready," Nyx called.

"Go—I'm coming." The only problem was, she couldn't undo her bracelet.

The second she stopped waving her knife around and tried

to get her trinket off, the goblins would swamp her. And if not them, the ogre who was clumping his way across the clearing would finish the job.

Nyx had his hands full, too, holding his sister and the talisman.

"Hurry," he cried.

"Please, please, just go now! You have to get Emmie to safety, or this was all for nothing."

An agonized look crossed his face. Nyx glanced at his sister, then at Marny. His eyes were stark with emotion—fear and hope. And love.

Holding her gaze, he cast his talisman into the heart of the purple flames.

The fire flared up, lighting the underside of the towering oaks and throwing violet reflections into the goblins' eyes. The queen rose from her throne and let out a cry of bitter anger. Frost swept through the clearing and the flames faltered, but it was too late.

Nyx and his sister were gone.

CHAPTER 26

Marny stumbled with relief, and the goblins surged forward.

"No you don't." She tightened her grip on her knife and waved it menacingly back and forth.

The goblins hissed and halted—closer than before. Their red caps were the color of old blood, and their eyes glittered with rage.

Stalemate, but only a temporary one. At least Nyx had escaped, along with his sister. Marny's heart squeezed tight; she was glad he'd made it out, but terrified of what her own fate might be.

The bonfire flickered weakly behind her, but she couldn't remove her bracelet. Even if she cut it off, the moment's inattention guaranteed that the goblins would swarm, overwhelming her and snatching it away. What a stupid talisman it had turned out to be.

Still, she wasn't going down without a fight.

"Take her," the Dark Queen said, violet sparks crackling from her hair. "We still have a mortal at our disposal. This one cannot be allowed escape."

Marny shot a look at Thomas, who remained near the bonfire. He gave a nearly imperceptible shake of his head. No help there.

The ground vibrated with the heavy tread of the approaching ogre. Panic tightened Marny's breath. Here she was, a lone human girl armed with a small knife, against the creatures of the Dark Court—including the queen herself. She was doomed.

"Tasty morsel," the ogre said, staring at her and licking his fleshy lips. "Hearty mouthful, that one."

"No eating her," the queen commanded. "She must be saved for the tithe."

Marny thought she might actually prefer being devoured by an ogre to being the blood sacrifice used to open a gateway between the worlds. She glanced at her blade. Turn it against herself? That might be the best solution, in terms of saving the world.

"Aieeee!" a shrill, raspy voice cried.

From across the court a small figure darted, pasty-skinned and bulbous-eyed. It dived in front of the ogre, then wove around the lumbering creature's feet, confusing it so that it swayed and halted.

"Korrigan!" Marny cried, gladness flaring through her. At least she wouldn't die totally alone and friendless.

"Seize him." The Dark Queen's voice was cold with displeasure.

The redcaps turned from menacing Marny and focused

their attention on the changeling. Such a foolish, brave creature who dared interfere with the queen's will.

The goblins were distracted, the ogre stopped—this was her chance, and she owed it all to Korrigan. Forcing back tears, Marny sliced the bracelet off her wrist.

"Korr—you are the best changeling ever!" she cried.

Then she whirled and threw her talisman into the fire.

Purple light flared and the Dark Court spun before her eyes. She caught a glimpse of Korrigan, grinning fiercely as he fought off a goblin, Thomas with the faintest of smiles curving his lips, and the queen's fathomless gaze, full of winter and night.

An arcing pain sizzled through Marny, as if she'd been struck by lightning, and everything went black.

NYX GROANED and opened his eyes. Afternoon light slanted through dust motes high above him. The ceiling of the warehouse swam into focus, and with it, the memory of what had just happened.

"Marny!" He sat up, shook off the dizziness trying to tip him over, and glanced around.

Emmie lay on the floor beside him, her eyes closed. Fear spiking through him, Nyx scooted over to her and felt for a pulse.

Alive, thank God.

Where was Marny? She should be coming through any second—but there was no sign of her. He scanned the warehouse, desperately hoping that she'd appear.

Time moves differently in the Realm, he reminded himself as the seconds ticked past. He waited, heartbeat ratcheting up as a minute went by, then two, and she still didn't arrive.

Okay. He made himself take a deep breath. He could deal with this, despite the panic scratching through his brain.

First, wake Emmie up. By the time he got his sister going, Marny would be back in the human world, right?

"Em." He gently shook his sister's shoulder. "Hey, open your eyes."

"Hmm?"

The sound of her voice made hot tears spring to the corners of his eyes. Her eyelids fluttered open and she blinked up at him.

"I had the weirdest dreams," she said, yawning. "Why am I out here in the warehouse? What time is it? And why are you smiling like that?"

"I just..." He gathered her into a hug. How could he even begin to explain?

"Okay, okay." After a moment she pushed him away. "Why so sappy, big brother?"

"It's a really long story. Are you sure you feel all right?"

"Did the club get broken into or something? Where's Sula?" She glanced around.

"Sula went home." He didn't bother telling her it had been a couple days ago, in real-world time. "And the enchanted forest had some...issues."

"Oh, okay." She yawned again. "I'm so tired. And hey, wasn't that Marny girl here? I remember her being around."

"Yeah, she was with us."

But where was she now? Still trapped in the Realm of

Faerie? Worse than trapped? Urgency beat through him. He stood and held a hand out to his sister.

"Can you stand up?"

"Of course." She let him haul her to her feet, then swayed. "Oh, dizzy. Oops."

"Let's get you back into bed. It was a rough night." Let her believe it was only the next day. He could explain more later.

After he rescued Marny.

He got Emmie tucked into bed in the spare room, still groggy and happy enough to go back to sleep. The relief that she was all right warred with the clutch of fear in his gut every time he thought about Marny. Was she fighting for her life in the Dark Court? Was the queen even now preparing to kill her?

Only one way to find out.

This time, Nyx armed himself with as much steel as possible. No more wooden spears or plas-metal shuriken. He needed iron to fight the faeries. He slammed back another Haydeez, ate a protein bar in three bites, then went to face the enchanted forest.

He'd briefly considered entering Feyland via the sim system, but ditched the idea. Going in by the forest was what he knew, and he'd *make* it take him into the Realm. Begging, tears, blood, whatever it took. No way was he leaving Marny at the mercy of the Dark Queen.

Besides, she'd saved him. He flashed on the memory of her warm brown eyes looking into his, the feel of her lips. Not for the first time, he decided she was the bravest person he knew. Especially since, when it counted, she'd been able to admit her feelings for him—and he had the suspicion Marny was not much into the lovey-dovey emotions.

Him, though, he'd gladly fall at her feet bearing a dozen tiger lilies. Once they were both safely back in the mortal world.

Nyx made a quick check of the various blades strapped about his person, resettled a couple of the knives, then squared his shoulders and strode into the soft light of the enchanted forest.

Over the last few days, Marny Fanalua had become as important to him as breathing. He hadn't known what his type of girl was before, because he hadn't met her yet: strong, serene, fiercely competent. And apparently embroiled in the magic of the Realm of Faerie.

He didn't know what the future held for either of them, but he wasn't giving her up without a fight.

CHAPTER 27

JUNE 30

Marny opened her eyes, then groaned at the pain flaring through her. She was lying down on something soft. Was she safe?

She turned her head, blinking to focus her gaze, and almost fell off her bed. Somehow, she was in her bedroom on the fortieth floor at Intertech.

No. How could that have happened? Slowly, she sat up. Judging from the light falling through the window, it was early evening. Her brain throbbed and she felt dizzy, but other than that she seemed unharmed.

A wild sense of victory flashed through her. They'd done it! She and Nyx had gone into the Realm of Faerie, rescued his sister, and escaped. She needed to message him right away, let him know she'd gotten out of the Dark Court. Thanks to Korrigan.

Earlier that year she'd saved the changeling's life, and he'd insisted that the fey folk always paid their debts. Guess they were even now. She hoped the little guy was okay.

Where was her messager? Marny rubbed her forehead, realizing it must be back at the club, along with her tablet. Maybe Anjah or Wil would let her borrow theirs. They might be the worst roomies ever, but surely they'd at least do that for her.

Moving carefully, she stood up and went out of her room. She peered through the half-open door of Anjah's room, grateful to see her roommate was there.

"Hey," she said, her voice coming out as a croak.

"Marny? Ohmigod!" Anjah jumped up from her armchair and rushed to the door. She reached out—her nails were fuchsia now, Marny noted—and set her hand on Marny's shoulder. "Where have you been? Are you okay? You are in deep trouble with von Coburg, let me tell you. Do you feel all right?"

"Slow down." Marny held up her hand. "What time is it? What day is it?"

"Tuesday evening—I just got home from work."

The answer sent a jolt through Marny, though part of her already knew it was true, after looking through that one arched doorway in the misty hall. She'd lost almost three days in the Realm of Faerie.

"Where have you been?" Anjah continued. "Come sit down, you look like hell. I'll make you some tea."

Marny blinked at her. "That's nice of you."

"Hey." The other girl gave her a wry look. "I haven't been the nicest person to you."

"Yeah, I noticed."

"I'm sorry." Anjah glanced at the floor, then back up at Marny. "I guess I was just jealous."

"Jealous? Of me?" Marny stared at her—gorgeous, stylish, smart. Anjah had it all.

"Of course." Anjah led her into the living room and settled her on the couch. "You're so relaxed and self-confident, and you'd created the most prime app of the century. How could I compete with that? When you disappeared..." She flushed, looking more uncomfortable—and real—than Marny had ever seen her. "I thought I'd driven you out by being such a bitch. And I realized that making you miserable wasn't really a solution to my own issues. I felt guilty as hell."

Whew. That was a lot to process. Marny leaned back against the cushions.

"How about that tea," she said. "And could I borrow your messager?"

"Sure." Anjah handed over her glitter-embossed messager, then hurried into the kitchen. Anjah nodded and hurried into the kitchen. The hiss of the electric kettle warming was strangely soothing. Normal.

Marny sent a quick message to Nyx, but there was no reply. Then to her family, reassuring them that she was fine and it had all been a misunderstanding.

"I was the one who found the medical report," Anjah said, coming back to the couch and sitting a little awkwardly at the other end.

"Medical report?" Marny frowned.

"When you didn't come back by early Monday morning, and I realized all your clothes and stuff were still here, Wil and I figured something must have happened to you. We called the hospitals, and Wil even went around to the unregistered clinics to see if you were there. Then I found the med-tech report about the accident at Club Mysteria, and we knew you'd been hurt."

"Right. That." It seemed like her injury had happened a thousand years ago.

"Are you okay?" Anjah peered at her arm. "It sounded pretty severe."

"It was. Is." Marny forced herself not to look at her completely normal arm. Better to pretend it was still hurt—because how could she explain away the fact that she was miraculously healed?

"Anyway. Wil went to the club a few times, but it was all locked up, nobody answered, and he couldn't get in. When we couldn't find you we... well, we covered for you." Anjah smoothed the back of the couch with her hand, like she was petting a cat.

"You did what? How?"

"We basically called you in sick. I showed your team the med-tech report, and said you were resting and shouldn't be disturbed. Then Wil kept looking for you, and I contacted your family to let them know you were missing."

"But you didn't tell Intertech?"

"Oh!" Anjah jumped to her feet. "Wil's meeting with Brenna right now. Let me message him."

Marny handed back Anjah's messager, and the kettle dinged in the kitchen.

"I'll get that," Marny said.

She needed a minute to collect her whirling thoughts—and

come up with some kind of alibi to tell her roomies. And her family.

"What did my family say when you contacted them?" she called over to Anjah.

"Your uncle is on his way." Anjah tucked her messager away. "Also, Wil and Brenna are coming up."

Marny fixed herself a mug of tea. It felt like forever ago since she'd bought her colorful mug. She made a cup for Anjah too.

"Thanks." Anjah came into the kitchen and picked up her cup. "Sorry. So much for taking care of you. I suck as a caregiver."

Marny gave her a half-smile. Despite herself, Anjah would always be a princess. But maybe a more thoughtful one in the future.

"I appreciate you guys covering for me," Marny said as they took their tea back in the living room. "And getting ahold of my family."

She was about to ask to borrow the messager again—she had to reach Nyx, and Uncle Zeg—when the apartment door slid open and Wil and Brenna came in.

"Hey!" Wil said, grinning when he caught sight of her. "You're here. Prime."

Brenna raised an eyebrow, the pale streak in her hair catching the light. "What's been going on, Marny? First we get accounts that you're injured and resting, then Wil comes to me this afternoon saying you've been missing for days, and now we find you sitting on the couch drinking tea."

"Well." Marny took a sip to buy time, then set her mug on

the table beside the couch. “As Anjah knows, we went to a club and I met a guy.”

Anjah’s brows went way up but she nodded. “Nyx Spenser. Ooh, you move fast, Marny girl.”

Marny felt a blush heating her cheeks—but that was okay. It helped create the impression she wanted them to have.

“Anyway, he’s a martial arts pro. We were hanging out this weekend—in fact, Mr. von Coburg’s guards can confirm that we had a breakfast date. So, Nyx was showing me how to use one of his spears, and I got hurt. I guess the pain meds the techs gave me were way strong or something, because I was knocked out for practically two days. Nyx took care of me, and brought me back here earlier today.” Kind of true, in a way. If by true you meant almost completely fabricated.

“Nice.” Anjah sent her a knowing look, clearly jumping to all the wrong conclusions.

“While I appreciate the camaraderie that prompted not immediately informing Intertech that Marny seemed to be missing, I cannot condone it,” Brenna said.

“Of course not,” Anjah said.

Wil nodded, looking contrite. “We just didn’t want her to get in trouble.”

“The company is liable for her safety,” Brenna said. “At the very least, you would’ve gotten me fired, since I’m your liaison. Plus, you could have opened Intertech up to a potentially huge lawsuit. This is serious business. I’m tempted to recommend that all three of your internships be terminated over this.”

Whoo, Brenna was bringing the hardass.

“This is entirely my fault,” Marny said. “I know I’m going to get the boot, but please don’t punish Wil and Anjah, too.”

Brenna raised one eyebrow, her gaze resting on Marny. "I'll have to sleep on this. Marny, do you need another day, or are you good for working tomorrow?"

"I can work. I don't want to let the team down any further —I know I missed a crucial meeting yesterday, and I need to apologize to them for that."

Somewhat mollified, Brenna gave her a short nod. "Then I expect you all to arrive at work bright and early tomorrow morning. I'll let you know my decision at the end of the day. Now get some rest."

This last was directed at Marny, along with a sternly sympathetic look.

"Right, boss." Although, strictly speaking, Brenna wasn't her boss.

And strictly speaking, Marny wasn't going obediently off to bed, either. She had to get to Nyx's club and make sure both he and his sister had returned safely from the Dark Realm.

CHAPTER 28

Nyx strode past the pale-trunked trees with single-minded intensity. He was going back into the Realm, and he was going *now*.

But the air didn't change and soften, and no faint chimes or tinkling laughter reached his ears. He had the sinking sensation that if he glanced back over his shoulder, he'd still see the dim interior of the warehouse through the trees.

"Hey!" he called. "White Stag—come and get me. Spriggans, goblins, pixies, ahoy! A mere mortal is entering your domain."

Nothing. He whirled and glared at the faint shadow of the juice bar beyond the silver-leafed branches.

Maybe he needed to do something more drastic. Though he hated the thought, he turned his back on his club and pulled out one of his shorter knives. Didn't the Dark Queen have a thing for blood?

"Hist," a high voice said. "Put away thy blade, Master Nyx, and bide a while."

"Puck?" Reluctantly, Nyx re-sheathed his knife. "Where are you?"

"Here, there, everywhere," the voice said. "But most measurably, perched above your head."

Nyx stepped back and craned his neck to see Puck sitting on a branch several feet above him, swinging his legs and grinning.

"Great, you're here." Nyx said. "Does that mean I'm in the Realm?"

"Not yet—though calling the dark fey with your blood would certainly tip you over. I do not recommend you do so, however. Having so recently escaped, do you truly want to enter that trap once more?"

"I have to. Marny's still in the Dark Court."

Puck laughed and leaped into a handstand. "T'would be a terrible thing, to return to the queen's court and find that your lady love is gone."

"Wait, what? Marny's not there?" A chill gripped him. "Where did they take her?"

The sprite tumbled forward off his branch, flipping in the air until he came to hover before Nyx. Sprigs of greenery were woven in his hair and cobwebs festooned his tattered tunic.

"Have you so little faith in Mistress Marny's prowess? She has escaped."

Relief whooshed through Nyx, but he peered distrustfully at Puck. "Then why didn't she return to the warehouse?"

"She was returned elsewhere."

"Elsewhere? Like, Crestview? Or somewhere else in the

Realm?" He tamped down on his frustration. Talking with Puck was like trying to navigate through a twisty maze, but getting irate at the sprite wasn't going to help.

Puck tilted his head like a bird, bright eyes twinkling. "She is nearby. And in this when, as well."

That seemed like a very good thing. For a second Nyx's heart twisted at the idea that Marny could've been sucked out of time, or taken anywhere, but he made himself relax. Breathe.

"Okay, so Marny's back in the real world." Although who knew what Puck meant by *nearby*. "I have your word on this? Is she hurt?"

"You learn quickly," Puck said. "She is well. And my time here is spent. Good eventide to you, Master Nyx. May our paths cross more lightly in the future!"

"Or preferably, not at all," Nyx said, but he was speaking to empty air. Only a shimmer remained where the sprite had been.

Fine, then. He had to believe that Puck was right, and Marny had made it back safely. Considering they'd used the sprite's magic to come back to the human world, it was probably safe to assume Puck knew what he was talking about.

And if he didn't, well, he'd basically confirmed that if Nyx went into the forest, cut himself, and called on the Dark Queen, he could get back to her court. If he had to. The idea sent a shudder of distaste through him.

Nyx cast one last, narrow-eyed glance at the shadows between the trees, but everything seemed normal. As soon as he got out, though, he was going to take away the anchor points and figure out what to do next. His mind shied away from the inevitable fate of the club and the failure of his grand project. First things first.

The second he walked out of the forest, somebody pounded on the warehouse door. Was it Marny? He sprinted across the floor, undid the locks and keypad, and flung open the door.

A big man with wild, frizzy hair stood there, the light of battle in his eyes. He raked his gaze up and down Nyx, and his face hardened.

“Can I help you?” Nyx said, shifting his stance to prepare for an attack.

“I think so,” the man said. “I’m looking for my niece. A certain Marny Fanalua.”

Ah, crap. “You must be Zeg. Come in.”

Marny’s uncle moved like she did—light on his feet and aware of his surroundings. As soon as he stepped into the warehouse, his gaze fastened on the enchanted forest.

“Oh, that there’s trouble,” Zeg said.

“I know.” Did he ever.

Zeg made a slow survey of the entire warehouse, then focused back on Nyx.

“Where’s Marny?” Zeg asked.

“Um. I’m not sure, exactly.”

The look on Zeg’s face darkened, and Nyx took a step back and raised his hands.

“Hey,” he said, “we don’t need to fight it out. She’s safe and unharmed.”

“Why isn’t she with you?”

Nyx stared at him. “How much do you even know?”

“Enough. And if you do anything to hurt my niece, now or in the future—”

"What, you'll challenge him to a Samoan-style duel?" Marny's voice was dryly amused.

Nyx looked up to see her leaning against the doorway, arms folded. The light from outside limned her in sunset tones, scattering red sparks in her wild hair and making her brown eyes glint almost golden.

She was big and strong and imposing. She was beautiful. Relief blew through him, a strong, rushing wind clearing away the last of his fear.

"Marny!" Ignoring her uncle, he hurried over to her, reached out, and took her by the shoulders. "You're here. You're okay."

"Yeah." Her smile broadened as her gaze met his. "Same to you. Is Emmie all right?"

"She's sleeping, and I don't know how to explain what happened to her, or if I even should."

"We'll figure it out. Now, are you going to hug me, or just stand there like a fool?"

With a huff of laughter, he drew her in close. Her arms went around him, and something clicked into place in his heart, something he hadn't even known he was missing.

"Break it up, lovebirds," Zeg said. "You've got some explaining to do."

"And a forest to banish." Nyx let go of Marny, closed the door behind her, then led them over to the couches by the dance floor.

Ruefully, he swept a look around his club. So much for the big experiment. The ashes of failure sifted over him, clogging his throat, but he had no choice. He had to close Club Mysteria

—for the night, before people started showing up. And then permanently.

"One sec," he said. "I have to go make a CLOSED sign."

"No worries." Marny gave him a sympathetic look. "We're not going anywhere."

As soon as Nyx left, Marny turned to Uncle Zeg and gave him a big hug.

"I'm so glad you're here," she said into his shoulder. "And I'm sorry for everything. This was almost a huge disaster."

"Hm." Her uncle patted her shoulders a few times, then let go. "Let's sit down and you can tell me how all this happened. I'll hear your young man's explanation when he gets back."

"He's not my young man," she said, dropping her gaze.

"Don't add self-delusion to your troubles. Now, start at the beginning."

Marny settled on the couch, Uncle Zeg across from her, and told him everything, starting with her first visit to the club. He listened and nodded, and asked a few questions, but mostly just let her talk.

When she got to their encounter with the Dark Queen, Marny felt her anger rise.

"And there we were," she said, "trapped on the back of the White Stag, and no help in sight. Then Nyx got hypnotized, and I was sure that was it—we were going to be the queen's sacrifice. Where were you guys? We really could have used a Feyguard!"

Uncle Zeg regarded her a long moment, his eyes warm and

understanding. “Did it ever occur to you that the reason the other Feyguard were not able to reach you was because there was already one on the scene—one with the power and ability to save you?”

“Well, who? Thomas couldn’t help us much, and Nyx was completely out of it.”

Her uncle smiled, the corners of his eyes crinkling. “You, Marny Fanalua. *You* are the hero you were waiting for. You are one of the Feyguard.”

Shock rippled through her, and she sat back. It couldn’t be true. Could it?

She thought back to all her encounters with the fey folk. The time she’d been drawn into the game against her will, the time she’d tracked and helped fight a goblin. And her adventures with Korrigan. When she’d saved him in the real world, during the other Feyguard’s epic battle against the combined power of the king and queen, she had glimpsed some of that fight. And she had seen…

“That black dragon,” she said softly. “It looked right at me.”

“At that moment you were recognized, my dear. You have the strength and fortitude of a Feyguard. I’m surprised you didn’t know right then you’d been called.”

“There was a lot happening,” she said, embarrassed. “And besides, I don’t even play Feyland. I don’t sim.”

“And yet you entered the Realm of Faerie and, using your wits and skills, helped rescue two other people. Playing the game of Feyland doesn’t make you a Feyguard, Marny. Strength and smarts and the ability to make good choices under pressure do. Plus, of course, an understanding of the Realm of Faerie and the creatures who live there.”

"Yeah." She blinked a couple times, sorting out all this new information. "I guess so."

She'd been so convinced of her role as a sidekick, as support staff, she'd never considered herself a hero. But apparently the world thought otherwise—and she'd have to deal with it.

"Now, about this Nyx Spenser," Uncle Zeg said. "I'm not sure he's the right guy for you."

"And why not?" She sat back up and looked her uncle in the eye. "Because he's handsome and white and rich?"

"Idiot." Uncle Zeg reached over and ruffled her hair. "No. Because he doesn't have the sense to listen when he's given good advice, and I'm not sure he can make a commitment, especially not to a girl who lives nearly a thousand miles away."

"How about you let us work that one out," Nyx said, striding from the back hallway, a sign in his hand. "Besides, Marny will be here all summer. We have time to figure out the details."

"Maybe not." Marny spoke around the lump of shame in her throat. "I blew my internship. They'll be sending me home tomorrow."

"Ah, no," Nyx said. He came over and squeezed her shoulders.

"Are you certain?" Uncle Zeg asked, giving her a close look.

"Well, not a hundred percent, but pretty sure. I'll know tomorrow night."

"Then we'll wait until tomorrow for the weeping, all right?" Uncle Zeg said.

She let out a breath, but really, there was no point in having a prolonged argument with her uncle about the fact she'd probably lost her internship.

"Let me put this sign on the door," Nyx said, his voice low.

He held it up. *Closed until Further Notice.*

Uncle Zeg gave him a thoughtful look. "I'd say you put a lot of effort into getting this place up and running," he said. "The idea of closing down must hurt. I know it would about kill me to shutter my simcafé."

"It was only open a week." Nyx gave a shrug that didn't fool anybody. It was clear he was desolated at the thought of closing Club Mysteria.

He trudged to the door and stepped outside to put up the sign.

"Marny," her uncle said. "Now that you know you're a Feyguard, what can you sense about the forest over there?" He waved his hand at the silvery trees taking up the back third of the warehouse.

Closing her eyes, she concentrated. She felt the magic of the Realm, but it was faint. Contained. What Nyx created really *were* bubbles, separated from the Realm of Faerie, but made from it, and therefore lightly connected.

"There's a... I don't know. A resonance?" She opened her eyes. "The forest isn't immediately dangerous, but it could be. Which is what I was trying to tell Nyx all along."

Uncle Zeg nodded. "I agree. Under most circumstances, this enchanted woods is a harmless amusement, sufficiently removed from the world of the fey folk to pose no danger."

"Circumstances can change." Marny gave him the eye. "What are you getting at, anyway?"

"I'll tell you in just a minute."

The warehouse door closed with a thud, and Nyx trudged back over and settled beside Marny on the couch.

"Your bubble worlds are fascinating," Uncle Zeg said.

"And severely dangerous." Nyx rubbed at his face, his voice tight with misery. "I'll get rid of it in a sec."

"I'm not convinced that's necessary," Uncle Zeg said. Marny and Nyx both stared at him in disbelief, and he let out one his rumbling laughs. "If there are safeguards, I think your club might be able to remain in operation. At least for a short time. Through the summer, maybe."

"What kind of safeguards?" Marny pursed her lips. She had an idea where her uncle was heading with this, and she wasn't sure she approved.

"Nyx is already in close contact with one of the Feyguard," he said, a twinkle in his eye. "Perhaps if she remains in Newpoint she can help keep an eye on things."

"That's not enough," she said, and felt Nyx beside her, nodding his agreement.

"Of course not. When dealing with the fey folk, it's always a good idea to have a couple layers of protection. Luckily, we happen to know a faerie inside the Realm who would probably be glad to take up temporary residence in this bubble world, or one much like it. Perhaps with a stream running through."

Marny's eyes went wide. "Brea," she breathed.

It was a kind of brilliant idea. Although...

"I'm not sure I'd want Roy underfoot all summer," she said. Because it was obvious that if Brea could come live in one of Nyx's creations, Royal would do everything he could to be there. And really, she couldn't blame him.

She shot a glance at Nyx, taking in his clean profile and

muscled shoulders. He turned his head, catching her looking, and smiled, and she went a little fluttery inside.

But it didn't mean she was weak. Just that she had a new burden to carry—one that she'd bear lightly, and full of joy.

Sometimes being strong meant opening up to the world, no matter how scary.

Whatever happened with Intertech, she knew she'd be spending the rest of the summer in Newpoint, figuring out how to keep her balance. How to be a Feyguard. And, maybe even more frightening, a girlfriend.

Taking Nyx's hand, she smiled back. "Everything's going to work out," she said.

And she believed it.

EPILOGUE

AUGUST 25

Marny sat across the expanse of black desk from Dettwiler von Coburg. Outside his immense office window, morning light lay over Newpoint, clear and bright. She glanced at the glass of cold water in front of her, then at Bruno the guard, hovering off to her right.

Unlike her previous encounter with the CEO two months ago, she felt relaxed and almost cheerful. As cheerful as a person could feel in von Coburg's presence, anyway.

He steepled his fingers and regarded Marny from icy blue eyes. "Well, Miss Fanalua, your internship here is concluded. I have never seen anyone with such a... rocky beginning end up with so many glowing recommendations."

Marny tipped up her chin. Yeah, the fact that she hadn't cooperated with his whole strong-arm technique for trying to cop VirtuMax secrets hadn't put her in his good graces. And then missing the first crucial team meeting had almost gotten her kicked out for good.

But, surprisingly, Brenna had decided that Marny—and Wil and Anjah—could have one more chance. In retrospect, it had been clever of the liaison. The three interns had buckled down, to the point that their team members mentioned they'd never seen such a dedicated, hardworking bunch.

In her limited off hours, Marny had spent a lot of time with Nyx. Thinking of him made her smile, but she quickly erased the expression. Nobody smiled around von Coburg.

"As you are no doubt aware," the CEO said, "during this exit interview, high-performing interns are occasionally offered a chance of future employment at Intertech. You are one such intern." His lips twisted a little, as if it pained him to say the words.

"Glad to hear it," she said, keeping her voice cool.

It was prime news—for most interns. But over the summer, Marny had gotten pretty clear about some things, including the fact that she had no desire to become a corporate drone. Even working for a company doing the kinds of cool things Intertech did. The *awesome* factor was severely offset by the work pace and byzantine politics. Not how she wanted to spend her life.

"To that end," von Coburg said, glancing down at the display on his desk, "Intertech is willing to offer you a position next spring, upon your graduation from high school. Provided you continue to earn sufficiently high marks, of course."

"That's quite an honor," Marny said. "But I think I'll pass. Thanks anyway."

A look of surprise jerked the CEO's eyebrows up, and for a millisecond his eyes lost that hard-edged shine. He recovered quickly, however.

"No need to answer right away," he said, as if she hadn't just turned him down. "Spend some time thinking it over. Our offer will stand until the end of this year."

"My answer isn't going to change." She stood up. "But I appreciate everything I've learned here." Especially the fact that corporate culture could be like a shackle around your neck.

"Do not forget the nondisclosure contract you signed, Miss Fanalua."

"Don't worry." She couldn't help it, she grinned at him. "I'm well aware of the proprietary nature of the work I did here this summer. All your secrets are safe with me."

Working with Intertech had opened her eyes to new things possible in the human/avatar interface. The last few weeks her mind had been swimming with notions about mods nobody had tried yet, and half-formed ideas about reality and virtual space and perception. She'd mentioned a couple of her thoughts to the Social Interface Design team, but the most prime ideas were still gelling in her brain.

When she was ready, though, she happened to know a business whiz who could help her take those ideas to the next step. And maybe a couple interns who could aid in making them a reality.

Later, though. For now, she was delighted to be leaving Intertech.

Even though it meant her time in Newpoint was almost over.

"Thank you," she said to Mr. von Coburg. "I've learned a lot here. It's been an invaluable summer." In so many ways.

The CEO rose and give her a chilly nod. "Good day, Miss Fanalua."

She tried not to skip down the plushly carpeted hallway as she followed Bruno's black-suited form to the VIP elevator.

It whooshed down, stopping smoothly to deposit her on the fortieth floor. Just before the doors closed, she gave Bruno a jaunty wave. His expression didn't change. It must be no fun being von Coburg's watchdog.

As soon as Marny stepped into the apartment, Anjah jumped up from the couch. Wil, who had been pacing around the room, gave her an expectant look. Both of them had completed their exit interviews—and both of them had gotten employment offers, too.

"Well?" Anjah asked. "Are you joining the ranks of the corporate drones next year?"

"Nope," Marny said. "But it's not because I wasn't asked."

Wil ambled over and gave her a high five. "And it's a sweep. Intern powers, activate!"

"Personally, I plan to attend the Data Technology Institute," Anjah said.

Wil shot Marny a quick eye-roll. The DTI was notoriously hard to get into, and Anjah acted like she was already admitted. Then again, you didn't reach the stars by stopping short at the moon.

"Eh, I might do it," Wil said. "Depends on what else comes along."

"Well, don't decide too quickly," Marny said. "I might have something in the works by the time next year rolls around."

"Ooh, Spenser-Fanalua Enterprises?" Anjah gave her a knowing look. "That boyfriend of yours is a serious powerhouse."

"Marny's no dim bulb, either," Wil said. "Oh, hey, I got you something. One sec."

He went into the kitchen and came out with a bag, which he held out to her.

She took it, eyebrows going up at the sweet scent drifting up as she opened the bag. Inside lay two foil-wrapped loaves, still warm to the touch.

"Coconut bread?" It was way more thoughtful of Wil than she'd given him credit for.

"I found a local bakery who'd do them up, special. Probably not as good as homemade, but..." He lifted a shoulder in a half-shrug.

Marny set the bag down, then swept Wil into a hug, ignoring his muffled yelp of surprise.

"You're the best," she said when she let go, then looked over at Anjah, standing stiffly to one side. "Get over here, princess. Group hug. You *both* are the best roomies a girl could want." Despite a difficult start.

Heedless of getting rumpled or smeared, Anjah joined them. When the hug broke up, her eyes were damp.

"I'm going to miss you guys," she said.

"Same," Wil said. "Except not the girly smells in the bathroom all the time. Perfume and ugh."

Anjah gave Marny a superior smile. "We women understand how to use all the tools at our disposal. You know, Wil, you should really consider plucking."

He gave her a panicked look. "Um, well, I gotta get my stuff together."

"Thanks for the bread," Marny said. "It means a lot."

"I owed you." He grinned at both of them. "Safe travels, ladies."

"Likewise," Anjah said. As soon as he was gone, she turned to Marny. "I owe you, too."

"We're way past that," Marny said. "I'll even wear some of the makeup you gave me. You have no idea how much forgiveness that is."

"I can guess." Anjah gave her a wry smile. "Stay beautiful, Marny."

"You too." Before either of them could tear up again, Marny hefted her backpack and duffel bag from where she'd left them by the door. "Ping me, anytime."

"Oh, I will. I want to hear all about how your *partnership* develops." There was a wicked twinkle in Anjah's eye.

"I'll keep you informed," Marny said, grinning, before slipping out the door.

Next stop, Club Mysteria. And more goodbyes she was not looking forward to.

Nyx was closing the place down, since Marny and Royal had to head back to Crestview. That pesky detail of finishing high school had to be taken care of, after all, and keeping the club open without any Feyguard around was way too dangerous.

Keeping it open *with* them there had felt risky enough, though they'd done everything they could to minimize the danger. Over the last few weeks, Brea had collared a couple minor fey folk trying to slip through and shoved them back into the Realm, and Roy had turned back a stray redcap. Other than that, though, the bubble world had stayed benign.

At least Nyx had made back his investment, not that he seemed to care too much.

"It was an interesting experiment," he'd said. "Time to try something else. Something less dangerous."

Then he'd shot her that smile that made her feel soft inside, and she'd folded her arms.

"I know that you and Royal are talking about a way to keep a bubble world going, for Brea," she'd said. "Doesn't sound entirely safe to me."

"Yeah, but it's not going to be a bubble where unwitting humans can wander in and out all the time, tempting the fey monarchs. Trust me."

She did, mostly—and she was relieved he was planning on setting up this next attempt in Crestview, where the Feyguard were thick on the ground. Although she was also a little scared of having him on her home turf. Uncle Zeg was coming around, but the rest of her family hadn't met Nyx yet. What if they hated him?

One thing at a time—and the next step was taking her leave from Brenna, who waited downstairs to collect her badge and see her out.

"Help you catch a grav-taxi?" the liaison asked as Marny handed over her Intertech ID.

"Sure." Marny took a last look at the spacious lobby, the huge vase of flowers—wildly colorful dahlias, this time—and all the busy worker-drones of Intertech buzzing in and out. She wasn't going to miss it.

"So, how'd the interview go?" Brenna asked as they headed

for the front doors.

"Good," she said. "You probably know I was offered a job."

"Mhm." The doors slid open, and they stepped out into the fresh autumn air. "And?"

"Much as I like you," Marny said, "and the rest of the Social Interfaces Design team, working for Intertech's not for me. Probably not a surprise to you, is it?"

Brenna smiled and tucked her silver strand of hair behind her ear. "I figured you'd turn von Coburg down. Our loss. I predict you're going to do some interesting things in the field."

Marny nodded. She was hoping to—but didn't want to say anything where Intertech's cameras and sensors could hear. She stepped forward and waved down a grav-taxi.

"It's been quite the experience," she said. "Thanks for everything."

"My pleasure." Brenna gave her a hug, then stepped back, her expression serious. "I admire you a lot, Marny. Keep being true to yourself."

"I will."

Even if that self meant encompassing a bunch of new ways of being. She'd spent the summer figuring them out: roommate, girlfriend, Feyguard. Not a corporate employee anymore though, thank goodness.

"Take care of yourself, too," she said to the liaison.

Marny stepped into the taxi and told the driver where to go, then waved at Brenna as they pulled away from the curb. Her last time paying exorbitant city fares.

The Intertech skyscraper cast a long shadow down the

street, but after several blocks they emerged into bright sunshine. In another minute, the grav-taxi dropped her off in front of what had been Nyx's club.

The warehouse door was open, but Nyx had removed the lettering on the walls. Only the faint shadow of the words *Club Mysteria* remained. Marny went inside, a pang going through her. The club had become so familiar, like a second home. It was hard to see it being dismantled.

No more dance floor and flashing lights, no more twinkly lights twined in green gauze. No juice bar—although that had been repurposed into a portable espresso cart that Emmie and Sula were going to run at their school. No doubt they'd end up making bank.

One thing remained, however, and it still made Marny's breath catch.

The enchanted forest.

The pale-trunked trees disappeared into shadows above a carpet of green mosses studded with white flowers. A small stream burbled along one side, silver-lit where shafts of sunshine struck it. The leaves stirred and whispered in the breeze.

On the bank of the stream a boy and a girl sat, holding hands. She had white flowers in her dark hair, and wore a gossamer gown. He was dressed in jeans and a sweatshirt, and though he was smiling, Marny could see the sorrow in his expression.

Yeah—she thought leaving Nyx was going to be hard, but her heart went out to Roy and Brea. It was never easy to say goodbye to the person you loved.

But they'd see each other again soon, when Nyx came to Crestview. And hopefully, something a little more permanent could be worked out for Brea. Nyx had even mentioned the idea of giving Brea tiny, personal anchors so that she could move around in the human world, while technically still being in the Realm of Faerie. If that worked, it would be a brilliant solution.

Nyx sat cross-legged on the warehouse floor, facing a little away from the couple in the forest. He looked up and smiled as Marny strode across the floor toward him.

"Hey," he said, patting the floor beside him. "Pull up a seat."

She settled beside him, shoulder leaning against his, and Roy glanced up, noting her presence. The sadness in his eyes deepened as he leaned forward to give Brea a farewell kiss.

"Don't worry," Nyx said, catching Marny's gaze. "I'll be in Crestview soon."

"I'm not worried. But I'll be glad to see you."

There were a million details to work out. Nyx wanted to rent an apartment, and though they hadn't talked much about it, she'd already started planning her next app. Then family, and school, and—oh yeah—the little detail about being a Feyguard, and things were looking fairly complicated for the near future.

That was okay, though. She'd never been afraid of having an interesting life.

Slowly, Roy stood up and walked out of the enchanted forest. He paused at the edge and lifted his hand in farewell, and Brea blew him a kiss. It turned into a white moth that flew to land in his reddish-brown hair.

"Ready?" Nyx called to him.

Roy's shoulders fell in a sigh, and he walked out from under the silver leaves. They rustled at his departure, and the moth took flight, disappearing against the pale trees. Further in, Brea stood, then dove into the stream. A bright splash, a shimmering ripple, and she was gone.

"All clear," Roy said, a catch in his voice.

Nyx opened his hand, where a shimmering leaf rested in his palm. He picked it up, held it between his fingers, and snapped it in two.

A single, clear chime sounded, resonating through the warehouse like it was the inside of a bell. Between one heartbeat and the next the forest faded, until only mortal sunbeams sifted through ordinary dust in the echoing space.

"Well," Nyx said. "That's the end of that."

"Not to sound all woo," Marny said. "But every end is another beginning. I thought you knew that, mister Zen philosopher."

That made Roy smile, just the faintest bit.

"Hi, Marns," he said. "I'll take your bag to my grav-car. Meet me out back when you're ready to go."

"Right."

She wasn't looking forward to the long drive back to Crestview with him, especially the way he drove. On the other hand, it beat taking the bus. And she figured they'd have enough to talk about. Royal Lassiter had turned into a fairly decent human being, after all.

As soon as Roy left, Nyx got to his feet and drew her up beside him.

For a long moment they looked into one another's eyes.

Hopes and dreams and unspoken promises flickered in the air between them, but there was no need for words.

Softly, patiently, their lips met—and that was all the magic Marny would ever need.

~*~

HOW TO BABYSIT A CHANGELING

The cafeteria at Crestview High was filled with the din of conversation, the clank of silverware on plasmetal trays, and somebody's tunes cranked up too loud, screeching tinnily out of their earbuds. Despite the noise, despite the smell of floor cleaner mixed with cooked cabbage, despite the fact that high school was all kinds of tedious, Marny Fanalua never let things get to her. It wasn't worth getting tangled up in small annoyances—and almost everything was small, when you took a breath and looked at it.

She sat across from her friends, slightly scruffy Tam Linn and rich-girl Jennet Carter. They'd all found out recently that life was a lot more interesting than they'd ever imagined.

A little *too* interesting at times, maybe. It wasn't every day a person discovered that their favorite sim video game was actually a portal into a treacherous magical world.

Marny leaned forward and rested her broad arms on the table, studying Tam's face. She'd known him a long time, and she could tell by the tightness around his eyes—what she could see of them behind the screen of his overlong brown hair—that something was severely wrong.

Wrong beyond the usual tweaked state of Tam's life, which was bad enough. Nobody could call scraping by in the Exe fun.

Maybe his mom had taken off again. In Marny's opinion the woman barely qualified for the title, other than the fact that she'd given birth to Tam and his little brother. So, either his mom had gone off her meds and left Tam and the Bug in the lurch again, or something freaky was going on.

And if it was something freaky, that meant magic. Fey magic.

"Okay, spill it," she said.

Jennet sent her a grateful half-smile, but Marny stayed focused on Tam. He clenched one hand, then smoothed it out flat over the scraped tabletop. Before speaking, he shot a quick glance at the neighboring tables, but nobody was paying attention to them. Why should they? She and Tam were misfits—always had been. And Jennet had become a lost cause to the status-conscious Viewer kids since becoming Tam's sort-of girlfriend.

"They've taken my little brother," Tam said, his voice tight.

Oh, crap. Marny narrowed her eyes. Tam's brother, the Bug, was a sweet kid, if a bit random.

"*They*, as in the Dark Court faeries?" she asked. Tam nodded, and coldness settled in the pit of her stomach. "How do you know?"

"I know because they left a changeling creature in his place." Tam swiped his hair out of his eyes. "My brother is being held hostage in the Realm of Faerie by the Dark Queen, in payback for Jennet and me meddling between the realms."

"Yeah well, your *meddling* is kind of crucial." Marny folded her arms. "It's keeping the fey from stealing human energy and opening a gateway to the mortal world. Stopping blood sacrifice. Little things like that."

"We never thought they could do something like this, though," Jennet said. "Tam's brother is in serious danger."

She would know, too, having encountered the queen a few times too many. The back of Marny's neck prickled. Personally, she was glad to have never encountered that particular being. One of the advantages of staying out of sim games. Especially Feyland, which had managed to use the game interface to open a gateway from the Realm of Faerie to the mortal world, with serious consequences.

"Also, my mom's gone again," Tam said, his gaze dropping to the dingy floor, as if it were his fault the woman had problems.

Double serving of trouble for Tam, then. Marny shook her head.

"How do we get your little brother out of Feyland?" she asked.

"We're working on that from the inside," Jennet said, laying one pale, slim hand on Tam's shoulder. "We'll get him back."

"Meanwhile there's a creature living in my house." Tam shoved his tray away, food uneaten. "I can't leave it there alone all the time."

Marny took a deep breath, instantly regretting it as the smell of overcooked spaghetti filled her nose.

"So, just to be clear—the Bug's been stolen away by the

faeries, and they left a substitute in his place?" she asked. "One that's now living with you?"

Tam nodded miserably.

"I want to meet him. It. Whatever," Marny said, before she even knew the words were going to come out of her mouth. Yet, it made perfect sense for her to get involved.

"What?" Tam jerked his head up, denial flashing through his green eyes.

"Look." She spread her hands wide. "You two have to deal with things in-game. The last thing you need to worry about is some freaky faerie dude pretending to be the Bug. Even though I don't sim, I can help with this."

Jennet nodded and looked at Tam. "She's right. We can't take care of the changeling, and beta testing Feyland, and everything else that's going on—not by ourselves."

"At least your mom's not around," Marny said. "It's crappy that she's gone, but the timing is decent. Considering. This way, if she comes home and you guys are, um, unavailable, I can run interference."

Tam and Jennet needed to get back in-game to try and rescue the Bug. And Marny *had* encountered the magic and creatures of Feyland before. She was up for this.

Looking after the changeling thing couldn't be much worse than the few times she'd babysat Tam's actual little brother, right? That kid was a ball of crazy energy.

The hubbub in the cafeteria was dying down, the tables emptying out.

"Okay." Tam swiped a hand through his hair. He looked like he'd barely gotten any sleep. "Marny, if you're free you can come over after school today and meet the changeling. Provided it's still there."

"It will be," Jennet said. "I think changelings have to stay close to home. Their pretend home, I mean. I'll read up in my folklore book and let you know what else I find out."

"Good." Marny nodded, her black hair tickling her cheek. "This should be interesting."

Tam and Jennet could have their adventures inside Feyland.

Gaming was fine, and she was good at it, as long as she wasn't simming. But Marny had always felt that real life contained more than enough weirdness for a person to deal with. And she never had figured herself for hero material, anyway. Sure, she was competent and smart and strong, but there were better-qualified people when it came to saving the world.

IT WASN'T Marny's idea of a fun time, going on foot through the Exe—basically the ghetto of Crestview—but there was no other way to get to Tam's house. They'd met up after school and she followed him down stinking alleys, stepping over puddles slimed with oil and decay. Past graffiti-layered buildings with broken windows staring like blind eyes, and through gang territory where a misstep could bring trouble raining down on their heads.

She was large, both taller and wider than Tam, and could handle herself in a fight—though probably not against an entire Exe gang. Still, she had a knife strapped to her calf, and the can of pepper spray her uncle insisted she carry everywhere. She and Tam would be all right.

But it wouldn't come to that. So far, they hadn't met any trouble. Even though she was big, she knew how to move silently as they picked their way deeper into the Exe.

Without speaking, Tam led her down the last block before his house. They carefully skirted the broken building where the yellow-eyed smoke drifters squatted. Marny wrinkled her nose against the sickly sweet smell, glad to see Tam's place up ahead.

The house was a rickety, two-room building perched on the flat roof of an old auto-repair shop, long closed. A blue tarp gone tattered and gray flapped across part of the shelter's roof, and the walls were patched with scabby pieces of corrugated metal.

Marny followed Tam up the rickety staircase on the side of the building. The railing wobbled under her hand.

"Watch the seventh tread," Tam said. "It's pretty rotted."

Yeah, last thing he needed was for a big Samoan girl to crash through and ruin his stairs. She skipped the seventh one, then waited at the top of the landing behind Tam as he used his ring of jingling keys to open the multiple deadbolts. Old tech, but reliable. It was too easy to hack a keypad system, and the authorities didn't care if your stuff got stolen, not here in the Exe. She doubted the cops even came out this far.

Tam slipped his keys into his back pocket. A shadow moved behind the wire-webbed window next to the door. Tam held up his hand, signaling her to wait, then pushed the door open and slipped inside.

Everything was quiet for a heartbeat. Two. Marny peered through the half-open door.

"Hiiiyyaaa!" a voice screeched.

The sound was wrong, something made from an inhuman throat. The hairs on Marny's arms rose. She banged open the door, to see a small creature clinging to Tam's shoulders. Its clawed hands were tangled in his hair, and bright eyes gleamed maliciously from a pale, wizened face.

"Hey!" Tam yelled. "Get off."

He tried to shake the thing loose, but it held on tight, like some gruesome parody of a kid taking a pony ride on its dad's shoulders.

"Gotcha!" The creature laughed, showing sharp teeth.

Marny was through the door in two steps. She swept up her right arm and put some power behind it. Not quite a punch, but enough to send the oddly-jointed creature tumbling down. It flew off Tam's shoulders, its screeching laughter ending in a squawk as it landed on the carpet.

"Nice," she said, staring at the creature's bulbous, eerie-looking eyes. Its skin had a greenish tinge.

"What is this?" it hissed, glaring up at them. "Another human to see me? Sheer folly."

Tam pivoted and shut the door, snicking the locks home. "What was that about, jumping on me?"

She could see Tam's urge to kick the changeling in his face —but he'd warned her and Jennet that however the changeling was treated, the same thing would happen to the Bug. Which meant no beating up the evil faerie creature, no matter how totally deserved.

"Tee-hee. 'Twas all a bit of fun. Surprised you, did I?" The changeling grinned up at Tam and leaped to its feet. "Now feed me."

"Quite a houseguest you have there," Marny said. Maybe she shouldn't have volunteered for changeling-sitting duty after all. "As annoying as your little brother is, I prefer the Bug to *this*."

"What you think matters little to me," the changeling said.

Marny rolled her eyes at Tam and followed him into the kitchen. He flipped the electric kettle on to boil, then rummaged around in the cupboards. There didn't seem to be much to eat. Dried noodle packets, a couple lonely cans of synth-meat. Tam grabbed a few protein bars and banged the cupboard doors shut.

"Here," he said, flipping a bar through the air to the changeling.

The creature caught it and held it up to the light. "What is this item?"

"Food," Tam said, then gave Marny an exasperated look as the changeling bit into the protein bar right through the plastic packaging.

"Feh." The creature spit on the floor. "Mortal sustenance used to taste much better."

"You don't eat the wrapper," Marny said. "Peel it, like this."

She took a bar from Tam and tore off the shiny plastic. The changeling watched her, then stripped off the wrapper and popped the whole bar into his mouth.

"Still tasteless," he said, squinching his already-wrinkled face into a sour expression.

"At least we agree on that," Marny said, handing her bar to Tam.

"What?" he said. "You don't like synthesized nut-flavored protein bars?"

"I prefer my uncle Zeg's cookies."

And it was obvious Tam didn't have a lot of food in his cupboards. She wasn't hungry, and even if she were, she wouldn't eat up his few supplies.

"Me too," he said, "but I don't have any of those lying around. Tea?"

"Yeah—mint if you've got it." Tea was cheap, and it would be rude to completely refuse his hospitality.

Tam pulled out two mugs and a packet of tea bags. Marny noticed he scarfed down two of the protein bars. Right—he hadn't had any lunch. Not that school lunch was any better than the dry, non-flavored bars.

"So." She turned to the changeling, squatting on the floor like a toad. "What's your name?"

"Are you trying to trick me, mortal?" His gleaming eyes narrowed.

She raised an eyebrow. "As in...?"

"Names have power in the Realm," Tam said. "Generally, they aren't freely given out."

Marny pursed her lips. Made sense. She took the cup of tea Tam handed her.

"Right," she said. "Then what shall we call him?"

Tam frowned and shot a look at the creature. "I've been thinking of him as not-Bug."

"Catchy—but we can do better." She looked down at the fey creature again. "Changeling, what name do you use when you're in the mortal world? Doing, you know, baby impersonations."

The changeling folded its spindly arms and glared up at her. "I am called by the child's name."

"Yeah." Tam set his mug of tea on the counter. "Except we know you're not my little brother. Either you choose something, or we will."

"Yoda," Marny said, laughing internally at the idea of naming the creature after an ancient film character.

"Too obvious." Tam looked the changeling over. "How about... Bilbo."

"Nah." Marny was too fond of the Hobbit characters to give this ugly creature one of their names. "If anything, it's a Gollum."

She was glad Tam still remembered the moldering old paper book they had both read the summer they were ten. Had the author based his stories on glimpses of the Realm?

"Stop." The changeling bared his pointed teeth. "If you insist, you may call me Korrigan."

He made a mighty leap up onto the counter and took a guzzling sip of Tam's tea.

"Hey, that's mine!" Tam reached for his mug, then paused, probably thinking he didn't want to put his lips where the changeling's had just been. "Fine. Drink up."

With an evil, triumphant grin, Korrigan slurped the tea down. The thing had no manners at all. When he was done, the counter was splattered with liquid. He let out a belch that sounded like a bellowing frog, and wiped his mouth with the back of his hand. Although he seemed satisfied, Marny kept a tight hold on her own mug, just in case.

"Well, mortals," he said. "I cannot set foot over the threshold of this dwelling unless Tamlin is with me."

"And thank goodness for that," Marny muttered under her breath. Crestview sure didn't need a rude changeling creature running loose through the Exe.

Korrigan shot her a narrow-eyed look, then continued. "Since I am trapped in this wretched space, what is there to do here that will amuse me?"

"What do you normally do?" she asked.

"I squall and mewl like an infant. I flail my arms and legs, and lie in the cradle."

"Doesn't sound all that fun." In fact, it sounded stupefyingly boring.

She'd bet good credits the changeling was happy to be recognized as a faerie instead of having to pretend otherwise. Although maybe *happy* wasn't an apt word. Korrigan seemed a grumpy thing at best.

"So, you usually pretend to be much younger children," Tam said. "Why did they send you this time?"

The changeling frowned, and Marny changed her opinion from grumpy to hideously grumpy.

"It is how the thing is done," Korrigan said. "There cannot be a taking without a replacement. Most stolen children are but infants. Your brother is a special case."

That was true enough, though Marny refrained from pointing it out. Just because the Bug was all kinds of random and had tried to burn down the house a couple times didn't mean he deserved to be spirited away into the Realm of Faerie.

"Yeah," Tam said, crossing his arms. "He's a hostage."

He sounded tired and depressed, like he was about ready to give up on everything. Marny could see that losing his brother felt like the last straw.

"Tam," she said, "did you get any sleep last night?"

He shook his head in a quick, sharp negation. The shadows under his eyes were proof enough that he was exhausted.

"Go lie down," she said. "I'll show Korrigan a few basic screenie games, okay? That should keep him busy and out of trouble."

Plugging kids into screen entertainment was a time-honored tactic for keeping them occupied, and she had a feeling it would work with Korrigan. She'd guess that part of his nastiness was from sheer boredom at being marooned in the human world. Not all of his foul temper, of course. He was a fey creature from the Dark Court after all.

Yet maybe if she treated him decently, someone would do the same for the Bug.

Worry zinged through her at the thought of Tam's little brother. But they couldn't help him right now. They were doing everything they could—and for her, that meant making sure Tam got some sleep and keeping his unwelcome guest distracted and out of trouble.

"Just don't let him onto the 'net," Tam said.

"Bug's account is locked out, right?" She glanced to the corner of the living room, at Tam's netscreen setup.

She could imagine the trouble Korrigan could get into with unfettered worldwide 'net access. Not a pleasant prospect.

"Yeah," Tam said. "Log him into that, it should be fine."

He yawned, and Marny gave him a push toward the single bedroom. It was where his mom usually slept, but since she was gone...

"Get some rest," she said. "I'll introduce the changeling to the joys of Kart racing."

"Show no mercy," Tam said, heading for the bedroom.

"I won't." She grinned.

It would be fun taking the creature down a notch. And really, even if Korrigan got super cranky, she could always just sit on him.

As soon as the bedroom door closed, Korrigan began leaping about. He bounded onto the back of the shabby couch that doubled as Tam's bed, and looked like he was going to make a leap for the light fixture.

"Chill," Marny said. "Or I won't give you any more protein bars."

"They are like eating dirt," the changeling said, but he subsided, sprawling his knobby legs out.

"You still gobbled it up quick enough." She wondered what he'd think of chocolate. Or that crazy-sweet sugar cereal the Bug liked.

On second thought, maybe hopping Korrigan up on sugar and caffeine wasn't a brilliant idea.

He made a face at her. "You see too much, mortal girl. It is not usual for a human to perceive my real form. Why, I wonder, were you able to?"

Marny went to the screen setup and flicked the power on. She could think of at least one good reason.

"I've had faerie ointment smeared around my eye," she said.

It was weeks ago, but maybe the effects were long term. Unsettling, the thought that she'd be able to see any fey folk hanging out in the human world. Not a power she was comfortable with—but it seemed like she'd have to accept it.

Korrigan shuddered. “Nasty human potion. Unfair, to see through our glamours so easily.”

“Yeah, well making that potion nearly trapped my friends in the Realm forever. So I’d say it was pretty hard won.”

She picked up the two gaming controllers and gave Korrigan a hard look. It was probably a good bet he’d never driven a car in his immortal life.

“Have you ever ridden on a wild beast?” she asked.

He grimaced. “Aye, the Hunt took me up and brought me to the queen, where my servitude as a changeling began. Not a ride I would wish to repeat.”

Marny nodded. She’d heard the Wild Hunt once, strange and eerie over the streets of Crestview. The clear cry of a horn had floated over the barking of eldritch hounds and the thud of hoof beats racing through the sky. She was just as glad never to have seen the elfin knights on their red-eyed mounts—and especially not the horned Master of the Hunt. It was enough hearing Tam and Jennet talk about the fearsome riders.

“Okay.” She studied the changeling’s wrinkled face. “You’ve never hopped on a fox’s back and steered it with its ears or anything?”

“Not if I wanted to keep my legs,” Korrigan said. “The vulpine creatures of the Realm are not to be trifled with.”

“Then we’ll have to take this slow.” Marny handed him the controller, which he immediately brought to his mouth. “Stop! It’s not something you eat.”

Korrigan wrinkled his nose and examined the plastic buttons. “Then what good is it?”

“Watch.”

Marny booted up the kart racing game and quickly selected

the easiest mode and course. She chose her favorite vehicle, the blue one with dark green stripes.

"This is my racer," she said. "I control the speed and direction here." She demonstrated the controls, pushing the buttons and levers that made her kart move.

Korrigan looked at the netscreen, then back to the hunk of plastic in its hands. "It is a magical device?"

"I guess you could say that." She supposed the mechanics of remote-controls and screenie games were close enough to magic.

"What else might I command?" The changeling pivoted and pointed the remote at the kitchen cupboard. "Bring me a bar."

When nothing happened, he threw the controller to the floor.

"It doesn't work that way," Marny said. "You can only influence things on the screen. Which is this." She leaned forward and tapped the side of the netscreen.

"Will it produce food and drink, or fetch items from the Realm?" Korrigan asked.

"No, it just plays games. But it's fun. Now pick a kart." She pulled up the choices and used her remote as a pointer. "Do you like any of these?"

The changeling peered at the screen. "The one on the end, with the flames."

"Good pick. Now grab your controller and I'll show you how to move. Then we'll race."

Korrigan picked up the basics surprisingly quickly, and before long was zipping around the track, muttering under his breath as he tried to catch up with Marny. He screeched with glee whenever he passed one of the game-controlled racers.

“Putrid bog fungi!” he cried as his kart spun off the course yet again.

“You’re taking that turn too fast,” Marny said.

“My velocity matches yours,” he replied, grunting as he waved the controller and got his vehicle turned back around.

“Yeah but I’ve got a few years of experience on you.”

“But I am a fey creature, and you but a mortal girl.”

“A mortal girl who’s kicking your ass,” she said. Still, maybe she was being too hard on him. “Do you want to try something different?”

He glanced at her, his pale eyes slitted. “Are you trying to trick me?”

“Always with the suspicion. No—I’m offering you some other options.” She scrolled to a new course, featuring a race through the mushroom swamp instead of the colorful hills. “Let’s do this one.”

“Ah.” Korrigan leaned forward, his ugly mouth splitting into a grin. “This is much more pleasant in aspect.”

“All right, then.” Clearly, the changeling’s idea of pleasant involved copious amounts of muck and slime.

The timer counted down, and at the buzzer they took off, their bright cars zipping through the murky trees. Marny lagged a little, letting Korrigan stay close, but by the end of another hour, his skills had improved enough that she didn’t need to give him a handicap. She still beat him in the overall scores, though.

“Hey.” Tam opened the door of the bedroom and rubbed his eyes. “You still here, Marny?”

"Yep." She glanced out the wire-webbed window. "Getting dark."

"You're not walking home by yourself," Tam said.

"And you're not walking back alone after dropping me off," she said. "I'll ask Uncle Zeg to come get me. It's not that far." She pulled out her messager and sent her uncle a quick note.

"As if that racketing guzzler of his is low profile. I can't believe he keeps that old car running."

"We'll be okay. Zeg can out-drive anything."

"I want to race more," Korrigan said, leaping on to the back of the couch. "Next time, I will be victorious, I am certain of it."

"You can practice against the game," Tam said. "You don't need a real person to play with."

The changeling made a face, but turned back to the netscreen and soon was accelerating through the swamp once more.

"You feeling better?" Marny asked, giving him a hard look.

The smudges beneath his eyes weren't quite as dark, and his mouth seemed less pinched with exhaustion and strain.

"Adequately," he said.

"The beta team plays tomorrow afternoon, right?" she asked.

"Yes." He ran a hand through his hair, then let the strands fall back into his face. "I hope Jennet and I can get some answers. We have to figure out how to make the game safe for normal players, instead of them getting sucked into the Realm."

"I'll come over after school again," Marny said. "Keep the freaky dude out of trouble."

"Okay. I'll get you the extra set of keys for the front door."

Tam glanced at the creature squatting on the couch, and misery flashed through his eyes. "I guess that's all we can do right now."

Marny patted his shoulder. "Hang in there."

She couldn't promise that everything would come out okay —who could? But she knew they'd all try.

IT WAS a sign of how upset and distracted Tam was that he didn't ask Marny how she was getting to his house that afternoon. After school, he caught a ride to the beta testing with Jennet, giving Marny a halfhearted wave as they pulled away.

She'd planned ahead, though, and arranged for her uncle to drop her off at Tam's on his way up to the VirtuMax compound. Going alone into the Exe was plain stupid.

In fact, Uncle Zeg was the only member of her family who knew she was, as she'd put it, "helping Tam with a project at his place." Her mom would freak if she knew Marny was in the Exe without Tam, and Grandma Harmony would lecture her, then insist on telling her for the thousandth time all the ways to keep the *aitu*, or ghosts, away.

Marny went up the creaky stairs to Tam's place, undid the multiple locks on the front door, then waved to Uncle Zeg. He putted away, leaving a cloud of oily smoke in the middle of the potholed street.

It was nice to be out of the house and have some breathing room, even if she had to share that room with a fey creature. Babysitting Korrigan made a nice change from the bustling, close quarters of her own home. It wasn't that much bigger than Tam's place, and felt smaller, with her younger brother's projects always underfoot, her older twin sisters arguing night and day, Dad's boisterous jokes, and Grandma Harmony's weird teas scenting the air with bitter and pungent herbs.

Marny pushed Tam's front door open. She was greeted by a swath of vines sporting bright, poisonous-looking flowers. More plants lurked in the corners, fringed with sharp teeth.

"Jump on me, and you're meat," she called as she stepped into the jungle of Tam's living room.

From overhead, Korrigan let out an unhappy sigh. He let himself down, hand-over-hand, on one of the ropey vines hanging from the ceiling. Squatting on the floor, he blinked up at her. He almost seemed happy to have company.

"What's with the foliage?" she asked, batting away a tendril that tried to fasten around her wrist.

"This human habitation is far too plain," Korrigan said. "I thought to enliven the surroundings."

Marny kicked at a groping root. "Well, how about you un-enliven things. I'd prefer not to be some plant's snack."

"I doubt it would find you palatable," the changeling said.

Marny gave him a look, and he sniffed and waved his hands in a complex series of gestures. The vines curled up into the ceiling and the hungry-looking plants in the corner disappeared. A nearby orange flower imploded with a fleshy pop, leaving a wet spot on the dingy carpet.

"Better." Marny dug in her pack and held out a handful of silver-wrapped protein bars. "I brought you a treat."

The changeling's eyes lit, and he snatched the bars from her as if he were starving. Quickly, he stripped off the wrappers and stuffed all three bars in his mouth at once. Brown drool ran from the corner of his mouth, and Marny had to turn away from the disgusting sight. At least she'd been right that, despite his complaining, Korrigan liked the taste of the protein bars. Either that or he was really really hungry all the time.

Good thing she had another half dozen bars in her pack. Never knew when bribery would come in handy.

"Ready for some racing?" she asked.

Korrigan wiped his mouth with the back of his hand. "I shall defeat you this time."

"Yeah, we'll see about that." She was tempted to let him win once or twice, but it felt too patronizing. The changeling was quick and clever. When he came in first, beating her, it would be on his own merits.

Marny flicked on the netscreen system, and soon she and Korrigan were jockeying for position as they sped through colorful caverns. He was getting much more skilled, she'd give him that—but he still wasn't as good as she was. They played for two hours, and she let him come in a close second a few times, to keep his spirits up.

"Okay, break time." Marny tossed the controller on the couch, then stood up and stretched.

Korrigan pouted, until she gave him another protein bar.

"So," she said. "What's it like, where you're from?"

The changeling let out a heavy sigh. For a moment the sneer fell away from his mouth.

"It is full of magic and mystery. Your mortal world is nothing but drab and weary." He flicked the brown carpet with one finger.

"You've only seen the inside of Tam's house," Marny said.

"There's a lot more to discover. I bet you'd be impressed with the ocean."

"We have seas in the Realm," he said with a sniff.

Still, she suspected he'd like to get out of the tiny house at some point. Maybe she and Tam could figure out a field trip. Though she really hoped the Bug would be returned soon.

"Why don't you go back there for a quick visit, and let Tam's brother come home for a bit?" she asked.

"The queen would never allow it." Korrigan shivered, then grabbed his game controller. "Let us commence racing."

Although Marny wanted to press for more information about the Dark Queen, she could tell Korrigan was done with that subject. For now.

They spent another hour mindlessly racing, until the rattle of the gas guzzler outside and the jingle of the locks signaled that Tam was home. He stepped through the door just as Marny scored another victory.

"Noo!" Korrigan flung down his controller.

"I win. Again." She glanced up at Tam. "Hey, how'd the beta testing go today?"

"Good." He sounded a little more upbeat. "I'll tell you about it tomorrow at school. Zeg's out there waiting for you."

"I know—the sound of his car is unmistakable." She rose and gathered up her back and coat. "See you later, Korr. Better work on those driving skills."

The changeling stuck his tongue out at her and crossed his eyes. "I shall master this ridiculous mortal game yet."

"He's totally hooked, poor guy." Marny shook her head, then headed for the door. "See you tomorrow."

She hoped whatever Tam and Jennet had managed to

accomplish in-game, they were that much close to bringing the Bug home.

MARNY WAS TUCKING her things in her backpack at the end of the school day when Jennet came rushing up, her big blue eyes wide.

"We need your help," she said.

"As in?" Marny closed up her pack, then looked at Jennet. There was a pleading in her friend's expression she mistrusted.

"Um. Tam's taking Roy Lassiter to his place to see the changeling, and you have to go with them."

"What? That's a terrible idea."

Not just having to share air with Roy, but exposing Korrigan to any more people. She was starting to feel oddly protective of the ugly little guy.

"I know." Jennet pressed her lips together in the way she did when she was upset. "But we have to prove to Roy that Tam's little brother is a hostage in the Dark Realm, so he'll let me and Tam use his sim equipment to get into Feyland. The only way to do that—"

"Is to introduce him to Korrigan. I see." Marny crossed her arms. "You better hope Roy doesn't sell you and Tam out. If your dad finds out you two are spending illicit in-game time together, things could get even more severe."

"I know. But saving the Bug is more important than whether my dad grounds me for a year. Now, will you come?"

Marny let out a sigh. Of course she'd go. She picked up her backpack.

"Fine," she said. "Lead on."

She couldn't help grimacing when she saw Royal Lassiter standing outside with Tam. Ever since Roy had used his faerie glamour on her to make her play Feyland, she'd pretty much detested him. Not only had he forced her in-game despite her claustrophobia, he'd also made her have a disgusting crush on him. The boy had a very sketchy sense of decency.

Jennet gave Tam one of her *Iloveyou* smiles. "Message me when you get up to the View, and I'll meet you at Roy's. Good luck."

Roy made a noise of disgust, either at the little love darts coming out of Tam and Jennet's eyes whenever they looked at each other, or the fact that Jennet was sure he'd let them onto his sim system. Probably both.

Marny turned her shoulder to him, and stayed a couple feet behind as he led them to the parking lot where his shiny red grav-car was parked.

"I'm sitting in back," she said as Roy waved the doors open. "Tam can enjoy the pleasure of your company."

She didn't even want to brush up against him accidentally. She couldn't believe she'd once actually wanted to kiss the guy. Of course, she'd been under a spell, but still. She'd rather kiss Korrigan, who at least was honest with his bad self.

Roy slid behind the wheel and started the car.

"I don't suppose you have a real address I can put in the navbot?" he asked Tam, sounding all superior.

"Not so much." Tam's voice was calm, but Marny could see him flexing his fingers. "I'll tell you how to get there."

As they drove to the Exe, Marny braced herself against Roy's wild driving and watched the neighborhoods change.

Already faded and dumpy around Crestview High, they quickly disintegrated until all pretense of normal suburbia was gone. Half the buildings were empty, and the other half, Marny didn't want to know who lived inside.

"You sure it's safe?" Roy asked, slowing to navigate over a pile of rubble in the street.

"Of course it's not," Marny said. "Just do what Tam says, and we should be all right."

She was a little worried Roy would get all bossy and make his own decisions, which couldn't end well for them. Luckily, he showed some good sense, following Tam's directions as they wound through the outskirts of the Exe.

They got to an area Marny recognized. Sure enough, Tam's blue tarp roof came into view. He pointed to the alley beside the old auto shop.

"Pull up over there," he said. "And put the alarm on."

"Of course," Roy said. "It's triple-alarmed."

Not as alarmed as Roy would be if somebody decided to mess with his car. As if a siren would stop anyone.

"You seriously live here?" Roy asked, and Marny wanted to punch the smug expression off his face.

"Shut it," she said. "Welcome to the real world, rich boy."

Some day, she hoped Roy would get his comeuppance. Something that would shake his world, like being disowned by his rich CEO mom, or falling in love with a girl he could never have.

As soon as the car stopped, Tam slipped out and hurried up the stairs. Marny and Roy followed, though she hung back. The last thing she wanted was Roy behind her, where she couldn't see what he was up to.

Tam had the door open by the time they got to the top of the stairs. Inside, his living room was back to being a crazy jungle. Marny laughed a little, quietly. She hoped one of the flowers took a bite out of Roy's arm.

"Korrigan?" Tam called as they stepped into the house.

The smell of rank vegetation filled the air, and orange flowers with serrated teeth grew on ropey vines hanging from the ceiling. There seemed to be a waterfall in the kitchen, too. Nice touch.

"You have a way with decorating, Exie," Roy said. Beneath the bravado in his voice, she could hear fear.

He reached a finger out to touch one of the flowers, then jerked it back when the blossom opened its mouth and hissed at him.

Marny reached into her pack and pulled out a protein bar. Better to lure the changeling out than risk another ambush.

"Come out, Korr," she called. "I've got a treat for you."

The leafy canopy overhead rustled, and Korrigan stuck his head out.

"Protein bar? Give it to me." He stuck out his hand, his claws extended.

"A little less jungle, please." She held the bar out of reach and waggled it back and forth. "And ditch the carnivorous flowers."

He grimaced. "You mortals have no appreciation for the spice of danger."

Marny glared at him, and Tam let out a frustrated breath.

"We have more than enough danger going on right now," he said. Then he glanced at Roy, who looked way uncomfortable. "Seen enough?"

"Yeah." Roy swallowed, his gaze darting from Korrigan, to the flowers now smacking their lips, to the slick yellow moss under their feet.

"So, you believe us?" Tam pressed.

"Fine, fine. You were right." Roy looked up at the changeling and winced. "I guess if we can be transported to Feyland, its creatures can come out."

"You have no idea," Tam said. "Let's go."

Marny nodded. Korrigan loved an audience—maybe a little too much. As soon as the boys cleared out, she'd be able to get the changeling to clean up the jungle, and then distract him with more racing.

"One sec," Roy said, pulling out his sleek messager. "Let me vid this."

Holding it up, he slowly turned in place, panning the room. When he got to Korrigan, he paused and Marny could see him zooming in.

"Smile," she said to Korrigan.

The changeling obliged, grinning wide enough to show his pointed teeth. His eyes slitted nearly shut, and the proportions of his face were very clearly inhuman.

"Nice." Roy thumbed the power off and tucked his messager away.

Marny wasn't too worried that Roy would try to do anything stupid with the images, like post them out on the 'net. Stuff like that could be faked all too easily, and everyone knew it, even with someone swearing eyewitness testimony.

"No more water features in the kitchen, ok?" Tam gave the changeling a stern look.

Korrigan grimaced back, but made no promises.

Marny hid her smile. Tam should know better by now not to try to bargain with the fey folk. Even she, who had only a fraction of the experience dealing with them, knew how tricksy they could be.

"You guys go have fun," she said to Tam. "I'll make him clean up. I have the rewards, you know."

"Protein bars." Tam sounded disgusted. He was probably just jealous he hadn't figured out how fond of them the changeling actually was.

"Go," she said. "And be careful."

Despite her earlier words, Tam wasn't going to sim for fun. Tam, Jennet, and Roy were headed back into Feyland. And no matter the growing fondness Marny felt for Korrigan, she really hoped they'd be able to get Tam's brother home. Soon.

"You be careful, too," Tam said. "Keep the door fully locked."

Oh, she would. The Exe might not be full of faerie peril, but there was plenty of human danger. Everything from the fact that Tam's mom could come home at any moment, which was more complication than threat, to the packs of gangs who roamed the crumbling streets, to the yellow-eyed smoke drifters who squatted in the abandoned building down the street.

As soon as Tam and Roy left, she did up all the locks, smacking the deadbolts home and sliding the chains and bars across. Then she turned to Korrigan.

"Race?" he asked, his bulbous eyes bright.

"How about you clean up, first."

He groaned, sounding like a human teenager, but the vines

curled into the ceiling and disappeared, and the waterfall slowly gurgled away down the kitchen sink drain.

"Better." Marny tossed him the second remote, then settled on the couch.

"I shall beat you this time, mortal," Korrigan said.

He tried, too. For nearly two hours they raced and zoomed, and the changeling managed to push Marny to her limit. She was hanging on to her wins, but just barely.

At last, back on the mushroom swamp course, Korrigan edged past her on a turn, and cackled.

"Prepare to lose," he said, his voice high with glee.

Marny bit her lip and pushed her speed to the max, but it was too late. With a screech of triumph, the changeling crossed the finish line a moment before her.

"Heehee!" he cried. "Victory is mine."

"Good job."

He'd worked hard for that win, and it was worth it to see the goofy grin on his ugly face. Who would have thought a faerie would enjoy playing screenie games so much?

Then his expression sobered and he lifted his head, all trace of gleefulness gone. He looked dangerous now, like the fey creature from the Dark Court he truly was.

"Someone approaches," he said, his gaze moving to the wire-webbed window.

Marny hit the pause button, cutting off the happy music tinkling from the speakers. The back of her neck prickled with unease.

"Is it Tam?" she asked, already knowing the answer.

"No." The changeling screwed up his face. "Many men, with evil intent."

Crap, and double crap. Either a gang or the drifters. She'd bet credits someone had spotted Roy's fancy red grav-car parked outside earlier, and drawn the wrong conclusions about what riches might lie inside Tam's house.

Reaching past Korr, she clicked off the lamp—a clunky brass fixture with old-fashioned wiring instead of a sensor plate. The netscreen sent a pale glow over them, the word *PAUSED* blinking like a silenced alarm. From the street below, Marny heard voices.

Then the clomp of footsteps on the stairs.

Crash!

She jumped at the sound of splintering wood. Somebody yelled, then cursed loudly, and she guessed they'd gone right through the rotted seventh step.

Her hand went to the knife strapped on her leg, under her jeans—but that was for closer fighting, one-on-one. It was not the right weapon to deal with a group assault.

Her heart thumping out a heavy beat in her chest, Marny slowly rose. The locks on the door would keep the intruders out. She hoped.

Korr gave her a quizzical look, and she held up her hand, signaling him to stay there.

"Hey!" The voice was accompanied by someone pounding at the door. "We know you're in there. Listen, just give us all your money, and we won't come in and hurt you."

As if Marny would crack the door open and simply hand over any nonexistent cash. Must be smoke-drifters; gang members would be more clever in their approach.

Which was good, and bad. Drifters were dumb, having numbed their brains with too much smoke. But it could also make them stupidly persistent when any normal person would go away after a while.

"I am ready to fight," Korrigan said, keeping his voice low. He flexed his clawed hands, a wild light coming into his eyes.

"I bet." He could be an asset, for sure.

But it sounded like at least a half dozen guys were outside. One group on the landing, another down in the street. The two of them against six or seven drifters wasn't good odds. Even with a scrappy fey changeling on her side.

"Come on." The banging on the door intensified. "We know you got cash."

"Begone, foul mortals," Korrigan screeched. "There is nothing here for you."

Marny sent him a sour look. Great. Although it hadn't been likely the drifters would simply leave, the chances of that happening had just evaporated to nothing.

"Some kid," one of the drifters muttered.

"Bring it up," another one said. "We'll beat the door down."

A few seconds later, the door shook with the clang of metal on metal. The drifters had found something large to bash against the door; one of those big metal burn barrels, maybe. If she and Korrigan were lucky, their attackers would only dent the door some, then go away.

But it didn't feel like a lucky night.

Clenching her hands, Marny quickly evaluated their options. She and Korrigan could retreat to the bedroom, maybe get out the window there and climb down the back of the building...

But even if she could squeeze through, the changeling

wasn't able to leave the house unless Tam were with him. Dammit. They couldn't escape—so they'd have to fight.

With the constant clashing thud of the drifters at the door as a background, Marny pulled out her old messager and keyed in a quick call for help.

Not to the police—they'd take too long, if they even came out at all. Tam said the authorities ignored the Exe as much as possible. And she didn't want to risk revealing Korrigan.

:Under attack at Tam's. Help. Bring firepower.:

Uncle Zeg would get her message and be on the way, hopefully with the big flamethrower he'd recently finished rebuilding. Her uncle was worth at least three or four of the drifters, and she knew she could take a couple. Korrigan would pitch in, and they'd repel the attack. They just had to sit tight until Zeg showed up.

She almost messaged Tam, too, but he'd be in-game, and doubtless fighting his own battles. No, she could handle this.

Probably.

"Korr," she said, keeping her voice low, "if they break in, do you have any offensive magic to throw at them? Not the jungle though—it could get in our way."

The changeling gave her one of his horrific grins.

"I can summon any number of nasty crawlies to bite and sting our enemies, should they breach the walls," he said.

"Good. Because I have a feeling things are about to get real."

Not that she thought the drifters would smash through the door, but she'd been keeping an eye on the shadows moving across the wire-webbed living room window. One guy had what looked like a big wooden club, maybe a baseball bat, and it was only a matter of time before he started swinging it at the glass.

She bent and unplugged the cord of the old-fashioned brass lamp on the table by the couch, then stripped the shade off. In this fight, she'd rather swing something heavy at an attacker's head than try to hit a vital spot with a small, pointy object.

The yelling outside intensified, and two of the shadowy figures turned to the window. One of them lifted his club and swung.

The first crack of wood against glass made Marny wince. No telling how long the window would hold.

"Get ready," she said to Korrigan.

He flexed his spindly, oddly jointed fingers, and nodded.

Another whack, and a spider web of cracks spread across the reinforced glass. It wouldn't be long. She took a deep breath and widened her stance.

The third blow shattered the window, square-edged pieces of safety glass flying into Tam's living room.

"Ha! Told you we could bust it out." The drifter with the wooden club poked at the empty wire, then shoved it aside.

He began to clamber through the wrecked window, but Marny was ready. She brought the lamp down hard on the top of his head, and he crumpled.

"Dude. Why'd you stop?" His companion toed him in the ribs.

A second later, a swarm of weird looking insects poured from around Korrigan and out the widow. Some of them paused to bite and sting the unconscious man, but the rest kept going.

"Hey! Ow! Get off!" the man right outside the window yelled.

Marny glanced at Korrigan. He was mumbling, his fingers moving in strange patterns, his concentration on the insects.

Two more drifters tried to rush the window, which was stupid, because they couldn't both fit through. Marny whacked at them with the base of the lamp. Various cries of pain issued from outside, and one guy ran screaming down the stairs. Still, most of the drifters were not as easily gotten rid of. They'd stopped trying to bang the door down, and turned to the shattered window.

In the distance, Marny heard the loud cough and rattle of a gas car engine, and she smiled through the grimness of battle. Uncle Zeg was on his way. She and Korrigan only needed to hold their attackers off a few moments more.

The gas guzzler pulled up with a screech of brakes loud enough to make the drifters turn. Marny struck the current window-broacher on the shoulder, and Korrigan sent a particularly nasty winged scorpion at his face. The man ducked away, grimacing.

Outside the broken window, a gout of fire lit up the night, reflecting off smoke drifters' yellow-tinged eyes and casting eerie shadows over the dilapidated buildings.

"Want a taste of this?" Zeg's voice called from the street. "I'll give you three seconds to clear out of here, and then things are going to heat up."

Relief surged through Marny, and she tightened her grip on the lamp base. Her uncle was here, and the attackers were toast. Literally.

Two more drifters pelted down the stairs, reached the

street, and kept running. The remaining men looked at each other.

"What now, Skeever?" one of them asked, glancing at the man who seemed to be the leader.

"We'll come back later," Skeever. "After this guy leaves."

Marny narrowed her eyes. It was actually a halfway decent plan. Uncle Zeg couldn't protect them for the entire night, after all.

Another blast of fire from the street.

"I'm running out of patience," her uncle called.

"Go." The lead drifter roughly pushed one of his men, and the rest followed.

They ran down the stairs, several of them still swatting at Korrigan's persistent pests. Welts and stings marred their faces and hands, and Marny hoped the bugs had gotten under their clothes, too.

Now that their enemies were fleeing, the adrenaline that had powered her faded, leaving a shaky sadness in its wake.

Tam's house wasn't safe anymore, and her heart wrenched at all the losses he'd been facing. His mom taking off again. His brother stolen by the faeries. And now this.

Uncle Zeg waited until the last drifter ran away into the dark, then, still carrying his flamethrower, slowly backed up the stairs. Marny didn't warn him about the missing seventh stair—she didn't need to. For a big man, her uncle was amazingly light on his feet, and constantly aware of his surroundings. He was pretty much her hero.

Without even looking behind him, he took a giant step backward over the gaping hole.

"You okay up there?" he called softly to them.

"Yeah," Marny said. "Nice timing."

He smiled, teeth white in the dark bush of his beard. "I try."

"Korr, make sure your creatures don't attack my uncle," Marny said.

"They have already returned home," the changeling said.

She didn't ask where home was. Probably some poisonous forest in the heart of the Realm.

"Letting me in?" Uncle Zeg asked from the dented-in door.

Marny set the lamp down, her hand stiff from clutching the brass base. She snapped on the kitchen light, then went and undid the locks. The metal door opened fine. Too bad the window was wrecked.

Her uncle stood a minute, just looking at her, then set his flamethrower down and enveloped her in a big bear hug. Not many people could do that. She buried her face in his shoulder, smelling smoke and gas fumes.

"Glad you're all right," he said, his voice vibrating through her.

Two wobbly breaths, and she was better.

"Yeah," she said, stepping away. "We're good. Uncle Zeg, meet Korrigan."

She gestured to where the changeling crouched, his bulbous eyes gleaming.

"Charmed," Uncle Zeg said with a nod. He actually meant it, too.

Korrigan blinked, then smiled. "Likewise, mortal man."

As soon as her uncle stepped inside, Marny did up all the locks again.

"I'm letting Tam know what happened," Uncle Zeg said, pulling out his messager.

"Good idea."

She was happy to let her uncle send the message. Her fingers still felt numb from the fight. Plus, she felt too sorry for Tam at the moment for her words to come out right. He didn't need, or want, her sympathy. Life happened, and sometimes you ended on the bottom of the pile. Pity from friends only made it worse.

"He and Roy are on their way," Uncle Zeg said.

"Good." Marny set her hands on her hips and studied the smashed-out window. "He'll have to move out—at least for a while."

"Yep. Drifters'll be back, and more vicious than ever."

"Good thing your flame thrower works," Marny said.

"Well..." Her uncle's smile was a little sheepish. "The flame part works great. The thrower mechanism leaves a little bit to be desired."

"What? You mean you couldn't have shot fire at the drifters?" She didn't know whether to laugh or cry.

Korrigan nodded in approval. "A show of force is often more impressive than the actuality."

"Then why the crawlies?" Marny asked the changeling. "Why not a big ogre or something?"

"I have no dominion over those kind," Korrigan said. "And I have no desire to be trampled flat beneath enormous feet."

"Fair enough."

"Your insects seemed quite effective," Uncle Zeg said. "From what little I could see."

It was true. Korrigan had come through for them in the fight, in his own peculiar way.

The changeling lifted his head and sniffed the air.

"Tam Linn arrives," he said.

Marny blew out a breath, letting the ache of pity go along with it. Tam would deal, as he always dealt.

She heard his light steps on the creaky stairs, his pause when he saw the broken-out tread, then his quick rush up to the door.

"Guys?" He tapped on the metal. "It's me, Tam."

Zeg undid the locks and opened the door. Tam stepped in, his expression grim, and Marny decided a big, enveloping hug was the best tactic. After all, it had worked for her.

"Tam," she said, letting go when she felt he was ready.

"Good to see you're ok," he said. "What happened?"

"A couple hours after you and Roy left, we heard someone coming up the stairs. The smoke drifters. They said if we gave them money, they'd go away." She grimaced at the door. "Then they tried to batter down the door."

"We fought them," Korrigan added eagerly. "Mistress Marny laid about with her club, while I sent poisonous crawlies to bite and torment."

"Club?" Tam glanced about, looking for her weapon.

"Yeah," Marny said, pointing her thumb at the lamp. "One guy started coming through the window, so I bashed him. Between that and Korr's bugs, we drove them off. With a little help from Uncle Zeg."

She could see the guilt in Tam's eyes. But it wasn't his fault.

"They haven't come back?" he asked.

"Yet." Uncle Zeg picked up his flame thrower. "But they will. Grab anything important, Tam, anything you want to keep for good. We're clearing you out of here."

For an instant Tam looked lost. "This is my home. I can't

just leave."

Marny squeezed his shoulder.

"Where's Roy?" Uncle Zeg asked.

"Waiting with the car," Tam said.

"Now that you are here and can accompany me, we may depart," Korrigan said, oblivious to the undercurrents. He scrambled into the kitchen, hopped onto the counter, and began taking protein bars from the cupboard. "We must take all these. And the screenie system."

Marny felt a wry smile twist her lips. The changeling had his priorities clear, for sure.

"Tam," she said. "It's not secure here anymore." She hated the look in his eyes, but he had to come to grips with the fact his home wasn't a sanctuary any longer.

"But, what if my mom..." He swallowed hard, then continued. "What will Mom think, when she comes home?"

"Leave her a note, and hope the drifters don't mess with it?" There weren't any good solutions.

"You can't stay here." Zeg unplugged the netscreen and began winding up the cords. "I'll take the system down. You go get your stuff."

Tam turned, moving like he was underwater, and started gathering things up—his clothes, a couple books, a battered teddy bear.

He stood there for a moment, arms full of his possessions.

"Here." Marny grabbed one of the blankets off the couch and spread it out, then took the teddy bear and set it in the middle. "Anything from the bedroom?"

"Yeah." He blinked, clearly trying to focus. "Picture album, jewelry box."

"Go get them."

Tam laid the possessions on the blanket, then headed for the bedroom.

"I'll take this lot to the car," Zeg said, arms full of the netscreen setup.

"Good," Marny said.

The sooner they got out of there, the better. She undid the locks for her uncle, then turned back to the living room. Korr was still rummaging around in the kitchen, filling a plastic bag with protein bars and anything else that caught his eye.

Tam came back out of the bedroom, carrying a few small items and a green dress that probably was his mom's favorite. Wordlessly, he added them to the pile on the blanket, and Marny twisted it up into a bundle.

Uncle Zeg bounded up the stairs and into the living room, his hair wild and frizzy.

"Hurry," he said. "There's something happening at the end of the street."

Probably the smoke drifters gathering. Marny gave Tam a hard look. Whether he was ready or not, they had to go.

Korrigan hopped down from the counter, dragging the plastic bag behind him.

"Let us away," he said, sounding like this was the best adventure ever.

Which, considering he now got to leave the tiny house and see more of the mortal world, it probably was.

"Anything else?" Marny hefted the bundled blanket over her shoulder.

"No," Tam said. "Wait—there's a brand new Zing sim system downstairs."

Uncle Zeg shook his head. "Hopefully the drifters won't think of the shop—or be able to break in. We'll come get it tomorrow."

"Once we repair the window, we can bring everything back," Tam said.

Marny wasn't so sure. The drifters were persistent, and dangerous. It would take more than a few days for them to calm down and slide back into their smoke dreams. Weeks, maybe. And where would Tam live in the meantime?

"Come, come," Korrigan called impatiently.

Through the open door, Marny could hear the rumble of voices borne on the chilly air.

"Marny, ride with me," Uncle Zeg said, starting down the stairs. "Tam, you and the changeling go with Roy."

"But—" Tam started to protest.

"Git 'im!" a rough voice cried from the street. "They're taking the loot!"

"GO!" Zeg shouted, pulling Marny with him down the stairs.

She leaped over the broken tread, and at the bottom of the stairs glanced back at Korrigan. She didn't like to leave him, but he'd be all right with Tam.

"Quick," her uncle said.

Down the block, the drifters were coming toward them, carrying torches. Looked like Uncle Zeg's flamethrower had given them some unfortunate ideas.

"Hey," Roy stuck his head out the window of his grav-car, parked right behind Zeg's guzzler. "What's going on?"

He shot a glance at the approaching drifters, and went pale.

"Start the car," Tam called, clearing the last step.

Marny was glad to see Korrigan right beside him. She sprinted to Uncle Zeg's vehicle and wrenched the passenger door open. It screeched loudly, and the lead drifter, Skeever, lifted his head, his crazed eyes fixing on Marny.

"Over there, ijidts!" he yelled, shaking his torch toward the cars.

The drifters surged forward, their torches leaving oily smears of light against the darkness.

"Get in," Uncle Zeg said, then whirled. "All of you, go!"

"Tam, hurry!" Roy yelled, sliding the passenger-side door open.

Marny buckled in, her fingers clumsy with fear. The drifters were almost on them, dammit. Why was Tam just standing there, staring down the street with that look on his face?

He turned to Uncle Zeg, expression tight with anxiety. And hope.

"My mom's out there," he said. "I have to get her."

Uncle Zeg paused, halfway in the car. "I'll help."

"No. Get Marny out of here. Meet us by The View."

Tam and his drastic heroics. She scowled at him and started to unbuckle her seatbelt.

"Young lady, you stay put," her uncle warned.

He glanced down the street, then, with a low curse, threw himself into the driver's seat and slammed the door. The guzzler started with a coughing roar, and he accelerated forward. The drifters started yelling. One of them grabbed a chunk of concrete from the street and flung it at Roy's car. It left a dent in the shiny red finish.

"We can't just leave Tam," Marny said to her uncle.

"We're not."

Uncle Zeg spun the wheel until they faced back toward the drifters. He thumbed on the high beams, and the mob halted, squinting. Tam picked up Korrigan and threw him into the back of Roy's car, the bag of protein bars clutched to his chest.

The leader of the drifters lunged and grabbed Tam's arm as he got into the grav-car.

"No!" Marny cried.

Uncle Zeg gunned the engine and the guzzler shot forward, but Skeever was already collapsing on the ground. She didn't know what Tam had done, but it had been effective.

Roy's car roared to life, and he skidded around into a U-turn. Sudden alarms and flashing lights split the air, and the drifters milled, confused.

"Roy's car alarm," Uncle Zeg said. "Good move. Now hold on—we're out of here."

"But Tam's mom..."

She watched, heart thumping in her throat, as the grav-car reached a slight figure in a yellow coat. Tam reached out and pulled her into the vehicle.

"They got her. And they'll catch up."

The night cracked again, this time with the sound of a gunshot.

Uncle Zeg accelerated hard, leaving the scorch of burning rubber behind. Marny swiveled in the seat, checking to make sure the red car was behind them.

A searing flash of light made her wince and blink. Then came a chest-rattling *whump* as Tam's house went up in flames. The blue tarp on the roof melted and curled from the gasoline-fueled fire racing over the building. The drifters had brought Molotov cocktails.

And now Tam really had no home to return to. Her eyes burned with smoke, with tears.

Once they got out of the Exe, Uncle Zeg drove quietly, taking the streets that led to The View. Halfway up the final winding road to the compound, he pulled over and killed the engine. The silence of the night pressed in around them.

"So," Uncle Zeg said. "Tell me about the weird creature."

He'd been remarkably calm about encountering Korrigan—but then, he wasn't ruffled by much. And they'd had more pressing issues at the time, like dealing with the smoke drifters.

"That's Korrigan," she said. "Tam's brother was stolen by the faeries, and they left a changeling in his place."

"And you ended up as his babysitter?"

"Someone had to watch the little guy while Tam's in-game."

Uncle Zeg turned in the seat to look at her.

"You didn't feel like mentioning any of this to me?"

Marny shifted with discomfort. "Tell you that faeries are real? Would you have believed it?"

"Yes." His voice was clear with honesty.

"I'm sorry. But everything's been happening so fast." She let out a breath.

"Tam and Jennet's odd character disappearances in the Feyland beta testing aren't just glitches, are they?" he asked.

"No."

She didn't say any more. The fact that Tam and Jennet were entering the Realm was their secret to spill.

Uncle Zeg tapped his fingers on the wheel. "I won't press you, though I suspect tonight will provide some answers."

"What's Tam going to do?" She could voice her worry to Uncle Zeg. "His house is toast—literally."

At least he had his mom, and a few of their most prized possessions.

Uncle Zeg scratched his beard. "The apartment behind my place has been empty since Grandma Tina passed."

"You know Tam won't take charity."

"It's not charity if he works for it. The place needs cleaning up. And he could do some jobs for me at the simcafe too. Don't worry, I'll make it comfortable for him to accept."

Marny nodded with relief. Tam and his family had a place to go. He might be too stubborn to agree on his own behalf, but he'd do it for his mom and the Bug. Provided they got the kid safely out of the Dark Court. Her stomach tightened with worry. What if they couldn't? Tam's life was dire enough without that fear hanging over them like a tornado poised to strike.

Her uncle glanced in the rearview mirror. "Here comes Royal."

Headlights illuminated the inside of the car as Roy pulled up behind them. Marny opened the passenger door, wincing as it squeaked again. She grabbed the blanket filled with Tam's stuff.

The door of Roy's grav-car slid open.

"Special View taxi at your service," Roy said, getting out and waving to the back seat. "Everybody in. We all need to go to Spark's."

"I figured something along those lines," Uncle Zeg said, clambering into the back. "I'm sure the gate guards wouldn't let my car through this time of night."

Tam was in the front seat, his mom on his lap. She looked small and fragile, her gaze unfocused as though she wasn't seeing at the real world at all, but some dream inside her head.

Marny put Tam's bundle on the floor, picked up Korr, and then squeezed in beside Zeg.

"Crowded in here," she said. "And no, Korr, you can't sit on my lap."

He made a face, but didn't protest as she set him down in the middle of the backseat floor. There wasn't much room there, between the bundle, her legs, and Uncle Zeg's, but the changeling would be well hidden from curious humans. Like the guards at the gate.

"We'll be at Spark's in a minute," Roy said, getting back in the car. "Sit tight."

"Like we have any other choice," Marny said.

At least wedged in like this, they wouldn't go flying when Roy took the turns too fast.

The grav-car slid under the plas-metal arch of the view, the guards waving them past without a second glance. Guess the CEO's son could zip in and out any time he liked.

Marny stared at the perfectly landscaped lawns and large houses. The View was so artificial looking. Nobody real lived that way—no toys in the yards, no weeds in the lawn, no character or color anywhere.

"What's the plan?" she asked Tam.

He turned his head, one arm still cradled protectively around his mom. "The beta team has to go in-game to rescue my brother. Tonight. We were going to use the vid Roy made of Korrigan to convince everyone, but..." He shrugged.

"Nothing better than the actual creature," Marny said.

She patted Korrigan on the shoulder. The shape of his bones felt strange under her hand.

It had been a wild night, and was getting wilder. She was thankful she didn't have to sim into Feyland with the team. There were enough of them that she wouldn't have to force herself onto a sim system—though if she really had to, she would. The thought made her shudder, and she distracted herself by counting up the beta-testing team in her mind: Tam, Jennet, Roy, Uncle Zeg, sim-star Spark Jaxley, and...

"Are you seriously going to ask Jennet's dad to come with you?" she asked.

"We have to." Tam didn't sound happy about it. "We need everyone. And Jennet has been trying to tell him about Feyland for months now. Maybe he'll finally believe her."

Marny hadn't met the man, but he seemed rigid in his opinions.

Then again, they had Korrigan.

"Here we are," Roy said, pulling up to an enormous mansion.

The place rose into the night, at least four stories of glass and steel. Behind the building, the lights of Crestview were spread out like a twinkling blanket. Marny looked, finding the smudge where the Exe glowed with a few sullen lights.

They all piled out of Roy's car, Tam carefully leading his mom, while Korrigan scampered out. For a second, Marny thought the changeling was going to throw himself on the lawn and roll around like a dog, but he managed to restrain himself.

"Okay, everyone—behave." Roy said.

Marny suspected he was mostly talking to Korrigan. And

maybe Zeg, who liked to mess with authority. She sent her uncle a half smile, which he returned. No matter how crazy or stressful, this was a prime adventure.

The huge front door swung open at their approach. Probably cameras and sensors all over the place, up here at the top of the compound. A blank-faced security guard stood sentry, and behind him Marny glimpsed a warmly-lit entryway and spacious hall.

"Hi," Roy said. "We'd like to see Spark."

"I'll inform Miss Jaxley you're here," the guard said. "Wait in the great room."

He flicked his gaze to Korrigan, and though his expression didn't change, Marny saw the flicker in his eyes. She hoped Spark's people were discreet.

Roy beckoned them all in, then led the way down the hall, clearly comfortable with the mansion's layout. They passed a table holding a vase full of white lilies, their sweet smell perfuming the air.

What a crazy parade they were. Arrogant gamer boy up front, Tam and his totally spaced-out mom next, Marny after them, trying to keep Korrigan from darting into the side rooms, and Uncle Zeg in the back, big and fuzzy.

The great room was, well, huge. Two-story windows on the far wall looked out over Crestview, the orange city glow washing out the sky above until only a few stars showed through. Tam steered his mom to one of the tan couches at the side of the room. She sat, staring out the window, and Marny hoped she wasn't completely lost. Surely she was inside there, somewhere, and would wake up soon.

Uncle Zeg stood by the door, and Marny took her place

beside him. Neither of them wanted to make themselves comfortable. Not until they knew what was going on, and where they fit in.

Roy grinned at Korrigan. "Take a seat," he said, pointing to the big couch in the center of the room.

Obviously he wanted the changeling to make an impression the second Spark walked in.

Korrigan gave him a toothy smile, then hopped up and squatted on the plush upholstery. He looked wild and matted and dangerous, incongruous in the middle of the fancy mortal trappings. Give him a carnivorous forest, or a treacherous stream, and he'd be right at home.

Did he miss the Realm? It was hard to tell, he was such an irascible creature, but Marny thought maybe he did, despite the lure of protein bars. Certainly he didn't belong in the human world.

Brisk footsteps approached, and Spark Jaxley appeared at the door. In person, she looked just as prime as the gaming posters featuring her image—same bright magenta hair, same intent, intelligent gaze.

She paused and raised one eyebrow when she saw them all gathered in the room. Then her gaze found Korrigan, and the other brow rose.

"Well," she said. "This is interesting."

The changeling stood, his clawed feet gripping the couch, and made her a bow.

"Well met, milady," he said in his scratchy voice.

"I take it you're not from around here," Spark said.

Marny pursed her lips in approval of the gamer girl's calm reaction.

"He's from Feyland," Tam said. "I know it's hard to believe, but the game connects our world to the Realm of Faerie. Which, as you can see, is real."

Spark's mouth firmed, her eyes narrowed in thought. "There have been some strange things in that game, I'll admit. Things not even prime-level programming could achieve. So does this mean that faeries are overrunning the earth? Should we be freaking out?"

"Not yet," Tam said. "But things might get dire."

Zeg leaned forward, absorbing Tam's words.

"What are we going to do about it?" Uncle Zeg asked. "I presume the beta team is going in-game. Then what?"

"Then we hope we get lucky," Roy said, a twinge of bitterness in his voice. "Tam and Jennet have apparently managed to score an epic sword and talk to the guardians between the realms, or something like that."

Tam gave Roy a serious look. "It wasn't all fun and games."

"Speaking of Jennet," Spark glanced around, "where is she?"

Spark slowly walked around the couch, keeping an eye on Korrigan, and then leaned against the back. Marny moved into the room, too. No point in standing around awkwardly, now that it was clear Spark wasn't going to throw them out.

"Jennet should be on her way over," Tam said. "With her dad."

"Her dad?" The surprise was clear in Spark's voice.

"There's no other way for us to get into VirtuMax headquarters and onto the sim systems," Tam said. "We need Mr. Carter's help—and his access codes."

"Like Zeg said, then what?" Spark asked.

"We'll make a plan," Tam said. "As soon as they get here."

"We're here," Jennet said from the doorway.

She glanced at Korrigan still crouching on the plush tan couch, then swallowed and looked back at her dad. Marny mentally crossed her fingers. She'd never met Jennet's dad, but his actions spoke plenty loud.

"What the hell is that?" Mr. Carter stopped, one foot over the threshold. His expression was a mixture of confusion and revulsion as he stared at the changeling.

Marny studied Korrigan. She'd gotten used to, and a little fond of, his bulbous eyes, the slash of his mouth filled with sharp teeth, and the unlikely arrangement of his limbs. But he was still a revolting, otherworldly creature.

"That," Tam said, "is a changeling from the Unseelie Court of the Realm of Faerie."

"I..." Jennet's dad blinked, clearly having problems processing what he was seeing.

Uncle Zeg stepped forward, his voice sympathetic. "Hard to take in, I know. I've seen a lot of things in my life, but this is one of the strangest."

"Is it real?" Mr. Carter took a few hesitant steps into the room.

Korrigan narrowed his eyes, unhappy that his existence was in doubt.

"Shall I conjure up my crawlies, the better to convince you?" he asked crankily.

"No need," Marny said quickly, shaking her head. "You're proof enough, Korr. Plus, your bugs are hideous."

If Jennet's dad saw the weird nightmarish creatures, he'd

probably run screaming out the door. Better to take things slowly for now.

"Can I… touch it?" Mr. Carter asked.

He approached the changeling, one hand out. Marny wanted to warn him it was a bad idea; but then again, letting Korr be himself was the best way to convince Jennet's dad of his reality.

With a hiss, the changeling swiped his thick black claws out, catching the sleeve of Mr. Carter's jacket. Korrigan pulled, and Jennet's dad stumbled over to stand face-to-face with the faerie. The rasp of Mr. Carter's breathing was loud in the watching silence.

"Close enough, mortal?" Korrigan bared his teeth.

"Let him go." Marny stepped up, ready to interfere if things got nasty.

It was one thing to prove he was real, but there was a line she couldn't allow Korr to cross. No injuries. Either to fey creatures or human allies.

The changeling grimaced unhappily, but pulled his claws free and released Jennet's dad. Mr. Carter took three hasty steps back. His face was pale, and a drop of sweat trickled down from his temple.

"All right," he said, pulling down the sleeve of his jacket. "I believe you."

About time, too.

"Finally," Tam said, echoing Marny's thoughts.

Jennet's dad studied Korrigan a moment longer, then rubbed his face.

"I owe you an apology," he said, turning to where Jennet stood beside Tam. "To both of you. Honey, I… you have to understand how impossible your stories sounded, I thought you were making up wild excuses."

Jennet crossed her arms, a stubborn look on her face, and Marny didn't blame her. A single apology wouldn't erase months of issues.

"This would have been a lot simpler if you'd believed me in the first place," she said.

"I know." To his credit, Mr. Carter sounded genuinely sorry.

"Hey." Uncle Zeg, always the peacemaker, clapped his hand on Mr. Carter's shoulder. "We all make mistakes. The thing is to keep moving forward. Speaking of which, it's getting late, and we have plans to make."

From what Marny had gathered about the beta testing, the two adults had spent some time questing together. They seemed an unlikely pair, but then again, stranger things had happened.

She glanced at Korrigan. He still looked grumpy. With a wink, she tossed him one of the foil-wrapped protein bars she'd grabbed from his stash.

Although he scowled at her, he deftly caught it.

"Zeg's right," Spark said. "Everybody, sit down. We need to sort things out."

Roy, of course, immediately sprawled in the most comfortable-looking chair. "I'm thinking we wait until after midnight to sneak into headquarters, in case anyone's working late."

Tam and Jennet moved to the small sofa, and Marny settled into one of the double-wide armchairs. Uncle Zeg followed her lead. Nobody sat next to Korrigan.

"I'll ask the cook to throw together some pizzas," Spark said. "No commando raids on an empty stomach."

Marny agreed. When was the last time she had eaten? Or Tam, for that matter—the boy was always hungry.

"Ok." Tam leaned forward, resting his elbows on his knees. "You've all met Korrigan. He's the changeling that..." He glanced over at his mom, who seemed entranced by the lights of Crestview sparkling below.

Tam swallowed, then continued. "The changeling that was left in place of my brother."

"I don't understand," Mr. Carter said.

"Dad," Jennet said, "the Dark Court faeries stole Tam's little brother and are keeping him hostage. Our job tonight is to rescue him."

"Let me see if I have this right," Uncle Zeg said. "The game of Feyland actually leads to fairyland—which is a real, magical place?"

Marny knew that her uncle understood—he'd gotten it right away. But clearly Mr. Carter was still a little lost. Didn't hurt to restate things for his benefit. Especially since they needed him on their side in order to enter VirtuMax's super-secure headquarters and log on to the beta-test sim systems.

"Yes," Tam said.

"That'll be something to see." Her uncle's brown eyes gleamed with interest. "So, we go in-game, find this Dark Court place, and rescue Tam's little brother."

"Except it won't be that easy," Roy said, showing a rare flash of good sense.

Spark nodded. "I assume we're in for an epic battle.

"Yeah." There was the bare edge of worry in Tam's voice. "Thing is, there are two courts, and apparently they've joined forces."

"So this is a bad thing?" Zeg asked.

"Extremely." Tam sat up straight. "Which is why we need everyone's help. Jennet and I can't defeat the king and queen, not by ourselves."

Roy made a noise, and Tam shot him a look. "Not the three of us either, Roy. You don't know what the Dark Queen is like."

Marny knew that Tam and Jennet, working together, had barely beaten the Dark Queen in battle once before. And that, with the addition of Roy, they'd managed to escape the Bright King's court. But Tam was right—if the two fey monarchs were working together, the humans would need all the help they could get.

AFTER CONSUMING the better part of five pizzas, the beta team had their plan of attack. Two plans, really. The first involved sneaking into VirtuMax, and the second was how to proceed in-game once they were in Feyland.

Marny didn't say much, just munched her olive and pepperoni slice and kept an eye on Korrigan. He seemed partial to the all-veggie pizza, which surprised her a little. Then again, she didn't really want to know what his idea of a gourmet meal was. Worms and dirt, probably. Raw fish.

Tam was feeding his mom pieces of cheese pizza. She was still in a daze, but maybe the food would help. Marny went to join him on the side couch.

"What's your mom's first name?" she asked.

It was obvious to her, if not everyone else, that she'd be staying at Spark's to look after Korrigan and Tam's mom. But if something went wacky, she wasn't sure the woman would answer to "Mrs. Linn." And definitely not to "hey, Tam's mom!"

"It's Lara," Tam said, a little catch in his voice.

Jennet laid her hand on his knee. "She'll be all right."

"Maybe." Tam took his mom's unresisting hand and turned it, holding her wrist to the light. "Do you see that?"

Marny squinted and leaned forward. Despite her fear she'd be looking at drug-related marks, the only thing on Lara's skin was a pattern of silvery dots. Almost like...

"A faerie handprint?" Jennet asked.

"Yeah. My mom said a 'shining girl' talked to her tonight, and told her to come home. I don't know if it was a malicious faerie, or one trying to help." He shivered.

"Good thing you got her out of there," Marny said. "Before—"

She made herself stop. The last thing Tam needed was a reminder that his home was now a burned-out shell.

"Okay!" Spark called, standing up and stretching her hands. "Are we ready to do this?"

Jennet glanced at her dad, who had set aside his half-eaten slice of Canadian bacon and pineapple. He nodded and stood.

"I suppose so," he said.

Tam rose, his worried gaze focused on his mom. "Stay here with Marny," he said. "I'll be back in a while."

His mom smiled at him, her expression still dreamy and unfocused. It was hard to know if she even understood what he was saying.

"Take care of her," he said to Marny. It was more a plea than a command.

"No worries," she said.

That was her, Marny Fanalua; babysitter to changeling creatures and zoned-out moms. Still, it was better than squeezing into a sim chair and enclosing herself in the stifling helmet. Even the thought of it made her throat scratchy with rising panic. Nope, small spaces and her didn't get along at all.

"Ready?" Uncle Zeg asked in his calm, rumbling voice.

For a half second, Marny wanted to jump up and grab his arm, beg him not to put himself and her friends in danger. But they had to go. It was what heroes did.

The rest of the beta team nodded and started moving to the door.

"Good luck," Marny said. "I'll keep an eye on things here."

Tam turned and pointed at Korrigan. "Stay in this building, and do what Marny tells you."

Marny raised her brows. The changeling would certainly do the first, and definitely not the second. But that was okay—she had a few more protein bars in her pocket.

Spark gave her tight smile. "If you need anything, ask my staff. I've told them you have the run of the place."

"We'll probably just hang out in this room," Marny said. She didn't want to go chasing Korrigan through a five-story mansion.

"There's a vidscreen on the left wall. The painting slides down and the controls are there." Spark pointed. "And tell the house if you want something sent up from the kitchen."

"Will do. Now go kick some faerie butt," Marny said. Korrigan squawked, and she sent him an exasperated look. "Present company excepted, of course."

Uncle Zeg gave her a big hug, and Jennet a more diminutive one. Tam squeezed her shoulder and she squeezed his in return, Roy sent her a jaunty salute, Spark waved, and Mr. Carter just looked stressed.

Then they were gone, trooping down the hall and out into the chilly night. The big mansion seemed way too quiet. Marny tried to ignore the little flare of jealousy that all her friends were going off to fight while she remained on babysitting duty. Epic battles were their thing, not hers.

Don't you think you're good enough? a voice inside her whispered. You're a better gamer than Roy. A better person.

Yeah, well. She might be both those things, but she was still plain old Marny. Not a brilliant gamer like Tam, or a brave rich-girl like Jennet. Not even a CEO's spoiled kid. Just an ordinary girl, who took up a little extra space in the world.

She let out a breath, then stepped back into the room and closed the door. It might be a "great room," but compared to the enormous expanse of the rest of the house, it felt downright cozy

Korrigan was rooting around in the leftover pizza. Tomato sauce made his claws look bloody.

"Are you done eating?" Marny asked.

"There is no more of the delicious kind left." The changeling frowned.

"Then let's get you cleaned up."

There was a lavish bathroom attached to the great room, of course. There was probably a bathroom for every room in the place. Before taking Korrigan in, she glanced at Tam's mom, but Lara seemed fine, caught up in some reverie only she could see.

"What is this?" Korrigan hopped into the big bathtub, then rapped on the sides. "A bin to put treasure in?"

"No. You fill it with water to bathe in. Like a little pond. And before you ask, I'm not running you a bath." Seeing Korrigan without his tunic and trousers would probably scar her for life.

He didn't press the point, which was good, though he did splash water from the sink all over the floor. Marny mopped it up with one of the thick cream-colored towels. The smell of floral soap perfumed the air.

When they went back into the other room, Marny was relieved to see that Lara hadn't moved.

"Let us kart race," Korrigan said, scrambling up to the back of the couch and giving Marny a hopeful look.

"I don't think there's a screenie system in here," Marny said.

"Then find one," the changeling demanded.

Marny shook her head. She wasn't going to impose on Spark's hospitality. And she had a feeling that asking the staff to accommodate a grumpy fey creature like Korrigan and get him set up for gaming would be too much.

"We can watch some vids, though," she said, heading over to the wall.

The control panel was right where Spark had said. Marny hit the button to activate the vidscreen, and the image of a newscaster appeared. Boring. She scrolled through the channels.

"See anything you like?" she asked.

"Yes! There." Korrigan pointed to the channel where a lion chased gazelles over the dry African plains.

They probably didn't have lions in the Realm of Faerie, but if they did, she could imagine Korrigan trying to take one down. Or tame it. The thought made her smile.

Once she got the changeling settled in front of the screen, she went over to Tam's mom. Maybe some contact with the real world would help her come back from whatever dreamland she seemed to be inhabiting.

"Hey, Lara." Marny sat down beside Tams' mom, who didn't turn her gaze from the window. "What are you looking at?"

"All the pretty lights. And wings," Lara said softly, rubbing the silver marks on her wrist.

Marny leaned forward and peered out the window. It was hard to see past the flickering reflection of carnage on the savannah.

There—a flicker of gossamer wings. A scattering of sparks moving through the sky.

"Um, Korr?" Marny said. "Do you see anything interesting outside?"

The changeling glanced out the window, then shrugged. "Only the pixies and faerie maids."

She swallowed. "You mean creatures from the Realm are flying around out there?"

"They are boring, insipid creatures," Korrigan said. "Lions are of far more interest."

"To you, maybe." Marny stood and moved to the window, letting her shadow cut the light from the room so she could see out more clearly. "Why are they there?"

"The boundary between the worlds is thinning," the changeling said. "I can feel the fey magic seeping out."

"Is this because of the beta team going in-game?"

"Perchance. Or because, with my presence in your world and the mortal boy's in the Dark Court, the connection here is strong. This city is becoming a nexus, where the two worlds may more easily overlap."

She didn't like the sound of that.

From the darkness outside, a faerie maiden suddenly swooped close to the glass. She was about as tall as Marny, but thin as a handful of sticks. Pale wings protruded from her back, flapping slowly. As they caught the light they shimmered, opalescent. Tam's mom let out a sigh.

"So pretty," she said.

Yeah, until you looked closely and saw the sharp teeth, the alien consciousness in those pupil-less eyes. Marny shivered. The team better rescue Tam's brother, and help stop whatever was letting fey creatures through into their world.

"Do we have to worry about anything dangerous getting loose?" Marny asked.

She made shooing motions at the faerie, but the creature hovered in place outside the window, staring at her. Creepy.

"Unlikely," Korrigan said over the cries of dying gazelles. "The gateway is not big enough to allow more than the lesser fey folk through."

"Let's hope that doesn't change." She squeezed her hands into fists. The beta team had better succeed.

Fewer things were worse than waiting around, powerless. The next few hours were going to crawl by.

"Gah!" Korrigan's strangled call made Marny turn.

He was lying on the plush carpet, pinned there by two small, squat creatures even uglier than he was. One of them raised a sharpened wooden spear.

"Stop!" Marny yelled.

Adrenaline jolting through her, she bent and whipped out

her knife, then dashed around the couch and shoved Korrigan's attacker away. The blade touched the creature's leathery skin, and it hissed in pain and retreated a few steps.

"Get off him," she warned, waving her knife at the one still holding Korrigan down.

It scowled at her, eyes full of malice, and slowly released the changeling. Korrigan scuttled back on all fours, then stopped and raised his hands.

"Begone, foul hobgoblins," he screeched. "Before I drive you forth with stings and bites."

The one holding the spear growled and shook it at Korrigan, but Marny put herself between it and the changeling.

"You heard him." She pointed her knife at the hobgoblins. "Or do you need more convincing?"

With a last, evil glare, the creatures muttered something that might have been a spell. Purple light flared, and Marny put up her arm to shield her eyes. When she lowered it, there was no sign of the hobgoblins. Her heart was pounding, the beat a steady thump, thump in her ears.

"Are they really gone?" She turned to Korrigan.

"Aye." He winced. "Kindly put away your blade, Mistress Marny. The cold iron burns the air."

"Right. Sorry."

She remembered Jennet telling her that the fey folk couldn't abide the touch of iron. Another good reason to carry her knife, evidently.

Marny glanced at where Tam's mom sat. The woman seemed oblivious to what had just happened, and was still staring out the window. At least the freaky faerie maiden was gone.

Korrigan let out a grunt and got to his feet.

"Are you okay?" Marny slid her knife back in her leg sheath, then hurried to his side. "Did they hurt you?"

"They meant to." He grimaced. "The queen sent them to kill me."

"But if you're injured while in the mortal world..." Realization iced her bones. "The queen wanted Tam's brother to die."

"A human's death in the Realm of Faerie carries great power. She still intends to sacrifice the child, but it will be more difficult now that your friends have entered the Realm."

"Wait, what? How do you know?" Marny had to raise her voice over the sound of roaring lions, and quickly muted the vid. A little too much excitement going on without the addition of the brutal soundtrack.

Korrigan looked affronted. "I am a creature of the Realm. I am aware of what transpires there, even from my entrapment here in the human world."

"Then tell me what's happening," she said. "The beta team can't have gotten there already."

"Time moves differently in the Realm," he said. "Your mortal friends are approaching the Dark Court."

"I want you to tell me everything you can. What exactly they're doing in there, how the battle is going, all of it."

Korrigan screwed up his face and grunted. Was this the prelude to a changeling tantrum?

"Look," he said, waving at the vidscreen.

The image was blurry, and strobing light/dark/light, but Marny could make out a group of characters gathered at a crossroads. On the hill above them rose a circle of standing stones, illuminated with eerie purple light.

"Is that the beta team?" she asked, squinting to see the figures.

"Aye." Korrigan sounded a little breathless. "And see, the Faerie Rade approaches."

They looked like an army—elfin knights in shining silver armor, redcap goblins capering behind, brandishing their wickedly sharp blades. Rank after rank of faerie folk, and in the center a woman astride a tall horse, with a crown of stars blazing upon her brow.

It was like watching some epic fantasy movie—except that this was really happening, to people she cared about.

The odds didn't look good. Marny crossed her arms, trying to breathe out her anxiety. Worry wouldn't help her friends, and would only tweak her out.

The image wavered, then disappeared. She was staring at lions again, now hunting a zebra.

"Hey!" She turned to Korrigan.

"The connection is difficult to sustain," he said. "As I told you before, time is not parallel between our worlds. I am doing my best."

It was true the changeling seemed tired, his brow furrowed and his skin even paler than usual.

"Okay," Marny said. "Don't hurt yourself. But if you can get the picture back at some point, that would be great."

He nodded. "Another moment of rest, and I will try once more."

"Have a protein bar." She handed him the last one in her pocket.

Judging by how quickly he ripped the wrapper off and devoured it, channeling the Realm of Faerie was hungry work.

When he was finished, he narrowed his eyes and stared at the vidscreen.

The African plains dissolved and the Realm came back, a little distorted. Marny leaned forward, worry crashing through her. The beta-team members had been taken captive, and were tied to different standing stones at the top of the hill. They were all in a state of bad to even worse. Marny sucked in her breath at the sight of one slumped figure who looked almost dead.

"Is that Mr. Carter's character?"

"Aye."

Uncle Zeg was tied to the next stone, and Marny breathed a prayer of thanks that he was upright. He glared at the two figures standing in the center of the circle—the Dark Queen and what must certainly be the Bright King. Red and blue flames coruscated between them—

The image shivered, shifted, and now Marny saw Tam's little brother being held by the king. The fey monarch lifted a needle-sharp blade. Both Zeg and Tam rushed forward, and behind them, Jennet sliced her own radiant sword down—

A huge black dragon hovered in the sky above the standing stones. It lifted its head, its gaze piercing, and Marny swore those centuries-deep eyes looked directly at her and Korrigan. She shivered. The dragon brought its ebony wings together in a thunderclap—

The vidscreen went dark, and Korrigan crumpled to his knees.

"Korr!" Marny went to her own knees at his side, and gently lifted him.

He felt nearly hollow, all knobbles and bone in her arms.

His pale, bulging eyes blinked up at her, and he gave her a crooked smile.

"Mistress Marny, do not fear for me," he croaked.

"Is Tam's brother dying? Are you? What's happening?" She wanted to shake him for answers, but he seemed suddenly so breakable.

"The guardians between the worlds have been called," he said. "I am being pulled back to the Realm."

"Are you sure it won't kill you?" Her heart was pounding, but there was nothing she could do.

"The transition is... difficult. But I will survive."

"Does that mean the Bug is coming back to the real world?" A whoosh of relief temporarily displaced her fear, and her eyes stung with hope. With dismay.

"He will arrive here shortly," Korrigan said. "And now I must bid you farewell."

Unexpected sadness pierced her heart. "Will I ever see you again?"

Who knew that she'd become so fond of this weird, aggravating little creature? She was glad he'd managed to beat her in their last kart race. A small victory to leave the human world with.

"Our paths have tangled and twined," he said. "And the Elder has gazed into your eyes. The mark of the fey folk will be upon you now, and who knows where that might lead?"

Probably no place good.

But certainly guaranteed not to be boring.

"Take care of yourself," she said, blinking to clear her vision of tears.

"And you, mortal girl. I am happy to have called you my companion."

He grimaced, even as his body started to fade. He grew lighter and lighter in her arms, until at last she was holding only empty air.

"Goodbye, Korr," she whispered, bowing her head.

A flash of light, and something heavy landed on her, knocking her nearly off balance. She ducked a wild kick, and grabbed at the arm flailing around in front of her face. The Bug had arrived back in the real world.

"Hey, hey," she said, doing her best to channel Uncle Zeg's super-zen manner. "Calm down. It's okay—you're back."

The Bug looked up at her, eyes like Tam's in a younger, more mischievous face. He froze for a second, then bent over and started crying.

Marny hoisted him up and took him to the couch where Lara sat. Or had been sitting. She was standing now, her eyes looking more awake, her arms outstretched.

"Is that my boy?" she said, her voice strained. "Peter?"

"Mom?" The Bug lifted his wet, snotty face. "Mom!"

Before Marny could tighten her grip, he'd launched himself from her arms and tackled his mom. Luckily the plush sofa was right behind them, catching them as they went down. Tam's mom was crying too, and rubbing her son's hair.

"I'll grab some tissues," Marny said, retreating to the bathroom to give them some privacy.

She couldn't guess how aware Lara had been of Korrigan's presence. Weren't changelings glamoured so everyone believed they were the replaced child? Yet clearly Tam's mom could see the fey folk. Maybe her shutting down had more to do with an inability to believe the enchantment trying to tell her Korrigan was her own son, when he was obviously a hideous-looking fey creature.

Marny might do the same, if half her brain wanted her to believe an ugly, foul-tempered alien creature was actually her beloved kid. She'd been taken in by glamour before, and frankly, it was impressive that Lara had managed to sidestep it. Even if it had made her practically a vegetable.

"Where's Tam?" The Bug's high-pitched voice carried into the bathroom.

Marny came out with a handful of tissues and handed them to Lara. She took them, then started wiping her son's face.

"Tam should be here soon," Marny said, though she wasn't at all certain of the fact.

Sure, Korrigan had returned to the Realm and the Bug had made it home to the human world. But that didn't necessarily mean everyone on the beta team was all right. Or even alive.

She swallowed, refusing to entertain the idea for more than a second. Whatever that big dragon had been, she didn't think it would let any of her friends die.

She hoped.

"I'll get the staff to bring up some hot tea," Marny said.

"And cookies?" Tam's little brother lifted his head hopefully.

"If they have any."

For a kid who had just spent two weeks in the Dark Court, the Bug was bouncing back remarkably well.

She stepped into the hall to summon one of Spark's security guys, but paused at the sound of voices in the foyer.

"Bug?" It was Tam's voice, echoing down the hall.

Quick as a thought, Tam's little brother pushed past Marny and pelted toward the front door, footsteps slapping against the marble floor.

"Tam!" he cried.

Marny smiled as the Bug ran into Tam's arms, then smiled even wider as his mom ran forward. Lara paused in front of her boys, and placed her hand on Tam's shoulder. Without looking up, he pulled her into the embrace.

Beyond them, Marny saw Jennet watching, a look of such tenderness and joy on her face that Marny's heart stung. Tam seemed to feel Jennet's gaze on him, and lifted his head. Their gazes met, and Marny could practically see the light moving between them.

Maybe one day she would have that. She didn't know how, or when, or if Korrigan had been right that there were more fey adventures in her future.

Only way to find out was to keep moving ahead one moment, one day at a time.

Meanwhile, there was Uncle Zeg, and the bulwark of his embrace. She leaned into him and let the tight string of worry wrapping around her go.

"You won?" she asked, though she knew the answer.

"Yes." He smiled down at her, teeth white behind his fuzzy beard. "We won."

That was all anyone could ask for. It was enough to keep the world turning—and the faeries at bay for another day.

~*~

Acknowledgements

As ever, it takes more than an author to see a novel through to final publication. I am immensely grateful to my wonderful editor, Laurie Temple, and my amazing critique partner, Chassily Wakefield. Thanks to Ginger, always, and to the fantastic Arran McNichol of Editing720 for his quick and stellar copy editing.

Mulan Jiang has done the special graphic design work for the six anniversary hardcovers and just hit it out of the park. I am so thrilled I get to work with such a talented designer.

Finally, special thanks to Colin, for fight scene choreography and youthful woodland adventures.

OTHER WORKS

THE FEYLAND SERIES

What if a high-tech game was a gateway to the treacherous Realm of Faerie?

THE FIRST ADVENTURE—Book 0 (prequel)

THE DARK REALM – Book 1

THE BRIGHT COURT – Book 2

THE TWILIGHT KINGDOM – Book 3

FAERIE SWAP—Book 3.5

TRINKET (short story)

SPARK—Book 4

BREA'S TALE—Book 4.5

ROYAL—Book 5

MARNY—Book 6

CHRONICLE WORLDS: FEYLAND

FEYLAND TALES: Volume 1

VICTORIA ETERNAL

Steampunk meets Space Opera in a British Galactic Empire that never was...

PASSAGE OUT

STAR COMPASS

STARS & STEAM

COMETS & CORSETS

THE DARKWOOD CHRONICLES

Deep in the Darkwood, a magical doorway leads to the enchanted and dangerous land of the Dark Elves~

ELFHAME

HAWTHORNE

RAINE

HEART of the FOREST (novella)

WHITE AS FROST

BLACK AS NIGHT

RED AS FLAME

SHORT STORY COLLECTIONS

TALES OF FEYLAND & FAERIE

TALES OF MUSIC & MAGIC

THE FAERIE GIRL & OTHER TALES

THE PERFECT PERFUME & OTHER TALES

COFFEE & CHANGE

MERMAID SONG

ABOUT THE AUTHOR

Growing up, Anthea Sharp spent most of her summers raiding the library shelves and reading, especially fantasy. She now makes her home in the sunny Southern California, where she writes, plays the fiddle, and tries not to game *too* much. Visit her website at antheasharp.com, friend her on Facebook, and be the first to know about new releases and reader perks by subscribing to Anthea's new release newsletter, Sharp Tales, at www.subscribepage.com/AntheaSharp